LOSING
JULIA

LOSING JULIA

Jonathan Hull

WHEELER
PUBLISHING, INC.
ROCKLAND, MA

★ AN AMERICAN COMPANY ★

Published in Large Print by arrangement with Bantam Dell Publishing Group, a division of Random House, Inc. in the United States and Canada.

Wheeler Large Print Book Series.

Set in 16 pt Plantin.

Library of Congress Cataloging-in-Publication Data

Hull, Jonathan.
  Losing Julia / Jonathan Hull.
      p. (large print) cm.(Wheeler large print book series)
  ISBN 1-56895-827-7 (hardcover)
  1. World War, 1914-1918—Veterans—Fiction. 2. Aged men—
Psychology—Fiction. 3. Large type books. I. Title. II. Series

[PS3558.U3973 L67   2000b]
813'.54—dc21   99-059959
                                                                        CIP

All art is a revolt against man's fate.
— ANDRÉ MALRAUX

PART
ONE

I was glad that it rained. Not just a drizzle but big furious drops that lashed against us and danced at our feet. Our discomfort seemed somehow appropriate, all of us standing there with tears and rain washing down our taut faces, overcome by so many names. The clouds were just right too, dark and solemn as they marched slowly past, heavy with grief. But what got me most were the birds, dozens of them in every tree, loud and insistent. I remember listening and thinking how familiar they sounded, so that I couldn't close my eyes for more than a moment without tumbling back.

It was my first trip back to France. I had taken a train from Paris to Reims, where I rented a car and drove five hours, getting lost twice. Charlotte stayed in Paris with our son Sean, who was three then, and her sister Margaret, who had traveled with us from the States. I knew Charlotte wouldn't join me for the service; she had no tolerance for battlefields or military reunions and rarely asked about my experiences at the front. I didn't blame her though, and I was glad that she didn't complain when I told her that I'd be gone for six days.

I never did come back. Not completely.

That was in 1928, a time when thousands of memorials were still being erected across

France and Belgium: great big arches engraved with row upon row of names; small plaques and crosses in little fenced-in plots; solitary obelisks and statues in village squares; every one of them attended by mothers and fathers and wives and lovers who still remembered; vividly.

Page and a few others were there, dressed in their old uniforms, subtly altered. I didn't bring mine. Charlotte said I looked foolish when I tried it on, but that's not why I left it. Standing in front of the mirror and looking at myself, I decided I didn't want to see myself that way anymore. Not ever again.

"It feels sort of strange to be here, doesn't it?" said Page, lighting his third cigarette in a row and cupping it in his hand to protect it from the rain. I thought he looked much older than his age and wondered how many years a war takes off a man. "I wasn't sure if I should come."

"Glad you did," I said.

"Makes me sad, thinking of the guys."

I nodded.

"At least this time we get to see France."

"Yes, at least we can do that."

I proposed that we meet in Paris on that Friday for a night out but he was leaving the next morning on a family vacation. Just in case, I gave him the name of the hotel where Charlotte and I were staying and told him to call, though I didn't think he would.

The monument itself, a long granite rectangle four feet high, was draped in a white cloth.

Nearby, two small tables were covered with food provided by a local committee of mostly overweight French women, who smiled incessantly and kissed our cheeks with great delight. After a few speeches the cloth was removed and a wreath placed at the base. During a moment of silence I closed my eyes tight and let the birds take me. When I opened my eyes I saw her.

I knew right away, though I'd never seen her before. All the long nights listening to Daniel describe her; straining to see her face as he read her letters out loud, his voice mixing with the muffled cough of distant artillery.

I stood up on my toes to get a better look at her, craning my neck above the small crowd. She stood farther back than anyone; I think she might have arrived late. I couldn't catch her eye but I could see her profile clearly. A little taller than I had imagined; darker hair, partially hidden beneath a scarf.

When the ceremony ended, she walked slowly over to the monument and rested both hands on it, as though praying. Then she leaned forward and searched through the names.

I stood immobile, watching. It had to be her. Julia. The woman Daniel had planned to marry. The mother of the child he never lived to meet. I remembered Daniel telling me how he felt the first time he saw her; how he just *knew*. I watched as she slowly ran her fingers along the granite, stopping at Daniel's name, then carefully tracing each letter. I looked at her slender hands and her narrow shoulders and the side of her face and her dark brown hair and the way she tilted her head slightly, as though adjusting to the sight of Daniel's name in stone.

Finally I approached her.

"Julia?"

She turned quickly and I saw those bright green eyes, and even in her sadness they were smiling, just like Daniel described them.

So it was her. And how perfect she looked, more perfect than I had imagined, with the kind of face that you instinctively want to touch and kiss and gaze at for hours. Even now as I recall her features: her sharp jawline, her small nose and pronounced cheekbones—what I remember most is the searing sensation of looking into her eyes for the first time, eyes that would haunt me for the rest of my life.

"I'm sorry, I should introduce myself. I'm—"

"But wait, I know who you are."

"You do?"

"Patrick. Patrick...Delaney. Am I right?"

"Yes, but how did you know?"

"I've heard a lot about you, from Daniel's letters." She offered me her hand. "I'm glad to meet you. I never expected..."

"I didn't either."

The rain started to come down faster and soon people were hurrying to their cars. I saw Page wave at me as he struggled with an umbrella.

"You're wet. Should we go?" I asked, wishing I had an umbrella to offer her.

"I don't mind it," she said. I watched a drop of rain run slowly down her cheek, hesitating at the corner of her mouth. I struggled not to stare.

She wasn't glamorous. There was even a certain plainness to her appearance—no fashionable bob or plucked eyebrows—but that's what made her so appealing. Her warm, soft features were strikingly natural, as though she'd look the same whether just getting out of bed or going out to dinner. Meanwhile, her shy smile and flashing eyes—what life they held!—suggested an interesting combination of strength and vulnerability. When I caught myself staring, I forced my gaze away.

One by one the cars pulled onto the road and sped off. We stood there awkwardly for a moment, then began walking slowly around the monument, reading the names. After a few minutes the rain let up.

"I spent two weeks in San Francisco looking for you," I said finally. "I even put advertisements in the papers."

"You did? Really?" She looked surprised.

I nodded, feeling embarrassed. "I had promised Daniel I'd find you, though I had no idea what I was going to say if I did."

"That was very kind of you." She touched my shoulder, and from the expression on her face I could tell she was moved.

"I wasn't too successful."

"I'm afraid I've moved around a lot. I spent

three years in Seattle after the war. I had a job teaching."

"Painting? Daniel said that you—"

"Yes, I'm still at it."

"I'd love to see some of your work."

"Give me a few more years." She removed her scarf and shook her hair, which was a thick brown, before running her hands through its wavy softness. Her gestures were slow and deliberate.

I put my coat down and we sat on the granite step that ran along the base of the monument and stared out at the sodden field, which was still marred with bits of barbed wire and marked off with signs that warned *TER-RAIN INTERDIT* (forbidden ground) in large red letters. Julia turned and ran her fingers along the freshly engraved names.

As we sat in silence I felt nervous in her presence and wondered what to say. Should I talk about Daniel? The war?

"You have a child?" I asked finally.

"Yes, Robin." Her smile returned. "A friend of mine is looking after her. It's the first time we've ever been apart."

I thought of Sean and how he always screamed with delight when I returned home from work, barreling down the hallway to the front door. Already I'd begun to miss him: his chubby little face, the way he mispronounced things, his endless noisemaking. Since he was born I'd even turned down business that would have taken me out of town.

"And you?"

"A son. He's with my wife in Paris. She's not much for this kind of thing."

"Not too many people are." She was right of course. I suppose that's why I was so glad that she had come. I knew it would have meant a lot to Daniel. Death is such a lonely thing that it seems important for loved ones to know where you faced it. And Daniel and the others faced it just yards from where we were standing.

I looked down at the wet ground, wondering what fragments of war it still held.

"Mind if I ask you a question?" said Julia, standing up and turning toward me.

I raised my hands. "Anything."

"Why did you come here?"

I shrugged.

"Wouldn't you rather forget? I can't imagine what you think about."

"I can't imagine explaining what I think about."

She stared at me so intently that I had to look away. I tried to think how to describe all the reasons I had to come back to France. "I feel closer to them here. Closer to a big part of me. It's hard to explain, really, but I had to come."

"To say good-bye?"

"To say hello."

A sad smile spread across her face. I stood up next to her and we both looked out over the meadow, which was gradually being swallowed by a thick mist.

I pulled out a pack of cigarettes, offering her one. Then I lit a match and cupped my hands in front of her face, watching the light play on her cheeks. Her face looked so lovely to me—those piercing green eyes set in a slight squint, as though she were concentrating extra hard—that I felt self-conscious, wanting desperately for her to like me, which always seemed to make me less likable.

"It's getting cold," she said, pulling the collar of her coat tighter around her neck. "Look, the fog has completely covered the field. Like a shroud."

The headlights of a passing car swooped across the field, briefly illuminating the monument.

Julia ran her fingers along the etched names once more. "It's so lonely here," she said.

"It sure as hell ought to be," I said, taking a long drag from my cigarette.

"It doesn't upset you?"

"Not right now. To tell you the truth I'm almost enjoying it." It was true: after ten years of being stalked by memories it felt good to be back; sad but good, as though I belonged here.

She gave me a sideways look. "So if I've got it right, you favor dark, lonely and rainy places?"

"Only with the right company," I said, stomping my cigarette butt out. She kept looking at me, smiling. I looked down at my watch. "It's getting late. Are you staying in town?"

"At the Hotel Concorde."

"So am I."

"Really?" A blush?

We began walking down the gravel path to where our cars were parked. "Any chance I could buy you dinner tonight?" I asked, hoping she wouldn't detect the nervousness in my voice.

"Yes, I'd like that," she said.

As she got in her car she turned toward me and I could see she was crying.

"Patrick?" she whispered. I leaned forward to hear her.

"Yes?"

She looked at me closely. "I need to know what happened. You must tell me exactly what happened."

◆　　◆　　◆

WHAT HAPPENED.

I'm still not sure. Not completely. Too many holes. But I keep asking the question, asking over and over until I am limp with exhaustion. And I always come back to that first day I met her; to that face looking up at me with those sad beautiful eyes and those trembling lips and that soft struggling voice.

I always come back to Julia.

I can still see her clearly, even with these fading eyes of mine. Not for much longer though. You see, I am eighty-one now and everything hurts, sometimes all at once. Feet, knees, hips, lower back, stomach, head. One false step and smash, old man Delaney will splinter into a thousand pieces of brittle bone on cold cement. Then pneumonia and slow suffocation with concerned faces staring down at me like I'm laid out under glass; thick, heavy glass pressing against my wheezing chest. And finally, a forced retreat through drug-induced mists with voices calling fainter and fainter and me unable to scream until Patrick Delaney, loving father of two children, three grandchildren and three great-grandchildren; failed husband to one failed marriage (long long ago and mostly my fault); lover of many (but not nearly enough, which causes me tremendous grief); fiercely loyal friend to a few (all dead now but one, who can barely hear); disappears with a last shallow and putrid exhale.

Shit.

I've planned the funeral. Nothing starchy or pompous. Just a few words of comfort to mislead the survivors (no use dwelling on what's in store for them), a few of my favorite songs—"If Ever I Would Leave You," "There's a Place for Us," "Shenandoah"; I keep a list— and an absolute ban on holy pabulum, since I don't believe a bit of it anyway. My ashes are to be discreetly scattered in the vineyards of Napa Valley—a deep, velvety cabernet, I've requested—giving me one last shot at the lips of an appreciative woman. The instructions, handwritten on two pages, are in an envelope in the top drawer of my bed stand. Waiting.

So am I, though with scant enthusiasm. The fact that I still floss is simply my way of saying, "Up yours, Lord; you can destroy my spirit but not my gums." Not yet.

Strange how we labor all our lives to preserve our teeth—the one body part most likely to reemerge a few million years later from beneath the sands of the East African Rift, our incisors the subject of award-winning documentaries. I look at my teeth and remember how, as a boy, the whine of the dentist drill and the sickly taste of enamel so rudely challenged my adolescent sense of immortality. Head back and mouth open in an animallike snarl, I squeezed the hand rests and struggled not to cry.

Where are you, boy? I stare into the wood-framed mirror just above the small oak dresser in my room, searching. Some days I catch just a glimpse of him in the corner of my eyes, a small and frightened youth now buried beneath the rubble. Come back here, boy!

Sometimes I see him in my hands, now gnarled and splotchy but still, unmistakably, his hands too. I see them fumble with a ball, work a mitt, dig in the sand for hours. He's a kind boy, shy and uncertain yet full of yearning. Baby fat still hides the knuckles. He runs with the awkward gait of a newborn colt. Always running. Come back!

Other days the hands look older and filthy dirty with broken nails and lacerations and I see them tremble as they grip a rifle. The noise is tremendous and I want to warn him but I can't and I watch as he scrambles up the dirt with those hands clawing to the top and he staggers to his feet and runs, running madly until he disappears into smoke and horror. Careful!

And me? Ha! I look like I'm 120, give or take. A small ember from a once-roaring fire. The older I get, the more out of place I feel, like a weekend guest still loitering around the cottage on Sunday night because he's got no place else to go. How awkward, to feel a burden. Better to pack my things and move on. But please, before I go, isn't there supposed to be some sort of resolution? A denouement before the final curtain? Redemption? Atonement? Extreme unction, perhaps? I feel none. Just loose ends that snap and crackle like downed electrical lines.

Some mornings when I confront the mirror—it's always a bitter confrontation—I recoil, shocked by the once-ruddy face that abruptly (at least that's how it feels) turned ashen gray before sagging into layers like cheap shingles on a tear down. My hair, once light brown and thick, is a deathly gray, not a color really but what remains when there is no color left; the stuff on old corpses that are disinterred so that promising Ph.D.'s can examine whether the poor bugger was poisoned with arsenic after all, which of course he was.

Staring at the gaunt silhouette in the mirror, which stares back with imploring eyes, I realize my body has abdicated. The anarchists are on the palace grounds.

You can't see me, can you? Not if you are young and still unbeaten. I am black and white fading to gray; you are living color. I am driven by pain; you by passion. I am a shadow, diaphanous and bent. An OLD MAN. A

SENIOR citizen. A GERIATRIC. At best, I've devolved into one of those quaint carica-tures, grandmas and grandpas with fishy breath and worn to the nub buttoned-down sweaters (buttoned down because we can no longer manage a pullover).

To you, I look as though I have always been old, a permanent disfigurement upon the human landscape and a painful reminder of the road ahead. (Though you don't *really* believe you'll ever look this bad, do you?) To me, the face in the mirror continues to tor-ment long after the initial, degrading changes, like being convicted and punished daily for the crime of simply hanging in there day after day.

Grant me that I did hang in there, never boarding a doomed plane, never inhaling a deadly virus, never crushed by a car. For eighty-one years I have ducked and dodged the slings and arrows of outrageous bullshit. Missed me, bastards! Six months on the Western Front and the whole goddamn German Army—the jack-booted Jägers, the Landwehr and the Sturmtruppen, the Scharfschützen and the Flammentruppen and the Prussian Guard—couldn't lay a fucking finger on me. (Well, maybe a few fingers, but not enough to do the job.) Kiss my ass, Ludendorff! (You butcher.)

Yet finally, I am brought to my swollen knees by a hundred thousand indignities, small slices of the blade that have drained the blood from my face.

And I'm so tired.

I HAVE A black and white photo of me at thirty-four, standing by the ocean with a child in each arm like Atlas himself, my hair slicked straight back by the sea, which I can still taste. Shadows accentuate my biceps, my jawline, my abdomen. My body, then loyal servant to my soul, was stronger than its master, and much more intriguing, especially around women.

How strange: one minute I was gazing toward the future, a head full of hopes and plans—endless plans—and the next thing I know, poof! I'm poking through the charred remains of my past, dumbfounded.

Old age is a bloody rout.

I thought dying old would be easier than dying young. Now I see how that very expectation makes it so much worse. Die young and fists clench with rage; die old and shoulders merely shrug. If you are young and dying, you are embraced with love and sympathy; charities exist solely to accommodate your final wishes. If you are old and dying, well you're right on course, aren't you? Take too long about it and the looks begin; subdued impatience at first, then glares as though you've been lingering at a window table in a crowded upscale restaurant long after your coffee has gone cold, the table cleared of everything but stains and crumbs.

How about some commotion, a stir caused by the spreading news of my imminent demise? If the world would just wince momentarily at my passing. No need for flags at half mast (though I'd *love* it), but just a flinch, a brief pause before everyone returns to the busy business of life. Please, some sort of fuss somewhere. Anything but that bitter rationalization that he's had a good life and his time has come and it's all for the better now isn't it dear oh I'm starving shall we order out Chinese?

I had intended to be braver at this age, a fearless old fart beyond intimidation. Even a role model of sorts for the young and afraid, like the last Civil War veteran leading the town parade, chin up, eyes glinting, seen it all and survived. After all, the worst possible thing that could happen to me is bound to happen any day now, so what's to fear but a little flatulence as I shuffle past the nurses' station?

And how I fear flatulence, which rattles the nursing home like car alarms in the city. "It tolls for thee," quips the ubiquitous Oscar Bellamy, wagging his finger at the offender as he patrols the hallways in his squeaky wheelchair. For the first time in my life, flatulence is no longer a source of mild bemusement but genuine alarm. A loss of control. A clarion call from hell.

Control. Here at the Great Oaks Home for Assisted Living—and dying—control means having possession of the call button. Everything else is careening out of control, which is why we are all here in the first place. We piss in our pants, we drool, we cry uncontrollably, we smell, we leak.

That's it, really. We have all sprung unstoppable leaks. We're hissing to death, deflating old rafts adrift in the sea, flat out of flares and shit out of luck.

I really must get some rest.

◆　　◆　　◆

Know your rifle. The rifle is the soldier's fighting weapon, given to him by the Government with which to defend his country and himself.
It is the soldier's best friend.
He should know it and understand it. He should learn its peculiarities, if it has any—that is, if it shoots high or low; to the left or to the right. And just as one makes allowance for the peculiarities of a friend, so should the soldier, in firing, make allowance for the peculiarities of his rifle—his best friend.
　　　　　　　—*Privates' Manual, 1917.*

◆　　◆　　◆

THIS MORNING I looked in the mirror and saw just the outlines of my uniform, new and neatly pressed. What am I? Nineteen? A freshly minted soldier in the American Expeditionary Forces. One of Pershing's doughboys. An eager transfusion for the drained armies of the West, bled silly in a monstrous, thunderous draw.

I sit stiffly next to Mother and Father at the

Hostess House at Camp Merritt, listening to their instructions on how to deport myself and what to avoid and most of all to stay safe. On the last day we are issued our steel helmets, and each man gets a new safety razor in a khaki kit with a trench mirror, a gift from the government. Early the next morning we march in the darkness to Cresskill Station, where we board a train to Hoboken. Then we march through the city to the docks, where we take coffee, doughnuts and apples from a table run by smiling women from the Red Cross, then fill out safe arrival cards to be mailed home from France.

Six ships of differing sizes await us, each dazzle-painted to confuse German subs. On the side of the largest ship the silhouette of a small destroyer facing backward has been painted. We point and laugh loudly as we march up the gangplanks, waving back at mothers and fathers and wives and aunts and uncles and children. Black smoke belches from two dark gray funnels as thick, python-like ropes are tossed onto the pier where seagulls flap over food.

France. Son of a bitch! I'm sailing for France. The war! I hear the band playing and flags snapping in the wind and the cool ocean air reddens my cheeks as I stand at the railing, leaning forward so I can look straight down and see the dark blue water sluicing by the side of the ship. Most of the men have been ordered below deck until we clear the harbor to prevent German spies from estimating our troop strength. But I and a few dozen others have been allowed to remain on deck to smile and wave our campaign hats, lest those waving from the piers and smaller boats feel ignored. A fireboat salutes us with great arches of water as we pass the Statue of Liberty, the brave sons of America steaming east to join the valiant sons of France and Britain and Germany and Russia and Italy and Austria and Canada and Belgium and Bulgaria and Turkey and Australia in the greatest test of manhood in human history. A worldwide war!

♦   ♦   ♦

ON SHIP we play cards and study phrase books and listen to lectures and sleep in shifts. The soldier whose bunk I share is seasick, and I am dizzy with the smell. During twice-daily abandon-ship drills I stare at the dark frothing water and try to imagine jumping in. No, the fire would have to be at my back. But what about burning oil? Does it really burn upon the water? I look out on the horizon and see one of our escorting destroyers, a thin trail of smoke rising behind the sleek gray silhouette as it zigzags toward France. We are seven days out, three to go.

As we enter the danger zone we are issued life jackets, which we must wear night and day. Lying in my bunk in the darkness, far below the waterline, I rehearse what I'd do if a torpedo struck. Then I try to imagine what the war will be like. Not what it will look like, but what it will feel like to be at the front. To be under fire. To shoot back. I peer out from my bedroll at the other men, some asleep, others just getting dressed. If they can do it, I can do it.

We disembark at Saint-Nazaire, a sea of olive-drab khaki ordered left and right by MPs with scowls and whistles pinched between their thin lips. On the docks and wharves hundreds of black stevedores dressed in denim overalls unload crate after crate, their biceps straining beneath sweat-stained shirts, while bands of sullen German prisoners under guard shovel coal. We fall in and march and stop and march until eventually we are led into straw-lined boxcars, much smaller than ours, labeled *"40 hommes—8 chevaux"* on the sides in big white letters. We sit for six hours before moving, guarded by more MPs who line the tracks. I watch as the freight cars are loaded with horses, mules, rolling kitchens, machine gun carts, baled hay, ammunition, water carts, supply wagons, artillery and objects I'd never seen before. We pull forward, then stop in a railroad siding for two more hours. Then finally, the train heaves and creaks forward, clickety clacking through the French countryside, which looks remarkably tranquil and unmolested. Certainly land worth defending.

At Langres we march and drill with bayonets and gas masks and grenades, Stokes mortars and Chauchat machine guns, and listen to lectures by hard-looking French and British liaisons who make us wish that we too were veterans. We build trenches and lay wire and then attack trenches with carefully orchestrated leapfrogs of one company over another until we are lost in clouds of dust. And then week after week of drilling until we are numb with boredom. We want only to face the Germans, to prove ourselves in battle! To show what Americans can do. Hundreds of thousands of Americans.

Then, finally, my turn. I am going to the front!

I run my hands along the smooth stock of my Springfield rifle. I strap my puttees on tight. I stand and salute. I march farther and farther east, bent under the weight of my pack.

If only you could see me now, Father.

Thunder in the distance. Streaming refugees. Our pace quickens. Now everything changes: trees are snapped and splintered, the thick-walled farmhouses are smashed, collapsed upon themselves in piles of stone. Dead horses. Rows of wooden crosses. Has some leviathan run amok? The earth convulses.

Father?

Mother?

Oh shit.

Father!

What was it that the British poet and war hero Siegfried Sassoon said, that the war was a murderous "exploitation of courage"?

Ferocious courage. Ferocious exploitation.

Peer pressure gone berserk.

Nurse? I think I have soiled my sheets.

There could never before in war have been a more perfect target than this solid wall of khaki men... There was only one possible order to give: "Fire until the barrels burst."
—*Diary of the German 57th Regiment.*

THE ROAD FROM the monument to the hotel was narrow and rough. As I followed Julia's car I tried to think of all the things I should tell her, but I couldn't, not clearly. I didn't know where to begin.

We got to the hotel just after seven P.M. My room was on the third floor facing the street; Julia's was on the second. After washing my hands and face in the enamel washbowl, I stood before the free-standing oval mirror, studying the red lines that fanned out from my corneas. In the corner of my eyes, the first traces of wrinkles arched toward my temples. I'd always assumed that I'd get better-looking as I aged, a consolation for my miserable teenage years, when acne and testosterone conspired to drive me to the brink of madness. That my looks might further deteriorate with time had only recently occurred to me.

I wasn't unattractive. Not too short, with a slight but sinewy build, fair skin, hazel eyes, a good hairline and a smile that seemed to make people trust me. I had good teeth too, even though they remained largely hidden in my smallish mouth. Though I lacked any obvious flaws, I remained eminently average-looking, in that no single feature nudged me into the better than average-looking crowd.

I walked over to the dresser, picked up my comb and tried to impose some order on my hair, which was light brown and unruly. Frankly, I hated being average-looking, especially since none of the women who appealed to me were average-looking, which meant I was always working with a handicap. And Julia? I thought of her full smile and the whiteness of her neck and the way her eyes were set deep beneath dark eyebrows. I imagined the fullness of her breasts beneath her dress and how it would feel to trace their gentle curves with my hands. But men like me could never touch women like her. Daniel, yes, not me.

I'd always been shy, my inborn confidence stripped by my ineptness at any and all sports, so that I took refuge in books, which helped neither my social skills nor coordination. And I'd always found girls—at least the ones that interested me—especially intimidating, certain they were acutely attuned to my every flaw. Altogether, high school was a disaster from which I still hadn't fully recovered. I was, at best, seen as a "nice boy," the kind that parents like to pat on the top of the head and teachers entrust with weighty missions to the office. When an attractive girl approached me, it was inevitably to confide how much she adored one of my strapping friends.

And yet, at the memorial, Julia had seemed attentive; interested even. I tried to imagine what she was doing in her room and how she felt about meeting me. The futile daydreams of a married man. Pathetic. My heart quickened and I stood in front of the mirror, staring.

Careful Paddy.

We met in the lobby at eight P.M. I was there early, sitting on a small sofa flipping quickly through a magazine.

"Oh there you are," she said. That smile. I stood quickly. She had changed into a white shirt and burgundy-colored pants—Charlotte wouldn't have been caught dead in pants—while her hair was pulled back in a bun and she wore a simple pair of silver hoop earrings. I had to keep from staring at the gentle curves of her hips, which suggested all sorts of other perfect proportions.

"You look...absolutely great," I said.

She smiled shyly. "Thank you." We stood in silence for a moment, then she looked down at her hands, winced and said, "I forgot my purse." She bounded back up the stairs.

When she returned she held the worn brown leather purse up, as if to demonstrate that it was now securely in her possession, then said, "I've had a few days to look around and I know a wonderful little café just four blocks from here."

"Lead the way," I said, placing my hand gently against the small of her back.

Outside the air was cooler and laced with the earthy scent of fall, which always made me nostalgic. We walked slowly, brushing each other, and I tried not to think of how long we would have before we had to say good-bye.

I studied the buildings, noting which were old and which had been completely rebuilt since the war. When we passed the clock tower I remembered that I once drank at a bar around the corner in a building that now housed a bakery. Perhaps the town's consumption of beer wasn't what it was ten years ago.

"This has been such an adventure for me," she said. "It's such a beautiful country."

"Oh yeah, it's one hell of a place," I said.

She gave me a strange look.

"I'm sorry," I said. "It's just that when I was in Paris listening to all these tourists gasping over the culture and architecture and cuisine, as though they'd completely forgotten that..." I couldn't think of how to finish.

"Forgotten what? Tell me."

"That the world damn near bled to death here, that's what." I pulled out a cigarette and lit it quickly.

She waited for me to continue.

"I don't mean to sound so bitter." I smiled to myself. "That's the one thing my parents kept telling me when I came home, that I'd become cynical. The funny thing is, before the war I didn't have even a hint of irony in me. I was so *simple*."

"I'm glad you're not simple anymore."

"Well if I sound too bitter, just shut me up."

"I'm not sure I'd want to." She gave me a longer look and a smile that made me want to kiss her. *What's with me?*

26

"How long have you been in France?" I asked.

"Two weeks, mostly in Paris. I've been here for a few days. It's quite a lovely little town, not anything like it was during the war, I'm sure. Maybe we can take a hike tomorrow? I'd like to see some of the countryside."

"Yes, I'd enjoy that."

Another day together. That was all right, wasn't it? Then I thought of Charlotte and felt a tightness in my stomach. Simple guilt? No, something more complicated. Charlotte. My wife. Mrs. Delaney. Sean's mommy. I pictured her familiar face and gestures. Certainly I loved her. She was a good wife and mother; kind and dependable. Very solid. More than most men deserve. So why did I feel so drawn to this other woman? I'd hardly been with her an hour and already I felt entranced like some besotted schoolboy. I flicked my cigarette butt into the gutter. Was it all those months fantasizing about her in the trenches, only to find that she was better in the flesh? I looked over at her as we walked side by side in the easy silence of old friends and imagined what it would feel like to kiss her.

Again I felt a surge of guilt, followed quickly by desire.

We walked six blocks before Julia realized she was lost, then another three to the right, two to the left, until finally we happened upon the restaurant she had in mind.

"I knew it was here someplace," she said, looking relieved.

"I never had a doubt."

We sat at a small corner table, lit by long yellow candles in white ceramic candlesticks. The light played off the small windowpanes and made Julia's face look warm and tan. I studied her lips and the shape of her delicate ears and how she crinkled her forehead when she smiled, giving her an appealing, innocent expression. She ate very little, with long pauses between bites, and I couldn't tell if she was shy or preoccupied.

"Where are you and Robin living now?" I asked.

"Monterey, but I think we'll move soon. Maybe Los Angeles."

"You move a lot."

"There's a lot to see." As she raised her wineglass to her lips I noticed her nails were bitten to the quick, which surprised me. A lifelong habit or did that start with the war? I couldn't imagine her actually chewing on them, but it made her seem more human to me. More vulnerable.

"I thought I'd travel more myself, but after the war I just got bogged down with work and family," I said, trying to smile.

"Do you feel bogged down?" she asked, smiling back at me.

"Only sometimes. You're lucky you have a skill you can take with you anywhere."

"Sometimes I only feel at home if I'm moving," she said. "Then everything seems fresh and alive, the way it felt when I was a child."

"And what is it you're looking for?"

"What do you mean?" The question seemed to make her uncomfortable.

"When you move. I thought you must be looking for something."

She was silent, looking down at the table.

"I'm sorry, I thought perhaps..."

"I guess I'm looking for what I no longer have. That sense of being completely alive. I can't really describe it. I just remember feeling it."

As I watched her eyes well up I sensed for the first time the depth of her pain. Another war casualty, only all her scars were on the inside. But some of those were the worst kind, weren't they, cutting off the flow of life with all the force of a tourniquet.

Completely alive. I thought about what she meant by that; about all the joy and wonder and passion that had slipped from her fingers. Then I thought of Daniel; of the power in his eyes and voice and his strong, handsome features and the way he listened to you so that you finally felt understood. Thinking of him made me feel tremendously inadequate again; plain-looking and ordinary and dull, with no business to be sitting across from this exquisite woman. Worst of all, I felt incapable of removing the sadness from her eyes.

She placed her elbows on the table and rested her chin on her hands. "You said you were an accountant?" she asked.

"Rather boring, I'm afraid. I'm not even good with numbers." My choice of professions was a constant source of chagrin to me.

"I'm sorry it bores you."

"The truth is, I just fell into it. The firm is my father's pride and joy."

"Tell me about him."

"His father was a coal miner in Pennsylvania. Died at Antietam at thirty-six, leaving six young children. My father was the oldest, so he went straight to the mines at fourteen, but he was too smart for that. So he taught himself to read and eventually won a scholarship offered by the mine owner."

"What happened to the rest of his family?" She was still leaning forward. Staring. I lit a cigarette, concentrating on the way the flame climbed up the wooden matchstick toward my fingertips.

"The two youngest boys went into the mines and only one came out. My Uncle William died in a mining accident in 1902. My aunts went to work in the textile mills. Grandmother died in 1903."

"What about you? What did you want to be as a boy?"

I wanted to be a man sitting across the table from you. The thought made me turn away from her. Then I said, "Well, I'm embarrassed to admit it, but I always wanted to be some sort of artist. I wanted to be the first Delaney whose life was not totally consumed by the struggle to get ahead."

"Why is that embarrassing?"

"Because I'm no artist."

"Well, you don't sound like an accountant."

"Thank God."

"You don't even look like an accountant," she said, smiling.

"Are you trying to butter me up?"

She laughed and cast her eyes downward.

"So what *do* I look like?" I braced myself as she looked back up and scrutinized me for a moment.

"An absentminded English professor."

I frowned.

"What's wrong with that?" she asked.

"Frankly, I was hoping for something with a bit more cachet. Famous author, that sort of thing."

"A lot of women swoon over their English professors," she said, smiling.

I blushed as I signaled the waiter for the check. Was she attracted to me? It seemed inconceivable.

When we stood together out in the street I asked her if she would join me in a nightcap. She nodded, standing close enough so that I could smell her breath, which was moist and inviting. I looked quickly at her lips and again felt a sudden burning sensation in my chest. The romantic heart does live in the chest, doesn't it? Always that tight, burning feeling, like a warning or urgent demand.

We stopped at a small bar on the corner and ordered two brandies. The men stared at Julia but she didn't seem to notice. She didn't act beautiful; on the contrary, she didn't seem concerned with her looks at all. As I sipped my drink I thought of how wonderful it would be to stay up all night talking, then watch the sunrise.

"Cheers," she said, raising her glass to mine. After she took a drink she placed her glass down gently on a paper napkin, then ran her fingers along the rounded edge of the table. She had a habit of moving her hands a lot, not out of nervousness but as though curious about the texture and feel of things. Several times during the evening she placed her hand on my forearm or shoulder while making a point and I wondered if she knew how powerful that was. I liked people who spoke with their hands, so long as it looked natural. I looked down at my hands, which lay immobile on the table, and commanded them to join the conversation. Soon I was enjoying myself, telling funny stories just so that I could flail my arms in a certain way. When I knocked over my brandy glass, she burst out laughing.

"I'm not sure brandy is your drink," she said, as she dabbed the brandy off my shirt with her napkin.

"It's the Prohibition. I'm out of practice."

She went up to the bar to buy me another drink. I watched her squeeze in between a row of men and then laugh with the bartender. No wonder she loved to travel; she seemed at home anywhere. "On me," she said, returning. I took the glass from her and thanked her.

"Were you shipped home quickly?" she asked, sitting close to me. I glanced down at her forearms, which were lightly sprinkled with freckles.

"Five months after the Armistice. Five god-awful boring months."

"You must have been glad to be home."

I shrugged.

"No?"

"You'd think so, but it just didn't feel the way I had hoped. We got our sixty-dollar bonus and a uniform, coat and shoes—they let us keep our gas masks and helmets for souvenirs if we'd been overseas—and that was it. After the parades and speeches it was like it never happened. There was no grieving, not like in other countries. Everybody just went back to work."

"It's not something people want to dwell on," she said.

"Maybe they should dwell on it," I said, feeling my anger return. I leaned back in my chair. "One minute you're picking up after a shell has landed in a crowded trench, and the next you're at a dinner party listening to people belittle someone for their taste in china. Hell of a transition, if you ask me."

She nodded very slowly, as if she truly understood.

I took a long sip of my drink, enjoying the warmth of the brandy in my throat. "It felt like such a betrayal."

"Of those who died?"

"And their loved ones and the wounded and everyone else whose lives were absolutely wrecked." I squeezed my fists together, then let out a deep breath. "Anyway, I'm sorry..."

"Don't be." She leaned toward me and

placed her hand on mine. I looked down at it, at the smooth white skin and thin fingers and the small creases at the knuckles. Beneath her hand my own looked exceptionally large and worn.

I felt suddenly overwhelmed with the desire not only to touch and kiss her but also to tell her things I'd never told anyone since the war, things I'd seen and done and endured. Is that what Daniel meant, that you could say anything to her? And is that what the poets write about; about two souls who find each other and can live apart from the rest of the miserable, lonely world? Who wouldn't give everything for such closeness?

"I hated Daniel for enlisting," she said, sitting back in her chair with both hands wrapped around her glass. "He was so damn stubborn about it." Her eyes reddened. "He was just doing it for his parents, to make them proud and win them back." Then she tried to smile and said, "He didn't like guns. I couldn't even get him to shoot the wooden ducks at a carnival."

I remembered my excitement the first time I shot an Enfield in training; the smooth feel of the stock and the tension of the trigger and the sudden crack of rifle fire.

"I knew he wouldn't come back," she said, wiping her eyes. "After we said good-bye I couldn't eat for days. It was only when I found out I was pregnant that I understood that I had to go on."

And how did Daniel feel when he said good-bye? Did he know too? I tried to imagine those last minutes together, then waving from a train.

I took another sip of my brandy and lit a cigarette, feeling unexpectedly drunk.

"I'm so glad you're here," she said, reaching out and touching my arm.

"So am I. I mean I'm glad that you're..."

"I know what you mean." She playfully squeezed my arm before letting go.

I sat up straight in my chair, trying to clear my thoughts. "Were you serious about wanting to take a hike in the countryside tomorrow?"

"I'd love it. Really."

She smiled and raised her glass, though her eyes were still full of sadness. After we finished the brandies we walked back to the hotel, pausing to stare up at the sky, which hung over us like an immense sieve, sifting the light. In the lobby the concierge gave us our keys and we said good night at the bottom of the stairs. I waited a few minutes before starting up the narrow staircase. In bed that night I lay awake for hours thinking of her and wondering how I could ever explain to her how so many men became names carved in stone.

◆ ◆ ◆

JULIA.

Julia Julia.

What are you doing to me? And what is it about beauty that intimidates; causing us to kneel somewhere deep inside and pray and

35

wonder just how close we might crawl before being banished from the sanctuary?

◆　　◆　　◆

" YOU EVER PUT your hand through a woman's hair and it's so soft that you have to look to make sure it's there?" Daniel asked.

I hadn't of course, but I wasn't going to confess that to Daniel. "Nothing like it," I said, closing my eyes as if lost in reverie.

Daniel MacGuire and I had been up all night laying barbed wire, and now sat in a communications trench smoking cigarettes, which we kept carefully cupped in our hands like captured butterflies.

"I had one photograph of her, taken in Mendocino. But I lost it."

"So describe her."

He leaned back, smiling. "I'm not sure where to begin."

"I have some suggestions."

He elbowed me. "For starters, she's got this great wild streak—did I tell you about the night we snuck into a small empty yacht tied up to the wharf? And she's—"

"Her appearance. You were going to tell me about her appearance."

"Oh yeah. Let's see, she's about five foot eight, slim but very strong, with these legs...well...what can I say about them?" I imagined silken legs stretching from San Francisco to Paris. "She's got this playful, innocent expression on her face and a wonderful laugh.

What else?" He flicked the ash from his cigarette. "She's got thick brown hair cut just above her shoulders and parted on the side, full lips and an adorable nose. And her eyes..." His smile grew. "She's got these bright green eyes set in a kind of permanent smile, and when you look at them real closely, you feel as though you're going to fall in."

Daniel fell first. I tumbled in shortly after.

Daniel? I am so sorry.

◆　◆　◆

SHALL I TELL you about Daniel and Julia? I'm not sure that I can, that I have the strength. Certainly not today. Not until I feel better. But I'd like to.

If there's time.

◆　◆　◆

I DON'T SLEEP that well, which is a shame now that I can finally sleep in whenever I want. I usually have a glass of red wine with dinner, then two thumbs of brandy around nine P.M., which I drink in bed while reading some book or magazine. I read for an hour at most, sometimes the same pages from the previous night—though I'm never quite sure—then fall asleep without much fanfare, my last thoughts lingering on a select (and top secret) group of women with whom I've enjoyed a lifelong masturbatory relationship. The trouble starts around two a.m. when I tumble out of my dreams as though shoved from a speeding train. I am careful not to move as I try to shimmy back to wherever I was but soon I am alert to sounds in the hallways. I peek at the clock by my bed, which I hope will say five or five-thirty but usually reads two, the shock of which wakes me further. Then I consider whether to chance a trip to the bathroom, which promises tremendous relief but risks cranking up what metabolism I have left, making sleep impossible; or whether to stay put, rolling on my side to relieve the pressure on my bladder as I attempt to sneak back into sleep like a teenager returning home past curfew. I suppose, on any given night, that a good portion of humanity is agonizing over whether or not to piss. Is anyone satisfied with their decision?

And does everyone feel so utterly inconsequential at two A.M.? So puny? Pathetic even, like the cowardly lion clutching his tail to his face and quivering all over, ready to bolt?

Each night I marvel that I have blundered through another day without making a total ass of myself, then lie awake remembering all the times that I have made an ass of myself. A colossal, epochal ass. I still shudder at the thought of events that took place nearly a century ago, like the time in high school when I went the entire day oblivious to a bleeding pimple on my forehead until sweet, precious Cindy Wheeler, the prettiest girl in Latin class, took pity and offered me a handkerchief (with her initials on it), thus sending my self-esteem into a tailspin from which it never properly recovered. Or the time in college when I stood before my philosophy class to deliver a speech on Hegel's *The Phenomenology of Spirit* and stood and stood and stood until it was obvious that I could not move my mouth and I was led back to my seat dripping and sputtering like the village idiot.

Or the time I said good-bye to the woman I loved, not knowing I would never see her again.

Maybe insomniacs have more guilt and fear than other people, or maybe they just have more time to feel scared and remorseful. Whatever the case, if you are an insomniac, not sleeping is what you do in life, one of your top two or three defining characteristics, like being fat or short or rich or shy or being a doctor or politician or a hemophiliac. Only worse, especially if you are already fat and short and shy.

While some people count sheep, I tend to tally my shortcomings, itemizing all the things that I don't do well. By about four A.M., I usually start to wonder which is worse, the things that have happened to me or those that haven't. I think it is the things that haven't happened, but it's a tough call, and one which I must make again night after night, weighing my missed opportunities against my egregious errors like some frontier assayer.

I usually fall back to sleep at about four-thirty, plummeting into a psychedelic dreamland that alternately thrills and terrifies me. (As a child I thought my dreams were God's way of telling me, in the strictest confidence, that I was absolutely unhinged.) We are all eccentrics in our dreams. Lunatics, even.

If I have managed to fall back asleep at four-thirty or five, I usually wake again by six-thirty and begin a mental triage of my pain before attempting to move. On bad days I remain in bed most of the morning, sometimes rocking back and forth to shake the throbs and aches and prickles. If I feel that perhaps this is it, I grab the small metal box with the red call button that hangs next to my bed and hold it to my chest ready to press it the moment I detect a heart attack or hemorrhage or glimpse my parents beckoning me from the other end of some brightly lit tunnel that I'd rather not enter.

I know they say that we come into this world alone and so must leave this world alone, but the leaving it alone is much much worse. On those mornings when my body feels at war with itself, I want somebody any-body to crawl in bed with me and hold me and tell me that the fever has broken and by tomorrow I'll be well enough for school.

On good days I always shave and shower, careful to cling to the metal bars that ring the bathroom. I still wash my hair every day, though you can't tell, and I put a small dab of cologne on each cheek to confuse the nurses. (How could something so repulsive smell so *good*?) The toughest part of dressing is getting my feet into my pants, as neither my arms nor my feet are willing to meet halfway. Sometimes I'll get help—though it depresses me—or if my muscles are really stiff, I'll turn on my side on my bed and try to squirm down into my pants until I can grab them and wiggle them on. If I wasn't so fastidious, I might just sleep in the damn things.

By eight A.M. I appear in the dining room for breakfast, usually some pieces of melon, coffee and toast. I used to eat tremendous amounts in the morning, great piles of pancakes and bacon washed down with freshly squeezed orange juice, the pulp crunching between my teeth. But now my body resists, unable to process more than a few feeble calories at a time. The nurses say I'm losing too much weight, but even pizza and ice cream have lost their allure, which is a scary thing, like finding out you no longer enjoy sex or music. (No, I'm not that far gone yet.) I wonder whether there was even a single day of metabolic harmony before I went from fighting to keep fat off to struggling to keep it on. If so, I would dearly like to know what I ate.

After breakfast I either sit down with a book or the newspaper, outside on the porch if it is nice, or if I have signed up for one of the morning activities I paint or play cards or bake cookies or fiddle in the small workshop where we make leather belts and wallets and trinkets to give to our grandchildren. (I loathe the sight of old people sitting around beading and weaving and eating Elmer's glue but say nothing.)

41

For lunch I prefer soup and a grilled cheese sandwich with sliced tomatoes in it and lots of ketchup, but of course I take whatever is being offered. Then I usually return to my room to listen to music on my small tape player. Chopin and Mozart and Rachmaninoff are my mainstays, a sort of holy trinity to which I long ago entrusted my soul, but late in life I became smitten by soundtracks: *Doctor Zhivago, Camelot, West Side Story, My Fair Lady, Zorba the Greek, Man of La Mancha, Exodus*. Sometimes I fall asleep, though usually I remain awake in the chair in the corner, which is orange and itchy. Then at two-thirty p.m. I go to physical therapy for a forty-five-minute workout, which I suspect is shortening my life span but breaks the routine nonetheless. I try to socialize a bit in the recreation room before dinner because afterward I am often too tired to do anything but sit and watch the nurses go by, which isn't a bad thing to do when you don't feel like much else. Then it's back to bed with my book and brandy, bracing for the night's demons and debauchery.

♦　　♦　　♦

WHERE TO START? With Daniel? Yes, dear Daniel.

I see him so clearly. Handsome as all hell. Smart as a whip too. Always seemed to know things I needed to know but never could figure out, like he was one of those people who are born with answers built right in. You were so young! My young friend Daniel, sit-

42

ting there cold and hungry in a tarpaulin dugout in the rain with your knees drawn up and writing page after page. Always writing.

Daniel MacGuire was from a family of San Francisco Irish Catholics who proudly traced their lineage to a treacherous trip around Cape Horn in 1851, the final leg of a two-year flight from the potato famine. His father Conor was a stonemason, as was his father and father before him. The second oldest of seven—the two youngest died of scarlet fever—Daniel was pulled from school at the age of fifteen to help his father, who was backlogged rebuilding San Francisco after the 1906 earthquake. But Daniel kept studying. "It was either stones or books, and what the hell did I want to spend my life putting one stone on top of another for?" he said. By sixteen he had published his first short story in a boy's adventure magazine. Though he wanted to apply for a job with a newspaper, he didn't have the heart to leave his father, who had a bad back and increasingly relied on Daniel to run the business. Then one day, on a Sunday afternoon in September, Daniel was walking along Stinson Beach when he saw Julia.

"She had this little chair and an easel and this look on her face like she was completely lost in what she was doing, and I just thought she looked adorable. I must have walked by her four times before I got the courage to walk up and ask her what she was painting."

"What was it?"

"What was what?"

"The painting?"

"Oh hell, I can't remember, I was so struck by her face. Absolutely thunderstruck, like I'd been physically hit. But she's a damn good painter. She may even make a name for herself."

Maybe I saw her sitting on the beach too, or maybe it was just the expression on Daniel's face when he talked about her, but for me, Julia soon became my own escape from the war; my personal guardian angel who beckoned me away from the madness every time I closed my eyes. Daniel offered hundreds of dots and I connected them, until the most beautiful woman I'd ever seen emerged, my angel in the trenches; my incantation against despair. My Julia.

Her father was killed in an accident on San Francisco's wharf when she was a child; her mother worked as a waitress in a coffee shop. After school each day Julia sat at one end of the counter doing her homework or drawing pictures. She preferred drawing pictures, mostly landscapes inhabited by children at play or workers at rest. Daniel said her portraits were all of poor people with callused but unbeaten expressions and I imagined that she had no tolerance for the rich or well-connected.

She grew up in a series of cheap one-bedroom apartments near the wharves and Daniel described how the dampness of the bay mingled with the smells of leather and sweat and wet wood and the fresh fish on display early each morning in the market stalls. Like Daniel (and me!) she loved to read from an early age, disappearing for days into books when the pressures of childhood threatened to overwhelm her. "My bookish beauty," he called her.

I struggled to picture such a thing. "Sounds like you've met your match—and I'm referring only to the bookish part," I said one evening as we sat in a trench after returning from water duty.

"Oh no, I'm entirely outclassed." He lit a cigarette and slowly inhaled. Looking past him down the line I could see the glow of other cigarettes dancing in the darkness like fireflies. "She once told me that she got her self-esteem through books and I asked how that was possible, and she said that through books she learned what other people, even great people, were really made of inside, and it wasn't anything that she didn't have."

When she was eighteen, she won a scholarship to study at the Art Institute but dropped out after her mother got sick. She divided her time between waiting tables and caring for her mother, painting only at night after her mother was asleep.

"She's not like other women," said Daniel. "At least not the kind I've met."

"How is that?" I asked, watching as he exhaled his smoke into the lice-infested folds of his uniform.

He looked over at me and smiled. "It's not

just her beauty. There are plenty of women who are prettier than her. But she's got this incredible charm. And she's completely unconventional. She doesn't want to live like everybody else with all their petty ambitions and fancy clothes and numbing routines. We've even talked of spending our lives on the road, just traveling and meeting people and seeing the world. All of it: South America and the Orient and even Africa." His face took on a wistful expression. "But the best part about her is that I can tell her anything. I never imagined that that would be possible."

"Everything?" I couldn't imagine divulging the contents of my soul—much less my imagination—to any woman without the severest of consequences.

He nodded.

"There is one thing about her though."

"What's that?"

"She's totally absentminded. It's almost scary. For example, when I met her on the beach, she'd lost track of time and missed her ride home."

"How convenient."

"You wouldn't trust her to heat a pot of water."

"She's an artist, what do you expect?"

"I just hope she doesn't forget she's in love with me," he said, smiling.

"Doubtful. Did you start dating right away?" I was hungry for details.

"Immediately. It was incredible. We'd meet as often as we could, sometimes at the beach or in a park or by the wharves. Often I would just sit and watch her paint and I used to laugh to myself because I knew that no matter how talented she was, nothing she could paint was as beautiful as the sight of her painting."

"Are you engaged?"

He laughed. "You kidding? My parents won't even meet her. She's not Catholic. Doesn't even go to church. 'It's not the girl we don't like, Danny, but by God you marry out of the faith and you'll split the family forever.' That's my father. Mother just kept quiet and wrung her hands, which is her way of voicing discomfort. 'The faith is all we have, Danny. It's who we are.'"

Two months later Daniel and Julia ran away, heading north along the coast up to Mendocino, where Daniel tried his hand at poetry and Julia taught art. His letters home were returned unopened. That was 1916. A year later he joined the army, figuring that his parents would be unable to resist a son in uniform, even with a Protestant at his side.

◆　◆　◆

I pray you may never encounter a modern bombardment, it is simply hell let loose. The sights one sees are too dreadful to talk about, no chance of burial for the dead, they slowly rot in the ground, mangled and re-mangled by shells, and the flies come in swarms. Imagine trying to eat food under these conditions, also up to the knees in mud and water for 4 or 5 days at a time. I pray to God it will soon be over and this madness of slaughter comes to an end.

—*Reginald Gill,*
Australian Imperial Force, 1916.

◆　◆　◆

I FIRST MET Daniel in France. I was a replacement; he was a veteran, at least in my eyes. I was hastily assigned to the eight-man squad he led after being assembled with other replacements at a crowded railroad siding south of Paris. Within an hour the replenished combat battalion was marching toward the front, part of a dusty column of men and horses and trucks and ammunition limbers that stretched across the rolling French countryside, hurrying to meet the great German spring offensive, which was pushing the exhausted French Army back across the Marne River for the second time since 1914 and now threatened Paris.

I liked him immediately. He was tall and broad-shouldered with tousled, reddish-brown hair, a slight gap between his front upper teeth and a habit of rocking forward on the balls of his feet even after a long march. He was very handsome with intense, hazel-colored eyes that maintained a constant, penetrating squint, a strong chin and thin lips set in a slight smile. He had large, powerful

hands, the kind where you can see the muscles and tendons at work, and incredible sta-
mina. When he laughed he threw his head back
and shook without making any noise. Though
I only saw him cry once I felt it sometimes, in
the darkness during a shelling or standing
next to me at a burial service. But what I
remember most about Daniel was that he
seemed to have complete self-control over
every muscle in his body, which is unusual when
you are under fire. And no matter what we were
doing, he always seemed to be preoccupied with
something more important, like someone
who is in the middle of making a momen-
tous decision.

He was a good soldier, much braver than I
was but not foolhardy, with an economy of
motion and agility that made him seem almost
graceful, which is no mean trick in war. Yet
he never seemed the military type, not the gruff,
cigar-chomping sort that inevitably intimidated
me. He was far too gentle and soft-spoken, with
a soothing, compassionate manner that made
you want to spill your fears and secrets to him.
(He was one of the few men that other men
felt comfortable crying in front of.) By tem-
perament, I think he would have made an
excellent doctor or priest.

"Fresh off the boat?" he asked, dropping back
to walk next to me.

"A few weeks," I said, broadening my shoulders.

"We got a good bunch of men," he said, sizing
me up.

"I'll do my best."

He nodded slowly, still studying me. Then he gave me a friendly smile and said, "I was scared shitless the first couple of times."

I shrugged. The first couple of what? Shellings? Bayonet charges? Gas attacks? I wanted to ask but didn't dare.

"It's amazing what you get used to," he continued, offering me a cigarette. I took it. "Though to be honest, I wish we didn't get used to it. Then it couldn't go on."

"You been here long?" I asked.

"Long enough."

"Pretty bad?"

"Worse."

I wondered if he was testing me.

"Why did you enlist?" I asked.

He was silent for a moment. "It's complicated," he said finally. "How about you?"

"Seemed like the thing to do."

"Yes it did, didn't it?" he said, with a distant expression on his face.

An hour later we entered a small village, where we were stopped for two hours by a huge traffic jam. At the center of the square an angry officer stood on the top of a delousing truck, bellowing orders.

By midafternoon the straps of my pack cut into my shoulders. I mentally itemized my load: a hundred rounds in my cartridge belt; two bandoliers, sixty rounds in each; a nine-pound rifle; my haversack, filled with extra clothes, my kit bag, mess tin, pay book, extra boots, pup tent, blanket and four tins of hard bread; my greatcoat, which was rolled on the top of my haversack; a canteen; a pistol; a shovel; a first aid pouch; a bayonet; a gas respirator, which hung around my neck, and my helmet. At least some of the men were smaller than me. I studied their faces, looking for signs of stress, then wiped my brow with my sleeve.

"Pershing's Ammunition Train," said Daniel, smiling.

"What?"

"That's what they call us."

"I don't mind it." I slid my thumbs under the straps of my pack, arched my shoulders and smiled.

Moments later I heard a low buzzing sound and looked up. An airplane appeared from the south, dropping low.

"It's one of ours," someone said.

As it skimmed the treetops the flier leaned over and dropped a small object, which fell quickly to the ground.

"What was that?"

"A messenger cylinder."

"Maybe it's from your mom," said a voice up ahead. Laughter.

♦   ♦   ♦

WE MARCHED with little rest for three days, sometimes cutting through fields and woods to avoid the endless caravans that clogged the roads. Daniel and I spent much of the time talking, and after that he rarely left my side, especially at the front. We talked about our childhoods and our hopes for the future and he told me about his writings and about the war and what it did to people and how difficult it would be to ever explain to those back home. At the time I didn't really understand what he meant.

"But won't you feel proud for what you did?" I asked on the third day, as we were ordered to strip down to combat packs.

"Proud?"

"Yes. Back home men are dying to get shipped over. They're afraid it'll all be finished before they get here." I pulled out my extra blanket and boots.

"No, I won't feel proud." When I looked at the solemn expression on his face I sensed for the first time that maybe the war wasn't going to be quite what I'd expected.

As we wound around a low ridge lined with poplar trees I looked down at the stone skeleton of a small village. One corner of a church remained; the adjacent cemetery appeared untouched. I imagined a grand wedding party pouring out of the church and into a line of black carriages and smoke arising from the town bakery on a crisp winter day. From the ridge I heard, for the first time, faint thuds in the distance, like the low growl of a very angry animal.

"The guns, of course," said a voice behind me. Those of us who were new tried very hard not to show any fear.

"Yes, quite a lot of them," said another voice.

"How far do you suppose they are?"

"Maybe a couple dozen miles yet, I'd guess."

"Sounds like a lot of guns to me."

"Mostly French 75s and German 77s."

"What about our guns?"

"We don't have any guns."

"We don't?"

"Not many. We use a lot of French 75s."

"They any good?"

"The best."

"You know something about artillery?"

"A little."

"You can hear them things all the way from Dover."

"Where's Dover?"

"In England. Across the Channel."

"No shit?"

"No shit."

"How far is that?"

"Far."

"Must be a damn lot of guns."

"Wait until we get closer."

"Goddamn. Isn't this gonna be something, huh boys?"

"You got that."

"Time to have a talk with Fritz."

"Yep. Time to talk to Fritz."

"Fucking Huns."

By late afternoon the faint pounding had become a thunderous beating of drums, as though in anticipation of some gruesome tribal ritual. At a bend in the road several men were gathered around a man lying on the ground next to a tree. Nearby, I caught just a glimpse of an Indian motorcycle on its side, its front tire rim bent.

"What happened to him?"

"He ate it."

"Huh?"

"Took the turn too fast. They say he broke his neck."

"Ever ride one of those things? Dangerous as all hell."

"Looks fun to me."

"Don't ever be a dispatch rider."

"Why not?"

"Because you'll eat shit, that's why. It's the fucking suicide squad."

We passed abandoned earthworks and broken wagons and huge piles of empty ration tins. Many trees were shattered, bent this way and that like cornstalks after the harvest. In an orchard on our left a battery of guns manned by the French was hidden beneath chicken wire covered with painted cloth and branches.

"My cousin's at the artillery school at Fontainebleau," said Jack Lawton, who eyed me suspiciously for a few days before deciding I was worthy of the squad, or might eventually be, if I wasn't killed first. A tough-looking carpenter from Michigan, he befriended me one morning by pulling out a wad of letters from his pocket and asking in a hushed voice if I might read them to him. Tall and muscular with dark blue eyes and thick, curly black hair that carpeted not just his head but his arms and chest and legs as well, Lawton was the strongest man in the squad. He also had the quickest temper, which struck me as an unfortunate combination until I realized he was quite harmless—so long as you didn't make fun of his mild lisp, which seemed to worsen when he was scared or horny (the latter condition arising with extreme frequency). Until I met him I never realized that someone so disarmingly dumb could be so pleasant. With his animallike instincts for danger and exceptional marksmanship—he could hit things the rest of us couldn't even see—I began to think of him as the ideal soldier, complete with an infinite store of extraordinarily dirty jokes.

"Fuck the artillery," said Vince Tometti, a hotel clerk from New Jersey. "What the hell do you think the German artillery is aimed at?" Tometti, who claimed to be nineteen, was the puniest-looking soldier I'd ever seen, with only a thin line of peach fuzz on his upper lip and the shoulders of a small woman. Fortunately, he also had one of the best singing voices on the line, which he used to redeem himself several times a week with a vast repertoire of Italian love songs. Most of them he dedicated to a girl back home named Teresa, whose picture he carried in his shirt pocket in a thin, black leather case, frequently removing it to study it and kiss it and show it to everyone he met. She was so pretty that we assumed he either stole the photograph or cropped out extensive deformities in her lower body.

I reached for my canteen and took a long drink.

"Easy," said Daniel. "Only one refill per day."
"No shit?" I felt my canteen. It seemed light.
Behind me a voice sang:

> *If the ocean were whiskey*
> *And I were a duck,*
> *I'd dive to the bottom*
> *And never come up.*

As we crossed a culvert I saw dead horses piled in a ditch, their bodies stiff and bloated. On the left side of the road old men and women and young children hurried past pulling mules and oxen and trundling large wheelbarrows teetering with burlap sacks of food and chicken coops and crates and folded featherbeds and furniture. Then a regiment of French poilus streamed past, their sky blue overcoats filthy with mud and their faces drawn and unshaven.

I couldn't keep from staring at the passing faces, some completely void of expression while others were set in a sort of permanent wince; the look of someone just about to burst out crying or receive a blow. I wondered what made a person look like that. Most of the poilus stared at the ground as they walked, too tired to look up. Several had their arms in slings while others limped. I looked at the overcoat of one soldier and saw crimson stains all across the front. I wondered how they got there.

"Your turn," shouted a poilu. His left hand was wrapped in bloody gauze.

"Turn back, it's useless," said another.

"*La guerre est fini,*" shouted a tall, hollow-eyed soldier.

I caught a Frenchman's eye. He nodded and slowed down.

"*Là-bas, c'est terrible.*" He shook his head.

"I don't speak French. Terrible, huh?"

"*Les Allemands attaquent de tous côtés.*"

"What's that?"

"He says the Germans are attacking everywhere."

"Oh."

"*Partout.*"

"Yes, well, we'll see about that," said a voice behind me in a southern drawl.

"Damn right," said another.

A distant whine grew louder and louder, howling through the sky.

"Take cover!"

We scattered into a ditch filled with horse-shit. *BANG!* The air slapped my face and snapped against my eardrums.

Again, then again.

Jesus Christ.

Back on the road, marching. I stared at the bobbing olive-drab canvas pack in front of me; at the bayonet strapped on the left, the small shovel strapped vertically to the back of the pack and the rolled greatcoat tied across the top. I struggled to keep my eyes open.

How nice it would be to lie down, just for a few minutes. The thought of going into battle without sleep made me want to cry, big vulnerable tears of protest spilling down my cheeks. Since I was a child sleep deprivation has always made me feel grossly inadequate to the day's demands, causing many weepy scenes in kindergarten, when I would simply collapse in great big puddles of frustration. But to fight? Hand-to-hand combat with knives and bayonets when I can barely put one leg before another?

I felt sick, sure that a terrible, irrevocable mistake had been made.

Farther up we passed a makeshift field hospital built in the partial ruins of a large church. Then a first aid station, where dozens of men lay in rows under blankets while others stumbled about bearing freshly bandaged wounds. That's where I first heard the moaning, which seemed a pitiable reply to the roaring guns. From the sound of it the war was like a shouting match between men and machines. Only you could barely hear the men.

We stood at the side of the road as five Ford ambulances passed, men clinging to the running boards.

"Gas," someone said. I looked and saw a row of men with their eyes blindfolded. They shuffled slowly to the rear, each man clinging to the shoulders of the man in front. We moved quietly to the side to let them pass.

"Look at them damn German sausages," said someone ahead of me, pointing to the sky. I looked up at the horizon and saw two silver observation balloons hanging in the distance. Could they see us? A few men waved. "Over here, you bastards."

At nine P.M. I entered a reserve trench, ate some hardtack and a can of corned beef—which made me thirsty—and curled up in the dirt, feeling the earth shudder and snarl as I withdrew into sleep.

♦　　♦　　♦

"YOU UP for a game of checkers?" It was the ever-flatulent Oscar Bellamy, who is constantly on the prowl for a partner. I was sitting in the lounge with an unopened book in my lap. Emily Dickinson's poems.

"Sure, I'll play you," I said, regretting my offer immediately. Oscar smelled unusually bad.

"Great!" He unfolded the board he keeps in the back pouch of his wheelchair and set up the pieces. I began first.

"So, how long've you been here, Oscar?" I asked.

"Four years. Six months after my wife died I had a stroke. Small, but scared the hell out of me, you know? I went to live with my daughter and her family, but after I fell and broke my hip we decided I'd be better off here."

"You miss being home?"

"Home's not an option anymore," he said, hopping his red checker over three of my black checkers. "Besides, I sort of like it here, what with the different levels of care. It's not just a bunch of critical cases, know what I mean? And with all the dances, sing-alongs, guest speakers and field trips, what more could you want?"

"Beats me. It's a wonder we don't get any honeymooners."

He ignored me, concentrating on his checkers. "After Rose died I couldn't bear to be in the house by myself. She did all the cooking and homemaking. Jesus, I never realized how hard she worked, my poor Sweets. I just about starved on my own. You ever try cooking lasagna? You've got to be a structural engineer just to put the ingredients in the right order." He skipped a king loudly across the board, scooping up my remaining two pieces. "Another game?"

"One more."

"What about you?" he said, pausing to fiddle with the oxygen tube strapped beneath his nose. "You've been here about two years, right?"

"Yeah, after my bypass operation..."

"How many bypasses?"

"Three."

"Had two myself," he said. "Wife dead?"

"No, we divorced many years ago."

"How many years ago?"

"How many? Oh God, I don't know. That was, let me see, 1932."

"No kidding?"

"She remarried. Lives in Florida. Some retirement community."

"Her husband's still alive?"

"Died years ago," I said.

"Now you were a..."

"Accountant."

"Ah yes, a numbers man."

The description made me wince. "I quit right after the divorce."

"Quit your job?" He raised his eyebrows.

"Quit my job." I smiled. "I traveled around the country a bit and then got a job teaching history at a small high school in Vermont. Later I quit that and opened a bookstore."

"That's why you read so much."

"No, that's why I opened a bookstore."

"So you were living alone before you came here?"

"Until my heart attack. Then I lived with my son for a year but his house is small and I felt in the way. When the doctors discovered cancer I decided to move out before I got worse."

"You've got cancer?" He perked up. "What kinda cancer?" Nothing so fascinates the elderly as diseases, especially cancerous ones.

"Stomach cancer," I said. "Seems to be in remission for the moment."

"Stomach cancer?" he said, slowly sounding out the words. "That's tough."

"Gotta go some way, right?"

"Yeah but Jesus, I'm real particular about which way."

"Nice if you have a choice," I said.

"For example, I can't stand the thought of drowning."

"That seems unlikely."

"You never know. You can drown in just a couple of inches of water. Did you know that?" He hopped over two of my checkers. "And fire. Oh Jesus I'd hate to burn to death. I don't even want to be cremated. Told my son I said, 'I don't want to take up a lot of space when I die but no way do I want to be shoved into some goddamned oven and toasted like some goddamned overdone Belgian waffle.' Of course, coffins scare me too. You know, some of the poor bastards aren't even dead. No kidding. Read an article once, I think it was in *Reader's Digest*, about how somebody dug up a lot of old caskets in England from the eighteenth century and found that ten percent of them had scratch marks on the inside! Ten percent! Imagine that? Awful way to go, eh? Worse than drowning, I'd say."

"I'll make sure you're out cold," I said, as he swept away the last of my checkers.

"Thanks Patrick, I'd appreciate that."

◆　　◆　　◆

Points To Be Remembered While Firing
    1. Don't breathe while aiming. Take a
    deep breath; let some of it out, and then
    hold the remainder until after you have
    fired.
    2. Get your sights aligned, and gradu-
    ally squeeze your trigger. Keep your
    eye open when you discharge the piece.
    Continue your aim for a moment after
    discharge.
               —*Privates' Manual, 1917.*

THE FIRST THING I killed in France was a horse. One of our horses, a small underfed animal requisitioned from some farm in France or Britain or even America. We were marching through the Aisne-Marne region alongside overloaded French *camions* and the sides of the road were carpeted with rotting animal carcasses, some distended with legs pointed straight and others crumpled in piles of fur and bone. As we passed one horse lying on its side with its legs bent at odd angles I noticed its large brown eyes blink once, then twice. I stopped.

"That horse is alive," I said.

"Not for long," said a passing voice.

"We can't leave it like that. Look at those front legs," I said.

"Both broken, it looks like," said John Giles, joining me by the side of the road. A short but powerfully built farmer from Ohio who hated farming but loved horses, Giles dreamed of being in the cavalry until he saw what artillery did to horses. I think that bothered him more than the human carnage. The animals had nothing to do with it.

He looked closely at the maimed horse. "Wonder how long he's been lying here?"

"I'm going to shoot him," I said.

"What?" asked Giles, whose boyish, well-freckled face and pronounced overbite defeated his strenuous efforts to look soldierly.

"I'm going to shoot him." I pulled out my pistol from its leather holster.

63

"Might get in trouble," said Lawton.

"For what, disturbing the peace?" I asked.

"Well, it ain't exactly no German spy you're shooting," said Lawton.

The rest of the battalion was steadily marching past. I leaned over the horse and stroked his head. His eyes were filled with terror but he didn't move.

"What an awful place for an animal to be," I said.

"How do you think we feel?" said a passing soldier.

"Where should I shoot him?" I asked Giles.

"In the head, of course."

"I know that," I said. "But where in the head; which way should I aim so that he dies instantly?"

"Well, the bone is pretty thick between the eyes," said Giles, leaning over the horse and pointing. "It's like a bear. You shoot a bear in the forehead and he'll keep charging you. Probably best up behind the eye, say right about here."

"Right here, huh?" I examined the spot closely. "You think so too, Lawton?"

"Yeah, that's the best spot," he said, stepping back.

I looked down at my pistol and then at the horse. Then I stood sideways to the horse, aimed my pistol, leaned back, and fired. After I put the pistol back in its holster, Lawton, Giles and I turned back to the road. An hour later I saw another crippled horse, on its side with its lips drawn back and its belly split open, revealing bright red and pink and purple colors, glistening. I didn't stop.

♦   ♦   ♦

THE HOTEL WAS completely quiet when I awoke. I must have dreamed about the ceremony because in my first moments of consciousness I could still see the names clearly, as though etched on the insides of my eyelids. I lay in bed for an hour watching the sunlight gradually cut through an opening in the curtain and illuminate a thin slice of dust particles that danced in the air. I imagined Julia lying in her bed and wondered if she was awake yet and if she was thinking of me.

After washing up I went for a walk toward the east side of town, hoping I could still find the house of a French couple I met in July 1918. The father had lost his father to the Germans in 1870 and two of his three sons had been killed on the Western Front, one on the Marne and the other on the Chemin des Dames, which means Ladies' Way, after King Louis XV's daughters, who used to ride their carriage along it. Daniel and I had billeted at their house for three nights and I had promised myself to return and thank them for their generosity.

The house was still there, a two-story stucco with a slate mansard roof. The dark red paint on the shutters was chipped and the flower boxes on either side of the front door were empty. I knocked and waited for several minutes but no one answered. Then I found a neighbor returning on his bicycle who told me that Mr. Luchère had died but that his son Pierre, an invalid, lived in the house with his mother. Perhaps they were out and I should try later. I thanked him and then went shopping for a basket which I filled with breads and cheeses and wines from three different stores. Then I sat on the street corner and struggled to write a note in my meager French, then left the note and the basket at the Luchères' front door.

When I got back to the hotel Julia was sitting out front at a small round table having coffee and reading a newspaper. The sorrow was gone from her eyes and I wondered if she was one of those people who begin each day completely healed from the previous day's lacerations.

"Hi!" she said, smiling with such enthusiasm that I nearly tripped over the curb. She was dressed in a lavender-colored chemise and her hair hung loosely around her shoulders. I couldn't detect any makeup and the only jewelry she wore was a small silver bracelet on her left wrist. From Daniel?

"Good morning."

I sat and ordered coffee, feeling anxious in her presence. Was I staring? Was my hair doing funny things? I discreetly reached up and patted it down, wishing I'd combed it properly.

"How long will you be staying here?" she asked.

I hesitated. "Four or five days. I told my wife I wanted to look around a bit. And you?"

"I haven't decided."

Her eyes looked even greener than before, the color of some sort of precious stone formed deep underground. I glanced at her lovely features, her nose and lips, her slender bare arms, before turning my eyes away.

She picked up her coffee cup, leaned forward and took a sip. Then she gently placed it back in its saucer, turned to me and asked, "Are you still game for that hike?"

"Sounds wonderful. I thought we might head toward the ridge east of town. I could show you a few sights, if I can still find them."

"Yes, I'd like that very much," she said, and from her eyes I could sense that she was eager to connect the descriptions from Daniel's letters with the actual roads and ravines and fields of France.

We drove, then parked in the countryside and walked for a while, stopping to rest against an old stone wall.

"Those were the German lines," I said, feeling myself tense as I pointed toward the low ridgeline about half a mile away across a broad plain. "And if you look closer, you'll see some of our lines still." She held her hand flat above her eyes and squinted toward the weathered trenches that snaked across the fields. I wondered if I should tell her that the soil wasn't soil at all but recycled human flesh; a vast experiment in fertilization. I picked up a clump in my hand and smelled its wet pregnant smell and I thought that this right here in my hand is a man in his afterlife.

"You can't really tell me what it was like, can you?" asked Julia.

I let the dirt fall from my hand, then brushed my palm off. "It never comes out right so I stopped trying a long time ago. It's enough that it never happens again."

"But you don't mind me asking?"

"Not at all." I looked down at the little clumps of dirt at my feet. I loved her asking.

"The truth is, I don't really know what to ask. I thought I'd have so many questions...."

She was quiet, looking out across the plain. A lone bird landed nearby, then flew away. I felt a sense of sadness in my throat.

"Is there any way to describe it?"

"You mean..."

"I mean the worst parts."

"Not really, no." *But go on, try.*

"What was it like, being around so much...death?"

I shrugged, then looked over at the nearest trenches, imagining them filled with men. "It was goddamn terrifying. But at a certain point I got so scared that I felt strangely calm. It was as though there was suddenly *nothing* to worry about."

"Because you'd accepted your death?"

I laughed. "Not graciously. At times it just seemed so inevitable, that such a tremendous effort was being made to bring it about that I might as well concede the inevitable."

"And Daniel, how did he take it?" She

tensed slightly, as though bracing for my response.

I thought for a moment. "I'm not sure. He always seemed so brave; almost fearless. But looking back, I don't know. It's more like he always knew he'd never make it. Some men just had that feeling. They were usually right."

"You think he knew?"

"I can't be sure."

"So we both knew," she whispered. I watched the quiver in her lower lip.

We slowly walked to the edge of a trench, which was partially filled in from the rain and wind. I made out the outlines of a rifle half-buried in the dirt. A Mauser.

"I wasn't scared of dying until I had Robin. The prospect of suffering frightened me, but not the idea of being gone."

I thought of Sean and how much he needed me; how much there was to teach him and to protect him from. Then I thought of Daniel and what a wonderful father he would have made, patient and loving; how his daughter would have been the highlight of his life.

"Freud says we're anxious about sex. I think we're anxious about death," said Julia. "It colors everything."

"I haven't read much Freud," I said, remembering Daniel's descriptions of her voracious reading habits.

"Don't you think it makes sense, that underneath everything we are all terrified of dying, only we can't bring ourselves to admit it, so we complain about everything else? Look at the way people live their lives; you'd think they had all the time in the world. It drives me crazy."

"You can't expect people to dwell on the fact that they'll ultimately lose everything they have and love."

"Why not? It might make them think about what really matters."

"What does really matter?" I asked.

She looked at me as though wondering if she could trust me with some immense secret. Finally she said, "Having someone to love. Being compassionate. Being fully alive every day so that you really see and hear and smell and feel things."

Listening to her made me think how wonderful and rare it was to hear someone talk that way. Was that what really drew me toward her, that she talked and cared about the important things? So few people seemed to that it left me with a certain unshakable loneliness, especially after the war.

"Do you feel fully alive now?" I asked, anxious as to how she'd reply.

She looked at me and smiled. "Yes, I do."

"Good."

I dropped down into a shallow trench and retrieved a battered canteen, the lid still screwed tight. I unscrewed it, then held it to my nose. "Old wine," I said. "Must have been a Frenchman." I turned the canteen upside down and watched the sour liquid pour out onto the ground, then tossed the canteen back into the trench.

"I don't see how one got the courage to

attack; to stand up and run toward the Germans." I noticed the muscles in her face tighten.

"It's amazing what you'll do when you don't have a choice. At the Somme one British officer offered a reward for whichever platoon could kick a soccer ball across the German front line first."

"They kicked soccer balls?"

"Yes, soccer balls. You know, good sport and all."

"Good God. Did anyone...win?"

"There were sixty thousand British casualties—on the first day. The Tommies called it 'The Great Fuck-Up.'"

Julia pressed her palms against her forehead and shook her head slowly.

"Did many men refuse to attack? The odds seemed so awful."

As she held my gaze I suddenly longed to be able to explain to her what happened; to make her understand what really took place here.

"Not many," I said. "If you did you'd be court-martialed and shot anyway. The French had quite a bit of trouble with that. Whole mutinies in 1917. Their generals were extremely fond of *l'attaque à outrance*—the all-out attack; the *Furia Francese*. That made it awfully easy for the German gunners. I don't think the poilus—that's what everybody called the French soldiers, it means the hairy ones, in honor of their unkempt beards—I don't think they minded defending their nation so much, it was the senseless offensives against machine guns they were protesting. It just became too much."

"So they were shot?"

"Or sent to Devil's Island. It was all rather hush hush. Still is."

Who shot them?"

"Other French soldiers."

"That must have been a wretched job. To be pulled from the line to shoot one of your own. I have the most terrible image of it: some poor young kid who simply can't take any more. My God, if a mother saw a thing like that." The lines of her face tightened again. "Were there many that were executed?"

"In 1915 a French battalion refused to go over the top at Vimy. The whole battalion was court-martialed."

"What did they do to them?"

"They didn't want to shoot them all—or at least they weren't sure they could pull it off—so instead one man from each company was sentenced to be shot."

"How were they chosen?"

"The commander of each company drew the name from a hat. It was worse in 1917, when the French Army nearly broke. The men would baaa like sheep on the way to the front."

Julia turned her head away. We walked for a while in silence and then sat by the edge of a large crater. She pulled out a cigarette from her bag, lit it, and then wrapped one hand around her silver bracelet and twisted it slowly back and forth. "You were wounded once, weren't you? Daniel mentioned it."

"I got gassed. Only slightly. Trouble with my damn mask. I was back in five days."

"What about on the day Daniel died?"

"I had some stitches in my shoulder. A concussion. Then in the last week of the war I got some shrapnel in my thigh. But no permanent damage. I was one of the lucky ones."

I watched her peer over the edge of the crater and remembered the wounded men who drowned in the filthy cold water that pooled at the bottom.

"I didn't realize there'd still be so many shell holes," she said. "The place is covered with them."

"We did leave rather a mess, didn't we? Men are such slobs."

She frowned at me, then asked, "What was it like to be shelled?"

I laughed out loud.

"If you'd rather not..."

I thought for a moment. *Try. Try to tell her.* "It was the random, helplessness of it, more than anything." I paused, suddenly feeling more upset than I wanted to. "There was nothing you could do. Nothing at all. You cowered and prayed and played these games in your head to keep you from going crazy. You told yourself all the reasons you probably wouldn't get hit, or you told yourself that if you were going to get hit there was nothing you could do about it anyway.

"The physical sensation was another thing

entirely. I could tell you that the earth shook and trembled but that wouldn't really be it. It was more like the earth was bucking and kicking as though trying to throw you off. And the sound, well it was like someone was hammering against your eardrums. And the air just came alive with objects, pieces of metal and wood and dirt and flesh and bone flying every which way, like a tornado."

"I couldn't bear it." Her voice broke. I longed to reach out and hold her.

"You had to. You just had to."

"But not everybody could."

"Some went mad." I laughed nervously. "We had to tie a few onto stretchers. Eventually they'd be sent to the rear, but not for long. It was different with officers. When officers broke, the army usually found excuses to whisk them away; a couple of weeks in Nice until their nerves were restored."

I stood up and walked over to the crumbling parapet of a trench that zigzagged for several hundred yards. "If I'm not mistaken we were positioned somewhere in this sector here. Ten years and you can still see our handiwork. Makes my back hurt just looking at it." She stood and walked toward me. I think she was waiting for me to say more but I couldn't.

As I turned and looked across the field I felt pressure in my ears and a shortness of breath. I stood perfectly still and concentrated on maintaining my balance. I closed my eyes tightly, and in the darkness I felt a rush of nausea as I saw the bloated, fly-ridden bodies with twisted limbs and blackened faces. I saw haversacks and broken shovels and helmets and rifles and boots and strips of clothing swaying in the barbed wire. There were deep shell holes half-filled with brackish water and bits of paper swirling in the wind and belt buckles and canteens and pieces of wood and smashed mess kits and cartridge belts and Chauchat clips and broken picks and shovels all littering the tortured earth. Then I heard the moaning. Terrible moaning and screaming while the acrid air began to burn my eyes and throat. Men cried for their mothers and for water and medics and morphine and some pleaded to be shot quickly please by either side it didn't matter. Good God the noise!

"Patrick?"

A rush of warmth in my chest. Blood? No, not that. I looked and saw Julia staring at me, her hand resting gently on my arm.

"Are you all right?"

I felt the wind hard on my face. Leaves scurried over the dirt. *It's over.* I blinked several times, then stepped down off the parapet. Steady. "I'll be all right," I said.

"Are you sure? I can't imagine what it looks like through your eyes."

My knees were shaking. "We'd better watch our step. There must be another war's worth of live ordnance still buried around here."

She was still watching me closely. What did she see? Could she see miles down into me?

We walked on awhile, then I stopped and lit a cigarette. I inhaled deeply, blowing the smoke out from the side of my mouth in a steady stream.

"There is something I've been wanting to ask you," she said, spinning her bracelet slowly around her wrist.

"What's that?"

"Do you believe in God?"

"No."

"Not at all?"

"Not at all."

"Neither do I. But that leaves a big hole, don't you think?"

"Enormous." I took another long drag on my cigarette. "There's a wooden calvary at the cemetery in Ypres where a German shell landed between the cross and the figure of Christ and failed to explode. It's still there, lodged in the wood."

"Do you think..."

"No. With hundreds of millions of shells fired, a thing like that was bound to happen. It's just interesting."

"Did a lot of the men pray?" she asked.

"Sure. I did too. Why not?"

> I dreamed kind Jesus fouled the big-gun
> gears;
> And caused a permanent stoppage in all
> bolts;
> And buckled with a smile Mausers and
> Colts;
> And rusted every bayonet with His Tears.

"That's Wilfred Owen. It's a habit I picked

up from Daniel: memorizing bits and pieces of things."

"It's a nice habit," she said, smiling at me. Then she added, "I don't think that most people can manage without the idea of some sort of heaven."

"They don't do so well even with the idea," I said.

She laughed. "But if you take it away from them, if they can't believe in some place better and kinder and fairer, then they have to somehow justify their suffering in their lifetimes. They have to make sense of things right here, on earth."

"Which nobody can."

"Exactly. But that's why there is such despair."

"Despair? What despair?"

She nudged me in the ribs. I nudged her back, then took her hand in mine.

As we walked back to the car she suddenly turned and said, "I heard a terrible story from a woman at the vegetable market the day after I arrived. Three years ago a young French boy came across a German…stick bomb? Is that what you call it? Anyway, his father must have plowed it up. When the father saw his son running across the field holding the grenade he yelled for his son to drop it and run away. But the boy threw it down too hard and it exploded."

"He died?"

"Three days later."

The wind blew her hair into her face and she

turned so that it blew back again. "And the thing that the woman at the vegetable market kept saying was that the boy's father fought for four years without a scratch."

♦ ♦ ♦

I THINK I'M being stalked. It only occurred to me this week, when I noticed that wherever I went, Helen McCrackle soon appeared. Either this is a remarkable series of coincidences or Helen has a crush on me. Unfortunately, Helen is completely ambulatory, which makes it much harder to avoid her.

She's nice enough, for a nonagenarian. But she hovers, always asking about my health and my grandchildren, sometimes twice a day. And she stares at me with her dull gray glassy eyes like a dog watching you eat. If I stare back, she smiles and nods knowingly, as though we have secretly pledged ourselves to each other.

I saw a picture of the former Helen. It's a black and white five-by-seven she keeps on her dresser in an ornate silver frame. At least she claims it's the former Helen. I have my doubts. The woman in the photo is standing at a railing, one hand resting on another, and looking out as though watching a ship recede on the horizon. I guess she is about thirty, and she is beautiful, her auburn hair cascading down both sides of her softly sculpted face.

The two Helens bear no resemblance. Absolutely none at all. To think that the one devolved into the other is almost inconceivable. I can't look at the elder Helen without thinking that she is some tragic mutation; an evil twin who killed Helen the Younger out of jealousy and spite, suffocating her with a pillow and burying her in the crawl space.

Now Helen the Elder pursues me relentlessly.

"How are you feeling today, Patrick?"

I stall a few seconds before looking up from my book, hoping she'll register my inattention.

"Fine, thank you."

"And the grandchildren?"

"Fine, thank you." I am talking into my book.

"Now how many do you have again? Four, right? Or is it five?"

"Three."

"Yes, three. Of course. And you've got a few great-grandchildren, don't you Patrick?" The lilt of her voice says: "You old goat you."

"Yes, I do. Three as well."

"Three and three." She always says three and three. "And how *are* they?"

"Fine, thank you."

Slowly, I raise my book higher and higher until it covers my face.

"What activities did you sign up for this afternoon? There's a papier-mâché class at three."

"I didn't sign up for any today."

"Oh. Well, neither did I."

Once I tried to shake Helen by walking out the front door and then hurrying around back as fast as I could. That's when I discovered that Helen is faster than I am.

Ding! It was Evelyn Stouffer's egg timer, which she kept in her lap in lieu of a short-term memory. Ding! Time for breakfast. Ding! Time for lunch. Ding! Time to take some pills. Ding! Time for bed.

The problem is that Stouffer is hard of hearing, so unless she feels the vibration of the bell in her lap she doesn't always realize that her timer has dinged.

"That's your timer, Evelyn!" I hollered.

"Huh?" She looked over with that befuddled, empty Alzheimer's gaze.

"Your *timer*, Evelyn. It dinged!" shouted Helen.

"Oh, my *timer*. Strange, I didn't hear it." She held it up to her face and stared at it. "Lunch already?"

"We just had lunch," I explained, wondering whether any of Evelyn's roommates had been driven completely batty.

"Huh? Well that's odd. I don't take my pills until right after dinner, on a full stomach you know. I wonder why I set the timer?" She held it up and stared at it again, as though awaiting an explanation.

I stood abruptly, hoping to leave Helen embroiled in Evelyn's confusion.

"Where are you off to?" Helen asked.

"The bathroom. I'm going to the bathroom."

She smiled that knowing sort of insider's smile that lovers flash, only her smile fractured along dozens of fault lines across her crocodilian complexion, like dried-out rivers and tributaries seen from space.

I turned and fled.

♦ ♦ ♦

THE BAYONET
NOMENCLATURE AND DESCRIPTION

The bayonet is a cutting and thrusting
weapon consisting of three principal
parts, viz, the blade, guard, and grip. The
blade has the following parts: Edge, false
edge, back, grooves, point, and tang. The
length of the blade from guard to point is
16 inches, the edge 14.5 inches, and the
false edge 5.6 inches. Length of the rifle,
bayonet fixed, is 59.4 inches. The weight
of the bayonet is 1 pound; the weight of
the rifle without bayonet is 8.69 pounds.
The center of gravity of the rifle, with
bayonet fixed, is just in front of the rear
sight.

—Manual of the Bayonet,
War Department, 1913.

♦ ♦ ♦

THE GERMANS began shelling us just after three
A.M. We were dug in to a farmer's field southwest of Soissons, bracing for their assault
when the first murderous concussions stung
my ears.

Oh shit, I can't take this. Clods of dirt
smack against my shoulders and helmet. I
press against the wall of the trench. Screams?
Who is that? I'm thrown backward, then down
to the ground. My cheek stings. It's wet. I
crouch lower and lower, curled up against

the earth. Something metallic strikes my helmet. My left hand hurts. A gas siren? No, that's the shells falling. Right? My box respirator hangs in a bag around my neck, but it feels tangled. Everything feels tangled. Something picks me up and throws me down again, hard. I feel seasick. I can't do this. Oh fucking Christ.

Back on my feet. Am I hurt? I look at my arms and legs and chest. Everything's there. Down the trench I see Tometti clutching his photograph of Teresa right up to his face and humming a song, tears streaming down his cheeks.

Another explosion. I'm down again. I feel a hand on my shoulder. Someone is pulling me. It's Daniel. He points to the left, where the trench wall has collapsed. Men begin digging. Daniel grabs a shovel and pushes it into my chest. Dig.

My arms ache as I stab at the dirt; down down down I must dig down farther. Something hits my face. My nose is bleeding. Am I crying? My face is so wet. I fall down again. Who's screaming? My ears are bursting. Stop the noise, *please*. What's that on the ground? A head. Johnson. I vomit.

The shells land farther behind us now. I am back on my feet, dizzy. Christ it's smoky. I can't see.

"Fix bayonets!"

Jesus God. My hands shake as I struggle with the steel locking ring. Come on come on come on. I hear dozens of metallic clicks up and down the line. Vomit burns my throat.

"The Germans are coming!"

Flares arch up from behind our lines and hover above, as if held by curious ghosts. To my right a Hotchkiss fires and men are shouting and firing and I hear tremendous screams over the parapet. I climb up and peer over the edge and see silhouettes of men running toward me; hundreds and hundreds of men with bayonets gleaming and rifles flashing. They are coming for me.

Holy mother of God.

I aim and shoot and load and aim and shoot as the figures come closer and now I see faces, faces of young men and middle-aged men hurtling toward me and my whole body wants to turn and run and hide from this horror. You bastards!

A sudden weight presses against my right side and I grab and push and pull until I see the face of Mark Castings, barely eighteen, illuminated by the moon. His jaw hangs sideways on his shoulder. I turn and load and fire. The figures are hesitating. I watch them drop to the ground. The rest turn and run back.

◆　　◆　　◆

I SEE THE moon, the moon sees me, the moon sees somebody I'd like to see...

◆　　◆　　◆

"SON OF A BITCH would you look at that," says Giles, who has a long cut across his chin and dried mud in his eyebrows. The sun is up and I peek above the parapet. There are dozens, maybe hundreds of bodies. Some moving, some still. And flies. Flies everywhere.

I can't eat.

"Don't be a goddamned idiot, Delaney," says John Galston, the platoon sergeant, pointing his spoon at me. A former police officer from Brooklyn who once clubbed to death an entire German machine gun crew, Galston is short and thick and all business. "A soldier can always eat. Anything, anywhere, anytime. Eat or I'll kick your ass."

So I eat, then vomit.

"You're a goddamned embarrassment. Ought to put you back folding the fucking laundry."

I would love to be folding the fucking anything.

◆　◆　◆

GOD BLESS the moon and God bless me and God bless somebody I'd like to see.

◆　◆　◆

THE NEXT MORNING we counterattack. Daniel squats beside me, snapping open and closed the ten pouches of his cartridge belt one by one.

"You okay?" he asks.

"I'm okay." I tighten the brown leather

chin strap on my helmet, then run my hand along the wooden grip of my trench knife, which hangs from the left side of my cartridge belt. At four A.M., our artillery begins. First the 155s, then the 75s. We go over the top at five A.M., when the covering barrage will begin rolling forward at a rate of a hundred meters every five minutes.

"Stay right with it," says Daniel.

"Yep, right the fuck with it," I say.

I am desperate to stop my shaking. Daniel puts his hand on my shoulder. I see his thumbnail is completely torn off. "Look, all you've got to do is get your ass out of the trench with the rest of us and run like hell and shoot at anything that moves. Don't be first and don't be last. Maybe we'll even get some souvenirs."

Yes. Right. Okay. Just crawl up and run. I can do that.

We are perhaps four hundred yards from the German front lines, which are bordered by barbed wire thirty feet deep in some places. Galston warns that several German machine gun teams will inevitably survive the bombardment. "Get to them and the rest is easy," he says.

"Yeah, no sweat."

At four-thirty A.M. I must piss terribly and hurry down the trench to the latrine, squeezing past dozens of huddled figures and tripping twice over bangalore torpedoes. So far the Germans are quiet, either in retreat or dug deeply in their trenches, which I've noticed are much better than ours.

Back in position I check my bayonet and make sure that all my pockets are buttoned. My eyes sting from the dirty sweat beading down my face. Someone to my left is saying the rosary. The smell of damp soil and sulfur and shit and urine seems unusually strong. "Anything happens to me, I want you to write Julia and send her my diary and make sure she's okay," says Daniel. I nod. "Anything happens to you, I promise that after the war I'll go visit your parents." Again I nod, imagining Daniel in a crisp new uniform sagging with medals and his hat in hand as he rings the doorbell and my mother placing her teacup back in its saucer and pulling the shawl around her shoulders as she walks to the door.

"Ten minutes, boys."

I tighten my helmet again, then tug on the haversack that hangs around my neck and holds my gas mask. Then I check the bolt of my rifle and run my hand along its smooth stock and finger my cartridge belt and grenades and the metal knuckle dusters on the handle of my trench knife and God my mouth is dry.

The bombardment from our artillery suddenly shifts forward. Across the field the Germans remain quiet. I look sideways and see Daniel and Giles and Lawton and Tometti, their faces rigid. Tears have started down my face.

Mother, I am nauseous.

The captain's whistle shrieks.

◆   ◆   ◆

SIX OF US are sitting in the day room, more sullen than usual. Emmett O'Rourke fell this morning as he rose from the breakfast table, smashing his left hip and elbow on the white linoleum floor. "Same thing happened to Walt Wallers and he was dead in a month," says Mitzie Smith, an annoyingly perky woman whose genial face testifies to nearly nine decades of smiling about God knows what.

"Well, I think Emmett is ready," says Bernie Mumford, shuffling in with his walker and pelting us with his ruthless smiles. "Ready to be reunited with Lyddia."

Bernie is the self-appointed chaplain of Great Oaks, constantly probing residents for remorse and possibilities for eleventh-hour reconciliation. This morning he looks particularly excited as he plunges into our silence, his furry eyebrows rising and dropping like window shades. "So, Jack, what would you do differently if you had it to do all over again?" he asks, pausing his walker to rest. Jack is actually gassy ol' Oscar, who is spared from his own perfidies by the oxygen tube he wears. But Bernie calls all the men "Jack" and the women "Dear."

"By God, I'd do it all differently," says Oscar. That's what I like about him: he hasn't lost his verve. If he didn't smell so bad I might even get chummy with him.

"Everything?" Bernie looks dumbfounded.

"He's pulling our leg," suggests Mitzie, rather gingerly. A rail-thin homo barely erectus blue-hair, the predominant species at Great

Oaks, Mitzie's spine is curled like a dried seahorse, so that when she stands her hunchback is level with the top of her head. She has heart disease and glaucoma and a habit of falling asleep in the middle of every meal, sometimes with food still left in her mouth, unprocessed.

"Everything except for that trifecta I won at Del Mar in 1967 and the time at Sycamore High in 1923 when I hit two homers against the Trojans to claim the state title." Several of us recoil, fearing that Oscar will launch into yet another soliloquy on his glory days at Sycamore.

"How could you feel that way?" asks Bernie.

"You want to hear about the thirty years I wasted in the steel business?" continues Oscar, sucking a big hit of oxygen in through his nostrils.

Half a dozen voices shout, "No!"

"So what would you have rather done?" I ask.

"I never would have married, for starters."

"I thought you loved Rose," I say.

"Sure I did. I'm just sorry I married her." He takes in another long hit of air. "What I really wanted to do was play baseball. The majors. And maybe date some movie stars. Only I ended up marrying Rose and selling steel. You see my point?"

"I see your point," I say.

"What about you, Mitzie?" asks Bernie.

"Gosh, I wouldn't have done anything differently," chirps Mitzie. When I first arrived at Great Oaks Mitzie seemed to have something of a crush on me, but lately she's been doting on Bernie. I couldn't be happier. "I'm proud of what I did. Proud of the way I raised my kids. Proud of my grandkids. I just thank the Lord for my blessings."

Amen. But I wonder: was Mitzie's life really better than most, or did she appreciate it more or just remember it differently? I suspect she remembers it differently, which is really the trick. If you want to age gracefully, remember selectively. Old age is best spent in the editor's booth, whittling a life down to its greatest hits, which are played over and over again until the tape finally snaps.

"I always wanted one evening where I was the most beautiful woman at the ball," says Helen, giving me the eye, or what's left of it. "Where all the handsome young men, the pick of society, were desperate for my attentions." She inhales dramatically, then winks at me. "Mind you, I had my good days." She presses her palm gently against her cheek, as if she had just awoken from an attack of the vapors. "Days when I felt so pretty, so put together, that I just had to get out to be *seen*."

"Anybody else?" asks Bernie, pursing his lips and beginning to whistle, which is the other reason he annoys me: he whistles constantly, as though he is doing us a favor by providing a little background noise.

"I would have studied piano," whispers Howard Bullard, who always whispers and always wears the same lime green cardigan with ketchup stains down the front. "Always wished

I could play the piano." Howard's sallow, pallbearerlike pallor makes him look like a younger man made up to look like a very old man. He blinks constantly from behind thick glasses that greatly magnify the size of his eyes, making him appear as though he is always right up close to you and fighting back tears or a sneeze.

"Why didn't you?" asks Mitzie.

"My mother played for years. Beautifully." He pauses and shakes his head with a pained smile. It occurs to me that Howard is one of the nicest men at Great Oaks. "I remember sitting in her lap after dinner and watching her hands skate across the keys." I can see Howard's mother in the animation of his face. "After she died I inherited her piano, a baby grand Baldwin. But when my son Chris got sick we had to sell it to pay the medical bills. The Depression and all."

"What about you, Jack?" Bernie peers over his walker at Jim Runyon, a much-decorated Korean War vet who at only sixty-five was enfeebled by a series of strokes.

I try to intercede, placing my hand on Runyon's arm. He looks confused.

"Let's try somebody—"

"I would have taken my son to Canada," says Runyon, his head bobbing slightly as he talks. Runyon's son—and only child—Timothy was disemboweled by a claymore in Vietnam in 1968 in a bid to emulate Dad. We are silent. I squeeze his arm. Runyon begins to cry, as he does several times a day and especially during meals, when he slumps forward in his wheelchair and stares back in time, looking for his son.

I walk outside and then stop, both hands resting on the carved wooden handle of the dark brown cane my children bought me for Christmas after my heart attack. The wind is picking up and the low clouds look discolored like fresh bruises. I raise my head slightly and notice that the air smells of an approaching storm, which is a pleasant thing to smell; seductive, even. I slowly close my eyes, then open them again as the wind buffets my face. That's the feeling of nature to me: cool, bark-laced wind against my face. Even the birds are silent now and the only sounds I hear are the wind brushing my ears and the gentle whoosh of air rushing in and out of my windpipe as though the earth were infusing me with its dewy breath. Strange, but as I stare at the large oak tree across the lawn I think I see a face in the shadows.

Daniel?

But it can't be, can it?

I grip the cane with all my strength.

♦　　♦　　♦

Humanity is mad! It must be mad to do what it is doing. What a massacre! What scenes of horror and carnage! I cannot find words to translate my impressions. Hell cannot be so terrible. Men are mad!
—*Alfred Joubaire, French Army,
diary entry May 23, 1916,
shortly before his death at Verdun.*

WHEN WE got back to the hotel that evening it was almost dark. On the sidewalk a Frenchman with one leg was selling tobacco. Had I seen that face on the Paris-Metz road?

In the lobby Julia took her knapsack from me.

"Can I buy you dinner?" I asked.

"I'm very tired. But thanks." She started toward the stairs, then stopped and turned back toward me. "I thought I might do some painting tomorrow. I was wondering if you'd join me?"

"I'd love to."

She smiled. "Tomorrow then."

I nodded. "Tomorrow."

After she had gone upstairs, I went back outside and bought a cigar from the Frenchman, who spoke no English but still managed with his expression to acknowledge our bond. Then I went across the street to a small bar and ordered a carafe of red wine. The bartender smiled and said something about America's Prohibition. Then he made his hands into a machine gun and made a ba-ba-ba-ba-ba sound with his lips, spraying me with saliva.

"Yes, silly, isn't it?" I said, carrying the carafe over to a small round wooden table in the corner covered with cigarette burns. I sat for an hour sipping from a small glass with a chip on one side and nodding occasionally to some of the men at the other tables, who played cards and laughed and smoked continuously.

So what in God's name are you doing, Patrick? I smiled to myself, suddenly overcome by a familiar sense of absurdity. That's what the war was really about, wasn't it? Final proof of humanity's vast, monstrous absurdity. Love and die, you pitiful bastards. The French and British understood that: how the war changed everything; how it made fools of mankind and all his feckless Gods.

And so here I sit with my wine and all I can think of is this woman I've just met. Also absurd. Impossible, really. You see, Paddy ol' boy, you've already got yourself a wife and family. A good wife and a beautiful son. And so now you're one scared son of a bitch. And the damn thing is, the goddamn thing is, you promised yourself after the war ended that nothing else would ever scare you again.

After I finished the wine I went for a walk through the town, weaving slightly down the narrow wet streets that were flecked with moonlight and half-expecting to come across bands of drunken soldiers singing to the night. I started on the north side and worked my way around in a gradual circle. The air was unusually warm and humid and I wondered if everyone else associated that sensation with childhood, with bare feet and wet grass and fireflies and heat lightning and repeated entreaties to come in for dinner.

When I passed a church I noticed a small graveyard on the right surrounded by a rusty wrought-iron fence. The headstones and statues pointed at odd angles like bad teeth, some still white, others worn and blackened. There were angels too, some bent with devotion, others standing with heads cast down and hands clasped together, bereft. I thought of Julia and Daniel and how maybe the important thing is to have somebody grieve for you; to know that angels will bow in sorrow.

I heard laughter and looked down the street to see a French couple walking shoulder to shoulder as though propping each other up. They must be young; older couples rarely walk that way.

That's how Daniel left Julia; frozen in time when they were young and still leaning against each other when they walked. She has the memory of perfect love forever, which would make it difficult to love again. Heartbreaking, to compete with angels.

I lit a cigarette, tossing the match into a small puddle.

So who is better off, those who share love long enough to see which parts inevitably fade or those who lose their love when it is still pristine? I think each is lonely in a different place, though if you lose your love while it is still perfect you at least have a clear explanation for your grief, while if it gradually crumbles in your hands you do not.

When I returned to the hotel I noticed that a window on the second floor was lit and I wondered if it was Julia's room. I stood in the street for a few minutes, hoping I might see a silhouette cross the light. Then I went into the hotel, waving at the concierge who was half asleep in a chair in the corner near the stairs. Once in my room I pulled off my shoes, closed the shutters and lay on the bed with my clothes on. I fell asleep immediately.

◆　　◆　　◆

I THINK I'M in love with you, Julia.

You're dreaming again.

But you're here. You're here with me. Tomorrow we'll be together again, and I'll watch you paint and make you laugh and tell you about all the things inside of me.

That was a very long time ago.

No, no it wasn't. How can you say that? Tomorrow. We'll be together again tomorrow. I'll have the concierge put together a wonderful picnic for us. I've so much to tell you! And you must tell me everything about yourself, about what you're thinking and about your hopes and...

But Patrick...

Did I tell you what a wonderful time I had today? More fun than I've had in years. You see, I haven't really talked to anyone for a long time. What I mean to say is that after Daniel died I never really met anyone else that I could talk to, not like that. Did you know that I'd given up? Could you tell? It's true. Before I met you I'd given up. But you changed that.

Patrick...

And did I tell you that I'm nervous around you? Funny, isn't it, a tough ol' doughboy being so scared of a woman. But I'm not like Daniel, Julia. I'm not that courageous. I wish I was more like him. Maybe then...

Good-bye, Patrick.

Good-bye? But I've so much to tell you. Things I want to ask you. What are you thinking about when you get that look on your face, when your head is turned and you're looking far away? And were you up late tonight too? Were you lying in bed thinking about Daniel or were you thinking about something else? Did you think of me at all? And how do you get your ideas for paintings? I'd be interested to know that. You'll show me some of them someday, won't you? And your daughter. I'd love to meet your daughter. I'm sure she's very beautiful. Do you have a picture of her? My son is beautiful too.

Good-bye.

But wait. What am I going to do in four days? What am I going to do when I go back to Paris? What am I going to do, Julia?

◆　　◆　　◆

" GOOD MORNING."

"Julia?"

"It's Sarah, your favorite nurse. Here's your medicine. Who's Julia?"

◆　　◆　　◆

IT IS SAID that life is too short and that's quite true, unless you are lonely. Loneliness can bring time to its knees; an absolute and utter stand-still.

I've always judged places and times by how lonely they felt. The entire Midwest, for example, strikes me as horrifically lonely, Indiana more so than Wisconsin and Wisconsin more so than Ohio or Illinois. Coasts are dependably less lonely than inland areas while the warmer latitudes are noticeably less lonely than the colder ones. Hardware stores feel lonely while bookstores do not. Mornings are lonelier than afternoons, while the hours before dawn can be devastating. Vienna is lonelier than Paris or London, while Los Angeles is lonelier than San Francisco or Boston. The Atlantic Ocean is lonelier than the Pacific while the Caribbean is not lonely at all.

And then there are nursing homes.

◆　◆　◆

EMMETT O'ROURKE is dead.

◆　◆　◆

I'M SLIPPING, aren't I? The ground itself fissuring at my feet. Sometimes it feels as though my mind's eye has become nearsighted; that clarity improves with distance. With time. And here I sit in the lobby and I don't recall deciding to sit in the lobby at all. Nor even what I had for breakfast. If I had breakfast.

I don't know when the confusion started,

nor just how far in retreat my brain cells have been driven. One mile, two miles? An entire army in flight across a hundred-mile front? Or has my mind been encircled like the German Sixth Army, stalled and freezing to death at the gates of Stalingrad? One thing I've learned, the fog of war has a peacetime equivalent: old age.

Some mornings I feel a certain bewilderment enshroud me like ivy upon an old house, causing me to mix days and months and even shoes. I forget: how clearly did I once think? How sharp was the focus? So many things that were once familiar now look strange that I cannot be sure of what should and should not be familiar. I cannot remember how much I might have forgotten. I imagine row upon row of ancient books that crumble at the touch.

I put everything I need to know on a small pad I keep in my shirt pocket. Sometimes I jot down old names and dates that leap from my addled brain like fish from a pond. I remind myself to take my pills and to return a borrowed book and even to check that my zipper is up.

I examine my bank statements very carefully, determined to reconcile every last penny. It's not that I'm cheap, it's just that I don't have a lot of earning potential left when what I've got runs out. I don't sweat it, though. Despite my remission, I'm confident that I will run out before my money does. The race is on!

Actually, I'm glad I'm not rich. I've gotta believe that it's harder to die if you are. Not only do you lose possession of all those *assets*, all that cash and those stocks and bonds and cars and antiques and silver and paintings and vacation homes, but in those final days and weeks there can be no denying that a tremendous amount of your life was spent accumulating and fussing over all those *assets*, time that could have been spent with family and friends or fishing or traveling or, quite simply, fucking. Imagine that, Old Boy, you could have been fucking all that time! I say, can you hear me Old Boy? That's right, I said fucking! No, not accumulating, fucking!

I did manage to sock away a little something. The small bookstore I opened after I quit teaching broke even in two years and then brought in a steady income up until I sold it in 1968. When I sold my two-bedroom house in 1977 I used some of the money to buy an annuity that pays for this nursing home. I squirreled away another $100,000 to leave for my family. My son Sean, fifty-five, and daughter Kelly, fifty, will split $60,000, or what's left after my final bills are paid. They divvied up most of my possessions when the house was sold, but I've still got a rental storage shed full of vague surprises. I've made a list of my favorite items and just who gets what. They can figure out why.

I'm leaving the remaining $40,000 to my grandchildren and great-grandchildren. Originally, whenever that was, I had hoped to leave enough money to pay for somebody's education. Then I read that I'd have to put aside several hundred thousand a year, or some such figure, and that by the year 2000 and what not, it would cost a trillion dollars per semester. So maybe I'll spring for a textbook instead. Or a party.

I often try to imagine the little ones as adults, wondering how their faces and minds and souls will fill out over the years. On some days I stare at their photos like I'm looking across a huge divide, with me too old and them too young for us ever to really know each other. And God forbid they should rely on the memories of their own parents or I'll pass through the generations as a series of incorrect and poorly told anecdotes. Or maybe I'll persist as a frozen face lingering in faded photos until one day a descendant stabs me in the nose with a pointed finger and says, "Who's *that*?"

Sean's grandson Kenneth is seven with outsize knees and elbows and skinny limbs trying to catch up and coordinate. He's got green eyes, curly brown hair, and big earlobes. Michael, five, is the little big man, blond, stocky and incapable of anything slower than a canter. Kenneth may have heart but Michael has fire. Which is better I do not know.

Then there's my daughter Kelly's granddaughter Katy, three, who has fat cheeks that roll back into explosive smiles and blue eyes like vacuums that suck in everything but sorrow. Every time she giggles my eyes redden reflexively, a counterbalance to so much joy.

When she visits I wait for her out front, knowing she'll sprint the last forty feet, leaning so far forward that she arrives headfirst, squealing like a pig.

My little piglet. Some nights when the pain won't break I lie on my side and think up appellations for her: Peaches, Honey Bear, Bunny Bear, Angel Face, Sweetie Pie, Sugar Bear, Lollipops, Pookie, Muffins, Snuggle Puppy. Sometimes when I hold her little white hand in mine I am mesmerized by it, staring like a tourist transfixed before *La Pietà*.

They don't visit much, the little ones, despite the presents I send and the big Easter baskets from the Senior Crafts Store along with cards that play songs when you open them and flat figurines that expand when you soak them in water. Instead, I get photos: smiles peering out from Halloween costumes or posed over birthday cakes or a pair of eyes set deep behind a football helmet. I keep them neatly tacked on the bulletin board above my desk, layered back to the day I moved into Great Oaks two years ago last May.

It's nothing to feel sorry for me about, them not visiting. I didn't visit my Grandpa Neil much either when he was old and dying. "You just can't imagine what it would mean for him if you and your sister would just spend a few hours at his bedside," pleaded my mother, who still felt guilty for not visiting her Grandma Claire more often before she died of consumption at seventy-six. "Mother,

Grandpa has breath like a dead fish and besides he won't remember if I do visit so what's the difference?" I said, heading out the back door to the woods where Jimmy and I were fortifying our clubhouse with planks stolen from the freight yard.

I'm all paid up now, Grandpa, just as my offspring will be when they are old and sick and lonelier than all bejesus and the grandchildren they long to hug or just stare at for hours don't bother to visit any more than is absolutely necessary, which is less and less these days.

Guilt and loneliness seesawing through the generations like a family curse.

◆　◆　◆

I SEE HER again: her face wet with tears, her eyes searching mine. Slowly, very slowly, I reach my hands out and trace my fingertips along her skin, first down her neck, so warm and fragile, then across her breasts and down along the curves of her hips. Then with all my strength I wrap my arms around her and pull her toward me, but she is gone.

◆　◆　◆

FROM MY BED I can see the moon tonight, so bright and ripe and salmon pink it looks as if it might drop from the sky. I imagine pirates on deck just before sunrise with the wood groaning and the moonlight streaking across the water in a straight line from the horizon.

Did Caesar see the moon exactly so as he strode down the Roman Forum on the way to some debaucherous celebration? And what about Moses and Galileo and some wretched young Londoner pulling a cart full of corpses during the plague? Or an American Indian crouched by a fire in a small clearing surrounded by huge primeval trees that glow orange from the flame?

And Julia?

◆　　◆　　◆

I LOST ANOTHER roommate today. Frank Denton. He'd only arrived three weeks ago. Must have been twenty years younger than me. Looked a lot healthier. I'm starting to wonder if God's crossing his wires.

"Patrick? You awake?" he whispered, two nights before he died.

"I'm awake."

"You ever find yourself getting disoriented in the dark, right after the lights are out?"

"Frank, I feel disoriented when the lights are on."

"I was just thinking about this girl I dated in college. Holy toledo, she was a looker."

"Yeah? What was her name?"

"Iris. Iris Perkins. From Rye, New York."

"They don't age in your memory, do they, Frank?"

"Not one bit. It's the strangest thing, but for a moment I thought..."

"What? What did you think?"

"I thought I was back at my dormitory at New York University, lying awake and fantasizing about Iris."

I imagined the young man lying in a bunk bed, hands clasped behind his head, staring at the ceiling.

"She had great ankles," he said. "Doelike and nimble. Like those tall champagne flutes."

"You're killing me, Frank."

"Yeah, me too. Jesus. The longing never goes away, eh?"

"No, just the ability," I said.

"Yeah," he laughed. "But the funny thing is, even when I had the ability most of the good stuff still took place in my dreams."

I thought of Julia; of her smell and the feel of her skin and the warm moistness of her lips.

"But not all of it," I said.

"No, not all of it."

Frank had been a second lieutenant in the Marines fighting the Japanese in the Pacific. At Tarawa he watched fourteen Marines drown in ten feet of crystal-clear water. "We came in to this beach under intense fire," he told me one afternoon as we sat on the porch playing cards. "Bullets smacking against everything and great big spouts of water splashing down on us. We were certain we'd be hit before we even made land. And God what a beach, beautiful white sand, water the color of robins' eggs. Honeymoon stuff, you know? Well, the captain in the landing craft next to mine must have panicked because he opened his ramp early and the boys went charging out into the water and sank straight away like stones. Jesus, Patrick, they just sank right to the bottom with their packs weighing a hundred pounds, and we could see them struggling clear as day but nobody could help them because we were all getting shot to pieces. A whole goddamn platoon standing on the bottom and staring up at us. Never forget it so help me God."

I saw the men, and their faces caused a dull pain in my abdomen.

"Of course, you were on the Western Front weren't you, Patrick? So that kind of shit is nothing new to you. But goddamn, you know, it sticks with you."

I wonder whether Frank was looking at those boys' faces under the water or Iris's ankles when an aneurysm in his chest burst and dropped him straight to the linoleum in the hallway just off the kitchen.

I hope he was looking at Iris's ankles.

◆　　◆　　◆

WE FOUGHT IN the Aisne-Marne region northeast of Paris throughout June and July, first repelling the German advance, then slowly turning them, farm by farm, village by village, as the U.S. Expeditionary Forces swelled into the millions. Everywhere the battered countryside was littered with the dead, who often lay unburied for weeks, so that you could walk for miles without getting away from the smell.

In September we took part in the huge American assault on the Saint-Mihiel salient south of Verdun, losing thirty percent of our company before being rushed north into the Meuse-Argonne during the final push to take the railhead at Sedan.

At the time we rarely knew where we were or where we were headed, and the days ran together in a strange tincture of terror and monotony, distinguished only by whether we were at the front or at rest. Most of the villages we passed through were in ruins by the time we reached them, their ancient buildings pocked with shell and bullet holes and their streets cluttered with debris and the carcasses of animals and burned-out trucks and tanks. Others we destroyed ourselves trying to drive the determined Germans out.

From May until the end of the war that November our battalion lurched from battlefield to battlefield, ordered about by invisible—and much cursed—forces up the ranks to plug a gap, make an assault or hold the line on the fast growing portion of the Western Front being held by the Americans. Sometimes we fought on the move, taking shelter in hastily dug rifle pits and funkholes. Other times we dug in deep and lived underground, bracing for the desperate German counterattacks and the unremitting shelling. Each day more men died and more replacements arrived. And somehow we continued.

The bravest and the meekest were the first to die. The rest of us tried our best not to look like cowards but sometimes, when asked to charge a German Maxim nestled in a concrete bunker surrounded by three belts of wire, a man would shit in his pants and there was no stopping it. The body goes berserk like an animal being dragged kicking and whining to the slaughterhouse.

We were all in awe of the stretcher-bearers, who as a matter of principle would risk everything to bring back the wounded and even the dead. I often looked into their eyes as they headed out and wondered why men will risk almost certain death in an attempt to save other men. I decided it was because men will do anything to give their lives some meaning and virtue, especially if it looks like they'll die anyway.

"In a way I envy them," said Daniel, the morning a stretcher-bearer from Minnesota was shot in the groin bringing a man in. We had just moved up in the predawn darkness from the reserve trenches to the front for our ten-day shift on the line and were struggling to repair the duckboards that were half-submerged in the mud at our feet.

"You're kidding."

"At least they can feel good about what they're doing."

"Until they're shot," I said, pulling at a wooden plank. "You're not a pacifist by any chance? Because as a squad leader that might—"

"I don't know."

"You don't know?" I yanked at a long plank until it came free.

"Yes and no."

"I didn't realize pacifism was a yes-and-no kind of thing."

"I should have been. It's too late now, so I'm not. That's what I mean." He picked up his gear and headed for the entrance to a large dugout thirty feet underground. Thick wet blankets hung from the entry to guard against gas. I followed him, pausing to let my eyes adjust to the candlelight before descending the narrow wooden stairs. Down below half a dozen men sat smoking, writing letters, playing cards and cleaning their weapons.

"So when are you two going to get married?" asked Giles, looking up. "Might as well make it official. We could even have a party."

"I'm just waiting for Paddy here to pop the question," said Daniel, smiling.

"Courage," said Lawton, looking at me. I flipped him off.

The chairs and bunks were taken so we sat on the floor against the wall.

I watched as Giles methodically cleaned his bayonet, pausing to test the blade with his thumb, which was filthy. His youthful face had grown somewhat slimmer while the sun had made his freckles more pronounced, so that some of the larger ones merged into reddish splotches. I thought he might eventually be considered handsome, except for his overbite and teeth, which went every which way, as though completely estranged from one another. Meanwhile his eyes, which were very round and dark brown, belied a softness he tried to hide by hunching up his shoulders and spitting a lot. Lately they'd looked unusually bloodshot and I thought I detected a slight tremble in his hands.

"What I need right now is a big fucking steak," he said, holding his bayonet up to eye level to examine it, then placing it back in its scabbard. I had grown to like Giles immensely, except for his habit of talking about food, which was almost pathological. I think he used food as a metaphor for all that he missed about civilian life, but regardless his descriptions were excruciating. "A great big juicy steak, cut thick, and maybe some—"

"Would you shut the fuck up," said Lawton, who was lying on his back on a wooden bunk, hands clasped behind his head. I'd only recently learned that Lawton's mother had died when he was five and his father had left him and his younger brother to be raised by an aunt, who beat them. He told Daniel all about it one morning, as though it was important for at least one person in France to know. Now when I looked at him, he reminded me of an overgrown puppy that had never been loved.

"Yeah, why the hell have you always got to talk about food?" said Lee Chatham, a Kansan with thick stubby fingers and a complexion that was frequently compared to no-man's-land. A preacher's son, Chatham had just joined the squad a few days ago, freshly minted and full of illusions. His brother had joined the Lafayette Escadrille two years earlier and been shot down over Verdun. Chatham was here to avenge him. I had tried to think if there was anything I could say to prepare him for what was to come but I couldn't. You never could. Instead I made a note to myself to stay close to him during his first shelling.

"I'd trade a herd of cattle for a good fuck right now," said Lawton, whose favorite pastime was torturing us with descriptions of what it might be like to do so-and-so with so-and-so. His lisp—so at odds with his great bulk— gave dirty words an amusing urgency. (I could thur use thum puthy.)

"Don't even think about jerking off in here," I said.

"Yeah, why don't you go up top and see if you can hit the German lines," said Giles, who would take a good steak over a naked woman any day. "I'll start a pool."

"I got ten Lucky Strikes says he can hit Berlin," I said.

"Aim for the Kaiser," said Giles.

"Or Ludendorff," I said. "Yeah, hit the old bastard right in the fucking eye."

"You ladies are just jealous," said Lawton.

"You know what you are, Lawton?" said Giles, pausing to clear his throat and spit. "You're a fucking goat."

"I know all about you farm boys from Ohio," said Lawton, flicking the stub of his cigarette butt at Giles. Lately I'd noticed a certain strain in Lawton's expression and I wondered whether maybe he talked about sex so much to cover up his fears.

"So besides fucking, what do you intend to do with yourself when you get home?" I asked. "You going to stick with carpentry or maybe open a whorehouse or something?"

"Hadn't thought of that. I suppose I could build one from scratch."

"Yeah, but you're going to have to share with your customers," said Giles.

"I'll give you a first-timer's discount," he said.

"Kiss my... I take that back, don't kiss nothing."

I turned to Daniel. "What about you? What are you going to do when you get home?"

He looked up from the letter he was writing. His hair was matted down and his lean face unshaven. "I don't know. I'd like to write, or maybe teach. The war has sort of changed what's important, don't you think?"

"So what's important?"

He thought for a moment. "Personally, I can only think of three things left that make sense doing."

"Well, let's see, we've covered eating and fucking... I'm stumped," said Giles, rubbing his jaw. Giles constantly suffered from toothaches (he'd had one pulled already), as well as debilitating heartburn, which he blamed entirely on the army diet, particularly the canned beef imported from Argentina by the French but widely derided as "monkey" or "Madagascar" meat.

Daniel smiled, then turned back to his letter.

"I'm listening," I said.

He looked back at me. "Well, I'd either like to reduce human suffering in some way, like being a doctor or helping the poor; create some sort of art, which is really a protest against suffering; or teach, especially young children, which might prevent further human suffering."

"Isn't Daniel a fucking sweetheart?" said Lawton, who was now picking at his teeth with a small splinter of wood peeled from a nearby beam.

"No shit," said Giles. "My money says he's gonna be famous someday."

"Bet you can get a scholarship somewhere," I suggested.

"Talk to Page, he's the college man," said Lawton.

Nathaniel Page, a Harvard student, glanced up from the corner where he sat reading. Despite his education, upper-class background and good looks—tall, square shoulders, strong jaw—Page never put on airs. Still, you could just tell he was smart by the way he reacted to things, not cautiously but with obvious deliberation. I liked him immediately when I met him, and I was fascinated by his efforts to grapple with all the war's larger implications. Here was Harvard meets Hell in the flesh: a guy who could speak three languages, including Latin; had actually read Newton's *Principia*; and yet couldn't find even the simplest words to describe the horrors of trench warfare. He was more fastidious than most of the men, which made him amusing to watch in a water-filled trench, yet he kept his discomfort to himself. He thought the war would go on until people at home in America and Germany and Britain and elsewhere realized just how awful it was, only there was no way to make them realize that. That was what bothered him most, knowing how indescribable it all was.

"What did you study at that fancy school anyway?" asked Lawton. "Fox-hunting?"

"Philosophy."

"I'd love that," said Daniel.

"It was a waste of time," said Page, who'd become increasingly sullen.

"Why do you say that?" asked Daniel, who looked almost hurt.

"Because it's the truth."

"No shit?" said Lawton. "You mean the rest of us aren't such dumb fucks after all?"

"Precisely."

"So what did you have to pay to learn that?" asked Lawton.

"Get off him," I said.

"A fortune," said Page, returning to his book. As I looked at him sitting there in the corner I felt suddenly sorry for him, imagining how desperate he must have felt inside when all his learning failed him.

"What about you, Delaney?" asked Giles, turning toward me.

"What about me?"

"What are you going to do with your miserable self when you get home?"

"The first thing I'm gonna do is to attend to several women waiting for me."

"How many sisters you got?" asked Lawton.

"Fuck you," I said.

"So seriously, what do you want to do?" asked Daniel.

"Hadn't thought much about it. I guess I'll go back to school, I don't know."

"I'm not in such a hurry to get home," said Giles. "I'd like to see Paris. Maybe find a French girl." For Giles, the great redeeming aspect of the war was that it offered an escape from farm life back in rural Ohio; I don't think he ever intended to go back.

"Good luck," said Lawton.

"I'm serious. I've been in France for six fucking months and I haven't seen shit. Where's all that great French civilization I heard so much about?"

"You're too late," I said. "Didn't you hear there's a war on?"

"Anybody ever been to Germany?" asked Daniel.

"My parents are from Germany," said Carl Frueller, a tall, skinny bank clerk from Pennsylvania whose shyness made me feel protective. Frueller was another recent replacement, and I wasn't sure he could hit a pumpkin from ten paces.

"You speak any German?" asked Giles.

"Sure I do."

"You got any relatives over there?"

"Some." Frueller looked embarrassed.

"Do you ever think about that, that maybe some of your cousins are in those trenches there?"

"I've thought about it."

"It doesn't bother you?"

"Not so much as I won't shoot them." He forced a smile.

"Too bad the Germans don't stick to making beer," I said, trying to change the subject.

"My mother got a letter back in 1914 saying two of her brothers had died on the Marne," said Frueller.

Nobody said anything.

"She hates the Kaiser."

"Is it true he's got one arm shorter than the other?" asked Lawton.

"Yeah, he keeps it tucked in his shirt like Napoleon," said Daniel.

"Did it ever occur to you all that maybe that's why this whole thing started?" asked Page. "You know, like Napoleon being touchy about his height? That maybe we're sitting here in this little hellhole because the Kaiser is embarrassed about his short arm?"

I thought about that for a while: a generation of Europeans killed because a man is shorter than average; another because a man's arm is shorter than the other. The absurdity of it made me laugh out loud as I headed up the stairs for gas duty in a sap that jutted out from our line twenty feet toward the German lines.

WE WERE on patrol in no-man's-land some time after two A.M. when Chatham coughed. He and Frueller were shot dead instantly while Daniel and I were pinned down in a shell hole for three hours. We decided not to say anything about Chatham coughing. It didn't seem necessary.

◆ ◆ ◆

CHRISTMAS MUSIC IS piped into Great Oaks from November through New Year's, typically fifteen hours a day. "Robert, do you have any idea how many times I've heard this song?" Robert is an orderly, and more orderly than most. In his twenties, he recently married a beautiful young woman named Debbie who paid a special visit to the ward after they got engaged.

"Kind of gets to you, doesn't it?" he says, smiling.

"Gets to me? Robert, my boy, I've heard 'Greensleeves' 738 times since Thanksgiving. I think 'Jingle Bells' started playing in October. We've got five more weeks to go, Robert. Five more weeks of nonstop around-the-clock Bing and Frank and Prancer and Dancer."

"You're just gonna have to hang tight, Mr. Delaney. Hang tight." He walks over and empties my trash can.

"And soon the Easter decorations will be up! Eggs and bunny rabbits everywhere, Robert! Hop hop hop!"

116

At Great Oaks it is always either Christmas, Easter, Independence Day, Halloween, or Thanksgiving.

A week before Christmas a young women's church group drops by with pets for the elderly to pet; lonely puppy dogs and kittens, which they plop in our lonely laps like Alka-Seltzer tablets into a glass.

I prefer dogs myself for the obvious reason that dogs prefer humans whereas cats think only of themselves. (Is there a more narcissistic creature on God's green earth?)

"Hello, my name is Anne and this is Baxter." A tall brunette with closecropped hair places a baby basset hound in my lap. I am more interested in Anne than Baxter but take what I can get. I look down at Baxter, who stares up at me expectantly, his rear flailing madly. I stroke his neck gently, enjoying his warmth. "That's it," Anne says. "There you go now." She addresses the old man she sees, not me. I tell the old man to behave and be thankful.

I remember hearing faint yelps and barking from the basement one Christmas Eve as I lay curled beneath the covers watching the snow gather on my windowsill. I couldn't sleep for hours as I thought of names for my new puppy: Rags, Scotty, Paws, Chester. I was six that Christmas; twelve when Chester was kicked by a horse on the street in front of our house. I held him as Father went to get the veterinarian and I remember that there was no blood but his fur was hot and wet. I also remember his eyes full of fluid and pleading and staring up at me with questions. "The doctor says they have to put Chester to sleep," said Father with his hand on my shoulder. I stared down at Chester through big tears that hung in my eyes and I felt that my throat would explode as they gently pried him from my arms.

Good night, Chester.

Good night, my broken-hearted boy.

◆　◆　◆

NEW YEAR'S EVE used to make me sad in that sentimental sort of way. Now it scares me. At Great Oaks the countdown starts in mid-December: who will make it to the New Year, which looms like red tape at the end of another senseless marathon? Few die just before Christmas; the expectation of family gatherings encourages survival. But New Year's Eve is for lovers and revelers, not family. Not a reason to hang on.

This year I watch Dave MacKenzie, a plumber who lost his left leg in a farming accident in Iowa when he was seven. I like MacKenzie, an utterly genuine man with a gentle voice and a pleasing laugh. The multiple wrinkles that stretch like rows of parentheses from the corners of his eyes to his temples suggest a merriment that has always eluded me.

"You know what really gets to me," he said one day when we were sitting out back by the trees.

"What's that?"

"I'm so goddamn full of good advice now and I can't use any of it." He laughed his gentle laugh. "Can't use it on myself and no one else will listen. Especially not my sons."

"Is any of it original?"

"Oh, I guess not. But it's still great advice. Could save a guy a lot of trouble. Tell me, Delaney, why is it always too late when you have finally figured out what's really important?"

"At least you finally wised up," I said.

"I don't know. It kind of makes it more painful, knowing all the mistakes I made."

"That's wisdom," I said.

"Wisdom? Ha! Wisdom is nothing but a consolation prize for growing old," he said. "A damn booby prize."

He was right of course. Better to be young and foolish.

Now bedridden by prostate cancer and nearly blind, MacKenzie is suspended between pain and pain-killers. This Christmas all five of his children and their children visit the center, wheeling his bed out to the patio and enveloping him in chatter. My own two children are vacationing with their families this year, but I don't mind. I am content to sit on my bench and watch as the MacKenzies pile presents on the patriarch's lap, opening each one just inches from his face.

"Look at this sweater, Dad. It's PERFECT for you." A daughter, maybe 40 and overweight, holds the dark blue sweater aloft. "And did you see these socks that Scott bought you? PERFECT, Dad." He smiles, the first smile I have seen on his face in months.

I watch as they leave, leaning one by one over MacKenzie's bed for a kiss and a whisper. MacKenzie is asleep as the nurses wheel him back to his room, his sheets still littered with wrapping paper.

◆ ◆ ◆

JULIA?

Yes, Patrick?

I'm so lonely, Julia.

I know you are, Patrick. I know you are.

You know that theme song to *Exodus*? I listened to it all morning on my tape deck until the nurses asked me to turn it down. It just seemed exactly right.

I didn't mean for it to be like this.

I know you didn't. I don't blame you a bit.

Maybe it would have been better if we had never met.

No, God no. I don't regret it at all.

You should have found another woman, Patrick. You're a good man. A wonderful man. I'm just a crazy woman who paints all day and can't even keep house.

I didn't want anybody else, Julia. I wanted you. I still want you.

It's too late.

Too late? Why is it too late? Don't say it's too late, Julia.

Patrick, my dear Patrick.

You're leaving, aren't you?

Soon.

Don't leave me. Why are you leaving me again?

I must.

Wait, please. Tell me you love me. I must hear at least that Julia, please.

But then I'll have to leave.

I know. But just tell me. Just say the words.

I love you, Patrick.

And how does the story of Patrick and Julia go, won't you tell me? You must tell me that before you go. Tell me how we start back in the beginning and every morning I awake to the smell of your hair and we read books together in bed side by side and we go to the symphony and we take our children camping in the summer can't you tell me any of that, Julia? Can't you?

I have to leave now, Patrick.

Can't you stay, just this once? Here, lie down beside me and we'll breathe each other's skin and I'll make breakfast in the morning and sneak out to the florist to buy you roses.

I love you, Patrick.

You love me, you really love me?

Good-bye, love.

Julia!

I awaken and stare at the clock: four A.M.

◆　　◆　　◆

MUCH TOO much pain today. Can't think straight at all.

Seemingly, as a miracle, all firing
stopped, and the silence was amazing!
Then, as we stood at our positions along
the trenches, we heard a chorus from the
German lines, which was only a couple of
thousand yards away, a beautiful chorus
singing "Silent Night." We stood there,
listening, and the strangest feeling came
over us.
—*Albert M. Ettinger, United States Army.*

◆   ◆   ◆

DECEMBER 31, I prowl the halls, whistling loudly
to combat the music. There are pictures on
the walls drawn by local schoolchildren who
flood us with artwork each holiday. I enjoy the
paintings but long for a Monet or Van Gogh
to break it up. The infantilism of old age
leaves me seething.

I stop at the entrance to the recreation
room, which is strung with red, white and
blue streamers. The TV in the corner, always
turned much too loud, celebrates another
year we had no part in. The room, otherwise
quiet, is filled with two dozen celebrants and
as many wheelchairs, walkers, canes and
colostomy bags. Those who can handle it—
and some who cannot—drink cheap champagne
from paper cups and stare at the flickering
images; images of a world that is increasingly
unrecognizable. I watch a nurse spoon-feed

chocolate cake with pink icing to a wretched-looking man who sits low in his wheelchair wearing a party hat cocked sideways. A balloon hangs from his IV drip and his shirt is covered with ice cream. Paper horns are blown. A cup is spilled. Someone begins to snore.

On my way back to my room I notice that MacKenzie's bed is empty.

◆　◆　◆

MACKENZIE'S FUNERAL is held in the small chapel on the hill behind Great Oaks. I sit alone near the back, cane between my knees. His family arrives: three daughters and two sons dressed in blacks and dark blues murmuring to spouses and towing neatly combed boys and girls adorned with bows and ribbons. Music begins as the family floats silently down the aisle; a mournful flute crackling from small white speakers mounted on the walls. I hear but two stifled sobs during the moment of silence.

Why do we suppress tears at funerals, fighting the sorrow until our throats ache? I want screaming Baptists who fall to the ground, writhing in agony. I want anguish in full orchestra and wails of protest and a pounding of chests. How dare you steal MacKenzie away from us! Damnation!

Too bad I can't attend my own funeral. What better way to see who really gave a shit? First, the cold shock of the phone call or the telegram. Then a few days for everybody to rake their memories before they are dressed in black and lined up shoulder to shoulder in creaking pews for a mixture of heart-wrenching poetry and music until their throats are constricted with grief. Louder and louder the music grows amid stifled sobs and rocking shoulders when suddenly I appear at the back of the church, striding forward triumphantly with hanky in hand. Take comfort, my friends, it's not too late to appreciate me! To apologize! For Patrick lives!

I leave the service before the final prayer. Good-bye, MacKenzie.

◆   ◆   ◆

The escort marches slowly to solemn music; the column having arrived opposite the grave, line is formed facing it.

The coffin is then carried along the front of the escort to the grave; arms are presented, the music plays an appropriate air; the coffin having been placed over the grave, the music ceases and arms are brought to the order.

The commander next commands: 1. Parade, 2. REST. The escort executes parade rest, officers and men inclining the head.

When the funeral services are completed and the coffin lowered into the grave, the commander causes the escort to resume attention and fire three rounds of blank cartridges, the muzzles of the pieces being elevated. When the escort is greater than a battalion, one battalion is designated to fire the volleys.

A musician then sounds taps.

—Infantry Drill Regulations,
United States Army War Department, 1911.

◆　◆　◆

A WEEK HAS gone by and I've nothing to show for it but a nagging feeling of having misplaced something. So all afternoon I've been going through my things, trying to figure out what I might have misplaced.

How absurd.

◆　◆　◆

"I'VE BOUGHT SOME flowers," said Julia, when I saw her in the lobby the next morning, holding a small bouquet in one hand. "I thought they might brighten my room." Her hair was pulled back and she was wearing a simple olive green dress, open at the neck and short enough to see her legs, which swiftly captivated me. Then I glanced at the curve of her hips and imagined her naked—or tried to. I thought of the women in the advertisements from the fashion magazines I used to peruse at the library as a teenager, stealthily cutting out photos of those I found especially appealing. Only Julia was so much more natural looking, with a warmth I never got from my magazine girlfriends, who died a fiery death one after-

125

noon when my mother found them in my desk and decided they were interfering with my development.

"They're beautiful," I said finally, realizing that I'd been staring.

"I'll just be a moment." She turned and headed for the stairs.

"I'll get our picnic and meet you here in the lobby," I said.

When she came back downstairs she was carrying a small folded easel, a rectangular framed canvas and her dark brown knapsack, which was slung over one shoulder. "Ready!" she said happily, with a full smile that showed her teeth.

I drove and she sat next to me with a map open on her lap and a cigarette in one hand. "Look at those graves there," she said, pointing out the window to a small cemetery surrounded by a low stone wall. "The crosses are all black."

"German," I said.

"It's an awful color for a cross," she said.

"Germans seem rather fond of black," I said. "Even their bread is black."

"But I don't think tombstones should ever be black," she said.

We parked at the edge of a thin gravel road that ended at an old wooden gate. Nearby beneath a tree sat the rusted chassis of a truck and next to it a pile of seventy-five-millimeter shell casings. I carried her easel and let her walk ahead. After forty minutes she stopped suddenly and turned back toward me.

"Right here, this is lovely," she said, putting down her knapsack. We were stopped by the edge of a cedar grove with a stream running beside it. There were several large rocks to sit on and toward the east, across a wide golden meadow, a granite-colored church spire still partly damaged rose from a gray stone village. I put down the picnic basket and looked around, trying to decide what it was that she intended to paint.

"Why did you enlist?" she asked, as she pulled a battered, flat wooden box from her knapsack, opened it and began selecting small silver tubes of paint.

"Because I was young and stupid."

"Any other reasons?"

"Young and stupid about covers it."

She eyed me sideways, smiling. "I'm not getting too far here, am I?"

"Sorry..."

"You don't have to keep apologizing."

"Then I won't."

She selected a brush and then ran her fingers through the bristles. "Do you have any heroes?"

"They're dead."

"All of them?"

"Yes, all of them."

She put the brush down and selected another. "People are funny about heroes. I read in the papers that two women in Los Angeles killed themselves after Valentino died."

"And what acts of heroism did he perform?" I felt the anger in my voice.

"That's just it. He didn't have to. He just had to offer a dream."

"Which was?"

"That a man like Valentino could save you, if only you could get close enough to him."

"Which you never can."

"No, we never get saved, do we? That's why the women killed themselves." She looked over at me and began to say something, then hesitated. Finally she said, "It's the same with our romantic relationships, don't you think?"

"What's the same?"

"We expect them to save us and they can't."

I didn't respond. Did she know what I felt? Was she telling me she couldn't help me? That nobody could?

She placed her easel facing toward the meadow and scrutinized the blank canvas, her hands resting on her waist. I studied her silhouette, the way her breasts pressed against her dress and how her forehead creased when she was concentrating and how her nose curled up just slightly at the end.

"So if Valentino isn't a hero, then who is?" she asked, turning back toward me.

I shrugged. "Someone whose life is somehow more meaningful than our own."

"So just being around them gives our own lives more meaning?"

"I suppose." I thought of Daniel.

She turned back to her canvas and began to paint.

"I think I'll just take a look around," I said. She nodded without looking up.

I jumped across two rocks in the river and entered the cedar grove, which grew increasingly dense toward the middle, fragmenting the light. Since we were northeast of town, I estimated that this ground probably changed hands several times in 1914, then remained just behind German lines until the summer of 1918, when it changed hands again several times before being secured by U.S. and French troops. I turned back and looked at Julia, whose distant silhouette, her back toward me, was framed between two slender trees. I stood there for several minutes, staring at her and listening to the birds just above me. Then I walked farther on until the trees closed her off completely. I stood perfectly still for a moment, then laid down on my back on the dry leaves, looking up toward the light. As I stared straight up the trees all seemed to lean slightly toward me as they arched skyward and I remembered the same feeling from when I was a child resting in the woods and wondering if the whole forest was going to fall in on me.

I thought of Sean and missed him intensely; his little laugh and the way he tugged on my pants leg when he wanted to play and the sweet expression on his face when he was sleeping. Then I thought of Charlotte and felt a guilty ambivalence. I pictured myself with her, then with Julia, then with Charlotte again. How could I have such different, incompatible sides to myself? Maybe other people are like mirrors that we see ourselves in; versions of ourselves that vary dramatically depending on the particular cut of glass. Do we marry promising images of ourselves, only to watch those images become hopelessly distorted? And what do I see now?

The thought of returning to Paris in three days made my stomach tighten. Was I so unhappily married? I didn't think so. Not at all. Maybe we weren't as passionate as some couples but we loved each other. We'd settled into a comfortable routine. We'd made a home together. A child.

So why did Julia change everything?

I knew why and it terrified me. She changed everything because she seemed to offer so much more; more than I'd ever felt before. But what exactly? I pressed my palms against my forehead, trying to concentrate. It was the chance—just the chance—to come fully alive; to love someone else so completely that you would never again feel alone. That was it, wasn't it? The promise of being engulfed by love and passion and intimacy; to connect in a way that gently sutured together the souls.

A butterfly fluttered past, then came to rest on a nearby leaf. I watched its wings slowly open and close.

So maybe Julia was wrong. Maybe our relationships—love—can save us, at least enough so that our lives are finally worthwhile, even with all the rotten misery and dying. All the slaughter.

I closed my eyes and concentrated on the sound of the wind through the leaves and the birds above me.

Three more days. Then what would I do? Just say good-bye and walk away from a woman who made me feel better than I'd ever felt in my life, just by her presence? And what about Julia? What would she do? She seemed more resilient than me, more daring. Like Daniel. And yet so vulnerable too.

I sat up, kneeling and leaning back on my ankles, my hands on my thighs. Of course she would marry someday, wouldn't she? Or would she and her daughter just travel around like gypsies; the refuse of a long-forgotten war?

And what did she still hope for in life? Real happiness? Or did she think the best parts were already behind her, so that her only remaining source of joy was her daughter? There seemed to be something deep inside her that was broken, as though severed, and yet she was still so full of life and laughter.

When I stood I noticed a curved lip of metal protruding from the dirt just to the left of a small sapling. I pushed it back and forth a few times to loosen it, then pulled hard. It was a German helmet, dented in the front but with the horsehair padding still intact. I banged it against a tree several times, knocking off the dirt. Then I carried it over to the river, downstream from where Julia stood, and rinsed it in the water.

"I found something for you," I said, holding it out as I crossed the river and walked toward her. "It's German. They changed helmet designs in 1915. The spiked Pickelhaube was a bit too impractical even for old Willy."

I handed it to her. She stared at it, turning it over and over in her hands. I watched her fingertips search the worn gray steel.

"We collected a lot of souvenirs during the war," I said. "Helmets, knives, medals, canteens, everything. They were very popular. You could get sixty dollars for a decent Luger."

She remained silent. Was she somehow offended?

"There is something very sad, very poignant about it," she said finally.

"Every artifact has its story. That's the attraction, I suppose."

"And all one can do is wonder what the story is. Was this helmet discarded in flight, or was a man killed wearing it? And this dent, where did this dent come from? A bullet? A shell? A shovel? Or was it dented after it fell off?"

She offered it back to me. "I don't think I want it," she said. "Perhaps you'd rather give it to your son." I took it from her, feeling suddenly foolish as I stood holding it. (I later tucked it into the picnic basket and brought it to my room.)

"I'm hungry," she said. "Let's eat."

We sat on the grass and from the corner of my eye I watched as she bent her legs together on one side and sat almost on her ankles, leaning back on one arm. I opened the basket and handed her the bread and a knife. Then I opened a bottle of white wine and poured two glasses. As I sat back and took a drink I was struck by the impropriety of a married man sitting in a meadow picnicking with a beautiful single woman. *But how good it felt.*

"Do you read much poetry?" she asked, resting her glass on the ground next to me.

"Just a bit."

"Daniel loved poetry. He used to say that the best poems were like little vessels that carry messages that can't be transported in any other way; miniature worlds like tiny paintings or Fabergé eggs."

"Do you write poetry?"

"Sometimes. Most of them are awful. But I like the feeling I get. Daniel said that what mattered was to look at things differently once in a while or you'd stop seeing them for what they are." She leaned back on her elbows and looked up at the sky. "Sometimes I think we only live a small part of our lives."

"The way you talk reminds me of Daniel," I said.

I saw an almost imperceptible look of pleasure cross her face, which made me think of how much we can tell from even the most minute changes in a person's face or voice or gestures, especially a loved one.

Then I noticed a tear on her cheek.

"I've upset you," I said.

She dabbed her eyes. "I'm sorry, it's just that I don't get much of a chance to talk about Daniel, except with Robin. I don't even know anybody else who's ever met him. Can you imagine that? After he died it was like he never existed. The only trace I can find is in his letters." She paused, and I watched her chest rise and fall slowly. "And in Robin's face."

I reached toward her, putting my hand on her shoulder. "I wish there was something I could say."

"You don't have to say anything. I'm just glad that you're here."

She pulled a piece of bread from a baguette and handed it to me. "I worry about smothering Robin with too much love. I just have no one else."

"There are worse fates for children."

She pulled out a piece of cheese and began unwrapping it. "There are so many times I wish I could ask Daniel what to do. I even try to imagine what he would tell me, how he would handle a situation."

I put my wineglass down. "There's something I have to tell you."

She looked at me expectantly.

"Daniel was writing you a marriage proposal."

Her expression froze.

"It was in the form of a long poem. He spent weeks working on it. It was dozens of pages long when he died. I promised to find you and tell you but I didn't know your last name. All your letters disappeared with him. Everything."

She sat perfectly still for a moment, looking down. I watched her hands, which trembled slightly. After a few minutes I asked, "How did you know he had died?"

She tried to smile through her tears. "We had this very simple system that allowed me to keep track on a map of where he was. I'd simply put together the second letter in every third line of his letters and they would spell out where he was and whether things were going well or not. So I knew he was at the front, and when the letters stopped coming, I knew he was dead."

She folded a cloth napkin and wiped her face, then took a deep breath and sat up straight. "I'm really not sure what I'm going to do with the rest of my life. Sometimes I feel like I'm already old, like all the best things in my life are memories, except for Robin."

"You can't think that way."

She shrugged, then handed me a piece of cheese. "My friends tell me it's time to put Daniel behind me and find another man and get married. They're afraid I'm going to end up an old spinster."

"I don't imagine that happening to you."

"But I don't want to get married. Why should I? Besides, I'm not what most men are looking for in a wife."

"I don't know—"

"It's true. I hate to cook and I hate to clean and I'm disorganized and messy and I don't like wearing makeup. I also snore."

"You snore?"

She blushed slightly. "Only when I'm really tired."

"I don't believe you snore."

"It's not like I rattle the windows."

"Daniel snored."

"I remember."

"I think he kept the Germans up a few nights. I used to worry that they'd try to silence him with a couple of well-placed mortar rounds."

"I used to kick him."

"So did I. Only with my boots on."

She laughed, then asked, "Do you like being married?"

"Do I like it? Sure I do. Why do—"

"I don't mean to pry. It's just that I see so many unhappy couples. I'd much rather be single all my life than marry the wrong person."

"Nobody plans to marry the wrong person."

"Of course not." She took another sip of her wine, then lit a cigarette. "It's always amazed me that so many people do find someone to marry. It seems like such a long shot, to stumble across the right person at the right time. Most of the men I meet are so utterly self-absorbed, prattling on about themselves for hours." She paused, then looked up at me with a laugh. "But you're not like that."

"Maybe I just don't have that much to prattle on about."

"I bet you do."

She leaned back on both elbows again, letting the cigarette smoke slowly rise from her mouth. I could see the outline of her breasts, her nipples pushing through her dress. "Do you believe in love at first sight?" she asked.

"Yes," I said, rather too quickly. "Or something awfully close to it."

"Is that how you felt about your wife when you first met her?"

I blushed. "No, I mean not exactly." I tried to find the right words. "I was attracted to her. She seemed nice. It was a more gradual process. It's funny that you ask because the guys in our squad had endless debates about love and romance. You have to realize we had a lot of time on our hands."

"Sounds like an unusual group of men."

"The best." I thought of Giles and Tometti and Lawton and Daniel, of our late-night talks curled up in a dugout or on duty or marching, all the funny stories and laughter and dirty jokes and hopes and longings and loneliness. "I think that's what saved me."

"And what did you all decide?" She was smiling.

"About love? Well for starters we decided we all wanted to fall in love at first sight, like Daniel had with you."

She looked momentarily flustered.

"But we couldn't decide whether love at first sight could last, whether that feeling, that intoxicating attraction, that passion, could be sustained, or whether it just wore off. Nonetheless, we were desperate to find out."

"I guess I'll never know that now." She took another slow drag of her cigarette, then extinguished it in the grass. "Tell me, did you have a girlfriend during the war?"

I suppressed the urge to lie. "No. To be honest, I was envious of Daniel."

"I'm surprised you didn't. I'll bet you were quite popular growing up."

"What, are you kidding? Pudgy Paddy?"

"Pudgy Paddy?"

I winced. "It was a phase. My mother used to make these cookies..."

"Pudgy Paddy. It's catchy. I was called Pinky."

"Pinky?"

"I had pinkeye on and off for most of sixth grade. It went from one eye to the other and then back again. It was quite charming."

"I had pinkeye the night of the high school dance."

"You didn't."

"Fortunately, I didn't have a date."

"You didn't either? Aren't we a pair?" She brushed her hand against my forearm.

I studied her face. She didn't *know* the power she held.

"I always kept to myself at school," she said. "I never really felt comfortable with other kids. They seemed so unpredictable to me. And I was teased because I couldn't afford the right clothes. Little girls can be quite cruel."

"Another loner," I said, smiling to myself as I pulled off another piece of bread, added a slice of cheese and began eating it.

"I prefer loners," she said. "They're the most interesting people."

"If you can get to them."

She laughed. "Before I met Daniel I didn't know you didn't have to be so alone."

Was I lonely, even with a wife and son? I was, and I hadn't even noticed.

She rose to her feet and brushed herself

off. "It's hard to find the right person, isn't it? Someone you can love without losing yourself?"

I nodded and stood up, feeling cornered by her questions. What if I simply told her what I felt? Would that scare her? Would she feel sorry for Charlotte? How could I explain to her that it wasn't just a physical attraction; that I wasn't another lecherous husband on the make? How could I tell her the truth without overwhelming her?

A biplane passed overhead, low and droning. I felt an instinctive chill of fear. We both watched it until it disappeared. Then Julia turned to me, looking suddenly serious, and said, "How did you let go of the war; of the things you saw and did?"

"I'm not sure that I have." I looked at her and she held my gaze. Her eyes looked curious, as though she were searching for something.

"How often do you see the other men, the ones who came home?"

"Used to be once a year. We'd drink ourselves into a stupor. But now people are starting to drift off. Either they don't want to be reminded of the war anymore or they're just too busy trying to raise families and make a living." She was now standing close to me.

"The saddest part is, it's not the same even when we are together. Most of the guys are so different now; preoccupied. I hardly recognize them."

"Life does that," she said, plucking a bright red leaf from a nearby branch and running her fingertips along its surface, as if memorizing its texture. I imagined her fingertips running across my skin.

I lit a cigarette, shaking the match hard before tossing it to the ground. "You know the strangest part of it all, the war I mean? I've never felt so alive in all my life. Everything: my hearing, sense of smell, my vision, my taste buds; it was all so magnified. I noticed *everything*."

That was the secret delight of war, wasn't it? That at least for once in your life, everything was on the line. *Everything mattered.*

"That probably had something to do with being shot at."

I laughed. "But doesn't it seem a little pathetic, that we have to have a gun to our heads to fully value life?"

"Yes, come to think of it, it does."

"Actually, I believe that falling in love has the same effect—without quite so many downsides."

"Oh really?" Her full smile pressed her cheeks back toward the outer corners of her eyes, lifting her nose slightly.

I imagined holding her face and kissing her lips, her eyes, her chin. Was I falling in love? No, I'd already fallen, from the first moment I'd seen her; her eyes and nose and hair and laugh and hands and her smell and the things she said and the warm tone of her voice and the shape of her ears and her gestures and her easy smile. Especially her smile.

I reached for the wine bottle and poured more wine.

"Do you mind if we stay longer?" she asked. "I'd like to paint some more if you don't—"

"Not at all." I handed her a glass and we stood facing each other. Above, plump white clouds slowly crept past and the air felt cooler. In the distance I saw several cows clustered on the slope of a hill. "I'm curious, have you always wanted to be a painter?"

She nodded, then took a sip of her wine. "Somehow it makes me feel better. After Daniel died it's all I wanted to do."

She was standing so close to me, her head tilted slightly up toward mine. I longed to reach out and grab her in my arms. Couldn't I? No, I couldn't. So many reasons why I couldn't. Yet none seemed convincing. I leaned forward and kissed her quickly on the lips, then stepped back to look at her face. I thought she seemed to blush as she dropped the leaf she was holding. She opened her mouth as if to speak, then stopped herself and turned and walked back to her canvas.

◆　◆　◆

I WAS SITTING in the lounge this afternoon when I looked up from my book and noticed that I was surrounded by the No Names. The No Names are people who no longer talk; people whose souls have long since fled and whose eyes are like the vandalized windows of an abandoned farmhouse, the grass coming up through the porch steps and the front door half open, leading to cluttered darkness. They just sit all day, sucking air in, and breathing it out. Just breathing. I call them the No Names because I can't bear to learn their names. Not after they've already died. Who wants to acquaint themselves with a name that no longer registers?

I closed my book and hurried back to my room.

◆　◆　◆

YOU'VE AGED well, Patrick.

You think so? I don't. This place depresses me. All these old people, most of them long dead only they don't know it.

I want to ask you something.

Please. Anything.

Just one question.

I'm ready.

Well, after all these years, after everything you've seen, do you still think life is a tragedy?

Oh yes, Julia, I do. But there are some very funny moments. This just isn't one of them.

◆　◆　◆

GILES AND I sat in a listening post near the ruins of a farmhouse under a full summer moon, straining to distinguish one sound from another. Coughing. A tap of metal on metal. Creaking wood from the duckboards. Laughter. And much farther, the braying of a mule. We'd been up against the Germans for three weeks with little rest and our nerves were completely frayed.

"What's that?" asked Giles.

"You mean that?"

"*That.*"

"That's behind us. That's our lines."

"You sure?"

"I'm sure."

Just after four A.M. the Germans fired a few rounds above our heads. I heard them slap into the parapet of the trench behind us. Bullets sound different when they hit flesh. A thouk, thouk, thouk. Then maybe a scream or a low groan.

No word yet from the Maxim somewhere off to the right. They do talk, fast and guttural, their angry messages tapped furiously in a Morse code that translates: HATE HATE HATE HATE. Sometimes, as the bullets sweep back and forth, I hear them inquire, "Where are you, Patrick? We're coming for you." When I first heard them, they reminded me of the woodpeckers we had out behind our house. They don't anymore.

Artillery doesn't talk, it just screams, convulsing the earth with grand mal seizures. But not tonight. Tonight the 75s and 77s and 155s sounded like muffled barks in the distance; the persistent cough of some primordial beast lurking in the forest, unable to sleep.

"Wouldn't some venison taste good about now? Say with a side of—"

"Don't even start."

He shrugged, then rubbed his jaw. "Did you see that Chaplin picture at the Y last week?"

"Missed it. Any good?"

"Pretty damn funny stuff." He scratched his crotch, then his back, then his crotch again. "I've been thinking about opening a motion picture theater back in Cleveland. Wonder what it would cost?"

"Hell of a lot more than we're drawing sitting here. 'Course if the war lasts another dozen years or so, you might just have yourself the down payment."

"Guess I might need some partners." He scratched himself again, then coughed quietly into his sleeve. I imagined him back in Ohio, all dressed up and standing out in front of his new theater on opening night with a line of people waiting to buy tickets. Even if it failed he'd find something else; Giles was like that, always scheming on ways to get rich. He'd already started a lucrative trade in German souvenirs and French brandy and was constantly trying to befriend the storeroom clerks at the Red Cross canteens. "I just want to be comfortable," he'd say. "I watched my parents sweat every day of their lives and for what?" His mother died when he was eleven; his father was now bedridden and cared for by John's younger sister and her husband, who worked the family farm.

"Look at that moon, just sitting there staring at us," I said. It looked much closer than I remembered the moon being, like a big piece of fruit hanging just out of reach. Squinting,

I made out craters and gashes but I couldn't see the face. I never saw the face on the moon. Under my breath I hummed, "I see the moon, the moon sees me, the moon sees somebody I'd like to see..."

"Shhh, listen." He crept up on the firestep.

"I didn't hear anything."

"Shhh."

A footfall against dirt? I raised my rifle so that the tip of my bayonet was level with the top of the trench line. The sudden nausea and pressure in my bladder. Giles pulled out a grenade, his fingers fidgeting on the serrated metal grip. We waited.

"It's okay, it's nothing," he said, relaxing. "It's too bright out for raids. They'd have to be fucking crazy."

"They are fucking crazy." I slumped down against the side of the trench.

He pulled out his pistol, wiped it down, and placed it back in its holster. A few minutes later he said, "You know what I miss?"

"What?"

"My dog. I miss my dog."

"What kind?"

"A mutt. Named Scratch."

"Scratch?"

"Her fleas have fleas."

"Ought to name you Scratch."

He jabbed me with his elbow. "I'm serious. I really miss her. She's gonna go nuts when I get home." He smiled broadly.

I thought of Chester and how we buried him near the base of an elm tree out in the woods behind our house. Katherine and I made a wooden cross painted white with large red lettering that said, "Chester, 1904-1910."

"Shh."

"What?"

"Did you hear something?"

"No, I didn't hear anything."

◆　◆　◆

WHERE WAS I? The portrait, that's right. Let me sit a moment and close my eyes. It's easier that way, to drift back. Back to when things were so clear.

◆　◆　◆

AFTER LUNCH I asked Julia if I could look at her painting but she told me to wait a few more hours. Had I ruined everything with the kiss? And what was she thinking? I studied her face for clues but found none. I lay on the grass daydreaming for an hour and then tried to read a newspaper she had brought along, but I was too distracted.

"You're being awfully patient," she said, after a while.

"Oh I don't mind. I like it here."

"You can come and look now, if you want. It's not nearly finished, but I won't do any more today."

I stood and walked over to the easel. She took a few steps back and watched me.

It was Daniel. He was walking across a

146

meadow, looking right at her. I could see the damaged church steeple in the background and in the foreground I could see the corner of our picnic blanket. Daniel was in his uniform, dirty and slightly bent under the weight of his pack. He held his helmet in his hand and his rifle was slung over his shoulder. But what was that look in his eyes? I couldn't tell if he was sad or happy, but I didn't dare ask.

Julia asked me what I thought but I couldn't say anything at all so I just looked at her and nodded and she nodded too.

◆　◆　◆

> Calm fell. From heaven distilled a
>   clemency;
> There was peace on earth, and silence in
>   the sky;
> Some could, some could not, shake off
>   misery:
> The Sinister Spirit sneered: "It had to
>   be!"
> And again the Spirit of Pity whispered,
>   "Why?"
>
> —Thomas Hardy,
> "And There Was a Great Calm."

◆　◆　◆

I CARRIED THE painting of Daniel back to the car. It was hard to hold it, trying not to smudge anything as we carefully picked our way alongside the stream and past clumps of barbed wire and more piles of shell casings and then back across a long pockmarked pasture to where we had parked.

We got back to the hotel at dusk. In the lobby I handed the painting back to Julia. She turned it right-side up and offered a weak smile that suggested either sadness or exhaustion.

"It was kind of you to come with me today," she said.

"I enjoyed it."

"I promised myself I'd write some letters tonight."

"Yes, well maybe I'll see you tomorrow then."

She turned and headed for the stairs. Everything she carried looked so tremendously heavy that I wanted to help. And I couldn't let her leave without trying to explain myself.

"Ah, listen, about this afternoon..."

She turned. "Don't," she said, shaking her head and holding her hand up. Then she smiled.

We stood in silence, looking at each other. Then I said, "I thought I might drive to Verdun tomorrow. I was wondering, would you care to join me, if you're not busy?" So nervous. Did my voice sound strange? It did to me.

"Verdun?" A pause. Her just looking at me. Not staring, just looking. And that painting of Daniel walking toward me across the meadow. "Yes certainly. I'm glad you asked."

◆　　◆　　◆

THANK YOU.

148

PART
TWO

I've been trying to draw Julia for years. Not that I have any talent. I took some classes long ago and I sign up whenever they offer drawing here at Great Oaks. Most of my efforts are so embarrassing that I tear them up immediately. A few I tuck away in my drawer, only to destroy them upon later scrutiny. The instructor says I lack a sense of perspective. Everything is a bit off, as though viewed through the funny mirrors at a county fair. But I keep trying, if only from obstinacy. Sometimes I draw landscapes, usually French scenery plucked from my memory. But most of the time I try to draw Julia. I haven't been able to get her right yet; not the eyes and the smile. But I haven't given up. I'd just like to once before my mind goes. That way I wouldn't have to worry about losing her forever.

I sketch some of the nurses too. And not always properly clothed. The truth is, I'm in love with three of them, or more honestly, I'm in love with one of them and smitten by the other two. At my age you may figure this is a mere case of high affections, a grandfatherly crush on "women young enough to be your grandchildren!" It is not. This is pure hot lusty love celebrated in every nook and cranny of this facility, at least in my head. It's longing

151

until you want to claw at your chest and fall to your knees and beg for just one pouty-lipped kiss and a slight press of the loins.

My favorite is Sarah, who strikes me as one of those rare women who could fulfill both the wife and mistress fantasies on the same date. A divorced mother-of-two with a sleek black mane, dark blue eyes and the softest hands in the nursing profession, Sarah is the Florence Nightingale of Great Oaks, relentlessly cheerful and optimistic (except when it comes to her own life), with the rare ability to convince you that she actually likes being around old people. Not quite as sexy as Janet, the young blonde on the west wing, but so sincere, so absolutely honest and right there in front of you, her hand on top of yours and those eyes examining you to make sure you're okay and what can I do for you? And she's got the best laugh, a throaty chuckle that doubles the size of her smile and causes her to bend slightly at the waist, which makes me wince. The amazing part— this really kills me—is that her husband walked out on *her*, like maybe Marilyn Monroe was waiting for him offshore with champagne on ice.

My darling Janet is married, which complicates things, but not happily married, which raises possibilities. She has no children, but wants them, which raises more questions, and she treats me like an elder statesman, which can be exciting, though I'd rather be seen as a sweaty stable boy.

Janet's thick blond hair is parted on the

side, curled behind her ears and cut just above shoulder length. She has, quite possibly, the most beautiful neck I've ever seen, which means something at my age. And her breasts! Even in winter they are indisputable, a flagrant and august presence beneath her noble sweater, which is not to detract from her mischievous fanny, ever beckoning as it recedes lockstep down the hallway, left right left right. Follow me. Anywhere, Janet, you gorgeous creature. If I could have just one woman for one night, it would be Janet, and I'd be dead by morning. Au revoir!

Erica is in her mid-forties, I'd guess, with green eyes, thick black hair and a dark, Mediterranean complexion. About five foot six, she has strong slender legs, darling kneecaps and exquisitely lithe arms. Already twice divorced, she has probably slept with more men than Janet and Sarah combined, and spit a few out for breakfast. But what strikes me most about Erica is how she manages to be both tough and feminine simultaneously, which drives me crazy.

I shuffle down the hallway toward the nurses' station, where Sarah is studying a clipboard. "Good morning Sarah," I say, wishing I could bury my face in that soft, salacious mane and start all over again.

"Hi, Patrick," she chirps, firing off a huge smile that makes me sad. She always seems so happy to see me that I cannot help but take it personally, though of course she does that to everybody.

"What a beautiful dress," I say.

"It's my uniform, you old clown," she says, making me feel very old indeed. She heads off down the hallway, clipboard pressed to her chest, her head cocked slightly to one side. I head for a chair, quaking.

I'd love to get laid one more time before I die. Seriously. And truth be told, I get a lot less picky as I get older. (Some nights I am kept awake by the faces of women I once turned away during my brief and misguided heyday.) I am, essentially, a horny eighteen-year-old trapped in the carcass of an Egyptian mummy. If youth is wasted on the young, and it is, recklessly so, then old age is wasted on the infirm: all that wisdom crammed into a dog that no longer hunts. And still I fantasize like a freshman.

But my lonely lust isn't what hurts the most. The worst thing is that nobody even wants to touch me anymore.

◆　　◆　　◆

OR IS IT all the regrets, those desperate creatures that hound each day and hour and minute of an old man's life? Sometimes when I feel the panic coming, I will pour a second glass of brandy and drink it straight away, but I try to be careful or the brandy and the pills I take will throw impromptu parties that I don't care to host.

Today I feel especially anxious, a gnawing

or buzzing just below my chest as though I'm infested with termites. I should go to lunch before the kitchen closes but I'm too nervous to leave my room, where I sit in the corner in the orange-colored chair with stained fabric that itches even through a cotton shirt.

My joints ache and my eyesight seems more blurry than usual. If I were younger I'd make an appointment with my doctor and tell him that something is wrong, but at my age things are supposed to be wrong. "Well, of course you feel like shit, Mr. Delaney, you're eighty-one. Your insides are shriveling up and you're going to die soon. What you need is a paleontologist, not a doctor."

I reach for a book from a stack in the corner. Aldous Huxley, *The Doors of Perception*. I turn the pages until I reach a passage I have underlined:

> Most men and women lead lives at the worst so painful, at the best so monotonous, poor and limited that the urge to escape, the longing to transcend themselves if only for a few moments, is and has always been one of the principal appetites of the soul.

Then I close the book, slowly rise from my chair and head for my closet stash to fix myself a drink.

♦ ♦ ♦

I GOT A new roommate today. A short guy with watery eyes, their color long faded, hysterically tiny feet tucked into baby blue loafers and big age spots all over his forehead. I didn't have the heart to tell him the fate of his predecessors. Anyway I've decided not to get too chummy. The good-byes are killing me.

His name is Martin Dansfield. His daughter Trudy wheeled him in. She's some big shot ad executive from Chicago. A real bitch, if you ask me, telling him where to hang his pants and which drawers to put his underwear in and not to make too many phone calls since she's footing the bill.

When she disappeared into the bathroom I leaned over to him and whispered, "Tell her not to use too much of the toilet paper because I'm footing half that bill."

He laughed so hard that I was afraid he'd expire on me.

After Trudy left I gave him a quick rundown on which nurses to avoid, which to seek out, and which I'd already claimed as mine. Then I took him down to the recreation room to introduce him around.

♦　　♦　　♦

"UP, UP, UP! You're going to be late for PT!" It's Cindy, my least favorite nurse, who storms into my room like the ringleader of an angry mob headed for Frankenstein's castle. I have fallen asleep after lunch, and she is standing next to my bed with a look of mild repugnance.

I don't think she likes old people, not that I blame her.

"How are we going to work those muscles if you're just lying in this bed? Up, up, up!" she barks.

I used to work my muscles in bed, but that's neither here nor there, especially to Cindy. I rise slowly without looking at her. "I can find my own way there, thank you," I say, taking the cup full of pills she thrusts toward me. Her forearms are huge and I wonder if she resents having to lift old people for a living. When I die, I surely hope she is not the one who finds me.

The exercise room is down two hallways past the recreation room. I walk steadily, wondering how long I can keep the wheelchairs at bay. I watch them glide past across the glassy linoleum sea bearing their ancient and often oblivious cargo to and fro.

Hanford, a tall black physical therapist with the largest smile at Great Oaks, and maybe even California, waits for me in the doorway, smiling. The first time I met him he told me, "You know Patrick, some people think life is too short to put up with shit and other people say life is too short to let shit get to you. My problem is that I think most people are full of shit."

He greets me by gripping my shoulders and guides me toward a treadmill. "How ya doing today?" he asks.

"Feeling like a coiled jungle cat," I say. "It's just a question of when to pounce."

"Easy on the oysters."

"Chrimeny, if they serve oysters one more time, I'm gonna have to call a hooker." I hold the handrails tightly and try to lift my knees high as I walk. Rain is pounding against the window as though searching for an opening. I remember the metallic ping ping ping of rain against corrugated iron.

"You were in Vietnam, weren't you Hanford?"

"Hundred and First Airborne," he says. Behind him in the corner a large silver fan sways back and forth.

"Nasty business," I say.

"Nasty business," he says. "You ever in the service?"

"Pershing's army."

He thought for a moment. "That's the First War, right? Early part of the century now, wasn't it?"

"I'm impressed, Hanford. Some folks aren't sure whether I fought in the War of the Roses or the Thirty Years' War."

"Frankly I thought you was on one of them Crusades."

"Don't push your luck."

He presses a button on the treadmill, raising the incline. "So you gonna tell me what it was like?"

"I'm running out of breath here."

He slowed the speed down. "Better?"

"Better."

"You on the lines?"

"I could smell the sauerkraut."

"Shit boy! How long?"

"Couple of months."

"Ever get shot?"

"Shrapnel," I say, tapping my thigh.

"Gassed?"

"Yep."

"What's that shit do, choke you?"

"Depends on the gas. With mustard gas it could be hours before you felt the effects. Then your skin started blistering like it was coming off, especially in your armpits and groin, and your eyes clamped shut with pain and it began eating away at your bronchial tubes. The severe cases slowly suffocated to death."

"Some nasty shit."

I nod.

"So what the hell was the point?" he asks, after a few minutes.

"The point?" I pause.

"Yeah, the *point*."

"Well, for starters we were going to stop German militarism once and for all. But I think the real point was that everybody's honor was on the line."

"Honor? Shit," he shrugs. "Screw honor."

"What about you, what were you fighting for?" I ask, wheezing as I step off the treadmill and take the small white towel he hands me.

"Oh that's easy," he says. "I was fighting to save my ass."

Then I lie down on a bed and he lifts my limbs one by one as we listen to the rain.

In the charge, I got within fifty feet of the German machine-gun nests when a bullet plowed through the top of my skull… As I lay there I could plainly see the German gunners and hear them talking. They could see I was not dead and I watched them as they prepared to finish me. They reloaded their gun and turned it on me. The first three bullets went through my legs and hip and the rest splashed up dust and dirt around my head and body. Evidently thinking they had done a good job the Boches turned their gun to other parts of the field.

—*Joyce Lewis, United States Marines.*

◆　◆　◆

BANG BANG BANG. I jolt up from sleep as a timber falls from the ceiling of the dugout, smacking my shoulder. Then another, dirt and smoke filling the air.

"You all right?" asks Daniel, pulling himself to his feet. Light from a flare pours through a large crack in the roof and illuminates his face, which is bleeding.

Another blast. We're on the floor again, Daniel's legs across my head.

"Son of a bitch," he says.

"Can you move?" I ask.

"Yeah, I'm okay. Let's get out before it collapses." I scramble up the stairs behind him.

Figures are crouched at the bottom of the trench. Others scurry back and forth, hunched over.

"It's like a fucking meteor shower," says a voice to my left.

To my right I see Lawton huddled near the entrance to the dugout and shaking uncontrollably.

I move down the line past Page. His face is rigid and his nose is bleeding heavily. I pat him on the back.

The explosions start again and we throw ourselves down onto the earth until I am clawing at my helmet and burrowing desperately into the dirt. Bits and pieces of metal and wood and debris fly around the trenches. I wonder if I am cut or bleeding but I feel nothing because my body has gone rigid, fully contracted. I hold on to myself trying to keep from being pulled apart by the concussions. I move down the trench until I stumble into Tometti hugging the dirt and softly singing an Italian ballad. Tears streak down his dirty face. I think of his girlfriend Teresa and wonder what she would think if she could see him this way.

Another tremendous blast. Am I buried? I push away at the dirt. No, I can breathe. But dirt is in my mouth and throat.

"Give me a hand!" cries Giles, standing near a collapsed section of trench. I see Daniel behind him. Thank God. We dig frantically with our hands and picks and shovels. Everything glows white then red beneath the volcanic sky, flickering and flashing through the smoke. I find a finger, then a hand. I tear at the dirt, searching for a face.

"Over here. Delaney's found one!" says Giles.

I feel a shoulder, then a chin and a nose. "Pull!"

It's Tometti. Dirt is packed tightly in his mouth and nostrils and ears. With my fingers I clear his mouth and turn him and shake him until he begins coughing. I turn to dig some more. Another body. No, a boot. I tug at it and it comes easily. The leg is severed at the knee.

Page and I struggle with a third body that seems to be buried almost straight upside down. A voice shouts, "Grab your rifles. Stand to! They're attacking!"

I hear shouts and I notice my fingers are bleeding as I search through the dirt and rocks and splintered wood for the upside-down man's face. I feel an ear, a clump of hair. I gently pull. The forehead is missing. Page? No, a young kid from another squad. Farm boy from Nebraska, I think. I lay the head down. Someone grabs me and pulls me away.

Where is my rifle?

A trench mortar to my right and two of the BARs we hauled up the previous night begin firing. I listen and watch as everything slows down until I feel almost completely removed; a distant observer to some strange and horrible catastrophe. My ears are ringing but I am not afraid. I look slowly left, then right.

Nothing matters but the firing of the machine guns. I listen to their ruthless work, raking back and forth with fierce mathematical certainty. That's it: we are fighting a tremendous numbers game. Bullets versus bodies, artillery shells versus battalions, bandages versus wounds, medics versus the wounded, gas versus lungs, flame throwers versus human flesh. What matters is volume and quantity, quantity of boots and canteens and rations and rifles and privates and lieutenants and planes and ships and submarines. Won't someone call the score?

The Germans are in our wire now yet I fear nothing. Anger surges. I scream. Did I scream? Destroy it all. Everything. Fury and destruction. Now! Come for this cornered animal, yellow teeth bared. Rabid.

Try me.

I pull a rifle from a body stretched across the duckboards, then struggle to pull a bayonet from its scabbard. The latch is broken. The bayonet is bent. I throw it down and search for another. As I look I can hear rapid German phrases, both angry and scared, and wonder if German is the language of war. It sounds like it to me, a series of urgent commands being passed down the chain of command. Does "I love you" in German really sound like "I love you," or is it more in the tone of "I'm gonna beat the shit out of you"? This is interesting to me because language has been an awful problem in this war, at least for those of us who would like to put it into words but can't because the necessary words don't and can't ever exist. Carnage; murderous fire; mass, ritualized slaughter; gaping and septic wounds blackened with disease and flies, white bone protruding from flesh; ten thousand men cut down in an afternoon, their bodies spread across no-man's-land like a grotesque quilt.

There, my bayonet is fixed. Cold steel. I am cold ruthless steel. My fists are tight and my temples hurt; the muscles in my neck are taut. I want to get my death over with. *Now*. I look up and see one then two then three Germans with their long field-gray coats and flared helmets dropping down into our trenches firing rifles and pistols and tossing stick bombs and lunging with their bayonets. I fire my rifle (did I close my eyes?) and then jab jab jab with my bayonet pushing and slashing in blind fury DIE DIE DIE.

Daniel grabs me and shakes me. Then Page and Giles and I crawl to the top of the parapet and lie on our stomachs and fire at the retreating shadows that flee like ghosts across the pocked, swaying earth.

For the rest of the day we repair our trenches, bury the dead and haul up more ammunition. I remember nobody talked much though we listened very carefully.

◆   ◆   ◆

LIEBER GOTT, *hilf mir! Bitte, lieber Gott! Bitte, lieber Gott...*

[Dear God, help me! Please, dear God! Please, dear God...]

THAT NIGHT in the darkness amid the moans and the lingering smell of cordite I realized that the earth itself was bleeding, its wrists slashed deep down to the arteries along a line called the Western Front. I wondered how long it would take to hemorrhage to death. A few more months? A year at the most?

◆   ◆   ◆

" I WISH they'd shut up," says Tometti, rubbing his palms up and down his face like a man who thought he had spiders crawling on him. The moans and screams of hundreds of men, mostly Germans, drifted across no-man's-land. Tometti takes out his knife and tries to cut a small piece of hard bread he pulled from his pocket but his hands shake too badly and he puts the knife away. Then he crosses his arms in front of him and jams his hands into his armpits.

Some of the sounds are remarkably animallike, the shrieking of dozens of creatures big and small that have stepped into steel traps. My knees feel weak and I wonder if sound alone can make you faint.

"They are fucking Huns," says Lawton, whose dirty face is nicked with cuts, some of them an inch long. He pats Tometti gently on the back. "Just fucking Huns."

"Yeah, fucking Huns," repeats Tometti in a whisper.

Whoever tries to interfere with my task I shall crush.

—*Kaiser Wilhelm II*

OUR FIRST STOP in Verdun was at the Cimetière National de Douaumont on the east bank of the Meuse. We walked among the rows and rows of simple white crosses that guarded a silence so absolute and dense that it pressed against my eardrums like water at the bottom of a very deep pool. That one there, he was a new father and next to him, the last of three brothers killed and that one there was to have been a poet and that one a teacher and over there a great scientist and that one a writer and that one a priest and that one there, there in the corner, well that one could have been you, *oui?*

Names, endless names impaled accusingly on endless white crosses.

"I always think of the mothers," said Julia, holding herself as though she was cold, her arms crossed in front of her. I remembered the sound of men calling for their mothers; how common it was, so that you came to expect it. Only once did I hear a man call for his father, and that was in German.

"Maybe they should bury everyone in the same cemetery," I said. "All of them, so that people could visualize the toll. Can you imagine it, millions and millions of head-

166

stones and crosses and Stars of David in row after row, with one war right next to another?"

"No, I can't imagine it," she said, leaning against my shoulder.

We walked back to the car in silence.

Driving to Fort Douaumont we saw several signs posted at various angles by the roadsides warning of leftover shells and grenades. The *Zone Rouge*. When we passed two laborers loading shells into the back of a truck, Julia asked if we could stop.

"Those are live shells?" she asked, as we stood near the stack of two dozen dirty cylinders.

I nodded. The Frenchmen smiled, then carefully picked up one of the shells, held it close to my head, tapped his ear and then shook the shell back and forth. I heard the swooshing sound of liquid inside.

"It's a gas shell," I said, stepping back. The Frenchman gently laid the shell down on a wooden palette in the back of the truck, then turned to pick up another.

"What are they doing with them?"

"Getting rid of them."

"Are there many left?"

"They're all over the place. The Germans and the French together fired tens of millions shells just here around Verdun, and some ten percent of them never detonated."

"They'll be cleaned up somehow?"

"Not in our lifetimes. France doesn't have the money or the manpower now to do much but cordon the worst battlefields off and hope the damn things rot."

"Will they?"

"Eventually."

"So they're just sitting out there in the earth?"

"Yes."

"My God."

At Fort Douaumont—a massive, concrete polygon embedded in the area's highest ridge—we walked to the top and stood next to a seventy-five-millimeter gun turret. Then we slowly spun around, sweeping our eyes across the rolling hills of the Meuse Heights. The few forests were sickly looking with the tallest trees barely a decade old and huge bare patches where nothing would grow. Everywhere the landscape looked churned and unnatural. "What is that?" Julia asked, pointing to a large building under construction.

"That's the new Ossuary."

"Ossua..."

"Where the unidentified remains are kept."

She looked over at me, then walked to one edge of the battered fort and looked down.

"You're standing atop what was considered one of the mightiest fortresses in Europe," I said.

"It fell to the Germans?"

"For a few months. But they say it still fought for the French."

"What do you mean?"

"There was an explosion, among the ammunition. It started a chain reaction and more than six hundred of the German occupants were killed. There was no way to bury them properly, not with the constant shelling, so the burnt bodies were simply walled up behind one of the casemates."

"They're still there?"

"Yes."

"Like the shells."

I came up next to her. "Like the shells."

◆ ◆ ◆

AT FORT VAUX we traced our hands along the crumbled and pockmarked walls and watched as a Frenchman—one of the many decorated *gardiens* of Verdun's memorials—chased three schoolboys who were climbing over the ruins aiming stick guns at each other. Another Frenchman in a wheelchair with medals pinned to his chest sold postcards while a third offered his services as a guide. "Hear the true story of Verdun," he said in a thick accent, as he pulled at one end of his mustache with two fingers of his left hand.

We smiled politely and walked away.

In the city of Verdun we explored Vauban's impregnable Citadel with its miles of subterranean passageways and galleries where thousands of French soldiers hid from the German guns and where, many years earlier, English prisoners rotted during the Napoleonic Wars. Then we walked down Rue Mazel and had lunch just across from where the massive Victory Memorial was under construction. In some parts of the city entire blocks remained cleared, waiting to be rebuilt. Scaffolding was everywhere.

"It's overwhelming," said Julia, as she spread her napkin out on her lap, "that feeling that the dead are here. Now. With us. If a person believed in ghosts..."

"They'd be here."

She signaled the waiter for menus, which we studied silently before ordering. "When I was in London I went to see the Cenotaph," she said. "It's a great big slab of concrete near Parliament; an empty tomb that was dedicated a few years ago. And there were twelve other women from all over Britain standing there staring at it, as though looking for traces of loved ones. Some of them had traveled across the country just to see it, like a pilgrimage. One woman, a mother from Kent, told me that during the Battle of the Somme she could hear the guns across the Channel, especially at night. She said they rattled the dishes in her cupboard so that her whole house made noise. She could actually lie in bed and hear what her son was going through. It was *that* close."

As I ate my lunch I thought of how grateful I was that my own mother never had to hear that sound.

◆　　◆　　◆

I DON'T FOLLOW the news anymore. I used to, folding the newspaper just so over breakfast and muttering about the various idiots that ruled the world. But now it all seems remarkably irrelevant, like the weather in Tahiti when you're stuck in Buffalo. I do read the obituaries each day, poring over them with the same intensity that brokers study the stock tables. I've noticed lately that most of those dying are considerably younger than me and to be honest, I find this a bit discouraging. Actuarially speaking, I'm on rather thin ice.

I prefer the shorter obits to the longer biographies, which can be a bit deflating for those of us who never cracked a code in the war or won a patent or forged a booming business that we'll bequeath to our well-groomed and valedictorianed offspring. And I always study the photographs. Are they submitted by family members? In almost every case I am certain there must be a more flattering picture of George or Henry or Martha or Carol. Good Lord.

I also notice that no matter how old people are when they die, their obit photographs invariably show a man or woman smiling from the safety of middle age, that glorious high-water mark of life before everything turns to shit.

Ah yes, middle age, the smug summit of life. How arrogantly we strutted our stuff, those of us now physically bent into submission as we shuffle along the nursing home corridors, clinging to our metal IV stands. We had our three-bedroom houses and winding drive-ways and symmetrical hedge-rows and rose gardens and barbecues and hammocks and swing sets. We had wall-to-wall carpeting and hard-wood floors and chandeliers and pantries and basements and dinner every night at seven sharp with children stampeding down the stairs and dogs barking. We had cars and bicycles and flatware and silverware and dressers and desks and reading chairs and sofas and work-benches and tool chests and by God all the responsibilities at work and home and the church and our community! The sheer impor-tance of it all! Honey, it's the phone for you, long distance!

What is it with all that busy-ness? All that stuff? Do we secretly entertain the hope that if only we are preoccupied enough, if we but accumulate enough, the Grim Reaper will mistake us for immortals?

Maybe the best way to calculate the precise pinnacle of middle age is by raw tonnage. On Tuesday, August 12, 1959, the dear recently departed, then a perky forty-eight, was the rightful owner of 2.9 tons worth of clothes, furniture and bric-a-brac.

Then it begins, a series of sell-offs, fall-backs and setbacks that cut you at the knees; retrenchments and retreats that lead all the way to a hospital gurney.

♦   ♦   ♦

" YOU'VE GOT GOOD color today, Patrick," said Sarah, standing next to me as I sat on my bed. She slowly brushed my cheek with the back of her hand.

"It's my Irish blood. That's why we look so healthy when we drink. Christ, I get red when I bend over to pick up a penny."

"And you should see him when he can't find the penny," said Martin, sitting on the edge of his bed and searching for his slippers with his toes.

Sarah laughed. "There's some sort of financial planner speaking in fifteen minutes in the rec room if you two are interested," she said.

"No thanks," I said. "I'm taking it all with me."

"And Patrick here thinks old King Tut packed light," said Martin.

"What about you?" she asked, looking at Martin.

"What the heck, I'm not doing anything." He pushed off the bed with a low grunt and headed toward the door.

After he left Sarah sat down on the bed next to me. "I want to ask you something," she said.

"Anything."

"Are men as awful as they seem or is it just me?"

"They are worse," I said. "Far worse."

"I just found out I'm dating—or was dating—a creep."

I felt a sudden jolt of jealousy. "So now will you have me?" I asked, wishing she would take my offer seriously. Lately my crush on her had become so consuming that just looking at her made me wince.

She smiled and leaned against my shoulder. "Why is it so hard to find one kind, semiattractive and intelligent man?" I suppressed the

173

urge to flail my hands in the air like a shipwreck victim trying to attract a passing plane. "It's crazy. All of my friends are either divorced or unhappily married. You should hear the things they tell me about their spouses! It's like everyone is just hanging in there for their kids' sake, only the kids are wise to them."

"The more I learn about love and marriage, the less I'm prepared to say."

"I think I'm going through a bad period."

"Well, if it's any consolation, so am I."

She smiled and patted my back. "You don't want to hear my stupid little problems."

"Beats thinking about my stupid little problems."

She hesitated a moment, then sighed and said, "I don't know, I just feel like I've got a lot of stuff eating away at me. I bought three self-help books after work yesterday. That's a personal record."

"Careful with those things. When I had my bookstore I met some of the authors and let me tell you, never have I come across such a bunch of neurotics in my life."

"That's not encouraging." She leaned closer to me, so that my nose was inches from her cheek. "I was reading this book last night about how I should be more accepting of myself and I thought, does that mean I should also accept the parts of myself that are anxious and self-critical too? Or am I only going to find peace by repressing the unpleasant parts?"

"Maybe peace is aiming a little high," I said.

"Maybe I just need a good pharmacist."

"That bad?"

She nodded, and I suddenly realized that she was one of those people who look happier than they feel, which changed my whole sense of her. Does that suddenly catch up with you, or can you go through life with all the scars on the inside?

"We're all quietly going crazy. Or some not so quietly."

"Like you."

"Like me. And to deal with it, with all the stress, everybody goes overboard on something: food or drugs or work or relationships or religion or what have you. Everybody needs to worship something. I've never met an exception."

"You're probably right."

"Damn straight I am. What matters is how destructive your particular obsession is. Can you live with it or are you going to weigh three hundred pounds by Christmas? That's the question."

She smiled. "I don't mean to bitch so much. I'm just having a bad day."

"You can bitch to me anytime."

She put her hand on my knee and rubbed it softly. The rest of my body began contracting toward the point of contact.

"You're so sweet," she said, standing up. As she reached the door she turned, blew me a kiss and whispered, "Thanks."

I nearly passed out.

◆   ◆   ◆

WE WATCHED A dogfight this afternoon. Two Fokkers were lazily dancing high over our lines like big black gnats when two Spads appeared from the southwest. The Fokkers disappeared into a cloud and the Spads went in after them. Moments later all four planes came out the other side, only this time one of the Spads was in the lead and a Fokker dropped down behind him and starting shooting. The machine-gun fire sounded tinny from the distance and was nearly drowned out by the approving roar of Germans in their trenches. Then the Spad started to smoke and it dropped down steeply, whining louder and louder as it sped toward the ground.

"He's trying to put out the fire," said Daniel. "He's got to put it out before he gets too low."

"Come on, come on."

How many men were watching this one man's struggle? Thousands? Tens of thousands? Odd, but his fate seemed so much more important than ours. So much more heroic.

"He's pulling up."

"No he's not."

"Oh shit."

The Spad slammed into the ground just behind the German lines, which erupted in applause.

Above, the remaining Spad and the second Fokker disappeared again in a big, lone cloud that hung high above no-man's-land. Then both planes suddenly emerged and headed toward us, one just above the other. They swerved left and right then left again and we could see the heads of the pilots.

"Come on, get behind him!" I yelled.

"Keep your heads down," said Page.

"Jesus, I don't think I could stomach that," said Giles, as the planes abruptly looped upward until climbing almost vertically. Then the Spad broke off to the west, dropped low and headed over our lines toward home.

We fired a few potshots at the German plane, which broke off the pursuit and banked sharply south and then east, dipping its wings as it passed over the German lines.

◆　　◆　　◆

I'VE BEEN taking my sketchbook everywhere with me. It's not very big and I like to have it handy in case I feel the urge to draw. I try watercolors and charcoal and pencil and ink and pastels. Some days I wake up certain that this will be the day that I get it right, though I never do. But I am getting better.

This afternoon I was sitting out back on a bench painting with watercolors when it started to rain. My picture actually improved as the first drops hit it. Julia's hair streaked down her shoulders and ran across her cheeks and her lips fattened before merging with her cheeks. I made no effort to cover her up. Instead I enjoyed watching the droplets bounce off of her as the colors gradually began to swim.

After I got back to my room I carefully laid

the picture out to dry on my dresser. When I came back from dinner and looked at it again, I was struck by how much the swirling reds and browns and oranges and blacks reminded me of the night sky in France during a bombardment.

◆　◆　◆

I MAY BE no artist, but at least I'm not hard of hearing. I may be the only inmate at Great Oaks—we are inmates, all of us, on death row—who can still hear the owl that lives in one of the trees out back. Yet everyone yells at me nonetheless, conditioned by the sight of white hair.

"GOOD MORNING MR. DELANEY!"

"HOW ARE YOU TODAY MR. DELANEY?"

"DID YOU ENJOY THE SOUP TODAY MR. DELANEY?"

If I go deaf, it won't be because of my age.

And then there are the things I am not supposed to hear, conversations that take place within my range as though I am deaf, dumb and blind, as oblivious as a suckling.

"I don't know. I think he's looking worse. He's so thin."

"Stomach cancer is the *worst*, poor dear."

"I feel sad for him. Not a single visitor at Christmas."

The hard of hearing are easy to spot because they miss so many cues. Their heads are always slightly cocked, not sure if they should

178

be smiling or frowning or even listening at all. At mealtimes someone's hearing aid is always buzzing or whistling or humming, while the changing of the batteries goes on day and night; ridiculously old people hunched over ridiculously tiny little devices trying to remove and then install shiny little silver objects that they can neither see nor feel, and certainly not comprehend.

"How in the world do they put E—LEC—TRICITY into something so small?" asks Helen, looking even older than usual.

"Oh damn, I dropped the battery again!" howls Oscar, issuing the second battery alert of the day. I once counted five battery alerts in one afternoon, though I'm sure that's not the record. We all stare at the ground helplessly, as if we were gathered around a pool where a child had fallen in and none of us could swim.

◆　◆　◆

JANET LOOKED through me today. I'm sure she didn't mean to. But she did. Right through me. As though I wasn't there.

That happens a lot now. In old age we are all Invisible Men.

◆　◆　◆

WE SPENT THE day hiding beneath trees to avoid detection by German fliers. We were some-where outside the town of Villers-Cotterêts near the rail line to Soissons. At noon a large truck passed by pulling a balloon on a long wire. A few hours later the balloon was shot down. We watched the observer fall.

Up until dusk no one was allowed to step beyond the protective canopy of trees without permission from an officer, which wouldn't be forthcoming anyway. I slept on the ground, then wrote a letter, then slept again. In my letter I tried to explain how we careen from intense fear to intense boredom, but I couldn't get it right.

We got mail today but most of the letters were unreadable. They had gotten wet somewhere between there and here and the ink had run, diluting entire paragraphs with blots of blue and black. I'll never forget the look on men's faces as they struggled to decipher page after page of blurry ink, which had dried like water-colors painted by a child. Some of those watercolors had announced births and deaths; others were responses to marriage proposals. Now all the men had were sheaves of crinkled paper, paper that they kept nonetheless on the off chance that it might one day reveal its secrets.

At dinner Daniel sat next to me and pulled out a small muslin sack of beet sugar. "Here, liven it up a little," he said. I sprinkled some on my trench doughnut of bread fried in bacon fat.

Daniel had just returned from a three-day leave to visit a badly wounded cousin at the hospital at Toul.

"How is he?"

"Won't walk again."

"I'm sorry."

Daniel shrugged, then continued to eat. After a moment he paused and said, "Would you believe that some of the orderlies are German prisoners?"

"No shit. They make you nervous?"

"Actually I liked a few of them." He put down his bread, wiped his mouth with his sleeve and sat back.

"So what happened to your—"

"Bullet in the foot. Got infected. They had to cut off his leg, just above the knee."

"Oh, Christ."

"To stop the gangrene. Looks like he'll live." He leaned forward over his plate again, picked up his bread and used it to sop up the remaining bacon grease. "They keep the worst gangrene cases in a corner behind a curtain. But you can hear them. And you can smell them. Once the flesh starts to putrefy, it just runs up the body until it hits the vital organs. You can watch the line rise day after day right up a man's leg or arm."

"Can't they do anything?"

"Just amputate. But if it goes too far up the limb..."

"Christ, I couldn't stand that."

"There was a bucket I saw."

"A bucket?"

"Full of arms and legs."

"Shit."

We finished our meal in silence.

After we ate we joined Giles and Page in a game of poker, until Giles had cleaned our pockets of cash and was now asking for rations. Then Daniel stretched out and took a nap, snoring heavily within minutes. I envied the relaxed expression on his face and wondered whether he ever had nightmares. I did, and whenever I awoke I rarely felt much relief.

I was glad that Daniel was back. I couldn't tell him how much I'd missed him. He'd become like an older brother to me, superior in almost every way but not so that it bothered me. He knew I looked up to him. I guess maybe it flattered him or reminded him of his younger brothers back home. I felt safer around him too, as though he were too good to be touched by the madness. I knew he felt protective of me. Maybe my innocence somehow appealed to him. But more than anything I think it was that he felt I understood him; his sensitivity and his love for Julia and how that gave him strength.

After dusk extinguished the last shafts of light we appeared cautiously like cockroaches, thousands of us emerging from woods and dugouts and barns and farmhouses, a silent army in search of prey. To the west muzzle flashes and flares punctured the darkness like great big lightning bugs dancing to the muffled thud thud of artillery. The road was swollen with limbers and trucks and mules stretching all the way across France in a somber procession that was fed at one end by factories and trains and boats and drained at the other by explosives, gas, bullets and blades. We were told to hurry.

"Germans broke through the French lines somewheres up north, that's what I heard."

"Well, shit. Now we're just gonna have to chase 'em back again."

"I got to tell you, I feel sorry for the Frogs. They've been doing this for four years."

"Four fucking years, imagine that."

I stared straight ahead at Tometti's pack, noting the stains. It smelled everywhere like sweat and urine, except where it smelled worse. I had had diarrhea for three days accompanied by cramps that caused me to jerk forward. Influenza? I prayed not. But everyone talked about it, how it had opened up a third front against humanity. A young kid from Indiana died just four days after he got sick. The pneumonia killed him. They say it's just like drowning. Julia wrote Daniel that Americans were wearing gauze over their mouths on the trains and buses while office hours were being staggered to reduce congestion. My mother wrote that three houses on our street were quarantined and that little Janey Morgan had died. There was not a man in France who wouldn't rather be shot in the kneecaps than die from some disease. It just seemed like such a pathetic way to go, coming all the way to France to get sick; to die in uniform with no hope of heroism, to die wondering if your name would even appear on the hometown memorial after the war.

I watched Giles's head jerk left and right as

he walked and I wondered if he was sleep-walking. What a neat trick that would be, especially for a soldier. I felt another spasm low in my bowels. Funny, but when I enlisted it never occurred to me that war would be so monstrously inconvenient, so that not one single thing was easy except getting killed. Again I stopped and searched the terrain beside the road for a place to shit. From behind a tree I looked back at the silhouettes, illuminated by a half moon, that were bobbing and snaking past in an endless column, as though the entire human race had decided to up and move all in one night. I tried to separate the different sounds: whining, groaning engines; banging metal; the clip, clop of horses; creaking wood; a mule baying; the low rumble of thousands of boots on dirt like a centipede walking across the snare of a drum.

I spent two hours pushing and dodging my way forward to catch up to my company, which was indistinguishable in the darkness from every other company. An hour later I stopped and searched for another place to shit.

♦ ♦ ♦

WE HAVE A lot of catching up to do.

I'm dreaming again, aren't I?

Patrick it's me, Julia.

It is you, isn't it? And I have so many things to tell you. Did I ever tell you about my brother? My younger brother Ian?

No, tell me about him.

He died of smallpox when he was six. I was nine then. It was awful, Julia. Everybody huddled in his room. My father sitting frozen in his chair in the living room. The look on the neighbors' faces when they brought by food.

That's so tragic, when children die.

After he died I'd go and sit in his room for hours. There is nothing in the world so perfectly still and quiet as the room of a dead child.

I'm sorry.

The priest tried to make sense of it but he couldn't, not to me. When children die it's always murder, Julia. Always.

Yes, I understand.

I had an older sister, Katherine. She died ten years ago in Arizona. I still miss her, even though we were never that close. I don't think her husband liked me. Thought I was a bit flaky, not being married all these years.

You're anything but flaky.

Thank you, Julia.

You don't look good today.

I feel tired.

Get some sleep.

Yes, I think I will.

Good night.

Good night.

◆　◆　◆

I CAN'T BEAR to leave my room today. I feel altogether too weak. Not the weakness that comes from old age or even from cancer, but the weakness that comes with sadness, which is much worse. I'm starting to think that sadness is organic; that sad people are cursed with more insight than others. While our smiles defy our bitter plight, our tears acknowledge it.

Maybe that's why the only people who have really interested me in my life—besides children—are those who have experienced the loss of a loved one. People who haven't felt the caustic burn of death are like students who haven't yet held a real job; the world is still theoretical; intellectualized, vigorously debated, but not fully experienced or comprehended.

Any search for the deeper meanings in our lives has to start at our deaths. That's the fundamental, overwhelming dilemma of our humanity. But the great absurdity of our lives—which I can only now see clearly—is our unwillingness to concede that we are in a bit of a pickle in the first place. It's quite funny, really: several billion people all feigning immortality, as though they each have some secret exemption, or at least an indefinite future, and thus can afford to run down the clock without the least sense of urgency. And the incredible thing is, you can live through a world war and still not make the most of the time that you've got.

♦ ♦ ♦

LAST NIGHT I dreamed that I met a young boy who told me with the saddest eyes that he was never born and I asked how could that be and he explained very slowly and quietly that his father had died at the front. And then I looked behind the boy and I saw hundreds of thousands of children, just standing there. Infinitely mute.

♦   ♦   ♦

Rapidity of fire. Men are trained to fire at the rate of about three shots per minute at effective ranges (600 to 1200 yards) and five or six at close ranges (0 to 600 yards), devoting the minimum of time to loading and the maximum to deliberate aiming....

Muzzle velocity. When the bullet leaves the muzzle of the rifle it is going 2700 feet a second, or roughly, 1/2 mile a second, or 30 miles a minute.

—*Privates' Manual, 1917.*

♦   ♦   ♦

LAWTON BECAME an accomplished sniper as the months passed, methodically picking off careless Germans from seven hundred yards with a patient squeeze of the trigger. Page seemed to grow more quiet while Tometti waxed on endlessly about Teresa and Giles amassed a small fortune trading in German souvenirs, using much of the money to supplement his diet with chocolates and jams and smoked meats. Daniel kept us all together with his calm confidence and unerring sense of terrain so that we each trusted him instinctively, even when he led us out on raiding parties loaded with sacks of grenades slung around our necks and shoulders and stumbling through the pitch-black darkness over ground churned like the North Sea by the shelling.

I turned twenty that July. In August Page's father died and Tometti spent a week in the hospital with a slight bullet wound in the arm. Except for the occasional shows at the Y or pickup games in the rest areas, there was little in the way of relief from the intense fear and boredom and loneliness that gripped us. Good news seemed unheard of.

Maybe that's why we made such a fuss on the day Daniel learned that Julia was pregnant, celebrating with brandy that Giles scrounged up and howling drunkenly into the night, until the MPs rounded us up and sent us weaving back toward our tents.

It was our first mail call in weeks and several of us were sitting against the side of an abandoned barn fifteen miles from the front, greedily tearing open letters.

"I'm going to be a father!" he said, shaking the pages. His voice was cracking. "Julia thinks it's a girl and look here, she has a list of names and wants me to circle the ones I like." He stood up and pranced around like a Russian dancer as he recited the names. Several of us slapped him on the back.

"What if it's a boy?" I asked.

"If it's a boy, we'll name him Patrick. How about it, assuming Julia agrees?"

I blushed, and hoped fervently that it would be a boy.

Daniel decided right away that he would marry Julia and spent weeks crafting his proposal, which he carried on a small writing pad he kept in his breast pocket. "I don't think she expects I'll ask, because of my family, but I always knew I would. Now we'll just have to marry by mail, if that sort of thing can be done, and to hell with what everybody thinks."

"Where will you live?" I asked.

"San Francisco, unless that embarrasses my parents. We could always travel down to Monterey or even Los Angeles."

I couldn't imagine such spontaneity.

"I don't suppose you've given any thought to how you'll make ends meet?"

"Julia can teach painting, and maybe even sell a few of her works. I could try to get a job writing for some newspaper or magazine." Daniel was always writing, even during bombardments. He said it was the only way he could understand what he was thinking. He had submitted three articles on the soldier's life to a magazine in New York and one had already been published, much to the delight of the battalion.

"I wish I could be with her," he said, sitting down next to me. "I miss her like crazy."

"Hell, even I miss her," I said, which made him smile.

"I never should have enlisted. What the hell was I thinking?"

"You weren't thinking. None of us were."
He closed his eyes and leaned his head
back. When he opened his eyes he read her letter
again, then handed it to me. "Look at this handwriting," he said. "It's almost like callig-
raphy." I studied the beautiful lettering and
imagined Julia sitting at her desk just after
breakfast, dreaming of the man I fought beside
as she caressed her pen across the page with
a gentle scratching sound, pausing occasionally to feel for the baby's heartbeat within.

◆   ◆   ◆

TODAY DURING ART class I thought I had her eyes.
I was so close: the curve of her lids, the thin
bridge of her nose. Yes, the shape was just right.
Finally. But I couldn't bring them to life.
Every time I drew the pupils they refused to
look at me, so that I wanted to lean forward
and blow life into them. But no matter what
I did they just stared straight ahead. Life-
less. When class ended I rolled my drawing up
and dropped it into the garbage can.

◆   ◆   ◆

I FOUND TWO Valentine's Day cards under my
pillow this morning. One from Helen and
the other from Sarah. (Do I have wide appeal
or what?) I haven't opened the one from
Helen yet. Its thickness suggests a depth of ardor
I don't want to contend with. I took Sarah's
card into the bathroom, locked the door and

sat on the toilet, studying the way she'd written my name on the envelope encircled in a big red heart she'd drawn. The card itself was store-bought, with pictures of flowers and hearts on the front. Inside she wrote:

> *To the last of the truly great leading men.*
> *(My love life confirms this!) From your*
> *not so secret admirer.*
> *Love,*
> *Sarah*

I immediately walked down the hall to the phone booth and ordered a huge bouquet of flowers to be delivered to her home. Then I took the bus into town and bought her a large box of chocolates, which I left with a note at the nurses' station.

♦ ♦ ♦

WHY DOES the longing for love have to be so acute, like a desperate thirst? Is it because love is wanting to be saved and we can never really be saved? Maybe love is really born of our fears. Love is the heart's desire for a pain-killer; a tearful plea for a great big epidural. Yes, that's it: love is the only anesthesia that actually works. And so people with broken hearts are really those who are just coming to, and if you've ever seen someone come out of general anesthesia you know that it looks a lot like the beginnings of a broken heart.

But to find it and touch it and hold it! What

relief, if only briefly, until love wears off or slips through our hands. Strange how love—that most fickle of emotions—creates the illusion of permanence right from the start, just as beauty, so fleeting and elusive, can seem so timeless and infinite to behold.

If love doesn't triumph, it ought to. For love is the one thing we have that feels more powerful than even death; the only respite from life's wretched absurdity. The magic of love is not that it contains all the answers, it's that it eliminates the need for so many pressing questions. For love makes us feel like gods— and that's what we're really after, isn't it?

◆　　◆　　◆

THE GAS SIREN goes off just as we are carrying planks along the communication trenches to shore up the firing trenches. Six seconds to don your mask. That's the drill. My hands fumble as the gas shells hit. There, it's on. Isn't it? I grab my rifle. The ghoulish mist creeps over the edge of the parapet and slides down into the trench like a snake. A slithering poisonous snake. Thousands and millions of them, hissing toward me.

Don't panic, Patrick. Please, don't panic. Take a breath. That's it. Is the hose connected? I run my hand along it. More gas shells explode. Shit, what was the drill? I remember. Breathe normally. Do not remove your mask, even if you feel you are choking. The mist clings to the dirt and my clothes and my mask and the lenses are fogging. Do not remove your mask. Am I breathing normally? Under no circumstance are you allowed to abandon your position. Stand to and maintain your vigilance. It seems hard to breathe, harder still with each breath. Am I getting air or is that gas I taste? Do not remove your mask. Never remove your mask. If only I could get out of the trench where the gas wasn't so thick. The shelling stops. I look up and wonder if the Germans are attacking. But I can't see the top of the trench. Not very well. Oh Christ, I think I'm going to puke. But not in the mask. I can't puke in the mask. But I really must puke.

◆ ◆ ◆

Their expressions, indescribably, seemed frozen by a vision of terror; their gait and their postures betrayed a total dejection; they sagged beneath the weight of horrifying memories; when I spoke to them, they could hardly reply....
—*French Marshal Philippe Pétain,*
describing the sight of soldiers
returning from Verdun.

◆ ◆ ◆

WHEN WE reached the outskirts of Verdun Julia asked me to pull off on La Voie Sacrée, the road upon which France hastily delivered its youth unto Verdun so that Verdun could

193

deliver them with equal efficiency unto eternity. The surrounding fields were littered with the fragmented hulks of farmhouses and rusty piles of barbed wire and sheets of corrugated elephant iron and debris from trucks and wagons.

"I can't believe it still looks so bad here," she said, standing by the car. "I guess I thought more of it would be cleaned up...erased."

"This was the only road open to Verdun," I said. "Just a narrow dirt road. To keep the convoys from sinking in the mud, thousands of men lined the road day and night and shoveled tons of gravel beneath the wheels of the trucks and carts. It's France's Via Dolorosa."

I wanted to tell her more than that; I wanted to tell her that she was standing on the aorta of France and that just up the road on February 21, 1916, the Germans had raised a huge glittering blade and brought it down with all the might of the Teutonic Empire again and again and again for ten months. I wanted to tell her that the blood of a nation—the terrified and exhausted fathers and sons of France—had come coursing down the Voie Sacrée toward thundering acrid oblivion.

I looked at her standing near the side of the road next to a ditch filled with rusted axles and engine parts and when she turned and looked at me I knew from her eyes that she saw what I saw: an endless bumper-to-bumper caravan of bulging transports and lorries and wavering columns of dirty and tired men tagging alongside, all of them doomed.

And there was nothing we could say to them as they passed. Nothing at all.

◆　　◆　　◆

OUR LAST STOP was at a barren hill near Verdun that the French call Le Mort-Homme, which means The Dead Man, though it might also be thought of as a sloped anvil upon which men were smashed to little bits, bits that French Army chaplains still collect each week and place in the bulging Ossuary after the wild boars have dug them up.

We walked slowly to the top and stopped near where a group of uniformed cadets were receiving a lecture from a severe-looking officer with a thick mustache and a chest full of medals.

"What do you suppose he is saying?" asked Julia, turning her back to the strong wind and pulling her hair away from her face as she leaned against me. Her brow was creased and her lower lip was tucked in. It occurred to me that she was one of the few people who are just as attractive when they are serious as when they are smiling, maybe more so.

I looked over at the French soldier, and then at the young faces of the students, riveted by what he was saying. Watching him and his dramatic gestures and the supreme pride in his face made me flush with anger.

"I'll tell you what he's not saying. He's not saying what it's like when a shell lands in a trench full of men. He's not saying what that

195

looks like and smells like and sounds like and how it feels to be covered with bits of flesh. And I don't suppose he's saying anything about the surprising heft of a decapitated head, how awkward it is to pick up for burial and how—"

"Please, no more," said Julia.

"But it's true. Look at their faces. They're ready to revenge their fathers. Ten years and people have forgotten. Christ, a couple of more years and everybody will be ready for a rematch."

"They're so young. They don't know any better."

"Maybe someone ought to tell them. Maybe we should have allowed the war to continue on one small section of the front, just a few hundred yards, enough so that anyone who starts itching for a little glory can have a taste."

Julia turned and looked east toward the Meuse; then northwest across low hills toward Montfaucon, site of the massive Meuse-Argonne American Cemetery, the largest in Europe. Everywhere the earth was deformed like the skin of a child pulled from a fire.

The cadets stood at attention, then saluted.

Julia turned toward me. "Can we leave?" she asked. Her fists were clenched and she avoided looking at me.

As we walked quickly down past the cadets and toward the car I wondered if she was upset with the war or with me for dwelling on it. But I needed to dwell on it. Wasn't that why I had returned?

We drove for an hour in silence. Finally Julia said, "I don't want to see any more memorials."

"That's fine with me." Was it? I'd wanted to see the Meuse-Argonne Cemetery. Perhaps another day.

"Maybe you want to, but I don't."

"I don't want to either. No more memorials."

"Good." She smiled. "Why don't we buy a bottle of wine somewhere and go for a hike?"

"Excellent idea." I stretched my right arm out on the seat rest behind her.

We found a small store run by an old woman with cataracts and no front teeth. On the counter she kept a German helmet brimming with red and green sweets; a shell casing in the corner held umbrellas. I noticed she kept staring at me and I wondered if she thought that she knew me. When we paid she offered us each a piece of candy and then pointed to a picture of a smiling, handsome young man hanging in a small wooden frame behind the counter. Then she placed her hand on her heart and dropped her head forward slightly. The gesture hit me so hard that I found myself unable to speak.

When we got back to the car Julia began biting her nails, then suddenly burst into tears. I turned and wrapped my arms around her and held her tight, feeling the heaving of her back.

"He's not dead you know," she said, pulling back from me.

"Who's not dead?"

"The man in the photograph. He's not dead."

197

"But she was indicating that—"

"I saw him. Just a glimpse. He was in the back room. He was horribly deformed. Like a monster. It was awful."

"*Les gueules cassées.*"

"The what?"

"The smashed faces. That's what the French call them. They're hidden all over Europe."

"I hate this place," she said, wiping her eyes with the back of her hands. "No, I don't hate it. I hate all the destruction. I hate the bombs and the debris and the graves and the wounds and the heartbroken mothers and fathers."

"Yes, I do too."

"And I hate helmets with candy in them."

As she leaned back against me she rested her head on my chest and began to softly cry again. I rubbed her back and rocked her gently like a child, then closed my eyes and lost myself in the smell of her hair.

♦   ♦   ♦

KELLY CAME to visit me today. She was in town for a one-day management seminar and dropped by at lunchtime. I looked up from my soup and saw her walking toward me and I felt the tightness in my throat that I always feel now when I see any of my children or grandchildren.

"Dad!" She bent down and gave me a tight hug and a kiss on my forehead. "You're looking good today. I'm glad to see you

198

eating." The very young and the very old are under enormous pressure to eat.

"You look beautiful, Kelly," I said, clasping her hands in mine. "What a sight for an old man." At fifty, Kelly looks barely forty, though her son David is twenty-six and his daughter Katy three. Maybe it's because she never drank or smoked, but I think it's probably because Kelly was born with a certain immunity to the low-level anxiety that grinds the rest of us down like old teeth. I used to think that people like Kelly were simply tougher than the rest of us; now I realize they are wired differently.

"You always knew how to flatter," she smiled. We walked outside and sat on the patio. I noticed that her shoes were worn and wondered if she was having money troubles.

"How are you feeling, Dad?"

"I'm okay. How's work?"

"The same. I'd quit if it wasn't for the money."

"I guess that's why most jobs include some form of remuneration. Any interesting men?"

Kelly has been single since she and Stewart divorced eight years ago. Stewart was a bland and bulky Dartmouth boy who followed his own father nose-to-ass into investment banking in New York, abandoning Kelly for all but a few disappointing hours a week.

"Not a one. Frankly, Dad, I don't care if I never get married again. I've got plenty of good friends. I'm not lonely."

"You're too pretty to be single," I said.

"Or maybe you're too pretty to be married. I'm not sure which anymore." As she smiled the corners of her mouth tugged more to the left than the right, just like her mother. I always loved that.

"Do you ever wish you remarried after you and Mom divorced?" She'd never asked me that before.

"I tried," I said.

"With who?"

"A woman I once knew. But it didn't work."

"Oh, I'm sorry. I never knew that. A heart-break, huh?" She tilted her head slightly as she looked at me and I wondered how Stewart could have been such a fool.

"Yeah, one of those," I said. Then I stood with my cane in one hand and held her hand with the other as we walked across the grass.

"I felt terrible that you were alone over Christmas."

"I told you not to worry about that. It's not like I'm ever alone here."

"I worry about you. You should be with family. Are you sure you won't come and live with me?"

"I'm fine right here. Besides, they've got great medical facilities." I mention the medical facilities every time my children suggest I move back in with them; I think it helps alleviate some of their guilt.

"You're not too lonely?" she asked, looking at me closely. She smelled of soap and I remembered plucking her slippery white body from the tub each evening after dinner and wrapping her in a big yellow towel and rolling her back and forth across our bed as she howled with laughter.

"Lonely? Christ, I can't get a minute to myself and you know what a loner I am."

"I hate thinking about you here, like we've abandoned you."

I put my hand up and shook my head.

She tried to smile. "Do you need anything? Books or something? I can send whatever you need."

"Got any recent photos of Katy?"

◆　◆　◆

MY STOMACH HURTS.

◆　◆　◆

"WHAT DO YOU do with your pennies?" Eleanor Kravitski was staring at me across the lunch table, her soup spoon frozen halfway between bowl and mouth.

"My pennies?" I asked.

"Yes, your *pennies*," she said. "In my eighty-four years I have never found a satisfactory method of disposing of all the pennies one accumulates. Have you?"

"Well, Eleanor, come to think of it, I don't believe I have. Let's see, you can keep them in a big jar..."

"But then you either have to spend two days stuffing them into those penny rolls, which always rip and bend at the edges, or you have to carry the jar to the bank, which I can't do."

"You can try to spend them as you get them."

"Never works. It's impossible to spend your pennies as fast as you get them unless you hold up every checkout line and count out a dollar's worth of pennies with every purchase, which of course you can't do. Do you know how long it takes to count pennies under pressure, especially when you have arthritis? The fact is, you can usually only spend about two or three pennies at a time to make exact change, and that's no way to dispose of a huge penny collection."

"You could refuse to take pennies."

"I do! I stopped taking pennies two years ago. Said I want nothing to do with them, thank you. But I've still got a huge jar of pennies on my dresser, which means I'll have to make exact change for another ten years or so to get rid of them all. Why, I don't even care about the money, I'm just tired of thinking about pennies." Her frozen spoon lurched back into motion and she slurped her soup.

Four days later Howard and I snuck into Eleanor's room and carted her pennies away in a wheelchair covered by a blanket. We buried them out back behind the largest oak tree, about sixteen dollars worth, we figured. Ever since, Eleanor has appeared positively radiant. I'm certain she believes her prayers were answered.

◆　　◆　　◆

I MISS Julia so much.

◆　　◆　　◆

DANIEL, PAGE, Lawton and I got passes to go to Paris for three days that August. Actually we won them for capturing three German soldiers dressed as Americans and attempting to cross over into our lines near Vierzy, south of Soissons. We were elated: passes to Paris were extremely hard to come by, especially for doughboys, who, if sent anywhere for relief, usually ended up in official "leave areas" run by the YMCA like the one in Aix-les-Bains ("Aches and Pains").

None of us had ever been there of course, and we were like giddy children when we got off the train and waded into a crowd of soldiers and civilians and women in beautiful long dresses all kissing and hugging and shaking hands. I don't know what I expected but it wasn't like anything I imagined. The stores were filled with goods while kiosks offered every possible thing you could want—at a price— including souvenirs like German helmets and belt buckles and medals and swords. Though many of the women wore black and hundreds of amputees sold pencils and newspapers on the streets, Paris seemed impervious to the war; smug in its certainty that such mindless destruction was beneath its massive, corniced dignity. The few buildings that were damaged from bombings by zeppelins and the long-range guns were already surrounded by scaffolding and there was no sign that only weeks earlier the German spring offensive had come close enough to the city to cause evacuations.

Somehow the dense beauty of the city disturbed me. I think it was the gaiety of it all, the picnics in the parks alongside perfect rows of flowers and the brightly colored parasols and neatly pressed livery and the theaters and the perfumes and the art shows; all this a few hours from mankind's greatest agony. Was Berlin like this too? Were the beer halls full of laughter and was a good seat at the opera still the height of achievement? I was suddenly seized with the awful sense that the war could go on indefinitely. That it wasn't *that* bad.

Lawton made it clear that he was not leaving Paris without getting laid, and hopefully more than once, but Page insisted that he first join us for some sight-seeing.

"It'll be good for you," said Page, putting his arm around Lawton as we walked. "Broaden your interests."

"A good fuck will be good for me," said Lawton, reaching for his groin and walking with his knees out wide.

"Come on, Lawton, just try to keep your pants on for a few more hours," I said.

"I'll give you until five o'clock. That's all I can last," he said.

We walked in silence at first, just wandering and staring. Everything seemed remarkably old to me, so weathered and tempered and ornamental and written about. I couldn't pass a single street or church without thinking of the millions who had gone before me, all those footfalls of forgotten history.

As we walked toward the Seine and stared across at the looming Conciergerie I wanted to ask Daniel what he was thinking but he seemed too absorbed in the sights to disturb. I watched the awed expression on his face as we entered Notre Dame, which was first on our list not so much to give thanks as to be able to write home and say we went to Notre Dame to give thanks. Then we headed toward the Dôme des Invalides to look at Napoleon's tomb.

We entered single file and stood in silence before the huge red sarcophagus.

"I read that he's buried in six coffins," said Page, who loved European history, at least up until 1914. "Like a pharaoh. The first one is tin, the second mahogany, the third and fourth lead, the fifth ebony and the sixth oak. All that was put into this sarcophagus. It's a single block of red granite."

"What do you suppose he'd make of the trenches?" asked Daniel.

"Hard to imagine him in a gas mask," I said.

"You don't see the Kaiser in no gas mask," said Lawton.

"How did Napoleon beat the Germans?" asked Daniel.

"Beats the hell out of me," said Lawton. "No way he had them outnumbered."

Afterward we walked to the Eiffel Tower, which was guarded by soldiers and closed to the public. Daniel looked up at it and laughed. "My parents would consider this just about the ugliest thing they ever saw," he said.

"What do you think?" I asked.

"I think it's great," he said, still staring up.

As we crossed the Seine again I noticed a large number of painters with their easels along the shoreline and I thought what a ludicrously peaceful thing that was to do. At the Place de la Concorde a tall juggler in a red hat was performing for a large crowd of mostly women and children and old men. The front of the circle formed around him was reserved for men in wheelchairs who smiled and clapped and twisted their wheelchairs left and right as they watched. After the performance we tossed a few coins into the juggler's hat and then stopped at a café for lunch before continuing on to the Arc de Triomphe, pausing to look at the captured German artillery on display along the Champs-Elysées.

"God I'm horny," said Lawton, who was now leading us toward the Bois de Boulogne, which he assured us was teeming with prostitutes. When we reached the edge of the park he turned to us and asked, "Any of you ladies care to join me?"

We shook our heads.

"Come on, Page, it'll be good for you. Broaden your interests."

"Not my class of women."

"Oh the dumb ones are the best, trust me." He pulled out his wallet and began counting out his money. "I know Daniel's hopeless. How about you Patrick? Get your pecker wet. How about it?"

"I don't think so," I said, feeling unsure of myself.

"Get your pecker wet in there and it's liable to fall off," said Daniel, who found Lawton's farmlike libido amusing.

"I've come prepared," said Lawton, tapping his pocket. "Come on, Patrick, what have you got to lose but your virginity?"

"No, I think I'd rather sightsee."

"*Sightsee*? Well, what do you think I'm going to be doing, closing my eyes? You'll have your pick, Paddy! France *owes* you. Then we'll get drunk."

"Maybe you should have gotten Patrick drunk before you asked him," said Page.

Lawton stood waiting for me.

"You go on," I said. "Anyway, we've got two more days."

"Meet you at that Vendôme thing—it's on the map—around seven o'clock," he said, turning and walking off rapidly.

We stood and watched him disappear into the park, then Page headed off to meet up with an old friend who worked at the American Embassy. Daniel and I walked around aimlessly for a while, then stopped at an outdoor café and ordered two beers.

As we sat there I tried to point out some of the prettier women passing by but Daniel seemed distracted, staring down at his glass with a sullen expression on his face.

"Something bugging you?" I asked.

He shrugged, then signaled the waiter for another round.

"Tell me."

"It's Julia. God, I hope she's all right."

"Sure she is."

"But who will help her with the baby? Her mother's not well, and she's got no one else. And God knows she has no money. And what if something happens to me?"

"Nothing's going to happen to you."

He looked at me, as though studying my face for assurance.

"'Cause if it did I'd have to kick the sorry shit out of you for abandoning your sorry-assed squad, and we can't have that happen now can we?"

He smiled in a way that reminded me of how handsome he was.

"Come on, let's get drunk," I said as the beers arrived.

"Yeah, let's get drunk."

◆　　◆　　◆

I mustn't be shown any more such spectacles... I would no longer have the courage to give the order to attack.
　　—*French Marshal Joseph Joffre,*
after pinning a medal on a blinded soldier.

◆　　◆　　◆

THERE IS A German helmet in my closet. The one I found in the dirt when Julia was painting her portrait of Daniel. It's my last souvenir.

That's why I made such a fool out of myself this afternoon. I was sitting in my orange chair looking at the helmet, just feeling its cold gray dead weight in my lap and running my hands along the dents and scratches, when I started crying. Nurse Cindy found me. "Gimme that stupid thing," she said, taking the helmet and tossing it back into my closet, where it landed with a crash. "Aren't you supposed to be at woodworking today? Stop your crying and let's get you to woodworking."

She pulled me up and then got me a tissue for my face before escorting me into the hallway and aiming me toward woodworking.

◆　　◆　　◆

I AM DRAWN TO Germany as one is drawn to a car accident or a crime scene or a great big scab. It's a generational thing, I suppose, but I instinctively divide all German men into former soldiers and future soldiers. As for the Nazis, well, who isn't fascinated by the Nazis? (To think that the Germans I fought were comparatively decent folk.) Who can resist staring at those photos of Hitler and Goering and Goebbels and Himmler and searching their eyes and skin and hair for clues? It's the Devil we're looking at, isn't it? The once allegorical fury of fire and brimstone now finally and forever has a human face;

many faces, faces that look not so different from our own faces.

The Devil doesn't have horns after all.

I went to Germany in 1965, one of the yearly trips abroad I made after I turned fifty and decided I'd better not wait to fall in love again to travel. I remember taking the train from Munich to Dachau and getting off at the station and sure enough the signs still said Dachau only now there were schoolchildren with book bags playing beneath them. There was a bus to the concentration camp but I chose to walk, studying the neatly gabled brown and white houses as I passed and imagining perfect little Reich children playing out front as men were being tortured and shot only a few thousand yards away. They say that a man who lives by a river no longer hears it. Is that also true for concentration camps?

The moment I walked through the stone and iron gate beneath the sign that read *"Arbeit macht frei,"* I felt a tightening in my stomach; not just revulsion but actual fear, as though I had entered the den of a dragon to examine the piles of bones in the far recesses, only I wasn't sure whether the dragon had really been slain.

I stood on the *Appellplatz* or roll call square in the gray drizzle and imagined thousands of men in perfect straight lines ordered to stand at attention in the freezing cold all night because a prisoner had attempted to escape. Did it always rain here? I thought of asking one of the guides if there was always a dark gray cloud above Dachau and was this rain or tears on my face?

Then I heard music in the distance, soft at first, then louder and louder. I turned and looked and from behind the *Strafblöcke* a prison marching band appeared; men in dirty white shirts and black-and-gray-striped pants with stains from dysentery down their backsides playing violins and accordions as they escorted a condemned prisoner to the *Lagerarrest*. Behind them two guards laughed and smoked cigarettes. And near a guard tower a man was hanging from his wrists with his hands tied behind his back.

I stood still and closed my eyes and rubbed my temples until all the prisoners and the guards disappeared and then walked over to the *Totenkammer* and the *Krematorium*, which I was afraid to touch in case it felt warm. Before I walked back to the train station I bought a postcard that said "Never Again" and tucked it into my pocket, but by the time I reached the station I had decided that never again was not nearly enough. Even if it was the best we could do it was not adequate at all; not even if not another single drop of human blood is spilled again in anger. But of course the blood keeps spilling, doesn't it? And as I stood watching the train approaching, I thought that maybe the real horror is not what happened at Dachau but what didn't happen after Dachau. Certainly we know now once and for all that humanity can never be brought to its senses.

The dragon lives.

◆　　◆　　◆

" SO WHEN ARE you going to show us a picture of your girlfriend?" I asked, looking over at Page. "Aren't you two engaged or something?"

We were sitting with Lawton, Giles and Daniel in a humid, smoky bar on our last night of rest before returning to the front, which was still audible some twenty miles away, like a far-off storm rumbling across the Kansan plains. The room was crowded with a mix of French and American soldiers and it was dif- ficult to hear across the rough round table where we sat. In the candlelight the dense air had an almost yellowish tinge and the room smelled of sweat and tobacco mixed with the sweetish aroma of spilled drinks that made the floor slightly sticky. I'd begun to feel a hint of nausea and I couldn't decide if it was because of the smoke and drinks or because I knew I would soon be back in the trenches.

"I don't have it anymore," said Page, taking a long drag of his cigarette. I looked at his hands wrapped around a beer mug and noticed that they were covered with various nicks and cuts, especially near the knuckles. I looked down at mine and they looked the same, with dirt buried deep under the nails and into the cuti- cles and a thin scar across the top of my left hand where I had snagged it on barbed wire.

Trench hands. So different looking than I remembered them; all scrubbed for church, gripping the rake in the backyard and piling up the red and yellow and brown leaves, anxiously tapping a pencil at school. I raised them up and opened them wide and then squeezed them closed a few times before reaching for my beer.

"You don't have it?" asked Giles, signaling the plump, elderly French barmaid for a fourth round of drinks. In his left hand he fingered one of two Iron Crosses he had found on the bodies of German soldiers after we captured their trench. He'd been in good spirits ever since.

"I don't have it."

"What did you do, sell it?" asked Lawton, whose large face looked unusually haggard while his eyes were fiery red from drink.

"She broke up."

"With you? She broke up with you?" asked Lawton.

"Shut up," I said.

"It's just a little surprising, I mean, if Mr. Page here isn't the catch of the century, then..."

"I'm sure you'll straighten things out when you get home," I said hopefully. I'd assumed that Page was as good as married and I had privately hoped to be invited to a big Boston Brahmin wedding after the war.

Page shrugged.

So that's why he'd been so quiet lately. I was sorry I'd mentioned her in front of the other guys. I tried to imagine his sense of help-lessness, being so far away.

"That's got to be tough," said Giles, shaking his head. "I'm sort of glad I broke up with Meredith before I enlisted. That way I don't have to think about her being unfaithful. Nothing worse than sitting in a fucking trench imagining some guy back home screwing the daylights out of your girl in some nice com-fortable bed."

"Would you shut the fuck up?" I said. I noticed that Page had tightened his grip on his beer mug.

"So who's buying the next round?" asked Daniel.

"I'm broke," said Lawton.

"So let me get this straight," I said. "You expect us to buy your beers so you can save your money for whores?"

"Seems reasonable to me," said Lawton, smiling his big impish smile.

"I'll get them," said Page, reaching for his pocket.

I stared at the small flame of the red candle that burned in an empty green wine bottle in the center of the table. The bottle was almost covered with layers of different-colored wax that had dripped down its sides. I thought of all the other men who had sat around it laughing and talking and wondered how many were now dead.

"I got a letter from my kid brother yes-terday," said Giles. "He wants to know how many Heinies I've killed."

"How many have you killed?" I asked.

"No idea." He looked around the table. "Do you guys count?"

"I counted the first three," admitted Page. "Then I stopped."

"'Course you can't always be sure," said Giles.

"No, you can't," said Daniel.

"Can't beat Lawton here," I said, slapping him on the back. A week earlier Lawton had shot a German spotter right out of a belfry from eight hundred yards.

"What about those guys in the artillery, firing those fuckers all day and night," said Lawton. "That's gotta add up." We shook our heads solemnly.

"So what are you going to tell your brother?" asked Daniel.

"I'm going to tell him that I'll kick his ass if he signs up."

"Why don't you just tell him what it's like?" I asked.

"Yeah, right."

"I'm serious."

He looked at me steadily. "I've tried. I can't."

"How about you, Page?"

"I stopped trying."

"Daniel?"

He shook his head.

"Well shit, if none of you learned men are going to tell the good folks back home what's going on, who the fuck is?" asked Lawton, raising his voice. I thought of a letter Lawton had recently dictated to me to write to his parents, how there was no mention of death or violence at all, as if the worst things were the inconveniences; as if we were all on a big camp-out and someone forgot the marshmallows.

"I wonder what the Germans write," I said. "'Dear Pa, it's just like shooting pheasant. Please send more schnapps.'"

"Their letters are probably not much different from ours," said Daniel.

"Do you think they still believe they can win?" asked Giles.

"I don't think they believe they'll beat us, but I don't think they believe we'll beat them either," said Daniel.

I pulled out a cigarette and lit it, then took a long sip of beer.

"Do you suppose they have many deserters?" asked Giles.

"Not nearly enough, as far as I can see," said Lawton.

"Does anybody ever get the feeling that this thing could go on forever?" I asked, looking around the table.

"I'll give it another year," said Page. "Two at the most."

"Two? Christ, I'm not putting up with this shit for two years," said Giles.

I tried to imagine two more years but I couldn't. The idea made my eyes redden so that I had to turn away. I reached for my beer and finished it off.

Nearby a table of French soldiers began singing.

"Fucking sheep to slaughter," said Lawton, who was visibly drunk.

We sat in silence, listening to the song. Watching the soldiers with their arms around each other and their drunken smiles and bleary eyes made me enormously sad. What if their mothers could see them now? Their girlfriends? And where would they be in a month? A year? And what about us? As I listened to them my sadness slowly transformed into intense anger; anger that we were here, that nobody who wasn't here could ever understand us, that the rest of the world just went on without us. The anger came more often now. It was easier to deal with than sadness or fear.

When they finished singing we clapped and turned back to our table. Giles pulled out a deck of cards and began shuffling. I tried to concentrate on the quick movements of his hands but my vision blurred. I slowly looked around the table; first at Daniel, then Page, then Lawton, then Giles. It struck me what fun I'd be having if only there wasn't a war and how much I'd miss them when it was over.

"Is life fucking absurd or have I been drinking too much?" I said finally, feeling a heaviness in my tongue.

"It's absurd," said Daniel, who looked tired and thin.

"Thank you." I belched loudly.

"Paddy here's got a hell of a point," said Lawton, both lisping and slurring. His red eyes flickered as he talked and his left knee bounced up and down under the table.

"I get the feeling Lawton needs to get laid," said Giles, as he began dealing. A cigarette dangled from his lips and after he inhaled he held the smoke in for a moment and smiled appreciatively before exhaling.

"Bunch of fucking fodder is what we are," said Lawton, leaning so far back in his chair I feared he would fall over.

"Well shit, you might as well just stand on the parapet and whistle at the Germans," said Page.

Lawton began to whistle.

"Give this man another drink," said Giles.

"Worm food. We're fucking worm food," said Lawton, leaning his shoulder against me and raising his glass. "To worms, who've never had it so good."

"The thing is, Lawton, the worms have always won in the end," said Daniel. "Live, love and die. No answers. Little justice. Never has been, never will be."

"I feel so much better," said Lawton.

Daniel continued: "So you can say life is senseless and cruel or you can make a stand and try to impose your own meaning and values on it."

"I'm afraid I'm no good at that," said Lawton.

"What about the people that are important to you?" asked Page.

"They keep dying off," said Lawton, draining his glass.

"So you think we're all mad?" I asked.

"Oh most definitely," said Lawton.

"To madness then," said Giles, raising his glass.

"To madness," we said, clinking our glasses.

♦ ♦ ♦

What is happening to me now is more tragic than the "passion play." Christ never endured what I endure. It is breaking me completely.
—*Isaac Rosenberg, British Army, in a letter written January 26, 1918. Killed in action, March 31, 1918.*

♦ ♦ ♦

"LET ME ASK you something," I said to Daniel as we sat in a dugout after spending the morning carrying ammunition boxes and Marmite pots of food along the communication trench to the firebay. Daniel had just finished shaving in a small mirror nailed to a wooden beam and now gently tapped out powdered toothpaste onto his toothbrush. "So do you think it's worth it, all in all? Living, I mean. Do you think the good outweighs the bad in the long term?"

"Most days I do," he said.

"I don't," I said. "I don't think that all the happiness in the world can make up for the misery. Not for one moment. After the first child died in a fire or the first mother ran out of food I think the whole bloody thing should have been called off."

Daniel turned and looked at me and I felt my anger in my face and noticed that my hands had tightened around my metal coffee cup, which was cold. After he finished brushing his teeth he sat down and slowly untied his boots, which were caked with dried mud. Then he pulled them off, scraped them clean with a knife and slowly removed his socks, which had to be peeled from his skin like adhesive tape. After massaging and inspecting his feet, he pulled out a fresh pair of socks from his pack, put them on and laced up his boots. After rolling his wool puttees he stood, walked to the entrance of the dugout and pulled aside the hanging blankets. Then he turned back to me and asked, "You've never been in love, have you Patrick?"

◆　　◆　　◆

"DANIEL?"

"Patrick, it's me Martin. It's Martin, Patrick."

Martin? Ah yes, Martin. Great Oaks. Infirmity. Senility. I slowly raised my head and stared at my hands, which lay limp on my lap looking splotchy and mottled. I had fallen asleep in the corner chair of our room, my chin pressing against my chest with my head swung to one side at a cadaverous angle.

"Hello, Martin," I said, rubbing my neck. He smiled at me and patted me on the shoulder.

I've grown to like Martin immensely in the months since he moved in. (I know, I promised

I wouldn't.) He is one of those gentle souls who are always at pains not to be in anyone's way. His growing dependency on others embarrasses him immensely.

Nobody visits him. Not his daughter the bitch—thank God—not his older sister Abby, who lives in Baltimore and is too sick to travel, and not his grandchildren, because the bitch never brings them.

His wife Doreen died nine years ago of lung cancer. Martin had recently retired from his job as a floor manager in a printing factory where he worked for forty-three years, earning a little medallion etched with an old printing press and his name. (He keeps it on his side of the long dresser we share, along with a silver brush and comb set he got in child-hood, a white clay mold of his grandson's two-year-old hand and a picture of Doreen standing in the surf on the Jersey Shore and laughing with her head tilted sideways as she holds her yellow dress up around her knees.) Martin and Doreen had planned to travel on cruise ships and play golf and dote on their grandchildren; when she died they were booked to sail to the Bahamas. A year later, Martin lost most of his savings on a real estate deal pushed by a young broker whose father also worked at the plant. Then his health went.

I took him along to Sean's for dinner last weekend, where he played checkers for two hours with Kenneth and entertained Michael with sleight-of-hand tricks. Every time Katy approached him he made those funny clicking sounds accompanied by strange grimaces that old men like to make around small children. She loved it.

A few weeks after he moved in, Martin and I were sitting on the front patio, drinking little paper cups of lemonade sold to us for a dime each by some enterprising grandchildren.

"Cute, aren't they?" he said, taking a sip. The lemonade began spilling over the sides as he brought the cup to his lips, which were extended.

"Hard to believe how ugly they are going to get in about seventy years."

Martin ribbed me with his elbow. "Christopher will be five next month. I asked Trudy to send me photos of the birthday party. Nothing like a child's birthday."

"Nothing like a child."

"Seems like yesterday, doesn't it?"

"Sometimes it seems like today."

We sat for a while and then he said, "I retired ten years ago today."

"Really? Congratulations."

A large smile spread across his face. Anniversaries were important to him.

"Did you really like working in that print shop all those years?"

"I enjoyed having a place to go." His head bobbed up and down as though mounted on a spring. He also stammered frequently, which made him seem even more shy than he was. "I enjoyed the camaraderie, the guys I worked with over the years. The routine."

"Not the work?"

"Not the work."

"What about Doreen?"

"Well, she was home raising Trudy, and then she got a job in a fabric store. Gave her a chance to get out, talk to people. She loved chit-chatting."

"How long were you two together?"

"Forty years."

"Was she your high school sweetheart?"

"Not exactly." He paused, staring into his now empty cup, then said, "We had to get married. She was pregnant."

"Ah."

"Fact is, I was in love with another woman at the time, but she was in Maine for the summer."

Martin looked straight ahead and I noticed that his shaking had increased.

"Doreen was also in love with someone else."

"What happened to him? No, let me guess. He was in love with someone else, too."

"Right. Broke Doreen's heart."

"So how—"

"We met one night at a party, both feeling sorry for ourselves. I don't think we ever intended to see each other again after that evening."

Car doors slammed in succession and a stream of children dashed across the grass toward the entrance, their mother calling after them. She carried a large shopping bag brimming with party favors.

"What about the woman you loved?"

He smiled. "Her name was Lara. Lara Tennant. She was Scottish. Loved bagpipes. We both did." He shook his head. "I could draw her picture like she was sitting here today. Short brown hair, hazel eyes. The sweetest smile. We'd only dated a couple of times, but I knew for sure she was for me. Too good really, couldn't believe she'd have me. I used to dream about our wedding: lots of bagpipes and dancing."

"Did she love you?"

"I don't know. I honestly don't. When she got back from Maine and heard the gossip, that was it. She wouldn't even see me."

"That's hard."

Martin turned to me. "It's my tragedy. Everybody has theirs, don't they?"

◆　◆　◆

I KEPT GLANCING over at Julia as I drove, wondering how it would feel to have her only in my memory. How long until I lost that face and those eyes and that smile? Months? A few years at most? Would I remember the sound of her laughter?

We headed northwest from Verdun through the Meuse-Argonne region, skirting the old Hindenburg line as it cut through woods and open fields and around small villages.

Julia sat quietly looking out the window with her hands folded in her lap. I couldn't decide if she was deep in thought or just losing herself in the passing scenery, but I was starting to think that she was a bit like I was: constantly teeming with more thoughts and images and memories than she knew what to do with.

She was difficult to read. One minute she struck me as the strongest, most independent woman I'd ever met and the next she seemed extremely fragile, like a person with injuries that won't heal. Sometimes, watching her, I noticed that she would physically prop herself up, almost imperceptibly straightening her back, lifting her head and shoulders and summoning a smile, as if determined to make the best of things. What amazed me was how genuine the smile always looked. I'd always thought that sadness and happiness took turns running the show; in Julia they seemed to coexist.

When we parked at the edge of a woods beside a deep ravine, I thought we might be near the *Kriemhilde Stellung*—the German name for one of the sectors of the Hindenburg line—but said nothing. Instead I concentrated on the graceful sway of Julia's hips as she walked down the narrow path in front of me and hoped that we wouldn't stumble upon any more memorials.

"I'm not walking too fast, am I?" she asked. "My mother always said that I walked too fast for a woman."

"No, you're not walking too fast." I imagined her as a young girl racing ahead of her mother, pigtails flying.

"You're an only child, aren't you?" I asked.

"My father died just after I was born. I think my mother always thought she'd have six or seven children."

"That must have been awful."

"You can't miss what you never had, right?"

I disagreed but didn't say anything. "Is your mother..."

"She died six years ago."

Another loss, which still registered in the wounded expression on her face. "I'm sorry. You two must have been close."

She seemed lost in thought for a moment, then said, "I felt very protective of her when I was growing up, which is a difficult thing for a child to feel. She was very loving but not very strong. I think my father's death just crushed her." Julia jumped up on a thin log that lay across our path and tiptoed along it, hands high in the air, before jumping off. "But she never lost her ability to laugh. She had such a wonderful sense of humor!" She smiled at the recollection. "We used to laugh so hard that we'd both get the hiccups."

"I hate the hiccups."

"Not as much as I do. They nearly ruined my childhood. I had them constantly." She laughed again, this time from deep in her chest. "Especially in places you're not supposed to laugh. Oh God, that always did it for me." She rolled her eyes, still laughing, then tried to stop but couldn't. "It got so that my mother was embarrassed to take me to church." The memory made her laugh harder, so that she

226

had to stop walking and lean against a tree. I thought she looked absolutely adorable.

"I even got them in the Christmas play. Can you imagine? I was supposed to be one of the presents under the tree, a little doll...." Tears were running down her cheeks now and her face was red. "My mother spent weeks on my costume...." Her laughter made it hard for her to talk. "And the only thing I was supposed to do was to stay perfectly still for one entire act."

"Let me guess."

Julia nodded, bending over at the waist and holding her stomach as she laughed. "And then all the other presents started giggling. I couldn't stop. The whole Christmas tree was shaking. They had to drop the curtain." Then she hiccuped. "Oh damn," she said, pounding her fist against her chest.

"I think they're cute."

She shook her fist at me. "Don't say a thing," she said, pushing me playfully on the chest, then turning away and hiccuping again.

"Maybe I should try scaring you."

"That never works," she said, hiccuping midsentence. "I've tried *everything*."

She began walking again. I followed close behind, watching the rhythmic convulsion of her shoulders, which only ceased after half an hour.

When we came upon a concrete bunker I stopped, examined the entrance, then carefully walked down a short flight of crumbling stairs and peered into the darkness. The damp smell was familiar, but without the urine and sweat. I could just make out the shadow of a chair and table against one wall and some boxes on the floor. Other shapes in the corner on the floor were unrecognizable. Had anybody entered it since the war? Or was everything exactly as it was hurriedly left, ten years ago?

"You're not going any farther are you?" asked Julia, standing behind me.

"Not enough light," I said, slowly turning and walking back up the stairs, wishing I'd had a candle.

We continued walking, careful to sidestep coils of rusted barbed wire. Julia was quiet. Was she sad again or not thinking at all? I couldn't *not* think but I envied those who could. I looked over at her, trying to see past her face. Her expression was placid, but her eyes were full of expectation.

I thought again of her mother, and how hard that must have been when she too died. What do you learn when everyone you love leaves you?

"What was your mother like?" I asked.

"She was shy, except around close friends. She loved music, especially singing. The choir at church just transported her."

"Was she happy?"

"She was when she laughed. She thought that things were either hysterically funny or extremely tragic. There wasn't a lot in between, or at least not that she noticed."

"She may have been on to something."

Julia eyed me thoughtfully. Behind her the sun streaked yellow through a tall stand of trees.

"A friend of mine married a man she met on vacation in Nantucket. Once they moved in together she realized she'd made a horrible mistake. She told me never to fall in love with a man I met on vacation until I saw him in his natural habitat."

Why would she tell me that? Was she saying she could fall for me? And was that little grin she gave meaningful or was I reading too much into everything?

I listened to the sound of the red and yellow and orange leaves crunching under my feet.

"Do you ever think about settling down somewhere?" I asked.

She shrugged. "Sometimes, but after a few months I get bored."

As I looked at her I thought that maybe she was restless because she feared she'd never be happy anywhere, and knowing that, her only hope was to keep moving.

"All that moving around must take a toll," I said.

The smile vanished from her face. "I do miss having roots. A home. And I get tired of being poor. I've quit more jobs than most people hold in a lifetime."

"You just quit?"

"Oh sometimes I make quite a scene before I storm out of the place. I'm not very good at taking orders." I watched the way she gestured as she talked and it occurred to me that she lived more fully in her body than I did.

"Who is?"

We walked in silence for a while, and I began thinking of Charlotte and Sean and how far away they seemed. Was I a family man already? Amazing. Little ol' Paddy married. A house. A career. How fast it all happened, and I barely remember making certain decisions.

I glanced over at Julia. Maybe this would just seem dreamlike when I returned to Paris. Maybe from a distance it would even seem silly, a brief and selfish indulgence, though I didn't think so. But it would be good to see Sean. I'd never been away from him for more than a few days. Does a three-year-old stop long enough to miss his daddy? Thinking of him brought a smile to my face.

"Do you want to know who one of my heroes is?" asked Julia, stopping by a small stream.

"Who?"

"Michelangelo. I read that someone once asked him what he was doing with his chisel and do you know what he said?"

I looked at her expectantly.

"He said he was trying to free an angel."

As we made our way over rocks in the stream I reached out and took Julia's hand. Neither of us let go as we headed up the gradual slope of the wooded hills and each time we passed a ruined bunker or trench or rusted bayonet or boot I felt the gentle squeeze of her hand in mine.

IT'S RAINING AGAIN, huge cold drops that beat upon us as we walk. The French say the war has changed the weather. That's something to think about. It reminds me of the African saying that when elephants fight, the grass suffers. We are some elephants.

Mid-September. We've been marching all night. Everywhere we see the signs of a huge buildup: newly erected field hospitals, camouflaged supply dumps, endless columns of soldiers.

We're somewhere southeast of Saint-Mihiel, just a few miles behind the front and rushing into position. I haven't slept in two days. At the next rest I should clean my feet but I'm afraid to take off my boots. Sometimes you can't get them on again. Maybe tomorrow.

A few hours ago we passed one of the naval guns, a fourteen-incher mounted on a railroad car. We also counted fourteen Renault tanks. We argued about which would be worse, being in a tank or a submarine. Most of us preferred the tank, but only slightly.

I vomited yesterday. Daniel feared I had the flu but I think it was just the smells; smells of rotting flesh and chlorine and gas and monkey meat and urine and shit. When no one was looking I pulled out a small bottle of cologne I carry in my pack, opened it and held it just beneath my nose. Then I closed my eyes and fought the tears.

All the trucks run with their lights out.

Sometimes we have to stop and push them out of a ditch. Men get run over too, which helps keep you awake.

"Fuck it's dark!" said Giles, bumping into me.

"Where the hell are the trenches?" asked Page.

"Another mile, maybe," said Daniel. "The jumping-off points are supposed to be marked with white tape."

"What?"

"Look for the white tape."

"Yeah, don't cross the white tape."

"Fuck no, I'm not crossing no white tape. Jesus it's dark out."

Then our bombardment started, the largest yet that we had witnessed.

"Would you look at that," said Daniel.

We stared upward at the huge firmament of white and orange and yellow streaks and flashes; a man-made aurora.

"That's more than a thousand guns, I'll bet," said Giles. I watched the light flicker off his face.

"You can't even count them," said Page. "It's like a drumroll."

We all stood still, watching and listening. The sounds of the explosions were layered on top of each other so that it was impossible to concentrate on any single one.

"At least we'll be able to see the white lines," said Daniel.

"Yeah, don't cross no white lines," said Lawton.

We walked the rest of the way in silence.

◆　　◆　　◆

I STEPPED on an American soldier. I felt something give beneath my feet and heard the breaking of ribs. Or was it a neck? The wheat field was covered with the dead and wounded and I was running headlong in a stampede of men and I could not avoid the bodies of the wounded and dead I could not.

I pray he was dead.

◆　　◆　　◆

DANIEL NEVER forgave Lawton for shooting the young German who raised his hands and yelled *"Kamerad!"* as we overran his machine-gun nest in a woods near Thiaucourt. The two other members of his Maxim team were dead beside him and he stood trembling with blood all over his face and his helmet at his feet. Daniel was walking up to him when Lawton raised his rifle and shot him twice in the chest.

"You son of a bitch!" yelled Daniel, grabbing Lawton's rifle and throwing it to the ground. Then he walked over to where the German lay and knelt beside him, checking his wounds. I stood beside Daniel and looked over his shoulder. The German couldn't have been any older than fifteen, with a smooth, unshaven face and freckles across the bridge of his nose. I knew he was dead.

"What's the matter with you, MacGuire? He's a fucking murdering bastard," said Lawton,

233

picking up his rifle. "You try raising your hands in the air next time you're up against one of them. Just try it."

"He's a boy," said Daniel, gently moving the German's head to one side and searching for a pulse on his neck. "He's just a boy."

◆　◆　◆

" GOOD MORNING, Patrick."

"Hello, Dr. Tompkins."

"Feeling all right today?" He was peering down through bifocals at a clipboard in his hands.

"Sure." I sat on the edge of my bed, trying to get my feet into my shoes.

"You're taking your medicine?"

"Yes."

"Is it helping?"

"A bit."

"Still a lot of pain?"

"Sometimes."

"The lab results are back."

"I see. And?"

"Not good, I'm afraid. But we've made tremendous progress in pain management." He began scribbling on his clipboard. "I'm going to try another medicine. Want you to take it three times a day. It may make you—"

"About the lab results..."

He stopped writing, took off his glasses with one hand, folded them neatly, slid them into the top pocket of his white lab coat and looked at me. "It doesn't look good."

"Well, of course not. I'm eighty-one. Nothing looks good."

He leaned forward and ran his hands along my neck, probing with his fingers. Then I lay back and he undid my shirt and pressed his hands along my abdomen. I winced.

"There?"

"Yes."

"And there?"

"Yes."

"How about here. Does this hurt too?"

"Yes."

After he left I went into the bathroom, stripped off my clothes and stood in the shower with my head under the nozzle. I turned the water temperature up until I could just barely stand it.

It's too much to bear, all this knowing; this acute self-consciousness. Who can stand it?

I turned off the shower, grabbed a towel and began drying myself.

If only I could sedate myself with amusing notions of self-importance. That's the trick, isn't it?

I dressed slowly, double-knotting my shoelaces so I wouldn't trip.

At least I am finally beginning to understand that all the other anxieties of our lives have a proper and inevitable lineage; that perhaps Julia was right: they are all just misplaced fears of death and decay, of the unshakable dread that we are mere cosmic nutrients, utterly and ridiculously superfluous. That's why we cling so desperately to religion and art: they are our most profound and eloquent responses to our vile predicament, bold assertions that our lives mean something after all.

I stood before the mirror and combed my hair, then flossed and put on my watch, pausing to wind it. After double-checking that my pants zipper was up, I headed down the hall to the cafeteria, trying to decide between Cheerios and Cornflakes and wondering whether Dr. Tompkins left all his patients in such good cheer.

◆　　◆　　◆

I CHOSE CHEERIOS but couldn't finish the bowl. Now I'm sitting on a bench in the hallway, desperate for a glimpse of Sarah or Janet or Erica; anything to ward off the despair.

It's this waiting that kills me. More even than the smell and the grayness and the infirmity; all of us waiting like cows in a holding pen, waiting to be shoved and prodded and pulled down the chute into eternity. Every day we are fed and dressed and pushed into common rooms like so much chattel to sit and wait and fart until finally it's our turn to be spirited away into the darkness, our Johnny coats flapping in the wind.

Death's inexorable approach puts extraordinary pressure on each day, so much so that instead of enjoying what I have left I simply seize up, unable to bear the tension. I don't just see the sand slipping through the hourglass I *hear* it, a constant flowing hissing sound that grows louder and louder with each passing hour.

That's why nothing's quite so important to the elderly as convincing themselves that they didn't squander vast chunks of their lives, which of course most of us did, frittering away the days like pocket change, which is why our seething resentments and regrets threaten to engulf us, until each thought begins with, "If only I..." or "I always wanted to..." In old age life's cowardice finally catches up with us. And we recoil at the waste.

That's what all the stories are about, the endless monologues that old men and women deliver to anyone who will listen. Our lives feel fuller when we can weave them into stories, even if not all the stories are true and even if we are really just filibustering, hoping our number won't be called—so long as we keep talking.

Time's a sneaky son of a bitch, no doubt about it. I don't think we ever really live in the present; instead, we're either just this side of the past or the future, wavering anxiously between anticipation and recollection. That's where I lived my life, always wanting, longing, wishing. And so, somehow, the days slipped by until I knew I'd never fall in love again; never remarry and live in a house with other voices and heartbeats. A few miscalculations early on and soon I'd sailed all the way into a neighboring galaxy with no chance of getting back. And just thinking about it makes me panic like I'm being held under water.

Oh well, screw it. Everybody here is way off course; light-years from the nearest inhabitable planet, just somersaulting through the miasma. No wonder such a big part of growing old is learning to lower one's expectations, only we call that maturity and wisdom so as not to sound too defeatist.

When you are young you demand ecstasy; when you are old you settle for anything short of agony.

Anything.

♦ ♦ ♦

I SUPPOSE that's why I write letters to Nurse Sarah. Love letters, if you must. It started as a lark six months ago, a hobby for an old man trying to unload what love he has left. Now I write her once a week, usually two pages or so, the musings of one person who finds solace in the presence—even just the existence—of another.

They are anonymous, of course, mailed to her home address in plain white envelopes. She even shows them to me. The first time I trembled as she read my words out loud, standing by my bedside one morning with one hand pressed against her chest. Now I fear she may be falling for this man, or at least with his words and their possibilities. I don't know how to stop without hurting her or me.

"Listen to this one," she said, putting her hand on my shoulder as she stood beside my chair in the recreation room, which was empty.

"He says, 'Beauty is the face of love, and love the feeling of enlightenment.'"

"Not bad."

"And look at his handwriting. I didn't know any man could write like that. It looks like the Declaration of Independence."

I agreed that the writing was quite striking and wondered aloud what that said about the author.

"He's obviously well-educated," she said. "God, this is torture!"

Yes, it is.

By now she has divvied up all the men in her life into three very distinct categories: those she hopes are the authors, a small group indeed; those she is certain are not the authors, which of course includes me; and those she fervently hopes are not the authors, the largest group by far. She scrutinizes everybody: the man at the checkout counter, the waiter at the restaurant, the policeman who issues her a speeding ticket, her friends' husbands. Especially her friends' husbands.

"I'll bet he's married and that's why he won't identify himself," she said one morning as she checked my pulse. "I mean, if he really feels this way about me, you'd think he'd want to at least ask me for a date, wouldn't you?"

"I'm sure he'd love a date," I said. "Maybe he's afraid there is something about him that you wouldn't like."

"Oh, like Cyrano de Bergerac?" She frowned. "You think maybe he's really ugly?"

"Or paralyzed or blind or deaf; it could be anything, really. Maybe he's quite young."

"Not with this handwriting. That's no teenager. Besides, teenagers can't write this kind of stuff."

"No, you're right."

"Well, I wish he'd give me some way to contact him," she said. "This relationship is very one-sided. I don't see what's in it for him."

I shrugged.

She folded her hands tightly across her chest. "Well, if he doesn't give me his address soon, I'm simply going to stop opening his letters."

That afternoon I took the bus into town and paid for a post office box.

The first letter from her was wary and full of questions. Gradually, she opened up. Now she is friendly, even passionate. Last week she sent me a picture of herself standing in front of a rosebush in her backyard. I picked the picture out myself.

"Which one do you think I should send?" she had asked, offering me five choices. None of them showed her figure—she wanted to be modest—so I chose the one where she was starting to laugh and reaching for her face. I keep it in my wallet. I wrote back that her face in the picture was like a talisman or amulet that gave me hope and purpose even though I knew that it was Julia's face I was really looking for.

Now Sarah has threatened to stop writing unless I too send a photo of myself.

" HEY DANIEL, you got any more cigarettes?" We were lying side by side in a hayloft a few miles from the front, passing a bottle of pinard back and forth and talking in the darkness.

"In my pack."

"Shit, I can't see a thing. Hold on." I reached for the candle stub I kept in my pocket.

"You got matches?"

"Yeah, here."

I lit the candle. The light flickered off the hay and bathed everything in a faint yellow glow. Something in the far corner of the barn flapped in the air and disappeared. Daniel fumbled with his knapsack, then pulled out a pack of Sweet Caporals.

We each lit one and lay back.

"I'm almost finished with the poem I've been working on," said Daniel, with a slight slur. I wondered if he was drunk. I rarely saw him drunk.

"The one to Julia? Your epic?"

"I was thinking of showing it to you before I send it."

"I don't know much about poetry," I said, taking a deep drag of my cigarette. I watched the smoke mingle with my words.

"You don't need to. That's the beauty of it."

"Sure, I'll look at it." I couldn't wait to read it.

"I don't know how I'll tell my parents," he said, flicking the ash from his cigarette

241

into his palm, then wiping it against his pants leg.

"Have you heard from them yet?"

"Nothing."

"I'm sorry. I don't understand how..."

"I keep writing."

"I wouldn't."

He looked at me. "Don't be so sure," he said.

"But why, if they don't write back?"

"Because I'm not in a position to hold a lot of grudges."

"Well, I'm sure they'll soften up."

He shrugged.

After a few minutes I blew out my candle and placed the stub back into my pocket. Then I lay back again and closed my eyes.

"Patrick?"

"Yes?"

"You're all right."

"Thanks."

"I mean that."

"You too."

He pushed the bottle of pinard up against my shoulder. I took it, sat up and brought it to my lips, swishing the rough red wine around my mouth before swallowing.

"Mind if I give you some advice?" he asked.

"Shoot."

"Don't let this war ruin you."

His comment took me aback. "Ruin me? It's not going to ruin me, so long as I don't get my balls shot off."

"I mean it. It's going to ruin a lot of people. Don't let it ruin you, all right?"

"I'll do my best—so long as I'm in one piece. Otherwise I may be a bit surly."

"Agreed." He took the bottle from me and raised it to his lips, then exhaled loudly.

"You know the thing that surprises me most about the war?" he asked.

"What?"

"It's so damn lonely."

"I hadn't really thought of it that way. There are so many shitty aspects to the whole enterprise that no single...hey, you're not making a pass, are you?"

He burst out laughing.

"Because I can sleep outside..."

"Dream on." He took another swig.

"I think you're drunk."

"I'm just unwinding," he said.

"Or unraveling."

He threw a clump of hay at me.

We were quiet for a few minutes, then he said, "If you could be anywhere in the world right now, where would you be?"

"A warm bed," I said, taking the bottle back from him.

"I'd like to be on a tropical island, lying on the sand so that the waves just lapped my feet," he said.

"Are you going to talk like this all night?"

"Actually, Julia can't swim."

"She can stay on the beach." I handed the bottle back to him.

"She's due next month. I hope she's okay," he said.

"Sure she is."

"You know it's funny, I really don't feel like I'm going to be a father. I mean it hasn't sunk in yet. It seems so...so far away."

He was quiet for a minute, then said, "Can you imagine holding a baby? Your own baby? Jesus."

"I can imagine holding yours easier than holding mine."

"I wonder what it'll look like. To think that it's some combination of me and Julia."

"It's gonna be a beauty."

He put out his cigarette against a floorboard. "I won't be able to afford a house. I have no insurance. Christ, what kind of a father am I going to be?"

I looked at Daniel lying on his back, eyes to the ceiling. "You'll be a great father. I know it." I imagined him with a child and how wonderful he'd be. Lucky child.

I closed my eyes again and listened to the distant thud thud of the guns. Suddenly a long, low rumble caught my attention. I sat up. "What was that?"

Daniel was quiet a moment, then said, "Thunder."

"Thunder?"

"Yes, thunder."

Again, a long deep growl in the distance.

"It is thunder, isn't it?" I said. "Doesn't that remind you of being a kid and lying awake at night, all warm and safe under the covers?"

The next rumble was louder. Five minutes later it began to rain, the drops slapping against the roof of the barn, which was just a few feet above our heads. Then lightning flashed through a small window just beyond our feet. Then again, followed by a tremendous crack of thunder. I jumped. "Jesus."

In the next flash I saw that Daniel was sitting up.

"You can't hear them," he said.

"Hear what?"

"The guns. You can't hear the guns." He was smiling.

I listened. "No, you can't, can you?"

"That's good," he said.

In the next flash I saw that he was lying on his back again with his eyes closed.

"Yes, that's very good," I said.

◆　　◆　　◆

JULIA'S BLOUSE was damp with sweat as we reached the hilltop and in the light breeze I caught the scent of her skin. I stood beside her and wiped the back of my neck and forehead with my handkerchief. We looked down at a patchwork of fields and woods that fanned out across a broad plain until the woods finally gave way to the fields. To the left old trench lines snaked across the ground like great big welts. And everywhere shell holes still gouged the earth as though from some ancient meteorite shower.

"What a gorgeous day," she said, smiling up toward the sky, where a thin white lace of high clouds inched quietly past, each cloud spaced perfectly apart like the folds in desert sand.

245

"I remember being a child and lying on my back in the grass and watching the clouds drift past," I said. "There was nothing else in the world but me and those clouds and the grass beneath me."

"Happiness to me was lying in bed at night during a thunderstorm and feeling warm and dry and knowing that my mother was just in the next room."

"I used to curl up in bed with my dog and read him stories by candlelight."

"You read your dog stories?"

"He was a smart dog."

She smiled, then kicked away leaves and sat down. I sat across from her on a rock.

"Happiness is different for adults, don't you think?" she asked. "Much too fleeting. Like something you can't see if you stare straight at it."

"I think for a lot of people happiness is just the absence of discomfort," I said.

"That's not enough for me," she said.

"It's not enough for me either. During the war we all insisted that whatever else we did in life we'd make sure we were happy, otherwise what was the point?" I laughed at the recollection. "Can't you see all these young men congratulating each other on how happy they were going to be if only they didn't get their butts shot off?"

"Well, I'm happy you didn't," she said.

"Me too."

"I hope you don't feel guilty..."

"For surviving? Yes, I do a bit, but it's more

a sense of responsibility; that I've got to make something of my life—get it right—because I was lucky enough to get a second chance."

"That's a lot of pressure."

"But that was the point of everything we talked about: we were going to *live* when the war ended. Take everything in. Make our own rules. Not waste a minute."

"But nobody can do that."

"No, but we can try," I said.

She reached into her bag and took out some grapes, carefully pulling them apart into two bunches and handing one to me. I took it and placed it in my lap, pulling the grapes off one by one as I looked out over the valley.

"At least you're not normal," she said.

"I'm not?"

"No, thank goodness. Don't you find normal people boring? They conceal all the important things." Then her expression grew serious as she said, "I really haven't enjoyed someone's company so much in years."

"Neither have I." I felt the burn in my chest again. Could she ever fall for me or was it just the friendship she needed? But who could remain friends like this? It was unbearable.

She stood up and brushed off her skirt. "Shall we walk?"

As the path narrowed, I let her walk in front of me. In the breeze I caught the lovely scent of her perfume. Strange, how emotional smells can be. And individual. As distinct as faces.

After an hour we stopped again in a clearing near a pile of splintered timbers. Behind them was a mound of rusty tin cans and next to them some empty and broken ammunition crates. I pulled out a bottle of wine and removed the cork. We had forgotten glasses so we drank from the bottle, passing it back and forth.

"What do you think about when you paint?" I asked.

"Everything." She smiled to herself. "Daniel thought that artists were trying to repair themselves, to heal themselves through their work. He admired them because he thought they salvaged something from human misery. But sometimes I think that art is more like the hot lava that spews from a volcano, originating miles underground."

"The accounting business doesn't allow for a lot of spewing."

"No, I wouldn't imagine it does." Her smile grew. Whenever she smiled her face reddened slightly, which made her expression seem unusually genuine.

"I think just about everybody would like to be an artist, if they had the talent," I said. "Art seems to get right to the point."

She took a swig from the bottle and handed it back.

"What inspires your painting?"

"I guess it's all the things that I want to say but can't. Not with words."

"And do you get to say them that way, with your brush?"

"I get to try to say them. That's enough."

She lit a cigarette, exhaling slowly. "Without art; without paintings, books, sculpture and music, the human soul would be quite impenetrable, don't you think?"

She looked at me with an expression I hadn't seen before, excitement tugging at the corners of her eyes, as though she had suddenly found something she was looking for. Then she stood and leaned against a birch tree, her arms stretched behind her around the trunk, and said, "When I was in Paris I went to the Louvre. It was my first visit. I was overwhelmed!"

I could see it immediately in her eyes and I thought of how wonderful it would be to wander through the Louvre with her, arm in arm and painting by painting, and then sit by the Seine and watch the world from the safety of our togetherness.

"I spent all day wandering up and down the hallways, staring at the *Mona Lisa* and Canova's *Psyche and Cupid* and the *Venus de Milo* and Caravaggio's *The Death of the Virgin* and hundreds of other works in all shapes and sizes and colors. My feet were killing me. And just before I was about to leave, I was staring at Michelangelo's *The Dying Slave*, and I suddenly realized that every single work I had seen expressed the same thing, the same intense longing for beauty and immortality and justice and compassion. It was as though all of these artists from throughout history were there in those long hallways crying out the same anguished plea in a thousand different languages. I burst into tears and started running. I just had to get out."

I said nothing as I watched the beautiful woman with tears in her green eyes running from the Louvre and then through the Tuileries, disappearing in a crowd.

"After that I didn't feel so alone anymore. Suddenly I realized that the deepest, most indescribable parts of my soul had been felt and understood and transcribed by these artists. But it made me sad too, because I realized that that is the best we can do: to express our longings and pain. We can never stop it."

"But is everything in the Louvre so sad?"

"Most of it seemed sad to me. Exquisitely sad, because it was so beautiful too. The entire human soul is on display there. It's all said."

"And the comfort is in knowing that it's been said."

She nodded. "And when I thought of what it took to make those works, painting or sculpting by candlelight with tired limbs and strained eyes, well I knew those artists must have been suffering tremendously deep inside. Can't you see them, toiling away all their lives because they have to?"

I tried, but I kept coming back to her smile and then the tears and the woman fleeing from the Louvre.

♦　♦　♦

DANIEL AND I were foraging for apples in an orchard when we came across a wrecked

Fokker, the front end smashed into the ground and the tail pointing in the air. The pilot was still in his seat, slumped forward and covered with flies. We both peered into the cockpit but the smell drove us away.

"How long you figure he's been here?" I said, walking slowly around the plane and staring at the big black crosses painted on the tail and wings and fuselage, which was punctured by a row of bullet holes.

"Couple of days," said Daniel, inserting his finger into one of the bullet holes.

Neither of us had seen a plane up close before and we spent several minutes studying it and running our hands along it and tapping it with our boots, as though we'd come across the carcass of a predator that we weren't convinced was dead.

"I wonder if he's one of those famous aces?" I asked, looking again at the pilot, whose face was so mangled that I had to turn away.

Daniel shrugged. "We should bury him."

"You're joking?" Though I knew immediately that he wasn't.

Daniel pulled out the small trench shovel from his pack, walked a few paces from the plane and began digging. We switched off every twenty minutes until we had a carved out a shallow but serviceable grave.

Then we crawled through the wreckage of the fuselage until we were on either side of the pilot. Grabbing him under the armpits, we counted to three and heaved. He didn't budge. We shifted positions, then tried again, squinching our faces at the smell and trying to blow away the flies.

"It's useless," I said, jumping down off the wreckage after we'd struggled for fifteen minutes. "His legs are trapped."

"We've got to get him out," said Daniel, yanking again on the pilot's arm.

"What does it matter? Christ, the guy's dead."

"Wouldn't you want to be buried?"

"I'm not sure I'd give a shit," I said. Did I? Neither option seemed appealing.

Daniel crawled up on the fuselage, then stood above and behind the pilot and began pulling frantically at his coat. "Come on, damn it!" He yanked again and again, until the sweat was pouring down his face, then finally he let go and smashed his fist against the plane. Then he slid down against the side of the wreckage and buried his hand in the crook of his elbow.

I'd never seen him lose control before and it unnerved me, like a child seeing his father cry. I went over to him and put my arm on his shoulder. "Come on," I said. "Time to go."

Daniel banged his free hand against the side of the plane again. I could see his shoulders shaking.

After a few minutes of silence he slowly stood up, packed his shovel and picked up his sack of apples. Then we walked on through the orchard and to the road and headed back to camp.

My senses are charred; I don't take the
cigarette out of my mouth when I write
Deceased over their letters.

> —*Wilfred Owen, British Army,
> in a letter home. Killed in action, 1918,
> seven days before the Armistice.*

◆   ◆   ◆

I SKIPPED dinner last night. Instead I sat in my
room at my desk and worked on a drawing of
Julia. I thought I had something for a while,
at least the mouth and the high curve of the
cheekbones. Then it fell apart on me so that
I couldn't even look at it anymore. I put it into
my drawer, next to the others. Then I went outside and sat and looked up at the stars until
my neck ached.

Ever since I was a child, stars have made me
feel wonderfully insignificant. Maybe it's
because the heavens are one of the few things
large enough to dwarf my own problems, to
place even my acute anxiety into some
perspective. I'm quite content to feel diminished
if my problems are equally demeaned, which
is why I love oceans and hate Sunday nights.

I closed my eyes for a moment. In the vast
darkness I saw my grandmother sitting next
to me on the front porch, rocking. She held
my hand in hers and sang, "I see the moon,
the moon sees me, the moon sees somebody
I'd like to see..."

I opened my eyes and wrapped my sweater tight and stared at the flickering pinpoints above, feeling the chronology of my life tumble out of order. I could be eight years old now, or twelve, or twenty-four, or thirty-four, or fifty-eight; the stars look exactly the same. How many other things in our lives remain constant even as we decay? Not enough.

Do I want an epitaph? I made a note to think about whether I might be willing to hang my hat on a pithy phrase for eternity, though I doubt it. What on earth would I say? THE JIG IS UP?

I read once that the sun will expire in about five billion years. Not an immediate concern but I can't help wondering: if we knew for certain that the human race and all we've created would eventually be destroyed in a great big solar surgical scrub, would it change anything? Certainly all of the world's problems would suddenly be cast in a more temporary light, though the same would be true for the planet's rain forests and art treasures. The knowledge of our ultimate annihilation would be no small blow to our illusions of self-importance and would make our Darwinian scramble to pass on our genes laughable. (After all, who would want *their* offspring to be around when the lights go out?)

I turned and looked through the large window into the recreation room, which glowed with a yellow warmth. It was bingo night and the white-haired men and women were hunched over their tables trying to find a three or an eight or a seven and I could tell by the way some of them looked sideways at each other that there was some confusion as to which numbers had actually been called and what game was actually being played. Then I saw Mitzie walk in and sit down with the slow, hydraulic movements of old age, and I thought of her dreaming of gentlemen callers who never called.

Returning to my room I walked past wheelchairs parked every which way, as though left over from some ancient and catastrophic traffic jam. Their drivers sat immobile, urine-scented blankets—the teddy bears of old age—draped over their laps. Urine and floor cleaner, that's the smell, with a trace of Bactine or some similar antiseptic. I tapped my cane softly on the floor as I zigzagged past, feeling remarkably nimble under the circumstances. The few other patients in motion moved so slowly that they appeared to be some sort of special effect, while the nurses and visitors looked almost Chaplinesque in comparison.

First I washed my hands, and then I carefully unbuttoned my shirt and hung it on the first hook in my closet, next to my blue blazer. After putting on the top to my pajamas—plain, light blue cotton with ridiculously large buttons—I sat back on my bed and struggled with my pants. Finally I got back up and brushed what's left of my teeth before returning to bed with a half glass of water. Martin was already asleep, flat on his back with the sheets tucked under his armpits and his bare arms resting on his stomach. Too tired even to read, I lay on my back and pulled the covers tightly to my chin. Then I closed my eyes and listened, first to the sounds of the hallway, the sounds of footsteps and muffled conversation; then to the sounds of my body itself. Gradually, as the sound of my breathing grew louder, I felt myself falling backward into oblivion, my arms cartwheeling in the air.

Will I comport myself with some dignity at the end, the proper carriage and grace, or will I shriek in holy terror like one of those Rhesus monkeys locked in some university basement with electrodes implanted on their exposed brains? More likely I will expire like most everyone else at Great Oaks: routinely and even meekly, my final diminuendo barely noticed. Then the sheet pulled over my head and away we go, the gurney squeaking down the hallway, my toes and nose jutting upward like goal posts as I'm hustled off to my eternal repose.

And after that? Pure nothingness? Are we expunged from the very earth itself? (Well, at least I like to think that death brings about a cessation of both anxiety and diarrhea, which is no small victory.) Or can I somehow triumph even in death? Failing religion, which has always failed me, what's the best I can do? Leave behind an achievement, some painting or structure that can withstand another couple of hundred years before it too succumbs? I haven't the talent. Do my children assure me some kind of biological immortality (though I shall be dreadfully diluted in a few generations), and if so, shouldn't I have scattered the seed with great profligacy? Or can I inoculate myself from extinction by sheer love? How about a noble deed or act of charity that might assure me goodwill beyond the grave, perhaps even a statue in the town square? Might I then be sustained as a fond memory in the hearts of others? What happens when those hearts fail, as they must?

Certainly the problem with money is that you can't take it with you, but that's true for everything else as well: Mozart's genius, friendships, love, a good recipe for crab cakes. And the more you have, the more you have to lose, which is why I no longer regret not learning a second language.

I rolled to one side and then another but couldn't get comfortable. I returned to my back but only briefly; ever since I was a child I have been unable to fall asleep in such an exposed position. Instead I curl up in a protective crouch as though bracing for blows. I think people who sleep on their backs are more confident than people who sleep on their sides and stomachs. Or maybe people who sleep on their backs are just asking for trouble.

If I intended to be buried in a casket—and I don't—I would insist on being placed on my side or stomach.

I rolled back to my left side and thought that the whole business of dying would be a lot easier if we had someone to blame. Instead we spend our last days shadowboxing with the vagaries of modern medicine. Mass genocide with no accountability whatsoever. I want war criminals in dockets and tribunals and convictions of crimes against humanity. I want, at the very least, someone to wag my finger at.

Dignity's what I'm lacking, no doubt about it. Why should I babble and quake before the firing squad when I can stand unbowed, perhaps even cheating my assassins of their cheap thrills? Why not flip them the birdie and leave this earth with a defiant smirk on my face, like a martyr who refuses to change allegiance even at the stake?

But a martyr for what? I'm tied to a stake with smoke filling the air and my lungs and my nostrils and I don't even know the charges. What are the charges? Will somebody please read me the charges?

♦　　♦　　♦

CAMUS WROTE that man carries on a kind of "gloomy flirtation" with God. I have stopped flirting altogether.

♦　　♦　　♦

I WANTED to take hold of Julia but I didn't. What would I do, just reach for her? Ask her? What would she do? Yet she was still grieving for Daniel, and I, well I was married. Maybe that's why she felt comfortable with me. I was a safe man. Like a brother. But I hardly wanted to be seen like a brother. And the days were slipping by. Was it possible that she felt none of the attraction that overwhelmed me?

She was quiet on the hike back to the car but on the drive to the hotel she told funny stories about her childhood, sometimes laughing so hard that she folded her hands tightly across her chest as though trying to keep herself from coming apart. All the sadness seemed to have fallen away from her so that she looked lighter as she talked, changing her voice to capture different characters and even singing bits of old songs. But as it got dark she grew silent again, concentrating on the single yellow flower she had picked from a field and now held by the stem with both hands.

"I've enjoyed spending this time with you," she said, turning toward me. "I'll never forget it."

"Neither will I."

"You'll be glad to be back with your family."

I looked at her, about to say something. But no words came. I turned away.

She spun the flower in her fingers. "I've decided that the preachers are right: if we can't find meaning in our suffering we won't find meaning in our lives. The pain just overwhelms everything."

"'A deep distress hath humanized my soul.'"

"Who's that?"

"Wordsworth."

"Say it again."

I did. Then I said, "I think he was saying that

his own sadness or pain made him more sympathetic to what others go through; that suffering should bring us together, bring out the best in us."

I slowed the car as a farmer led a donkey across the street by a thick, frayed tether. To my right I noticed a small street sign with faded German lettering nailed against a white, mortared wall.

After a moment Julia said, "I think that most people feel that their lives are private martyrdoms to some secret fear or passion."

I turned and looked at her. She held my gaze. "Can't you see it in people, especially older people?" she asked, tilting her head slightly. "I saw it in my mother: in her eyes and the deliberate way she controlled her gestures and the way she walked with her neck straight and her chin up. Maybe that's what courage and grace mean when we grow old; maybe they mean not talking about it."

◆　◆　◆

ABOUT WHAT, Julia? What?

◆　◆　◆

"MARTIN?"
"What is it?"
"I don't feel so good."
"You want me to call the nurse?"
"No, I just wanted to say that I don't feel so good."

260

"I understand."

"I know you do. Too bad we didn't meet earlier. We would have made great roommates. Can you imagine us with a nice walk-up in Greenwich Village? We would have had a good time, you and me. Think of the parties."

"But I was married then."

"I know you were. I'm just dreaming here," I said.

"Yeah, I'm with you."

"You never complain, do you?"

"No use in it."

"What do you think about, lying there?"

"I don't know. Places I've been, that sort of thing."

"Nothing in particular?"

"No, not in particular. My mind sort of wanders."

"Yeah, mine too. After all these years I think of it as an old dog who still explores every inch of the backyard each day even though he's been living there for years. He trots back and forth, smelling the same old bushes and the trees and checking for openings in the fence."

"You always find something new, don't you?"

"Yes, you do, don't you?"

"I hope you feel better."

"Thanks."

◆　　◆　　◆

I CAN ALMOST feel her hands on me. And her lips and the press of her soft skin against

261

mine. So many years ago, and yet, suddenly, there she is, staring right into my eyes, pulling me toward her, whispering my name. Over and over and over again.

Will you drive me mad?

◆　◆　◆

I AM SITTING outside on a wooden bench near a stand of pine trees out behind the center with an old paperback edition of *King Lear* in my lap. All day I have been feeling lousy and now I feel even worse, sometimes gripping the sides of the bench to fight off dizziness. I carefully take off my glasses and clean them with the corner of my dark blue sweater, bending my head down to slide them back on. Then I pull out my small notepad from my shirt pocket and scan my notes. The top item says, "check zipper." I glance down at my fly. It's wide open.

Damn.

After I zip up I watch two young boys play on the front lawn, turning somersaults and cartwheels and firing at each other with stick guns. Their mother must be inside delivering yet another shipment of See's candy to Grandma.

"I shot you! You *have* to fall down."

"You didn't shoot me! You missed."

"What do you mean I *missed*? I was *this* close! I shot you right in the head."

"Bang! Now I shot you."

"You can't do that. You can't shoot me. I

already shot you. You gotta fall down. You're dead."

"I'm not dead, you are. Bang! Gotcha, right in the face."

"No, you didn't!"

"Bang! Now I got you in the stomach."

"Stop that!"

"Bang! Right in the eyes."

"If you don't die, I'm not going to play anymore."

"Bang bang bang!"

"You keeping that bench warm enough, Mr. Delaney?" says June, the big-butted and big-hearted cleaning lady who pushes a big dolly of very dirty sheets down this path twice a day.

"I'm just sitting here watching all the pretty ladies go by," I say, feeling suddenly cold.

She smiles and then leans into her dolly, giving it a great big shove. I wave and then fold my hands in front of my chest, shivering.

I used to generate tremendous heat, sweating in anything above seventy-five. I fought with every woman I ever slept with over the window and the thermostat.

"Look honey, there is only so much I can take off," I'd say, standing in my boxer shorts and perspiring profusely, "while you can simply keep adding layers until you're comfortable."

At Great Oaks the temperature is a source of constant and bitter recrimination. "Excuse me, nurse, is there a window open somewhere?" says The-Woman-Whose-Name-I-Can-Never-Remember, a little bitty thing with hands like bonsai trees and the demeanor of a Jack Russell terrier.

"I've never been so cold in all my life," sputters Helen, who wears several sweaters at once, even in summer.

"It's a disgrace they don't heat this place," says a tiny creature in the corner, whose great big hooded eyes are always oozing some fluid or another. "Just criminal."

"A draft! I feel a draft!" howls Mitzie, tugging at her cardigan.

Slowly, we are all turning cold.

◆　◆　◆

NUMBING COLD. We sat close for warmth: Daniel, Page, Giles, Lawton, Tometti and I. We were huddled together in the back of a *camion*, part of a long convoy that spilled over the sides of a muddy road, drenched by an icy October rain. I kept rubbing my hands together but they refused all but the simplest commands. As the truck bobbed and lurched I had to hold on to keep from falling off, which made my hands even colder.

"When's the last time the Germans and French fought a war?" I asked, stomping my feet on the floorboards.

"That would be in 1870," said Page, who was still recovering from a broken nose caused when an explosion threw him against a beam in a trench. I wondered if his looks would ever recover.

"What was that all about?"

"Nationalism," said Page.

"Who won?"

"Guess."

We all nodded.

"The Germans had Paris surrounded," said Page. "Nearly starved it. The only way out was by balloon."

"Balloon?"

"One of the French leaders actually escaped from the city in a balloon to try to raise an army from the countryside."

"There's a lot of bad blood in Europe."

"No shit."

"Fuck it's cold."

I looked out the back and saw an old man on a sickly looking horse pass by. His black beret was tipped rather elegantly on his head, which he held inordinately high, as though in defiance of the whole catastrophic mess. Farther up, soldiers with the Signal Corps were erecting telegraph wire, while nearby, others were standing around a small fire, holding their hands above the flame.

"The French and the English used to fight, didn't they?" asked Giles.

"Like cats and dogs."

"Didn't the French fight in the Revolutionary War, on our side?" asked Tometti.

"You're not such a dumb fuck after all," said Lawton. "At least not for a pushcart Italian."

Tometti sputtered some Italian insults.

"That's Lafayette," said Page.

"Where the fuck are we headed anyway?" asked Lawton.

"This cozy little hotel just up the road. Great big featherbeds. Nice restaurant. Not a bad whorehouse next door either," I said.

"Funny."

I looked out the back as we passed the ruins of a farm and saw German prisoners in long gray coats building a fence. A lone elderly Frenchman stood nearby, a rifle resting in the crook of his arm.

"Anybody get laid in Reims?" asked Giles, speaking into his cupped hands, which he was trying to warm. "Heard you get a half hour for five francs."

"Well then, Giles you could drop a franc and get change," said Lawton. He hadn't been lisping much lately and I wondered if the cold had dampened his libido.

Tometti found that incredibly funny.

Giles ribbed him with his elbow. "One of these days, Tometti, you're going to hit puberty and that voice of yours is going to go to shit—unless we cut your balls off."

Tometti began muttering Italian epithets again. At least I assumed they were epithets, though in Italian they sounded quite lyrical, almost complimentary.

"They had MPs keeping Americans out of all the whorehouses. Pershing's a goddamn Puritan," said Lawton. "Bet he's never even been laid."

"His wife and children died in a fire back at an army base in San Francisco," said Page.

"No shit."

We were quiet for a few minutes. Then

Lawton said, "I heard the whores were pretty ugly anyway. And old. Fat and old."

"I thought you liked the fat ones," said Giles.

"No, he likes the old skinny ones," I said.

Lawton rolled his eyes. "I ain't even seen a single pretty girl since I got here," he said. "I thought French girls were supposed to be pretty." His lisp crept in again. I imagined he must get completely tongue-tied during sex.

"They're hiding the pretty ones from us, you fool," said Giles. "After the war is over and we've been shipped back home the villages will be crawling with them."

We each contemplated villages teeming with French girls; busty French girls in white lace with big toothy smiles and thick hair and picnic baskets slung on their silky smooth arms.

"I figure if you're a young Frenchman who lives through the war, the odds have got to be heavily in your favor," I said.

"Shit, they'll probably be fighting over the ones who aren't crippled," said Giles.

"You can't beat American girls," I said, thinking of a pretty girl named Nancy who lived on my street and wondering again why she had steadfastly refused to look at me since her family moved in to the neighborhood nine years ago. Maybe a few medals would change things.

Tometti reached into his shirt pocket and pulled out a small, black leather frame, reverently opening it. "Ain't no one as pretty as my Teresa," he said in a high-pitched voice that made me wince.

I leaned over and glanced at the photo-graph. "You really expect us to believe that this gorgeous creature is carrying around a pho-tograph of you?"

"Identical frame," said Tometti, beaming. "We bought them at the same store in New York."

Several of us shook our heads.

"What do you do, stand under her window and sing?" asked Page.

"I used to, till her father threatened to shoot me."

Daniel leaned forward and gestured for Tometti to hand him the photograph. He took it and studied it carefully. "What is it about a beautiful face that makes it beautiful?" he asked, handing it back. He had been quiet all morning and I wondered if he was thinking of Julia or the cold. It seemed to me that if you were in love like he was it helped you during the tough times but it also meant that you had a lot more to lose.

Tometti shrugged.

"Think about it," said Daniel. "What makes one face so much more attractive than another?" Lawton and Giles and Page turned toward him, their dirty and unshaven faces suddenly creased in thought. I tried to picture Julia's face but all I could think of was how warm her skin must be and how cold mine felt. I imag-ined crawling in bed with her, naked; the feel of her full breasts and her smooth stomach and her thighs and hips and neck. The thought made me sick with longing.

"Think of two women with similar facial features, only one woman is rather plain looking and the other quite striking," said Daniel. "Why does a centimeter here or there make such a difference, so much so that you'll walk by the one and risk your life for the other?"

"I'd take either one," said Giles.

"Seriously, why does a certain look make us feel so emotional?" continued Daniel. "What does that particular face trigger?"

"Didn't your daddy have a talk with you?" said Lawton.

"It's an interesting thought," said Page.

I looked out the back of the truck and saw a field lined with rows of wooden crosses. On the far end more German prisoners under guard were digging fresh graves. The symmetry made me smile.

"I sometimes wonder whether we don't each contain a template within our minds of a certain woman who is just right for us," said Page, rubbing his palms up and down his thighs.

Daniel lit a cigarette, then said, "The first time I saw Julia I felt as though I had found something that I had lost. There was something so familiar about her."

"That's it, they look familiar," said Page, smiling. "You see them and there is a strange sense of recognition. I remember once I was walking across the yard at Harvard and I looked up and saw this woman passing by me and I felt absolutely awestruck."

"Start with her tits," said Lawton, now lisping heavily.

"No, that's just it. She wasn't sexy. I mean, she was but that wasn't it. The point is, I *knew* that face. It was as though I had come within inches of my own salvation. Her face still haunts me."

I cupped my hands and blew into them, then stomped my feet again.

Page continued: "I'll bet there are no more than four or five of those faces out there in the whole world."

"You really think it's only four or five?" I asked. "I can't work with odds like that."

"That's why most people settle for less," said Daniel.

"This is depressing," said Giles.

Tometti placed his photograph of Teresa against his lips and kissed it.

"What about Julia?" I asked. "Did she feel the same way when she met you?"

"I got lucky," said Daniel, turning toward me and smiling.

"So where do we get these images?"

"I get mine from this little magazine I bought once in Chicago. Woo eee!" said Lawton.

"I think that face must be some sort of composite," said Daniel, ignoring Lawton.

"But of what?" I asked.

"Of our dreams; of women we've known and liked. But it's more than that. I look at Julia and I think: she's what I'm missing."

"So now you're complete?" I said.

"It feels that way."

"Remember Plato's allegory?" asked Page.

"Plato's allegory? What the fuck is this, a philosophy lecture? I ought to get a diploma listening to this shit," said Lawton, stomping out his cigarette.

"The one about how humans used to have four legs and four arms and two faces until the Gods split us in two so we wouldn't pose a threat to them, and how we've been searching for our other halves ever since?"

"I've heard of that," said Daniel, pursing his lips.

"You have?" I asked, looking at him.

He smiled back.

"What do you think?" asked Page.

"It's pretty good."

"But do you think it's true, that there is only one other person out there for us?" I asked.

"I don't know," said Daniel. "Giles, what do you think?"

"Well, personally, I can think of three girls from my hometown that I'd give my right arm for, and it's a small town. So, if there are, say, fifty counties in Ohio, each with at least..."

"You have no taste," said Tometti, turning his attention back to Teresa.

"So let's say you're lucky enough to find this person, does it last?" I asked.

"The love?" asked Daniel.

"No, not just the love. My parents love each other. I mean more than that. What you were talking about earlier. That magic."

"I don't know yet," said Daniel.

"I have my doubts," I said. "I'm not sure that we ever feel like we're whole for long."

"I think Delaney's right," said Page. "Besides, I've always felt there was something sad about beauty."

"Is that what they teach you at Harvard?" asked Lawton.

"Because it's usually unattainable," I said, agreeing with Page.

"Or we know we won't always be around to enjoy it," said Daniel.

"So even beauty is about death," said Page.

"You guys are fucking nuts," said Giles, spitting out the back of the truck.

"Or maybe the allure of beauty is that it defies death, at least temporarily," said Daniel, who had his hands folded under his armpits. "It's like looking at heaven."

"So now we're talking about angels, am I right?" asked Lawton.

"Am I following here?"

Giles spit again.

"Here, hand me that," said Page, extending his hand toward Tometti's photograph. When he was done I took the photo but my hands shook so badly that I couldn't see her clearly. I handed her back to Tometti, buried my hands into my armpits and spent the next few hours imagining crawling naked into bed next to Julia.

◆ ◆ ◆

"SO, WHAT'S she like in bed?" It's a question I'd been wanting to ask for months and as Daniel and I stood guard by a huge stack of ammunition crates in the predawn darkness, I decided to give it a shot.

"I'm not going to tell you what she's like in bed."

That's another thing that was unusual about Daniel: he didn't boast about his conquests, real or imagined. In fact, he was the only soldier I ever met who didn't like to talk about sex, as though it was too fine a thing to be bandied about with a couple of louse-ridden men.

"Just in general."

"In general?"

"Yeah, in general."

"She's passionate."

"How passionate?"

He looked at me and grinned. I longed for a cigarette, but we were under strict orders not to smoke. "Very passionate."

"As in..."

"As in, *very* passionate."

"I see."

For the rest of the day I tried to visualize *very* passionate. By evening I was practically lisping.

◆　　◆　　◆

THIS AFTERNOON I fell asleep in a large brown reading chair in the recreation room and dreamed about precious little Amy Sperling, the sweet-smelling apparition who hypnotized me throughout the eighth grade. Is Amy really in her eighties now, with East Bloc ankles and reverse biceps that sag and sway like the gullet of a pelican when she walks? I don't believe it. Not my Amy Sperling. To me, Amy will always be fourteen, her soft features framed with even softer blond hair that made barrettes do things that barrettes haven't done since.

Amy was one of the smartest girls at Winthrop Junior High. She had perfect posture and perfect clothes and a melodious laugh that ricocheted around her perfect teeth before dancing off down the hallway like a shiny stone skipping perfectly across the water. Even the way she carried her books, clutched to her breast with one or both hands, caused me enormous grief. (To be one of her books!) And the way she stood at the blackboard and made her letters, so flawless and ornamental, while my illegible efforts caused the blackboard to shriek with horror no matter how I held the chalk.

When I knew she wasn't home I would walk by her house just to stare at the windows and wonder which one was hers and what on earth did her bedroom look like? No matter how I tried to picture it, the details of her room were inconceivable to me; I saw only a holy place bathed in blinding light. What I would have given for just a swath of her sheets, a relic of my dear sweet Amy with the perfect barrettes!

I don't think Amy ever looked at me more than twice during that school year, but when she did, adrenaline flooded my insides and I felt the same giddy feeling one might get in the presence of royalty or fame. To my mind, Amy had the power to transform mere boys into White Knights with just a glance. Sitting but three seats away from her I felt, finally, that I was ensconced right smack in the sultry center of the universe.

I wasn't always faithful to Amy. After all, Nina Zumbrowski and her long black hair and blue eyes were only six seats away. Nina didn't look at me much either, but never mind. That made it easier to stare without being noticed. And how I stared, absorbed in the delicacy of her wrists, her neck and her shoulders, which seemed to twitch back and forth in unison with her fanny. I knew with certainty that if Nina but kissed me, I would get straight As for the rest of my life, and I knew with certainty that Nina would never kiss me.

◆　◆　◆

I ARRANGED for a piano to be delivered the Tuesday morning of Howard's birthday, just after lunch. It was a small beat-up black upright that I had rented for a month for twenty dollars. "We'll get him some lessons and see if he takes to it," I told Martin.

"You got him a piano?"

"I rented him a piano. From the Yellow Pages. Nothing fancy. Besides, this place needs a piano. Whoever heard of an old folks' home without a piano?"

"Oh boy, I hope he's got his inhalator handy when he sees it."

I smiled as I turned off my reading light.

Three months later Howard held his first recital, a stripped-down version of "Lara's Theme" from *Doctor Zhivago*. He wore a light blue seersucker suit and a red bow tie and an extra splash of cheap aftershave. I served brandy from the private collection I keep in the back of my closet and wore a blue blazer with a white handkerchief tucked into the breast pocket, which isn't like me, which was the point. Helen wore a bright green dress that strained at her waistline and her normally garish smile was exaggerated by lipstick that traveled a good way toward her ears. "Oh, I'm just percolating!" she announced as she plopped down in a chair next to me.

The-Woman-Whose-Name-I-Can-Never-Remember looked like Glinda the Good Witch wrapped in various pink gauzy things with her blue hair shaped like topiary while Mitzie wore a long purple evening dress with a great big purple scarf swirled pythonlike around her shoulders. "You know what this is, don't you?" she asked me conspiratorially. Her front teeth were covered with lipstick and her breath smelled of Kaopectate. "It's a soirée!"

Howard's hands trembled at first as they hovered over the keys, as though waiting for some signal from on high. We sat silently and then nervously, eager for him to drown out the rasp of Oscar's labored breathing.

Then Howard leaned forward, closed his eyes tight and began, breathing deeply and swaying back and forth as he gathered speed. He played seven encores that evening as we sat in a circle around him sipping our brandy from Dixie cups and humming and clapping. I wondered if anyone else saw the young boy perched on the piano stool and radiant with pride but I couldn't be sure. Anyway, I think he was about nine.

♦　　♦　　♦

SOME DAYS music is the only thing that makes sense to me, the only experience that confirms what I've never been able to articulate even to my closest friends. I wonder if music is the only expression of the soul that is not hopelessly compromised in communication. I think so. In fact, I'm quite certain of it.

Damn. I should have been a musician. Better yet, a great musician married to another great musician, and in the mornings we would leave scores on each other's pillows.

That would be love, or more precisely, the pure expression of love.

I remember sitting at the symphony in Boston in 1947 and feeling as though I were partaking in a mass seance with the crowd, the music filling in the tremendous gaps between us until it was possible to travel from one to another as though walking on water. Alone in public each of us shared the most intimate and ineffable feelings, feelings that we also shared with Handel and Mozart and Beethoven. It felt, momentarily, as if we were all holding hands somewhere deep inside, bound at our strongest point. When the music stopped, all hands let go. I walked quickly out of the concert hall, desperate to avoid conversation.

◆　◆　◆

MAYBE WHAT life needs is a good soundtrack, especially during the long stretches when nothing interesting is being said. A soundtrack might dignify things a bit, ennobling us with the proper drama and tension and pathos.

I stroll the hallways, shoulders back, chin up, humming softly. "'People stop and stare, they don't bother me, for there's nowhere else on earth that I would rather be...'"

Andrew Lloyd Webber and Rodgers and Hammerstein and Leonard Bernstein and Stephen Sondheim and Alan Jay Lerner and Frederick Loewe and Jerry Herman and Maurice Jarre to the orchestra pit now please, Patrick is on the march. Something inspirational, electrifying even, if you would. Thank you kindly.

If life were cast to music, I fear we might all drown in our tears.

◆　◆　◆

I'VE VOLUNTEERED for patrol tonight. With Daniel and Tometti. We head out in fifteen minutes to repair our wire, cut some German wire and with luck bring back any Germans we find doing the same thing. Orders lately stress the need for prisoners to interrogate. We all assume that means an offensive is imminent, though whose we are not sure.

We blacken our faces with burnt cork, which seems to make the whites of our eyes unremittingly obvious; luminescent, even. Then we work our way along the duckboards down to the end of a sap. Page is on sentry duty and nods at us as we pass. Tometti crawls out first, carrying the wire cutters. I follow right behind, my face trailing the worn soles of his boots. Daniel is right behind me, pulling a coil of wire. We slide down the front side of the parapet and through the opening in our entanglement, a secret passage that zigzags through twenty feet of wire. At the other end Daniel motions for me to grab one end of the wire he is carrying, which we stretch in front of a gap in the entanglement caused by a shell.

The noise of the wire scratching the dirt seems overwhelming, and I feel my ears ringing so much they hurt, as though I were holding my nose and blowing as hard as I could. SHHH...THUNK! A German star shell hurtles skyward. We slither into a shell hole twenty feet ahead just before the shell ignites and hovers like a hawk circling in search of prey. Then silence; miles and miles of enormous silence blanketing hundreds of thousands of men dug into the earth. We are perfectly still, frozen like mice trying to creep between two very large cats when one suddenly stirs. I smell decaying flesh to my left but do not turn my head. Instead, I slowly bring my left hand closer to my body.

Daniel signals with his hands: wait five minutes, then we move toward the German wire. I look at Tometti's boyish face, which is pulled tight. I see glimpses of panic in his eyes and turn away quickly before it overwhelms me. I feel my own lower jaw quaking and wonder if my teeth are chattering. I press my chin against my rifle and concentrate on my breathing, which feels difficult, as though I have fallen down into a great big black maw and the earth is closing up on me. Yes, that's it, I'm sandwiched between the two angry halves of the world like a coal miner on his back in a two-foot seam miles underground when the earth gives way.

Daniel taps me on the shoulder. My head rises slowly out of the shell hole as I crawl forward, my helmet tipped low over my eyes. Swivel left, swivel right, like a baby wiggling across the floor.

A sniper's bullet is the best way. A popping, thwopping sound that explodes the cranium like a watermelon hurled at the pavement. Better than being blown apart, torn limb from limb by shell fire, splattering your friends. And better by far than a bayonet. All that cutting and slicing of the intestines and trying desperately to stop it with bare hands and the look on the face of the German when he knows he's got you.

I crawl around a stinking pile of dirty khaki,

bracing, bracing, bracing. My jaw aches and perspiration stings my eyes. Will I feel it? Not a head wound. Some men don't know they've been shot, right? I don't feel anything. Did I hear a shot? No, but the silence is so *loud*. We are closer and closer. Ten feet to the wire. Down the German line I hear a cough. We are at the wire. Tometti moves gently, gently, cutting the wire as he goes.

Daniel and I point our rifles into the darkness. Can I see? I feel blind, not sure whether my eyes are open or closed. I rub them. Another cough. It sounds closer.

You should see this, Father. Damn! Your son, Patrick, right up against the German lines! Goddamn, Father, would you believe it? Your son! Look at me, Father, look at me dangling both feet over the edge of the universe, jumping the moon, soaring up and up farther than anyone has ever gone.

I've gone too far, haven't I, Father? How do I get back I want to get back. I remember being a boy and climbing to the top of a neighbor's tree and I couldn't get down, I couldn't find any footing below me and my hands were getting tired and I screamed and screamed and I remember Father running and I could just barely look down over my shoulder and see him looking so small staring up at me and telling me to hang on. I remember how he climbed the tree and I felt his hand on my shoe guiding it to a branch and then on my other shoe guiding it down until he grabbed me and I buried my face into his shirt and the damp smell of his chest and the sudden feeling of safety made me cry even harder.

Father?

Snip. Snip. Cough.

Daniel jerks his thumb back toward our line. Tometti hands me the wire cutters and I slide them into his pack. Then we turn on our stomachs and head back, and I wonder if anyone is behind us but decide not to look.

SHHHH...THUNK! We roll down into a shell hole, which has a foot of cold, pasty water at the bottom.

SHHH...THUNK! We press against the dirt, hiding from the glowing eagles that hover overhead, searching. Pop pop. Pop pop. Sniper fire down the line. And farther, the whine of a shell. Whhizzzzz BANG!

We wait. Daniel's face, made ghostly white under the flare, is expressionless. I don't even see him in his face and wonder if he stayed back in the trenches, perhaps to write poetry. Tometti's face trembles the way my grandfather's did in the months before he died. His pupils are shoved toward the top of his sockets as they scan the sky and he has one hand pressed down hard on the top of his helmet.

If I die and all my friends die, then who will carry the story of my death back across the ocean? I'd much rather that someone who knew me lived. Somehow my extinction wouldn't seem quite so complete.

Pop! Pop!

Sometimes the expectation of violent death

is so painful that you want to lunge toward it and be done with it, like the child crouched behind the couch in a game of hide-and-seek when the seekers are drawing closer and closer until the tension is unbearable and the breathless child jumps up and surrenders, gasping with relief.

Tometti starts over the lip of the shell hole. Daniel and I crawl behind him. Now the gravity of fear shifts. What if our own troops misidentify us? A frequent tragedy. Who is on sentry duty besides Page? I strain my eyes toward our line.

SHHH...THUNK! How many seconds until the flare ignites? One, two, three... We rise to our knees and crawl as fast as we can and then to our feet falling stumbling clawing forward toward our trench when everything goes white then POP POP POP POP as we run though the opening in our wire and tumble into a rifle pit gasping.

Daniel yanks my shoulder and I turn and stare at the hole in Tometti's throat which is foaming and bubbling. Daniel runs off to find a medic and I hold Tometti who is staring at me expectantly only I don't know what to do for a throat wound. I unbutton his shirt and hold him and rock him and he keeps staring at me demanding with his eyes and shit Tometti breathe breathe breathe what do I do for a throat wound shall I press my hand against it so you can stop leaking air or are you breathing from your throat now? Which is it Tometti nod or something Christ BREATHE

TOMETTI BREATHE TOMETTI
BREATHE MEDIC GODDAMN IT MEDIC
OH SHIT TOMETTI I'VE GOT YOU I'VE
GOT YOU I'VE GOT YOU.

♦ ♦ ♦

WE BURIED Tometti with Teresa's photograph
placed on his chest. It was Daniel's idea. It was
there in his breast pocket, where he always kept
it. Only no one wanted to look at her now.

On the back she had written: "So you'll
never forget me."

♦ ♦ ♦

I have changed terribly. I did not want to
tell you anything of the horrible lassitude
which the war has engendered in me, but
you force me to it. I feel myself
crushed.... I am a flattened man.
—*Marc Boassan, French Army,*
in a letter to his wife.
Killed in action, 1918.

♦ ♦ ♦

EVERYONE TALKS about the midlife crisis but not
the one after that, the latelife crisis when it's
too late even to get divorced and buy a motorcycle, though I must confess that I have lingered over the leather jackets at Henry Shay's
Store for Men, which might at least restore the
shoulders I once had.

Why didn't I ever buy a motorcycle? I could have afforded one. And after the kids were grown, who cared if Dad was smeared across Route 66 like a wayward possum? But by then I felt too old to buy a motorcycle, which in retrospect seems rather stupid.

This morning during rehab I asked Hanford if he knew anything about motorcycles. "My kid brother has one," he said. "One of those real loud ones, you know that high, whiny scream that announces testosterone from three blocks off. What do you want to know about motorcycles for? You going to buy your son a motorcycle? I'm telling you, don't buy him no damn motorcycle. Donorcycles is what I call them."

"I wasn't thinking of my son," I said.

"Oh," he said, stretching my left arm back over my head.

"I was thinking about me."

"You?" He laughed. "What are you going to do with a motorcycle?"

"Well, I was thinking of riding it, for starters. You know, travel Highway 1 from Canada to Mexico with a leggy lass on the back, arms wrapped around me. Think of it as unfinished business, Hanford."

"I knew you were kidding me," he said.

"No, I'm not kidding. I'm thinking about buying a motorcycle."

"No shit?"

"No shit."

"They won't allow you to have a motorcycle."

"I won't keep it here. I'll keep it in town."

"I see," he said. "What kind of motorcycle?"

"Well, like I said, I don't know much about motorcycles, but I think a five hundred CC should do it. Used, probably. Maybe I'll bequeath it to you."

"No thanks," he said. "My wife would kill me even before the bike did. What do you want with a motorcycle?"

"Same thing your kid brother wants," I said. "I had this friend, must of been about thirty years ago, who told me that riding his motorcycle was better than sex. I've never forgotten that."

Hanford was silent as he finished stretching my right arm. Then as I sat up he said, "I'm not sure you've got the strength to handle a motorcycle."

"Only one way to find out," I said.

"Maybe my brother could give you a ride," he said.

"No, I'm not that crazy," I said, waving goodbye as I headed out the door.

◆　　◆　　◆

ON THURSDAY morning I rode the bus into town and walked five blocks to Ray's Motorcycles. The glass door chimed as I opened it and a young man in jeans and a black T-shirt emerged from a back room. I nodded at him and walked over to the motorcycles lined against the wall, their front ends all pivoted to the left in perfect formation.

"Can I help you?" he asked, looking distracted. Did he think I had meant to enter the pharmacy across the street? Maybe I should act like I think this is a pharmacy and see what he's got for piles. Or perhaps I should just slam my wallet down and ask for the biggest, fastest damn hog he's got. With chaps.

"Oh, just thinking about buying a bike for my grandson. Thought I'd take a look," I said. I noticed a bikini-clad blonde staring down from a calendar tacked up behind the cash register. She was Miss June, which, given that it was August, suggested that she was better looking than July or August. I wanted to ask to see August, just to compare, but decided against it. Do pretty women really sell motorcycles? ("Yes, I'll have whatever she's sitting on. Same color, same style, everything.")

"How old is he?" asked the salesman.

"Ah, about twenty-five."

"An experienced rider?"

"No, not really."

"Is the bike for commuting or just recreation?"

"Mostly recreation."

"On or off road?"

"On road."

"A lot of highway riding or just local stuff?"

"Local stuff mainly."

"How much you looking to spend?"

"Couple thousand, I guess. Haven't really made up my mind yet."

"Well, they go from real light to real heavy," he said, motioning toward the bikes.

"What's a good light one?" I asked. "Just for short trips. Kind of a knock-around bike."

"A knock-around bike? Try this one here." He slapped the black leather seat of a bright red Kawasaki.

I put a hand on one handlebar and turned the front wheel. "May I sit on it?" I asked.

He studied me briefly, then pushed the bike forward and into the center of the room. He held on to one side as I worked my right leg over the back and then sat on the seat, which was firmer than I had imagined. Then I grabbed both handlebars and swung them left then right. He stepped back and smiled. "You look all right, man," he said, nodding his head up and down. I tilted the bike a few inches to the left, then a few inches to the right, getting a feel for the weight. Balanced properly, the machine was almost weightless. I imagined igniting the throaty rumble between my legs. Then, as I leaned the bike to the left again, it went a few inches too far, and suddenly its weight surged against my left arm and leg. As I pulled the handle with my left hand the front wheel swiveled left and I felt myself and the bike falling when the salesman lunged forward and caught me.

"Careful there! You all right?"

"Yeah. It's heavier than I thought."

"You ought to try some of those monsters," he said, pointing to the much larger motorcycles at the other end of the row. "If they fall over, it takes two men to pick them up."

"And four of me," I said. "Thanks for your

help. I'd like to think about it." My left wrist was beginning to throb.

"No problem, we're open Sundays too."

The door chimed again as I opened it and in the reflection of the glass I caught just a glimpse of Miss June before heading across the street to the pharmacy.

◆　　◆　　◆

THE FOLLOWING Saturday I took the bus back to town and paid twenty-one dollars to a man who rented me a little red moped for three hours on the assurance that I would not go too far too fast. I mounted it gingerly and then sat there in front of the shop, trying to look preoccupied with my watch and my pockets as I waited for the owner to go back inside before I attempted to ride. But he had no intention of missing my departure so he preoccupied himself by sweeping the sidewalk over and over again. After examining the controls and testing the weight and the brakes, I finally gave it a little gas and raised my feet, uncertain if I could maintain my balance. Once on the street I made a wide turn and then, after some searching, my feet found the foot rests. More gas. I was flying.

I crossed Fourth Street and headed west out of town, then followed a series of rural roads that looped back around behind Great Oaks, where I made a full-speed flyby just as Janet was walking to her car. (She did a double take but never said anything. I think the idea that I might be scootering past my own nursing home was just too much of a stretch.) Then I drove past Sarah's house (I had long ago plotted her address on a map), pausing to imagine that it was my home too and wondering which room was her bedroom and what it looked like. I was one hour late and offered to pay the difference but the owner waved me off.

"How did it go?" he asked, looking amused and not a little relieved.

"She purred like a cat," I said, struggling to dismount. "Thank you. I know you didn't have to do that."

"My pleasure. Glad you had fun."

I walked the five blocks back to the bus stop, then returned to Great Oaks. That evening, I was in bed by seven P.M., unable to shake a sense of sadness in my throat.

◆   ◆   ◆

"WORD IS we're going to hit the Hindenburg line," said Page, walking somewhere in front of me. I looked over at Lawton, who'd been unusually quiet lately. He didn't look back.

"What exactly is the Hindenburg line?" asked Giles.

"Their main defensive line," said Page.

"Oh shit."

"How far do you suppose we'll go?" I asked.

"To Berlin," said Page.

"Berlin? Shit. That's far, isn't it?" asked Giles.

"Not so far as we can't get there," said Page.

290

"I'd just like to get my hands on some of that beer," said Giles.

"And a fraulein or two," I said.

"War'll end before we get to Berlin," said Daniel.

"You really think so?" I asked.

"No way. Not the Germans. We're going to Berlin," said Page.

"How long do you think the war will last?" I asked Daniel.

"Maybe another year," he said.

"Maybe forever," said Giles. "Like one of those hundred-year wars."

"Jesus, you think so?" asked Lawton. Giles nodded grimly.

"Wouldn't you hate to be the last guy to get shot before the war ends?" I said.

"Soon as we get to Berlin, it's no patrols or raids for me," said Giles.

"Just how exactly do wars like these end?" I asked. "Is there like a bell or something?"

"Both sides announce that it's over," said Daniel, sidestepping a large pothole in the road.

"Like at a certain time?" I asked. "Like, keep shooting each other until right after lunch and then call it quits?"

"Something like that," said Daniel.

"How the hell are we going to know that they know that the war is over?" asked Giles. "I mean, what if we think it ends at three p.m. and they've been told four p.m., or they're on Berlin time or whatever?"

"I'm not putting my goddamn head up," I said.

"Well, they'll have to surrender. We'll just wait for them to surrender," said Daniel.

"I just don't see those bastards surrendering," said Giles.

"That's because we haven't beaten them yet," I said.

"So we've got to take the Hindenburg line," said Page.

"Yeah, maybe that'll do it," said Lawton.

"What exactly does the Hindenburg line look like?" I asked.

"Big fucking trench," said Lawton. "Tons of wire, machine-gun nests pointing every which way."

"No fucking worry," said Giles, clearing his throat to spit again.

◆　◆　◆

I mustn't show them that I'm afraid—
because one of the things that spreads
quickest of all is fear. If people in
trenches start to shout and scream with
fear it spreads like a flame so the best
thing is to quieten the bloke, either brain
him or, if need be, finish him.
　　　　　—*C. Miles, British Army.*

◆　◆　◆

AFTER MARCHING most of the night we sat near a burned-out farmhouse and had a breakfast of rice with Karo syrup, then marched another two miles to a rocky clearing, where we were ordered to dig rifle pits. Daniel and I made a two-man pit, then sat down and lit cigarettes. As he smoked, Daniel ran his fingernails along the seams of his clothes, squishing lice. I pulled out an old letter from my father, reread it and placed it back in my pocket. His tone was unusually sentimental, which made me worry that he was ill. Or maybe he was afraid that there were things he wouldn't get to say if his son never came home. Would I come home? I searched again for some gut feeling, the kind of intuitive certainty that so many other soldiers seemed to have about their lives, but felt none.

"So it's true, that you've never been in love?" Daniel was staring at me.

"In love? Not really. Why do you ask?"

"It changes everything. Even the way things look and sound."

I nodded.

"But it's different than I had imagined," he said.

"Better?"

"Yes. But more frightening."

"Why is that?"

"Because you can't imagine what you'd do without that person."

"You don't have to worry about that."

"But you think about it. The amazing thing is that it was just chance that we met. That's what it gets down to in life. A bit of luck."

"Well, at least you've got it."

"So far." He pressed his thumb into the seam of his pants.

Watching him made me itch. I scratched myself and then swung my hand at the flies that hovered over my head, bouncing blindly off my hair, which was matted with sweat and dirt. "Wish they'd spray some creosol."

Daniel blew smoke at my head.

"Thanks," I said.

"The strangest thing is that I couldn't tell you why I'm in love."

"But Julia sounds wonderful."

"She is. I just couldn't tell you what exactly it is that I love. I can name the parts, but not the whole. I can't tell you why I love her and not other women who are attractive and smart and funny and kind."

"But so long as you feel it."

"Still, I'd like to know, to have some understanding of it. If we can't really grasp why we are in love, then what's to keep us from falling out of love just as mysteriously?"

"That doesn't sound likely."

"No, I don't think so. But I wish it didn't feel so inexplicable, like a spell or something." He pulled out a letter from Julia and began reading it. "She's volunteered making bandages. Says if she wasn't pregnant she'd join the Red Cross and try to get shipped to France."

"Then you're lucky she's pregnant. Christ, I hated the crossing, sitting below deck at night with all the portholes covered up and just those little blue lights to see by, waiting for torpedoes to start slamming into the hull."

"She'd be a wonderful nurse."

"She can nurse you when you get home."

He grinned. "You'll come visit us?"

"Of course."

He closed his eyes for a minute. Then he said, "You know something, I'm not afraid anymore."

"You never seemed very scared to me." His remark made me uncomfortable.

"Oh, but I was."

"So what are you saying?"

"I'm saying that since it makes no difference whether I'm afraid or not, I've decided not to be afraid."

"You've decided that?"

"Yes, I've decided that."

Galston approached us. "MacGuire, Delaney, grab your shovels and go with Giles."

Giles waved us over. "Back behind those trees there," he pointed. We followed him.

"Trenches?" I asked.

"Graves," said Giles.

"Oh," I said. Daniel was silent.

There were three neat rows of bodies in a small clearing, each covered with a sprinkling of chloride of lime. Two other soldiers sat resting near a row of shallow pits.

"Another three feet deeper," said the tall one.

"Gotcha," said Giles.

I looked over at the corpses, at the boots just like mine with the heels together and the toes splayed out sideways and the puttees just like mine and the torn and bloodied pants and shirts just like mine only they were dusted with lime and far too small now for their bloated occupants.

"Which battalion?" asked Daniel.

"I don't know," said the smaller soldier, wiping sweat from his forehead with his forearm. "They passed through yesterday, going north. Shell got these boys."

"Are we supposed to bury them?" I asked.

"No, you just dig the holes."

I stripped off my gear and began digging.

◆　　◆　　◆

I COULDN'T find Julia the next morning. I sat at one of the tables in front of the hotel for over an hour sipping coffee and waiting, but she didn't appear. I walked around town for a while, stopping at a bakery to buy a baguette, which I ate on the spot. Then I returned to the hotel and sat in the lobby reading a book for two hours and listening to the tick tock of a large grandfather clock in the corner. When it chimed noon, I approached the concierge and asked if he had seen her.

"Your American friend? Why yes, she was up very early this morning. Left around six A.M., I believe."

"But she didn't check out?"

"No no, she didn't check out."

"Did she say where she was going?"

"It wasn't my business."

"No, of course not."

"You are concerned?" He scrutinized me with raised eyebrows.

"No, everything is fine, thank you."

That afternoon I called the hotel in Paris

and left a message for Charlotte saying that I would be back the next day around dinnertime. Then I went shopping for a present for Sean, finally settling on a small wooden sailboat painted red and blue with thick canvas sails and a working rudder. After I organized my things on my bed, I sat down in front of the hotel again and had another cup of coffee, followed by a glass of white wine. Was she lost? I couldn't imagine her finding the hotel on her own—or even the town for that matter.

Just after six P.M. she appeared, walking quickly down the street toward the hotel and carrying her shoulder bag, which looked heavy. When she saw me she waved and smiled, and then asked if she could buy me dinner after she had a chance to clean up. I never asked her where she had been. I could tell she didn't want me to.

◆ ◆ ◆

"MARTIN, what day is it today?"

"Tuesday. No, Wednesday. Heck, I'm not sure." He went out into the hall, struggling to tie the belt of his bathrobe as he walked, then returned. "It's Monday," he said.

Ah, Monday. Miserable Monday. I lay back against my pillow, sighing deeply.

I've always hated Mondays, the whole lot of them. Too much whiplash, snapping the tired masses to attention. God's way, perhaps, of reminding us that we are not masters of our fate, no matter how deluded we became during the weekend respite.

Twelve years after retiring I still awaken Monday mornings with a sense of dread, that "Here we go again" feeling low in the gut as the roller coaster click click clicks to the very top and then AAHHHHHH!

It starts Sunday afternoon between four and five, depending on the season, when the weekend and all its once-protean possibilities suddenly sputter out and I find myself feeling remarkably ill-equipped to deal with the coming cataclysms; as though, in just two days, I had lost all my muscle tone, my wits, my courage and my defenses for the rough-and-tumble of the big nasty world where I must soon present my miserable little self for duty. On Sunday afternoons I realize that I have gone completely and utterly soft.

Screw Mondays.

◆　　◆　　◆

THE BOOKMOBILE came by today. I think of it as the elderly person's Good Humor truck, only I can't get out the door quite so fast. I borrowed four books: a biography of Tolstoy, Hemingway's *The Sun Also Rises*, and two weighty-looking tracts on Eastern philosophy, which I've decided to reconsider. (When Western philosophy fails me, as it inevitably does, I flee to Eastern philosophy, then back again in frustration. Why spend hours sitting in an uncomfortable position struggling to achieve nothingness when death should do the job rather more efficiently?)

I miss my books. I gave most of them away when I sold the house. I had 2,142 of them, not counting the books at my store, which I considered mine as well, my darling pets up for adoption. The kids took what they wanted and the rest I gave to a local library. I've felt naked ever since, like a soldier stripped of his weapons.

Like most bookworms I read so as not to be alone, which often annoys those who are trying to make conversation with me. Lately I've taken to rereading the classics of my youth—a rare chance to relive the past—though I must confess that some of the books aren't what I remember at all.

Books aren't just my defenses, the sandbags I use to fortify my position; they are also the building blocks of my soul, and I am the sum of all I read. The truth is, reading about life has always proved much more satisfactory than living it, and certainly reading about people is far more interesting than actually sitting across from them at, say, a dinner party. On the page people come alive: they have sex, they travel, they reveal their deepest thoughts, they struggle against overwhelming odds, they search for meaning. In person, well, few dinner partners do any of these things.

Reading has gotten a lot harder, which depresses me more than most things. My eyes strain too quickly, and what information does make it to my brain is often misfiled or simply discarded. I dread the fate of Mitzie, who reads the same three books over and over year after year (*The Yearling, Main Street,* and *The House of Mirth*). "I like them and I know they'll be good," she says. "I say stick with a sure thing." It helps, of course, if the old slate wipes itself clean every few months.

If I had two lives, I would devote the first one to reading (and maybe the second as well). I understand that up until the early 1800s a learned person could read almost every book of consequence ever published, a prospect that titillates me to no end.

I buy new books once a month, taking the 42 bus to Cooper's on Fourth Street. The selection is appalling: a few literary titles squeezed among row upon row of business tracts and weight-loss manuals and brightly colored self-improvement guides with retouched photos of pharmacologically enhanced men and women on the cover. (Doesn't anyone realize that the best self-help books are in the literature section?) But Cooper's is the only bookstore left since Hartley's, a family-run business, closed down two years ago. Last month I went to Cooper's looking for Pershing's memoirs, which I had a sudden urge to reread. In the aisle marked "military history" I found three rows of books on Vietnam, four rows on World War II and one book on World War I: *The Guns of August,* by Barbara Tuchman. On the bus ride back I couldn't stop wondering if all those men would have died quite so willingly had they seen that bookshelf or whether they were just so many trees falling silently in the forest.

◆ ◆ ◆

Have you forgotten yet?
Look down, and swear by the slain of the
War that you'll never forget.
                    —*Siegfried Sassoon,*
                    "Aftermath, March 1919."

◆ ◆ ◆

DANIEL SITS on an ammunition box in the dugout writing by candlelight as we wait out our bombardment of the German lines. Our attack begins at five a.m. I feel filthy and tired as I sit and clean my rifle. Three weeks in the Argonne and I haven't removed my clothes. Not once.

A loud explosion rattles the dugout. Bits of dirt fall on my helmet and clothes.

"That ought to cut a pretty path through their wire," says Page, tightening his puttees.

"Bullshit. They've always got wire left. Since when don't they have any fucking wire left?" says Giles, fingering a tooth that has been bothering him all week. "How are you supposed to get your hands on the bastards when they're always hiding behind all that fucking wire?"

I look over at Daniel. It strikes me that he always seems much older than me, though we're the same age. I watch as he rereads what he has written, his forehead creasing before a slight smile comes to his face. Does Julia have a photo of him? She must. Does she look at it every day, trying to remember the gleam of his eyes and the tone of his voice—deep but full of compassion, like a good minister's—and his broad shoulders and the strength of his large hands? Does she show it off to friends or keep it on her bed stand and how does it make her feel to look at? Is it even worth having a lover who is halfway around the world at war? At least the men know their lovers are safe—maybe not always faithful but safe— but the women? How do they even sleep?

When Daniel finishes reading he tucks the letter into his shirt pocket, then adjusts his helmet and reaches for his rifle. Soon we are side by side in the line waiting to go over the top, our helmets tipped down to our eyebrows. Lawton is on my left and beside him is Page.

"You scared?" asks Page, offering me a cigarette.

"Yeah, I'm scared."

"Me too," he says.

"Just up and over," I say, trying to calm myself.

"Yeah, just up and over."

He finishes his cigarette and then quickly lights another.

"What time is it? I gotta go take a shit," he says.

"You got about two minutes."

"Oh Christ, forget it."

I look down at my hands, which are shaking uncontrollably. My breathing is fast and shallow and I feel sick to my stomach.

I look over at Daniel. He turns his head toward me, then tries to calm me with his eyes, the way a parent does with a child about to perform a recital. Then he reaches out and pats me on the back.

"You'll be all right," he says. "Just stick near me."

I nod, then check my gear again. Daniel uses his sleeve to wipe the sweat from his eyes.

"You know something, Patrick?" he whispers, leaning close to me.

"What?"

He hesitates, staring at me.

"What is it? Tell me."

"I finally..."

The whistle shrieks and we scramble up over the top and begin running, thousands of us streaming across the sunken field through thick black smoke toward the German line, which erupts in fire. Men to my left and right start dropping and twice I stumble. I catch a glimpse of Daniel up ahead of me, then lose him. A concussion knocks me down. I scramble back to my feet. The air is filled with things. Something is in my eye. Ahead of me a figure crumples. Then another. I jump over them, struggling to stay on my feet.

Now I'm at the German wire. Which way to go? Panic overwhelms me. To the left? I can't see through the smoke. I crouch among men struggling to find a way through. A hand grenade explodes nearby, then another. I reach for my wire cutters and soon my hands are raw and bleeding as I cut at the entanglements. A machine gun to my left sweeps back and forth. Am I hit yet? *Any second.* I feel so numb.

"There is no break in the fucking wire!"

"Move! Move! Move!"

The wire cutters slip from my hands.

"We can't get through!"

"The fucking artillery missed the wire!"

"Try to the left."

"Bring up a bangalore goddamn it!"

"Ah, Jesus!"

"Son of a bitch."

"Stop that machine gun!"

"Help me."

"Quick, hand grenades."

Another explosion, so close.

"Oh God I'm hit."

"Ow shit goddamn!"

"Medic! Medic! Medic!"

"My leg my leg my leg!"

"You bastards!"

"I can't see I can't see!"

"Get down goddamn it!"

"Don't leave me here. Please don't leave me."

Dear God.

I run to the right and then drop and crawl and I see men hung up on the wire like clothes on a line and the clothes are tearing and screaming and clods of dirt are jumping from the ground. I lie on my stomach and look through twenty yards of coiled wire and I can see German soldiers peering over their trenches and firing at me and I fire back and crawl but the wire keeps tearing at me.

Any second.

Am I dead, Mother? Father? But I can't be because the screaming won't stop. Then everything goes slow and I see Giles pulling himself forward in the dirt. *John, this way, over here.* But he doesn't have a jaw where is your jaw John your jaw?

Blood is soaking through my shirt. Must keep moving.

Daniel? No, who is that? I crawl closer. Figures hurry past. Someone steps on me.

Lawton? Is that you, Lawton? Lawton is on his knees vomiting and trying to stuff his intestines back into his shirt but they won't fit and they're filthy. *I'll help you Jack; get you a medic. They'll know what to do.* A shot hits him in the face. Then another.

Any second.

Another explosion. Something wet hits me in the face. In front of me I see a severed hand, palm facing upward. Mine? No, one of the fingers bears a wedding band.

And who is crying? I hear someone crying. There are dozens of screams maybe hundreds of them but one of them is so close, sobbing like a lost child. Who is sobbing? I hear you sobbing who are you? I think I see him, a shadow caught in the wire to my left but I cannot see his face. Just a shadow suspended in wire and sobbing.

I'm coming for you I'm coming for you

hold on. I tear at the wire and scream and shake myself in fury.

"Turn back turn back!"

Someone is pulling on me.

"Go go go!"

Not yet not yet. *Don't leave them.* A hand pulls hard on my shirt. "Get out of here!"

I'm running now but something catches my boot and I fall. Oh shit my shoulder is burning I'm on my knees now Mother and Father crawling on all fours but I'm going to faint.

A shell hole? Yes. I fall into it, rolling down into blackness.

Daniel?

◆　　◆　　◆

Losses in retreating over a fire-swept zone are greater than during the advance. If the main attack is effectually stopped, either by obstacles or the enemy's fire, or both, the troops remain where they are, under such cover as the ground affords or they can improvise, until night, the withdrawal being then effected under cover of darkness.

—*United States Army Field Service Regulations, War Department, 1913.*

◆　　◆　　◆

SEAN CALLED me today. I could tell from his voice that he was thinking about losing me and how it was going to feel never to say "Dad?" again. So he called me. Old people can sense that, when friends and relatives are calling just to hear a voice that will soon be extinguished or visiting to take one last look because they've got a premonition. Then they hang on to each gurgled word as though it may be the last, as though Gramps might finally excrete some cosmic wisdom or at least the location of a Swiss bank account. The pressure can be enormous, though it hasn't made me any more eloquent. What will my last words be? "Where's the Metamucil?" "What day is it?" "Who the hell are you?"

I guess I haven't really given much thought to last words. Perhaps I should. "Death, where is thy sting?" is sort of catchy, though not so convincing when rasped from clenched teeth. What about "Oh shit," or "Fuck" or "Damn!"? Too knee jerk, I suppose, though certainly to the point. "Help!" seems rather appropriate, though such a cry would inevitably rattle those standing helplessly by. Maybe I'll just try to wink and let them read into it what they like or mouth some gibberish that will keep me topical for years as family members puzzle over what I was trying to say. (If I didn't love my children I might expire with the words, "The treasure is buried beneath the..." so that I could go to my grave cheered by the thought of them digging holes for the rest of their lives.)

Sean's voice makes me sad too, not so much because of what's happening to me but because of what will happen to him when I'm no longer there. Growing old will be the one phase of his life where he won't be able to call me and say, "Christ, Dad, you won't believe what happened to me today! You've been through this shit before, how the hell did you manage it?"

"So how's it going, Dad?" His voice was softer than usual and I wondered if something had happened.

"Fine, just fine. What's up with you?"

"Same old shit. You know, I was just thinking..."

"Yes?"

"Well, remember when I was a kid, maybe six or seven, and I used to say how much I wished that we were kids at the same time?"

I remembered, and looked down at the little face with a sprinkling of freckles across the ridge of his nose; the face that was always looking up at me when I visited and saying, "Watch me Dad watch me look!"

"I wish you were in your fifties now," he said.

"How the hell do you think I feel?"

"What I mean is, I was just thinking how nice it would be if we could both go away for a few days, go fishing in Alaska or something. Drink some beers, talk. We never did go fishing."

"I hate fishing." He laughed.

"You know, Dad, the older I get the more I feel like I understand you, or least some of the things you must of been going through."

"You poor bastard."

"It must of been awful when you and Mom

divorced, watching me and Kelly crying and begging you not to leave after each visit."

"It's still awful," I said.

"Did you guys ever think of sticking it out for our sake? I'm not saying you should have, I'm just wondering if you thought about it."

"That's all any parent thinks until they feel as though they are going to burst inside. You ask yourself, 'I'd happily lay down my life for my children, so why can't I just keep the family together for their sake, for a few more years?' But one morning you wake up and you realize that there is not enough air to keep the family alive, that if you don't leave you'll all suffocate. But that doesn't make you feel any less guilty. It just pushes you out the door."

We were both silent and I was thinking of something to say when he said, "I think a lot about your experiences in the war and I wanted you to know that you've always been kind of a hero for me, even when I was so angry at you for divorcing Mom."

"A survivor. I'm definitely a survivor, though my skills are being a little taxed these days."

"How's your health?"

"It's okay."

"You sure?"

"Sure."

Pause.

"I wish you had visited more when I was young."

"So do I. I think I missed more than you did."

"When I was a kid I couldn't believe you and Mom were no longer together, and now I can't believe you were ever husband and wife."

"Neither can I," I said, adding quickly, "though I loved her."

"Dad, Sally and I are in marriage counseling."

"I see."

"Things have been pretty rough. Now that the kids are away and it's just the two of us, well, it seems too quiet."

"It's worth the work, Sean."

"Yeah, I know."

"You okay? You want to talk about it?"

"I'm okay. I'm late for the office but I just wanted to call you. I'm sorry I don't call more."

"Don't worry about it."

"All right then, I'll talk to you soon."

"Good-bye."

After I hung up I went back to my room and sat at the desk that Martin and I share. After a few minutes I pulled out my stationery and began a series of letters to Sean and Kelly to be opened when they turned sixty and seventy and eighty. It took a month to finish them but when I was done I decided to write one more letter to each of them, to be opened when they were eighty-one and a half years old, if they made it that far. I wanted to see what it felt like to address my children not as a spokesman of the impenetrable past but as though we were a couple of old farts sitting right next to each other, say on a bench overlooking the ocean or by a fire, and we were just sitting and gabbing and catching up after all these years, all of us the exact same age.

I'm just sorry I won't be there to see their faces when they open the letters.

◆   ◆   ◆

"DANIEL?"

I pull myself to the top of the hole but the machine guns are still firing so I sink down and load my gun and stare at the torso at the bottom of the pit.

God the screaming is awful.

And my shoulder hurts.

Am I the last one alive? No, I hear voices behind me. How far am I from our line? I'll wait until dark, then crawl back. But if the Germans counterattack? I'll play dead. Can I do that? I don't know that I can. Should I be on my stomach to protect myself? But if they are going to bayonet me I won't see it coming.

I hear Daniel.

Yes, I am sure it is Daniel. Dirt rains down on me. Someone's throwing hand grenades. My shoulder's bleeding.

"Daniel!"

I know it's you Christ where are you? I crawl back to the top of the hole and listen and peer out between clumps of dirt and I see hundreds of figures through the stinging smoke running and squirming on the ground and quivering in the entanglements.

"Daniel?"

Oh shit Daniel what are you doing out there come back.

"Daniel?"

Dear God is that you in the wire? No please it can't be. Is that you Daniel? Is that you in the wire?

◆　　◆　　◆

I REMEMBER Daniel twisting in the wire.

◆　　◆　　◆

TODAY FOR a few minutes I couldn't find my room. It was just after lunch and I wanted to retrieve a book from my bed stand, but I didn't know which way to go.

"Now what's that expression all about?" said a woman's voice. It was Sarah, my Sarah. "You heading outside, Patrick? Beautiful day, isn't it?" I stood still, one hand on the shiny steel railing that runs along the length of the corridor. Could it be Erica?

"Yes, I'm heading outside." I saw sunlight and headed toward it. Left foot right foot left foot right foot careful with the cane. Sarah? Sarah my jaw feels numb and I'm lost. Sarah?

◆　　◆　　◆

SCOTTY WESLEY, a nineteen-year-old chicken farmer from Arkansas, lasted in no-man's-land for forty-eight hours. Or at least that's how long we heard him. But I hear there's a German down the line who hung on for four days before a shell silenced him.

◆　◆　◆

THIS AFTERNOON I watched Sarah sitting outside during her break. She was drinking coffee and reading the newspaper but then I saw her put the paper down and pull out an envelope from her sweater pocket and read one of my letters over again. I went back to my room and closed the door and put the soundtrack to Camelot into my tape player and turned the music up loud.

◆　◆　◆

DANIEL STOPPED crying just after eleven P.M. I hope his eyes were closed.

◆　◆　◆

I GOT A new photo of Katy this morning. She's wearing pigtails and a little blue dress and patent leather shoes and she smiles on the verge of a laugh. I sit in the corner of my room and stare at the photo, which I cup gently in my hands. What is it about the photo of a great-grand daughter that makes an old man in a nursing home break apart?

It is everything. I head back outside to my bench, walking faster than usual.

IF, ALL TOLD, eighteen million people died in World War I, how many broken hearts is that? How many individually crushed, aching, shattered hearts? A multiple of three? Four?

How many simply stopped?

◆　　◆　　◆

I HATE YOU God.

◆　　◆　　◆

KATY?

◆　　◆　　◆

DANIEL'S BODY remained in the wire for three days until it disappeared during a bombardment. We took the German line that afternoon and I looked for Daniel but all I could find were pieces of clothing and leather and belt buckles and helmets and boots and metal and paper and bone all blended together in utter filthy anonymity.

Your letters Daniel, what about your letters? I don't even know Julia's last name.

◆　　◆　　◆

A KID FROM New Hampshire died the cleanest death I ever saw. Just after a barrage we found him curled up near the latrine like he was sound asleep. We yelled his name and shook him and rolled him over looking for wounds but there was nothing, not a scratch. So we checked his breathing and his pulse and opened his mouth and ripped off his shirt looking for what was wrong and he was already going cold.

"What the hell happened to him?"

"Damn heart attack?"

"Beats me."

"You sure he's dead?"

"Can't be gas."

"Stroke?"

"That's no damn heart attack that's a shell concussion."

"Shell concussion?"

"Yeah, just from the blast. Seen it at Château-Thierry."

"The air knocks you dead?"

"Sucks the air right out of you."

"Shit."

"Never seen nothing like it."

"Here, you take his legs."

◆　◆　◆

THE WHISTLE shrieks. I'm up and over the top running. So much noise and fear. Then a sudden blow to my leg. I look down. Blood's coming fast from my thigh. A bullet? Shrapnel? I step once, then stumble. I rise and step again, then fall to the ground. Again I struggle to my feet, but they give way. My pants are soaked. I turn my head sideways and see figures running past. I push up to my hands and knees, crawl forward, then collapse again. So tired. Something knocks my helmet off. Then a sharp pain in my right arm. I'm up again, on my knees. Which way? To the right? Too much confusion. A figure runs past, knocking me over. I try to rise again but cannot.

◆　　◆　　◆

THE GUNS SHOOK my hospital bed that morning right up until eleven A.M. on November 11, 1918, when the Western Front finally went completely mute, as though someone had ripped the vocal cords from an angry beast. A doctor stood in the center of the room and called out the minutes. We laid in our beds and listened, knowing that somehow the world was about to change. Next to me a badly wounded young blond boy with the letters *GP* (German Prisoner) painted with silver nitrate across his cheek mumbled and struggled to raise his head.

I'm not sure that any of us lying there really believed that the guns would actually cease. Can four years of violent momentum be stopped cold? I couldn't believe that war was so containable, that you could blow a whistle and stop the whole thing like a football game. Was bravery at 10:59 A.M. really just common murder at 11:01 A.M.?

My thigh throbbed with pain but it wasn't that bad, not as bad as for the ones hidden behind the white curtain on the far side of the room, which is where men were placed to die. I was certain that the man on my right was next. His lungs were destroyed by gas and all they could do was put zinc ointment on his blisters and castor oil on his eyes and tell him lies. I tried to talk to him but he couldn't hear; everything was drowned out by his own fight for air. I felt particularly sad for those who couldn't hear well through their pain and bandages and fevers, because the change from war to peace was certain to be such an audible thing.

At 10:45 A.M. the guns increased, escalating toward a cataclysmic grand finale. They were our guns mostly, and I wondered whose idea it was to lob a few more shells before time was called. Or was the point to contrast the noise of the barrage with the sudden, breathtaking silence of peace when the larks finally reasserted themselves? But how long would it take the farthest shells to land? Technically, wouldn't a shell fired at eleven A.M. shatter the peace?

But most of all I wondered how many men died that morning, and I thought how much worse that would be than dying at any other time during the previous four years, especially if you were lying behind the white curtain when everything went still.

♦ ♦ ♦

I WISH YOU could hear this, Daniel. The silence is so enormous.

317

◆　◆　◆

On the Fourth Army front, at two minutes
to eleven, a machine gun, about 200 yards
from the leading British troops, fired off a
complete belt without a pause. A single
machine-gunner was then seen to stand up
beside his weapon, take off his helmet,
bow, and turning about walk slowly to the
rear.

—Herbert Essame, British Army.

◆　◆　◆

GOOD–BYE, DANIEL.

PART
THREE

S ix weeks after I returned from France I took a train to San Francisco to find Julia. The train was full of soldiers and I listened carefully to the stories they told their girlfriends and mothers and fathers. The ones who hadn't fought told tremendous tales of battle while the ones who had were at a loss for words. I kept to myself and alternated between gazing at the landscapes rolling by and reading one of several books I had packed.

I got off in Oakland and took a boat across the bay to San Francisco, disembarking right at the wharves where Julia grew up. It wasn't San Francisco to me but Julia and Daniel's town and I looked at every street and store wondering how often they had passed by that very spot. I wanted to scan all the faces of the pedestrians until I found Julia but instead went straight to the library to look up the address of Daniel's parents. Three hours later I arrived in front of a slightly run-down light gray two-story house in time to see an elderly looking man pull up in a small wagon drawn by a tired-looking horse. "MacGuire & Sons" was painted on the sides in bright red.

"Mr. MacGuire?" I said, removing my hat.

He turned and looked at me, rather more warily than I expected.

"You must be Mr. MacGuire?"

"I am indeed," he said, in a deep brogue.

"Sorry to disturb you. My name is Delaney, Patrick Delaney." I paused, searching for the right words. "I was a friend of Daniel's."

"Oh Lord, come right in." He jumped down off his wagon, shook my hand vigorously and gestured toward the front door. "Mrs. MacGuire is at her sister's. Won't be back for a few hours still. Here, let me get you a beer."

We sat down on the front stoop.

"Been to San Francisco before?"

"No, never."

"Ah, lovely city. A pity what burned, but still lovely to look at, especially in the fall."

"Yes, I look forward to a little sight-seeing."

He quickly drained his beer and opened another. His hands were extraordinarily thick and callused and he made a habit of slowly opening and closing a fist, as though testing for soreness.

Finally, he said, "So you were with Daniel."

"Yes. Yes I was."

He placed his bottle of beer down beside him and then looked straight ahead. "My poor boy." He shook his head slowly and then mumbled something, a prayer maybe. Should I say something?

"He was very brave. We all respected him a great deal."

Mr. MacGuire nodded, his head slung low between his knees and his hands clasped out in front of him.

"When he enlisted the first thing his mother

said was, 'Daniel is much too brave to be a soldier.' She was right."

"I'm so sorry."

He placed his head in his hands for a minute,
then looked up.

"Daniel was in the business with me. Good
worker, that boy, never complained." His
voice trailed off. He took another swig of his
beer. "Then he met some woman. Well, you
probably know the story. Ran away. Broke our
hearts, he did."

"I know some of the story, not all of it."

"Oh blessed Mary mother of Christ, why
would my son run all the way to France for a
woman?"

"I don't think he went to France for her. I
don't think that's why he joined the army."

"You don't, eh?" He turned and looked at
me. His face was red and his heavy features
showed his age. "What then do you think
was in his head?"

"I think he wanted to make you proud."

His face broke and he turned away. I wondered what he knew of Daniel's death and if
I should try to make the best of it and tell him
more about how his son never flinched and how
even the captain seemed to look up to him, or
should I say nothing? Was there anything
Daniel wanted me to say? There must have
been, we talked about it, didn't we? But I
couldn't recall the words, the proper words.
At least I could say that he was felled by a single
bullet to the heart. Never saw it coming.
Never felt a thing. Or should I tell him that

last rites were said? That Daniel had just enough time to see Mary coming for him.

I cleared my throat. "I was wondering, do you happen to know where Julia lives, how I might contact her?"

"Haven't the faintest notion," he said quietly, tugging at his chin.

"Do you remember her last name?"

"Never laid eyes on her."

We sat for another half hour but both of us were at a loss for words. Before I left he asked me if I needed work. I thanked him for the offer and told him I'd try to stay in touch, though I knew I wouldn't because it made me too sad to think of him and his wife and their lonely conversations with God, not knowing what they did wrong.

"You know, Daniel's mother and I, we're simple folk," he said as I started down the front steps. "We work and we pray and at night we are thankful for the chance to rest." I nodded nervously. "My grandfather *starved* to death back in Ireland, do you understand?"

"Yes, well, no, that's awful."

He started to say something and then stopped. At the curb we turned to each other and shook hands.

"Daniel's with the Lord now. Sooner than we'd wish but with the Lord nevertheless." I nodded again then turned and walked down the sidewalk, trying to imagine what on earth the Lord would make of Daniel and vice versa.

After stopping twice for drinks and then for

a loaf of sourdough bread I rented a small room on the third floor of a sailor's hotel near the wharves. Then I returned to the streets to look for Julia. I searched for nine days, asking bartenders and waitresses if they'd heard of her, checking with art galleries and sometimes sitting all day at trolley stops watching the faces stream by. I even took a ferry across the bay to Sausalito and rode the train that zigzagged up to the top of Mount Tamalpais, from where you can see the entire bay and even the Sierra Nevadas on a good day. Partway down the mountain I got off the train and took a coach down to Stinson Beach in hopes that I might see a woman with brown hair and bright green eyes sitting before a canvas and painting the thrashing surf. Instead I found dozens of sand dollars that had been coughed up by the tides. I wrapped the three largest in my handkerchief and stuffed them in my pocket but they all broke before I got back to the city. I tossed the pieces into the bay.

Before I went back east to study accounting I placed an ad in newspapers in both San Francisco and Los Angeles with Julia and Daniel's names in boldface and my name and address in small print below. After a month I stopped paying for the ads. Two years later I met Charlotte at a Christmas party and a year after that we married. I knew within weeks of our honeymoon on the Carolina coast that something was missing and I remember lying in bed at night in the small flat we rented and wondering whether anyone else felt the same way so soon or whether I was just an absolute fool. Either way there seemed to be nothing to do about it at that point but settle in and hope for the best. Besides, I was busy with work and Charlotte was soon pregnant, so our lives took on a certain inevitability and routine, like everyone else's, I suppose. I tried to forget about Julia and Daniel and the war but of course I couldn't. Not even for a night.

♦ ♦ ♦

THE BOTTLE arrived five days after Easter. The halls were still wallpapered with pictures of bunnies and baskets while the smell of rotten eggs lingered from the annual Easter egg hunt, when the number of eggs hidden invariably exceeds the number found.

I was walking by the nurses' station when Erica stopped me. "It's for you," she said, pointing to the small wooden crate on the counter. "And be careful, it's marked fragile."

"Me? Oh God, not more Easter eggs."

The return address was written in large block letters with a black felt marker: Marblehead, Massachusetts. I felt confused, then sick.

"What is it, Patrick?"

I closed my eyes for a minute, then opened them. "Could you just put the box on my bed?"

"Sure. You okay?" She placed her hand on my forearm.

"I'm okay."

I didn't open the box that day. I couldn't. I just stared at it. Martin knew enough not to ask.

◆   ◆   ◆

"PAGE DIED," I murmured. We were sitting on our beds the next morning.

"Who is Page?" asked Martin.

"Nathaniel Page. The only other surviving member of my old squad and company. He was the Harvard boy." I smiled wistfully, trying to slow my breathing. Martin waited for me to continue.

"Just after the war twelve of us met for dinner in New York and after drinks we decided to pitch in on an expensive bottle of Scotch—bootlegged stuff, quite good—which was to be kept by the oldest living member of the company, and then passed along after he died. The last man to get the bottle, the last survivor, would open it. The joke was that he'd need a stiff drink, if he could still handle the stuff."

"And now that's you?"

"Now that's me." I pulled the bottle gently from the crate, where it rested in wads of brown wrapping paper. The label was crowded with signatures, some small and angular, others large and florid. I saw my drunken scrawl and John Galston's and Nathaniel Page's. I noticed a chip on the bottom of the bottle and wondered who dropped it and how relieved they must have felt when it did not break. I wished it had broken.

I put the note from Page's widow on my bed stand and washed up for breakfast.

◆　◆　◆

Cut off from the land that bore us,
*   Betrayed by the land that we find,*
The good men have gone before us,
*   And only the dull left behind.*

So stand by your glasses steady,
*   The world is a web of lies.*
Then here's to the dead already,
*   And hurrah for the next man who dies.*
*   —From the mess song of the*
*   Lafayette Escadrille, a squad of*
*   American volunteer airmen.*

◆　◆　◆

"WILL YOU BE leaving tomorrow then?" Julia asked, as we walked down an uneven brick-paved street after having dinner at a small restaurant on the south end of town.

"Yes, back to Paris. What about you?"

"I think I'll stay a few more days. The place seems to have a bit of a hold on me." She was walking close to me now, so that our shoulders touched.

Was there any way I could stay longer? A few more days? I thought of Charlotte and Sean and felt all the guilt and confusion again.

"Your wife is very lucky," said Julia, stopping and turning toward me.

"Thank you."

"But I'm lucky too." I waited for her to continue. "Because now I know that Daniel wasn't the only one."

"What do you mean?"

"I always thought he was the only man I could really talk to. The only one who would understand. Then I met you."

I felt the skin on my face redden and I had to stop my arms from reaching out and pulling her toward me.

"I don't want to go," I said.

"And I don't want you to go."

I thought of the sailboat I'd bought for Sean and how his cheeks would fill with a tremendous smile when he saw it and how he wouldn't let me out of his sight for hours once I returned, even following me into the bathroom. "I have to."

"I know that."

"I don't know what to do," I said finally.

She held my stare.

"I have this terrible feeling that I'm going to lose my chance..."

"But you already found someone. You're fortunate. I don't want to..."

"It's different. It's so different, Julia."

She started walking again. I knew she didn't want to hear the things I wanted to say. Was she afraid of what I might say? I knew I was.

"I'd like to go back to the memorial tomorrow, perhaps try to paint it, though

I'm not sure I can. Not the way I'd like to,"
she said.

"I thought I'd stop there on my way to the
train station. Maybe I could meet you?"

"I'll be there early," she said.

"So will I."

She turned and looked at me for a moment,
then nodded. When we reached the hotel
we stood in the lobby for several minutes,
talking nervously. Finally she took both my
hands in hers, thanked me for the dinner,
kissed me quickly on the cheek and said
good night. I tightened my grip on her hands
just slightly, then felt them gradually slip away
from mine. From the landing she turned
and looked at me again and her face seemed
full of pain.

◆   ◆   ◆

"YOU WANT TO take a walk or something?"
Martin looked at me hopefully. It was just after
nine A.M. and we were both sitting on the
edges of our beds, unsure how to proceed.

"Sure, I'll take a walk."

"Not a long walk."

"No, not a long walk."

"Good, let's go on a walk." He leaned forward and pushed himself off the bed with a low
grunt, then went to the dresser to brush his
hair. I rose and finished buttoning my shirt in
the mirror, then followed him out the door and
down the hall.

Outside the sun was just piercing the morning

mist. It smelled of wet evergreens and I had a vague memory of watching my father chop wood and then helping him stack it, careful to shore up the ends of the woodpile.

"Nice day."

"Yes, nice day."

We walked slowly, looking down a lot the way old people do, scanning for danger.

"I always wanted to go first," he said after a while.

"Go first?"

"To go before Doreen. I always hoped I'd go before Doreen."

"Oh, you mean *there*."

"Yes, *there*. She was much stronger than me. She would have been okay."

Most men feel this way about their wives. Fortunately for them, most men get their wish.

"I guess I always just assumed that I'd go first," he said. "I didn't give a lot of thought to it being the other way around."

"Well, if it's any consolation, I hope I go before you," I said.

"Oh no, I hope not." We looked briefly at each other and exchanged thin smiles.

"Do you suppose everybody has somebody they hope will outlive them?" I asked.

"Sure they do. The only thing worse than going first is going last. We lived next to a couple, the Bennetts, who had a son who died in a skiing accident. Ed and Nancy hardly left their house for a year. One day Ed told me— I'll never forget it—he told me that God better not exist, because if he does there's a madman on the loose."

We walked on in silence. Then Martin said, "For two years I didn't throw out her clothes. Nothing. Sometimes I'd stand in her closet— she had a big walk-in closet that she loved, double-tiered hangers and lots of cubbyholes, she loved cubbyholes—and I'd look at her things and I'd smell her, just like she was there."

I patted him on the shoulder.

"And then I'd imagine her voice coming from the shower, asking me if she should wear the red dress or the green dress. She always laid out several outfits on the bed before we went out, with matching shoes and purses and earrings. Sometimes just before we got into the car, she'd decide her outfit was all wrong and run up and switch into the other one. But she wasn't lavish; she made a lot of her clothes herself."

"You want to keep walking?"

"No, I'm kind of tired of walking."

"Me too. Let's head back."

"Yes, let's head back."

We turned and slowly walked back.

◆   ◆   ◆

I WAS AWAKE when she knocked. I was sitting in the chair by the window, listening to the creaks of the hotel and watching the moon. It was sometime after two A.M. I hadn't been waiting exactly, just sitting and thinking and

332

hoping and praying, unable even to close my eyes.

When I opened the door she stepped in immediately, closing it quietly behind her. I could just see her face in the moonlight. It was wet, streaked with her tears.

"Thank God," I said, putting my arms around her and pulling her toward me. I could feel her back tremble.

"I had to," she whispered, cupping my face in her hands and staring up at me. "I had to be with you."

"Julia, I want to tell you something."

"Please don't." She pressed her finger against my lips. I kissed it, then pulled it away and kissed her hard on the lips and then her face and neck and down along her shoulders. I felt her hands in my hair and then searching down my back, frantically. I pushed her toward the bed and tore at her clothes and struggled to keep from saying the things I wanted to say.

We made love for hours, exhausting ourselves against each other's lips and mouths and skin until the bed was soaked with our sweat. Sometime during the night I promised never to let go but I must have, for when I awoke at dawn she was gone.

◆ ◆ ◆

I'VE BEEN STARING at a blank page of my sketchbook all day but nothing is coming to me. Maybe tomorrow.

SARAH CAME into my room this morning just as I was struggling with my pants. She invited me to her house for the Fourth of July. "We're having a little backyard barbecue, me and the boys, and we thought you might like to join us. It'll be fun. We've got sparklers and those little black snakes that smoke and there'll be lots of ice cream. I can pick you up and bring you back. It'll just be for a few hours."

"I'd be delighted, if you're sure." I held the top of my pants closed as I tried to sit up on the bed.

"We'd love it." She patted me on the shoulder, then turned and left.

That afternoon I took the bus into town and stopped at Henry Shay's Store for Men, where after some debate I settled on a new shirt: dark blue with a modest button-down collar. When did I last buy a shirt? Five years ago? I used to like clothes, in so much as women liked men who understood clothes. But the clothes I wore never felt right; they never said what I wanted to say. Not that I wanted my clothes to say much; rather, I just didn't want them to say the wrong things, to say too much too loudly. Yet I couldn't find anything that would just shut up and let me be: understated said boring, conventional said conservative, casual said kicked-back in a premeditated sort of way, formal said uptight.

A short and balding salesman with a tentative, commercial smile measured my sleeve and then my neck. Didn't I used to be a forty-two long instead of a forty regular? I'm sure I was. And how old were the clothes I now owned? Did I look like some threadbare cat-food-eating miser? I decided to go through my closet as soon as I got back to my room and toss out everything with a stain or a rip.

Before returning home I stopped at a liquor store and bought a bottle of Grgich Chardonnay—the merchant's recommendation—which I hid in the back of my closet next to Jim Beam. I thought of getting a gift too, something for the house perhaps, but decided not to overdo it.

The thing was not to act desperate.

◆　　◆　　◆

ON FRIDAY morning I awoke extra early, and before my shower I carefully clipped the nose hairs that began growing like ivy once I hit seventy. (That the last healthy cells of my body should be devoted to the manufacture of nose hairs is a fact I find almost unspeakably perverse.) I was dressed and ready by eight and sat in my corner chair with the bottle of wine in a bag next to me. (I'd purloined a strip of red ribbon from the crafts shop and tied it around the neck of the bottle, though my efforts to make it curl at the ends using scissors had left it frayed and limp.)

As I waited I tried to remind myself that Sarah hadn't invited *me* to her house but rather an elderly man she perhaps felt sorry for. Nonetheless I felt extremely nervous and kept checking myself in the mirror to be sure everything was where it was supposed to be. I couldn't bear to make a fool of myself. Not today.

I was out front by twelve-thirty, sitting on a bench near the taxi stand searching the street for Sarah's yellow VW Beetle convertible. She pulled up five minutes late and jumped out to open the door for me.

"Beautiful day, isn't it?" she said, guiding me into my seat.

"Great day for a barbecue." I tried to strike a casual balance between enthusiasm and rapture.

"I hope you don't mind having the top down. Is it too windy for you?"

"Not at all."

"I'll put the top up."

"No, please. I haven't been in a convertible for years. It's wonderful." I leaned my face out the window like a curious dog just sprung from the kennel.

Sarah was wearing a light blue summer dress cut low in the back and just barely reaching midthigh. Her legs looked tan and I wondered what she'd do if I put my hand on her thigh, which suddenly seemed profoundly accessible. Scream? Call the police? Medicate me? Smile? Of course she wouldn't smile, but it was a pleasant thought. Very pleasant. I held my hands together in my lap.

"How are you feeling?" she asked, pulling off her sunglasses with one hand and placing them on the top of her head, the ends tucked into her hair.

"Not bad, thanks." I was sorry she was so familiar with my medical chart.

"You look good today."

Did I? But of course she was just saying it. Yet I did *feel* good.

"Me? Why you look just beautiful."

"Oh aren't you a sweetheart." She spun her head and flung me a smile.

Ten minutes later she pulled into the driveway of a white, ranch-style house with a single maple tree on the left and a small patch of overgrown grass on the right. A few scrappy-looking rosebushes ran along the front beneath a bay window that looked into her living room. At the door two boys appeared, the smaller one tucked safely behind the larger one.

"Jeffrey, this is Mr. Delaney. Can you say hello to Mr. Delaney? Jeffrey's in fifth grade now and doing a great job, aren't you, Jeffrey?" He smiled shyly as we shook hands. "And this here is my baby boy Kevin, he just turned five. Kevin, can you say hello?" I caught sight of his big brown eyes and dark lashes before he slid around behind his mother.

"I'll save a handshake for you, Kevin," I said.

Sarah motioned toward the living room. "Well it's not much, but then they don't pay a lot at Great Oaks."

"Why should they? All you do all day is alleviate human suffering, it's not like you're trading futures."

"I guess I'm lucky they pay me at all." Her voice trailed off into the kitchen.

I walked slowly through the living room,

examining the plates hung on the walls and the framed photos that covered nearly every available inch of table space. The room looked freshly painted and the white carpet and yellow-flowered sofa made it seem almost unnaturally bright. I imagined lying on the sofa with her after the boys were in bed and talking about whether the rosebushes were getting enough water and should we take the children to Disneyland this year. But enough talk for one night...

"It's charming, very warm," I said.

"The air-conditioning's out."

"No, I meant..."

"Come on. We'll sit out back in the shade." I followed her out through a screen door that slammed shut behind us. Jeffrey opened a lawn chair and motioned for me to sit down. He opened another one and sat next to me. "I'll get some iced tea," Sarah said, heading back inside. The door slammed again. I turned toward Jeffrey, who was sitting with his hands tucked under his thighs.

"Your mother said you were in sixth grade?"

"Fifth."

"Yes, fifth. I hated fifth grade. How about you?"

He looked at me sideways. "It's all right, I guess."

"What sort of things are you studying?"

"Math, English, Spanish."

"Play a sport?"

"Soccer."

"Any good?"

"I'm okay."

"You don't mind being interrogated, do you?"

He laughed. "Mom says you're cool."

"Extremely cool."

"Are you sick or something?"

"Do I look sick?"

"No, not really, but you *are* a lot older than me."

"You're pretty blunt for a fifth grader."

He locked his ankles together under his chair.

"Since you're not beating around the bush, I won't either. How are the girls in your class?"

He smiled, then leaned forward. "There are some real choice ones," he said.

"Choice? You mean like, worth choosing, if you had the chance to choose?"

"Choice means pretty."

"Ah. Well I like choice women myself. Anyone special? I won't tell your mom."

"No, not really. I'm not what you'd call one of the most popular guys."

"I see. And why is that? You look kind of choice to me, in a man's kind of way, and your mother said your grades are good, so it's not like you don't have something to bring to the table."

"I don't know, I guess it's because I'm shy."

"All the wrong kinds of people are shy, don't you think? I always figured it would make much more sense if the assholes were shy and the nice guys were all outgoing, but damned if it's not the jerks who do all the talking."

He laughed, then turned serious again. "I got in a fight last week—but you can't tell Mom."

"Oh no, I won't. Want to tell me about it?"

"There's this guy at school, his name is Richard, and for some reason he doesn't like me. So one day after school he and a couple of his friends—real jerks—jumped me near the bike racks. I wasn't hurt too bad but it was kind of embarrassing."

"Kind of? It doesn't get any worse than that, and I'm a war veteran." I thought about buying him a can of pepper spray. Would he be expelled? Probably. Ah, but to be a shy fifth grader with a can of pepper spray in your pocket when the bully comes at you; most men go a lifetime without such pure satisfaction.

"What's it like being a veteran?"

"Piece of cake. Being a soldier was the hard part, at least when it wasn't boring."

"You did real fighting?"

"Real fighting."

"Wow." He smacked a mosquito on his forearm, and then flicked it off. "My grandfather was in the navy but I'd rather be a fighter pilot."

"Is your grandfather still alive?"

"No, he died two years ago."

"See much of your dad?"

"Naw. He's remarried, and he and Jean—she's my stepmom—have a baby."

"I meant what I said about how tough it is, being a kid. First off, you live under martial law, no two ways about it. You're practically a prisoner until you reach sixteen. And the thing about prison is, the other prisoners are much more dangerous than the guards. To tell you the truth, I think adulthood is a cinch in comparison."

"Really?"

"Damn straight. Even being really old is easier than being a kid, and that's saying something. The curse about being young is that you are much more dependent on what others think about you, and those others tend to be," I lowered my voice, "pricks."

He laughed.

"But when you get older, you see that the world is a much bigger place and you can do without those people. What I'm saying is it doesn't get any worse, what you're going though, but it gets a lot better. Only I didn't know that when I was a kid and the cool guys excluded me. I figured it was just the beginning of a lifelong siege and I thought to myself I thought, holy shit, this *sucks*."

He slapped his hands on his thighs and smiled a great big smile. Then Sarah appeared with iced tea and lemonade, which immediately attracted more mosquitoes.

"A good time for the fireworks," I said.

Jeffrey was just opening the first box of snakes when a man appeared at the back door holding a small blue and white cooler.

"Oh Peter, you made it," said Sarah, jumping

up and walking quickly toward him. She kissed him on the cheek and led him back to the chairs. "Peter, I'd like you to met Patrick Delaney. Remember I told you about him?"

I rose and shook his hand. The new boyfriend. Of course. Silly me. I sat back down and looked at him, at his sleek, implausible smile, his strong hairy forearms and thick curly black hair and his thin leather shoes and the mirrored sunglasses suspended from his top shirt button. And worst of all his smug, self-absorbed expression, the kind worn by people who drive across the country with their turn signal on, and not one of those quiet ones but the kind that go DING DING DING DING! with a great big green arrow flashing on the dashboard.

Peter sat down and opened his cooler and pulled out a dark green bottle of foreign beer, flipped off the top, took a big dramatic swig and wiped his mouth with a loud "ahh." Then he turned to Sarah and started to talk about his efforts to close a real estate deal with a wealthy Korean who preferred to talk business at bars with table dancers. She folded her hands gently in her lap and listened with nods and uh-huhs that seemed unnecessarily attentive.

After Peter and the boys lit all the fireworks he stood by the barbecue flipping burgers and swigging and ahhing. Then we sat at a small picnic table in the corner to eat but I wasn't hungry so I just sat and listened to Peter eat and talk and ahh his way through two burgers and three scoops of potato salad that Sarah dished out from a large yellow and white bowl. When Sarah noticed me nodding off she went to get her car keys to drive me home but Peter insisted on taking me himself, which delivered him from doing the dishes and, I presumed, scored him some brownie points that he would cash in later in the evening. Sarah kissed me on the cheek as she leaned through the car window and I saw Jeffrey wave from the front door.

I fell asleep on the way home and don't remember how I got into bed.

♦   ♦   ♦

JULIA SAID that when the man you love dies young, a part of you never ages. But what if you are old and unable to find the woman you have loved almost every day of your life? Then what, Julia?

I need to know quickly.

♦   ♦   ♦

WHAT HAS slipped by? A week? A month? The foliage looks different and I don't remember it changing. I looked in the mirror this morning and saw that my beard had two days' growth. Yet I shave every day.

How horrifying this is.

♦   ♦   ♦

EMERSON WROTE that "a man is a god in ruins." That certainly covers a lot of ground, but now I must ask, what is a man in ruins? That's what I want to know.

◆　◆　◆

JULIA WAS already standing at her easel when I parked and walked over along the gravel path, careful not to step in the puddles swelled by the early morning rain that stopped just as I left the hotel. She turned and watched me as I approached.

"You must have gotten up awfully early," I said, feeling nervous to see her.

"The light was perfect. I wanted to see what it looked like at sunrise." Her hair was tucked behind her ears and she was dressed in a khaki-colored chemise, knee-length and belted at the waist.

I stepped forward, wanting to hold her, but she averted her eyes. Should I kiss her?

She kept painting for a minute, then put her brush down. "Patrick, I just want to... I want you to know that I didn't mean to, that I'm sorry. No, not sorry, just..."

"Please don't feel bad. I—"

"Don't say anything." She put her fingers on my lips. "Please."

"Julia..."

"*Please.*"

We stood looking at each other and I could hear the birds again, several of them up in a tree behind the monument, loud and unanimous. Then she picked up her brush and turned toward the canvas.

I walked partway out to the meadow and stood still for a minute, eyes closed. When I walked back toward her she was staring at me.

"May I look?"

"Oh, I've only just started. You'll have to come visit me someday if you want to see it." She looked away.

I sat along the edge of the monument, which hadn't yet been warmed by the sun, and I ran my fingers along the names, murmuring each one aloud.

"You won't be in Paris in the next week or so?" I asked.

"I'm going to Florence, just for a few days before sailing home. I'm afraid I've spent everything my mother left me on this trip. It wasn't much, from waitressing. But at least I've made it to Europe. I'll never forget any of this."

She turned back to her canvas but I noticed that she looked up at me frequently. I lit a cigarette and tried to think of something to say. Couldn't I just hold her?

A bird landed on the monument, took a few steps and then flew away. I stood and slowly walked around, trying to remember everything so I could describe it at the next reunion. The effort made everything seem unusually vivid.

"You have my address," I said.

"Yes."

"You'll send me yours when you settle down again?"

She nodded, then wiped her hands on a rag tucked into her belt, took a few hesitant steps toward me and stopped. "You'll miss your train." Her lower lip quivered.

"Julia, I don't know if I can—"

"Patrick." Her eyes offered me strength, just as Daniel's had done. She stepped closer and held out her hand.

"How—"

"Good-bye, Patrick," she whispered.

I took her hand in both of mine and then she came closer and buried her face in my neck and we held each other, arms wrapped tight and our bodies swaying slowly back and forth. I waited until she loosened her grip and finally dropped her arms and then I pulled back and kissed her desperately; her face, her neck, her lips. I couldn't let go. She finally drew back, her eyes filled with tears. Her hand went up to her mouth and she turned away. I began slowly walking toward my car. After a few steps I stopped and turned back to her.

"Come to Paris!" I shouted. "I'll be there for two weeks."

With her back to me she shook her head.

"Please! I'll look for you at the Arc de Triomphe. At noon. I'll check every day at noon. Please!"

She raised her hand, then said, "Please go." Her voice was breaking. My chest ached and I longed desperately to turn back and grab hold of her.

"*Please*, Patrick."

I turned and walked quickly to my car and drove off down the blurry, trembling road.

◆　◆　◆

The picture I have of you has a hole in it from a piece of shell. I have four bullet holes in my overcoat, and my trousers were torn to pieces by a grenade, but I only had my knees cut besides the bullet in my shoulder. The strap to my field glasses was cut by a bullet, my gas mask was cut in half by shrapnel, and my helmet has a dent from a bullet. But they did not get me.
—*Maurice V. Griffin, United States Army,*
in a letter to his wife.

◆　◆　◆

"MARTIN?" He had just begun to stir and I heard him fumbling for his glasses on his bedside table. Inevitably he knocked over a bottle or two of pills during his search, which helped explain his ruinously high pharmaceutical bills.

"Huh? What?" He pushed his glasses on and began fiddling with his hearing aids.

"I've been thinking about Lara."

"Huh?"

Each morning Martin and I spend several minutes just sitting on the edge of our beds, making sure our rusty gyroscopes are right side up before we stand. At a certain age system checks must be performed before any significant move, while the movement itself must be methodically plotted out in advance. Whoever slips up, dies.

"Lara. Your old flame. How old would she be now?"

"Why do you ask?"

"I'm just curious."

"Seventy-six," he said quickly. He sat in his light blue boxers, white T-shirt and black knee-high socks, his hands braced along the sides of the bed, palms down. "But why do you ask?"

"Well, you figure she married, right?"

"Yes."

"So chances are, she is still alive and her husband, whether he was husband number one or two or three, is dead."

He winced.

"So why don't we find out where she lives?"

"Patrick, that was almost sixty years ago."

"Not to you." He said nothing. "Why not call her, say hello?"

"Jesus, Patrick, are you *crazy*?"

"More so by the minute."

She wasn't hard to find. Martin was sure she'd still be in the Northeast—if she was alive—and he knew she was closely connected to her church. I talked to the minister who said that Mrs. Lara Tennant Hutchinson lived alone in a large house just five blocks from St. Marks. Mr. Hutchinson had died three years ago. Massive heart attack. Collapsed in his golf cart, which rolled into a pond.

I never actually heard what Martin said to Lara when he called her but I could see his face from across the lounge, all flushed and wiggly. We had rehearsed his opening lines.

"Just tell her you heard she was still alive and you just wanted to say hello, since, coincidentally, you're still alive too."

"You mean, 'Hello, Lara? This is Martin, as in the twenty-year-old who loved you but got another woman pregnant only now I'm almost eighty and can hardly piss so what's new with you?'"

"Close enough. And talk loud. She's probably hard of hearing."

After ten minutes by the phone booth, hand on the receiver, still safe in its hook, Martin retreated, requesting a small glass of brandy. He cringed as he took a sip, then another.

"Courage, my boy," I said as he put down the glass. "She's just an old lady, remember? An old bag. Probably ugly as sin."

"Yeah, that's right," he said, shuffling back toward the phone booth. "An old biddy. A granny. Probably got one of those purple Afros that she keeps by her bed stand at night next to her teeth and her hearing aids." He did a little shuffle dance as he approached the phone.

When he shuffled back across the room a half hour later he patted me on the shoulder and whispered, "Thanks." Then he padded off down the hallway toward our room, humming a song I did not recognize.

MARTIN AND LARA got to talking once a week. He also wrote her letters from his bed nearly every morning, propping himself up with pillows and using a piece of stained wood from the arts and crafts shop, which he placed across his lap.

"It's still her voice," he said one night as we lay in our beds.

"Well, whose voice did you expect?"

"But it was so long ago."

"I don't feel so different. Do you?"

"No, I just never imagined she would still sound so familiar."

Martin didn't like to talk about Lara too much, as though sharing her might spoil it, but I did manage to pry a little out of him. She had married twice, had two kids from each marriage, was in remarkably good health and financially secure. Her first letter, written on light blue finely textured Crane's stationery with matching envelope, arrived just six days after their first phone conversation. Martin handed it to me.

"You don't mind?" I asked.

He gestured for me to read. It began:

> *My Dearest Martin,*
> *You damned fool, I went away that summer because you never asked me to stay. Don't you know I was absolutely devastated when I found out? I loved you....*

350

After I finished it I handed it back, then stood up, patted him on the shoulder and headed to the cafeteria. When I returned he was still sitting on his bed, the letter on his lap.

Two months later he sat down next to me on a bench outside and announced, "I'm going to Boston."

"To visit Lara?"

"Yes."

"When?"

"In three weeks. She's offered to pay, said she has all the money she needs and then some. I just made my reservations." His head and hands shook more than usual.

"Wonderful. Absolutely wonderful." I tried to smile.

"I may need some help packing." He nervously rubbed his palms on his knees.

"Clean underwear. Bring clean underwear."

◆　◆　◆

WHAT IF Julia is widowed? The thought has been nagging me all day. But where did she live and what last name did she go by? I didn't know where to begin.

And I couldn't begin. I couldn't search again. Not anymore. And if she had died I didn't want to know. I couldn't bear that, to be the last of the three. And I couldn't bear to have her see me like this: such a wreck of a man.

No, I couldn't stand to lose her all over again.

◆　◆　◆

OSCAR DIED this morning, or sometime in the night. I saw them wheel him out just before breakfast, which ended any chance of working up an appetite.

I never did get to double-check his pulse, but I've made a note to contact his relatives and make sure he's not cremated. Oscar would have hated that.

Neither Martin nor I felt like doing much all day, but after dinner we decided to play checkers in Oscar's honor. His board was still there, tucked into the back pouch of his wheelchair, which was parked by his empty bed. Howard and Mitzie joined in and soon we had a feisty tournament going, which Martin won. After we finished we took a vote on whether to keep Oscar's checkerboard or put it back with his other belongings. By unanimous proclamation we decided to keep it.

♦   ♦   ♦

TODAY COULD be better than most days. Considerably better. Possibly even great. After months of pleading we've finally been promised a real live model for art class. A woman. Maybe even a naked woman. I've always dreamed of livening up Great Oaks's art program with a model; some biologically blessed local college student looking for a few extra bucks. Usually we are asked to sketch vases and plastic fruits laid out on a card table, sometimes the same vases and plastic fruits that we painted the week before and the week before that too. I often refuse, preferring to draw my landscapes and portraits from memory. But today I am willing to break new ground.

I arrive at the classroom door half an hour early, determined to get a front-row seat. When the door finally opens at ten sharp, several dozen of us, including many men attending their first art class in over sixty years, hurry in. A large curtain is hung over the front left corner of the room. I claim a seat directly in front of it, overjoyed by my good fortune. Then I open my pad to a fresh sheet of paper and carefully lay out my pastels. The instructor stands before the curtain, hushing the class. "Today, as promised, we have a beautiful model who has agreed to sit for us." I rub my hands together, then strain for a glimpse beneath the curtain of a collegiate toe or two. A shadow moves. Was it clothed? How utterly sublime. Then with one grand motion the instructor pulls the curtain away and stands back, both arms in the air.

There in the corner, with a bowl of apples in her lap and matching lipstick smeared all over her front teeth, sits Mitzie Smith, dressed (thank God) in her favorite lime green dress and hat and smiling ear to ear. "Surprise!"

♦   ♦   ♦

TIME IS doing strange things again, so that the present seems increasingly irrelevant while the past comes ever sharper into focus. Some days I am plunged backward as though dunked under water, suddenly remembering things I had forgotten for years. It's really not a bad sensation. In many ways I enjoy it; the feeling that I'm drawing closer to people and places long left behind. Maybe the past doesn't keep irrevocably receding. Maybe in old age time loops back on itself so that we can return to the things that meant the most to us (and flee the mounting horrors of the present).

Today, for example, I could almost insist it's 1941. Sudden news about a place called Pearl Harbor. Frozen faces held near large wooden radios that crackle with distant voices. Clumps of people in the streets exchanging questions, shopping bags at their feet. The trees are bare and there are Christmas decorations in the shop windows. Everybody moves fast and there seem to be more cars on the road than usual. So it's war then. Is San Francisco safe? Where's the Japanese fleet? How quickly will we mobilize and how old will the army draft 'em this time?

And that sick feeling low in my stomach as I sit by the window of my small cottage near the high school campus where I teach, a pile of student papers in my lap. I am dressed in a dark gray sweater and slippers and watching as the low white sky turns gray and then bluish-black.

Europe has already gone mad again. Hitler in Paris. The Luftwaffe over London. My God, the Great War was just the beginning.

IT WAS STILL light when I got back to Paris. I stood outside the hotel for a few minutes before I went in, watching my reflection in a windowpane, then smiled as best I could when Charlotte opened the door to our room. I tried to tell her about the memorial and the trenches and the forts at Verdun but I couldn't find the right words and I was worried that I sounded nervous. Then I sat in a chair in the corner with Sean on my lap and listened as she told me all the places that she and Margaret had been and where they'd eaten and what fun they'd been having.

As I sat there with my chin resting on the top of Sean's head and my arms wrapped around his waist I stared at Charlotte and reminded myself of all the wonderful things about her: her smile and her laughter and the way she was with Sean and her soft hair and smooth hands and then all the things we'd been through together. As I watched her and listened to her stories I knew that I still loved her and that I could never leave. But I also knew that I would never feel the kinds of things that I felt with Julia. Not even close.

Sean loved the sailboat. From the minute I walked in the door he followed me everywhere, one fist locked on my pants leg. We wrestled on the bed with the pillows, then used a blanket to build a makeshift fort in the corner where we sat in the semidarkness enjoying the cozy sense of safety and secretiveness. After I read him three books I tucked him into bed, lying next to him until he fell asleep, head against my chest. Then I went down the hall and took a shower, gave Charlotte a kiss and a hug and crawled into bed, telling her I was tired. The next day, a little before noon, I walked to the Arc de Triomphe and waited for Julia.

♦　♦　♦

I'M SITTING at the breakfast table, hemmed in by wheelchairs and staring down at my uneaten food, and suddenly I miss Daniel. Terribly so. It feels like a hunger, or the cravings I felt when I quit smoking. Only worse. I feel tearfully desperate for something I can't have.

One person dies and the whole world looks sadder, hollowed out so that you hear echoes in places where there aren't supposed to be any. Each passing day and month and year is an accumulation of absences; of people, places and events that a loved one will never see or know about. When you have suffered a terrible loss you look at things and think: I wonder what he would have made of that? Wouldn't he have enjoyed this and oh God he would have hated that and shit this reminds me of him.

When people die it's as though the earth itself opens briefly and swallows them up.

The last thing people do when they die is to change all the people who loved them. I can still feel the dead reverberating through my own life, sometimes with the delicacy of ripples on a pond, other times with the force of shock waves. And the strangest thing is how much talking the dead still do; talking in our heads. I've actually grown quite fond of it.

But I can't shake the sadness. Sometimes nostalgia swamps me like a flash flood and leaves me floating facedown amid the flotsam of the past. Not the nostalgia that comes with the change of the seasons—which is as good as sad gets; a rusty, blood red if you gave it a color—but the deeper, more funereal longing. Melancholy, if you will.

I know that the act of remembering the past changes it and it's a bloody good thing too or growing old would be utterly intolerable. At a certain age you realize that living life is only the first step, then you've got to figure what to make of your experiences, which is actually much more critical than the experiences themselves. That's what old age is for, when you pass the days scouring your memory like the wretched Filipinos who scavenge Manila's city dump, sorting images and sensations into various heaps that are then relentlessly revised, resorted and repressed until finally, when you are wheeled out for display each Thanksgiving and Christmas, you respond to each and every inquiry with a polished reiteration of your accomplishments before nodding off.

◆　　◆　　◆

I WAS CLOSING the bookstore on a Friday evening in November when a woman in a

357

long gray raincoat knocked on the glass panes of the front door. The rain beaded down her hat and onto her shoulders and strands of dark brown hair were stuck to her cheeks, which were flushed. When I opened the door she smiled and thanked me.

She resembled Julia, only younger. Julia would be in her late fifties then, as was I.

"Do you mind? I just want to get one book."

"Not at all, come in." I switched the main light back on. She took her hat off and shook her hair. I felt a burning sensation in my chest.

"Take your time. Can I help you find something?"

"D. H. Lawrence, *Women in Love.*"

"Right over here."

"Oh great. I finally have a night to myself and I promised I'd read a good book. No TV or junk magazines." She carried the book over to the counter. I rang it up.

"Feel free to browse some more. I'm in no hurry." Can you ask a woman to read with you? No, not a stranger.

"I'm all set now, thanks." She held up the book. "Have you read much Lawrence?"

"A bit."

"I read this once in school only I don't remember any of it."

"I don't remember things I read last week," I said.

"I don't think people should read the really important books until they are at least thirty, not unless they promise to read them again."

"What do you like to read?"

"I used to enjoy reading history and biographies, that sort of thing. But a couple of years ago I just stopped reading books. Don't ask me why. Anyway, I've decided to start reading again only this time I want to read fiction. I've missed so much."

Should I ask her for a cup of coffee? No, she's twenty years younger than me. She's a customer. But God the resemblance.

"I don't think I've seen you in here before."

"I live on the west side. I was in the area."

"You're not from California by any chance, are you?"

"No, why do you ask?"

"You remind me of someone."

"I have a cousin..."

"Julia?"

"No, Ann."

"Well anyway, I hope you come back."

She smiled. "I will." She picked up her book, turned toward the door, then stopped. What eyes. "Are you the owner?"

"Yes."

"It must be nice to own a bookstore. I'd like that."

"It's not very profitable."

"Oh, I wouldn't care about the money. Just to be around all these books." She looked around. "I've even thought of taking a job in a bookstore."

"What do you do now?"

"I'm not working at the moment."

"Let me know if you're looking for a job. I

might need somebody." Ridiculous. I'd go bankrupt in a month.

"I will." She paused at the door. "Maybe next time you could recommend a book for me?"

"I'd be happy to. Any particular author or subject?"

"No, you pick it. I'd like that." Another big smile, full of promise.

"Why then I will."

After she left I turned off the overhead light, went over to the display window and watched her walk across the street and down the sidewalk. It was still raining but she hadn't bothered to put her hat on. When she turned the corner I turned the lights back on and began going through the shelves, looking for ideas. I stayed until after midnight, finally making a pile of twelve books I thought she might like. But which one? *The Brothers Karamazov*? *A Room of One's Own*? *Anna Karenina*? The poetry of John Keats or perhaps John Donne? *The Good Soldier*? *Look Homeward, Angel*? *Lie Down in Darkness*?

The next day I took away some books and added more. After a week I had whittled the stack down to six books, which I kept on the counter behind the cash register. I thought if I offered her six, she could take her pick and that way I wouldn't feel so awfully responsible. A week later I suddenly switched two of the books, then switched them back again. I also kept a list by my bed stand, in case something came to me in the night.

The hard part was imagining her reading each

book. Would she be in bed—by a husband, perhaps—or by a fire, or sitting at a table in the kitchen with a cup of coffee? When she read would she ever think of me, looking for what it was that made me recommend the book? Can a person fall in love that way? No, of course not.

After a month I moved the books to the shelf beneath the cash register, where they stayed until two weeks after that, when I moved them to the back room. Then one day two months later I reshelved the books. When I got home I tore up the list.

◆　◆　◆

I WAITED for two hours at the Arc de Triomphe, walking back and forth and then sitting at a nearby café and drinking three cups of coffee. I thought I saw her once but it was someone else. All I could think of was the sound of her knock on my door and the look on her face with those tears rolling down and the way her skin felt against mine.

When I got back to the hotel there was a note from Charlotte saying that she and Margaret had gone out for lunch and then sight-seeing. Sean was playing with a sitter they had hired, the daughter of the concierge. I paid her and pulled out Sean's stroller and then took him on a walk through Paris, following the route that Daniel, Page, Lawton and I had taken ten years before.

I WAITED the next day and the next one too, standing in the cool rain from eleven-thirty A.M. until twelve-thirty P.M., then hurrying back to the hotel to meet Charlotte and Margaret. My matches got wet so I lit one cigarette off the other, until I finished the pack. Still, I was glad that it rained.

◆   ◆   ◆

I WAS DOZING on the blue chair in the recreation room, sketchbook on my lap, when Sarah tapped me on the shoulder.

"You'll miss lunch."

"I'm not hungry."

"Oh come on now. I'm not going to let you wither away."

"You can't stop me from withering away."

"Now don't get started." She sat on the edge of my chair and rested a hand on my shoulder. "I want to ask you something."

I looked up, slowly grazing my eyes across her neck.

"Jeffrey's school is having Voices of History Week next month and we—he—was wondering if you might speak."

"Me? About what?"

"About being a veteran. About the First World War."

"To fifth graders?"

"It'll be the whole school and parents are invited too. It would mean a lot to Jeffrey."

362

"I'm not much of a speaker."

"Baloney. You'll do fine and Jeffrey will be thrilled. It's three weeks from this Friday. I'll drive you."

♦   ♦   ♦

Our artillery had been bombing that line
for six days and nights, trying to smash
the German barbed-wire entanglements,
but they hadn't made any impact.... The
result was that we never got anywhere
near the Germans. Never got anywhere
near them. Our lads were mowed down.
They were just simply slaughtered.
—*W. H. Shaw, British Army.*

♦   ♦   ♦

THE STAGE was much brighter than I had expected and I had to squint as I sat in a chair near the podium waiting to be introduced by an extremely tall and thin and dire-looking principal named Mrs. Pertosi, who smelled distinctly of Play-Doh. I regretted immediately not bringing my cane. But at least I could hold on to the podium. I pulled out my small notebook from my breast pocket and scanned it, making sure I hadn't forgotten anything, then glanced down at my fly.

"And now it's my pleasure to introduce a very special friend of Jeffrey Fields from Miss Meyer's fifth-grade class. At the robust age of eighty-one, Mr. Patrick Delaney is still going

363

strong some sixty-two years after defending our nation's values in the First World War, which, in case some of you have forgotten, was the one that came before the Second World War." Scattered laughter.

"Let's all extend a big hand to Mr. Delaney."

The applause was louder than I had expected, which felt good. I stood slowly and headed toward the podium, careful to watch my footing. I shook Mrs. Pertosi's hand, which was large and damp, and then grabbed on to the podium with both hands to balance myself. The microphone, too high at first, was too low after Mrs. Pertosi's adjustments. I stooped toward it. "Thank you, yes, thank you." The room hushed, except for a low drone of coughs and sneezes.

"Well then, war."

Looking out at all the faces turned up toward me I searched for one I could lock in on, but they all seemed to homogenize into an indistinguishable mass teetering between curiosity and boredom. The stage lights felt warm and excessively bright and I wondered if they were magnified through my glasses, which I'd forgotten to clean.

"Well, perhaps the first thing you should understand is that—contrary to popular belief—the First World War was not conducted in black and white." Laughter. "Nor, as I try to tell my grandchildren, was my own childhood." More laughter.

"It's actually an important point, if you think about it." Silence. "Maybe some of you have seen old footage of the war. Let me assure you that we did not march that fast." A few laughs.

"It was early 1918 when I landed in France. The war had been going on since 1914, when Germany invaded Belgium and France for all sorts of complicated reasons. And it was, well, it was like nothing I had ever imagined. Certainly not like the books I'd read with glorious saber charges and all that."

I felt a stabbing pain in my abdomen.

"There is an old saying that hatred for an enemy increases with distance from the battlefield, and even though we felt the Germans were our enemy, I think that's true. A Frenchman named Marie-Paul Rimbault once wrote, 'There's nothing so like a German soldier in his trench than a French soldier in *his*. They are both poor sods and that's all there is to it.' And I can tell you another thing: a dead German soldier looks a hell of a lot like a dead American."

The faces remained unmoved. Just coughing and the creaking of wooden seats.

Silly, isn't this Daniel, me standing up here trying to put things into words. I'm no good at this. What should I tell them? That war is bad? Well, we can't have Hitler running the show now can we? That even winning is not that much fun? That war is the best foundry for friendships? That's an interesting point, isn't it? That if only war didn't kill it would be the best thing to happen to most people, showing them how much they need each other, how important every moment and every friend

365

is. But then the war took those friendships away. Shall I tell them that, too? Shall I tell them how war strips everything down to its elemental beauty and horror, so that you can behold every nook and cranny of the human soul? But how?

There was a large blue pitcher of water on the podium and I poured myself a glass, which was difficult because when I picked the pitcher up it felt unexpectedly heavy and the ice cubes came tumbling into my glass much faster than I had anticipated. I used both hands and when I finished I took a sip from the glass and thought of what to say next. When I leaned back toward the microphone the sound system made feedback noises, which stopped when I tapped the microphone with my finger.

"There is one thing that scares soldiers more than dying and that's being forgotten. Maybe it's different now but I don't think so. When World War II started, the War Graves Commission from the First War still hadn't finished accounting for all the dead. Well, if you ever go to France you'll see all the cemeteries and monuments, the dead from one war right next to another. It's quite something, to think that a soldier from the Second World War could take cover behind the headstone of his father who fell in the First War.

"But you're probably more interested in what the war was like from a soldier's point of view." I took another sip of water. "Well, believe it or not it was awfully boring at times. There's a great deal of marching and waiting around and just trying to keep comfortable. We were in trenches most of the time. Sort of a technological stalemate. Why, a person could walk from the North Sea to Switzerland without poking their nose above ground. The first gas attack—by the Germans—was during the Second Battle of Ypres in April 1915. Caused terrible panic. The first tanks were used in September 1916 by the British during the Battle of the Somme. But it was really the artillery and the machine gun that ruled the day, though dogfights were something to watch.

"But maybe I should tell you about the stretcher-bearers. There was this young fellow...now what was his name?"

I stopped again and sipped more water. My face felt hot and I wondered if I could ask that the lights be turned down. Was that Jeffrey down there in the front? I looked for Sarah but couldn't find her.

"Let's see, where was I? Well, there were different types of gases. Chlorine gas. Phosgene gas. Mustard gas. There was nothing to do for the victims but watch them suffocate. Maybe the best way to tell you about the effects of gas is to read a passage from something I've brought along."

I searched my coat pockets twice before finding the piece of paper folded in an inside pocket. I opened it and laid it flat on the podium, pressing the creases with my palm. "It was written by a nurse. She wrote:

"'I wish those people who write so glibly

about this being a holy war...could see a case—to say nothing of ten cases—of mustard gas in its early stages—could see the poor things burnt and blistered all over with great mustard-coloured suppurating blisters, with blind eyes...all sticky and stuck together, and always fighting for breath, with voices a mere whisper, saying that their throats are closing and they know they will choke.'"

I folded the piece of paper and placed it back in my jacket pocket. When I looked out again I could only see the lights. I felt dizzy and leaned hard against the podium.

"The first day of the Battle of the Somme was the bloodiest day of the war. The British alone suffered some sixty thousand casualties. Can you imagine such a thing? Rows of men fourteen miles long walking shoulder to shoulder into German machine-gun fire? The hospitals were so swamped that thousands of wounded were sent across the Channel to Britain without even having their wounds cleaned. The trains—endless gray trains—pulled up to Charing Cross and Paddington stations in London, full of the wounded. And over at Victoria Station, well that's where many of the men began their journey to the front, hundreds of thousands of them waving good-bye to loved ones. If you go there you might stand still for a moment, close your eyes and then look for the sea of khaki on the platforms. Try to see their faces, if you can, and then look at the faces of their mothers and fathers and wives and children. During the war the stone archway there became known as the Gate of Good-bye."

I paused and pulled a handkerchief from my pocket to wipe my forehead. "Did you know that on the eve of World War II more than three thousand British veterans of the previous war were still confined to mental asylums? No you didn't, did you? And even now, around Verdun, some ten million unexploded shells still sleep in the soil." I took a few steps back, struggling to maintain my balance. "Well, what else can I tell you about the war, about being a veteran of the war?" I wiped my forehead again, slowly folding the handkerchief before returning it to my pocket. Then I looked out into the white lights and felt a tremendous sadness that made it difficult to talk.

I can't make them understand, Daniel. I can't make anybody understand. Maybe you could have but I can't. I never have been able to. Except for Julia. She understood.

I steadied myself and cleared my throat. "You probably didn't know that I'm the last of them, did you? It's true. All gone but me, an old cracked vessel that holds their lives frozen in my memory. But after me?"

I took another sip of water and then felt another sharp pain in my stomach as I gripped the podium. There was lots of coughing and throat-clearing, or maybe it wasn't that. I listened closely, closing my eyes to hear better.

"Who's out there?" I squinted into the lights but could not see. "Daniel?"

"Mr. Delaney?"

"Is that you, Daniel?"

"Mr. Delaney?"

"Our artillery hadn't destroyed their entanglements. There was just no way through."

"Sir, please?"

I stepped back, turning my head to listen. "Daniel, are you in the wire?"

"Please, Mr. Delaney."

"Daniel's in the wire."

"Please, sir."

The sudden wet warmth in my pants. Blood? Have I been hit? Oh God.

"Come sit down, Mr. Delaney."

◆　◆　◆

I SPENT all day writing notes of apology to Jeffrey and Sarah and the school but nothing sounded adequate. Maybe tomorrow the proper words will come. Right now I must sleep.

◆　◆　◆

"IT'S BEEN two weeks since I last got a letter from my mysterious friend," said Sarah, holding her clipboard up to her chest.

"Maybe he's not well."

"Wouldn't he tell me? I hope he hasn't lost interest."

"I don't imagine that."

"If he was ill I'd want to help him."

"Yes, of course you would."

"Funny how important his letters have

become to me. Can you miss someone you have never met?"

"Oh, I think so."

"Well then I miss him."

♦　♦　♦

ON THE FOURTH day I saw her. She was sitting at a café near the Arc de Triomphe drinking coffee and sketching on a small pad. She looked up as I approached and smiled.

"Julia." I ran toward her and hugged her, feeling my eyes water as I held her and kissed her head, which she buried in the crook of my neck. "Thank God."

"I had to come," she said, whispering into my ear.

I pulled back from her and looked into her eyes, then hugged her again. After a moment we sat down. When the waiter came I ordered white wine for both of us.

"Can you stay for a while?" I asked.

"A few days."

"Spend them with me."

"But what about—"

"She's off sightseeing and shopping a lot with her sister. I can get away, for a few hours at least."

She studied my face, then looked down. "I didn't know if I should come, but I had to."

"I waited for you every day."

She smiled and caressed the side of my face with the back of her hand.

When the wine arrived I took a long sip

and pulled out my cigarettes, offering her one. She took it, then put her other hand on mine as we watched the pedestrians stroll by. Then she said, "You never told me how Daniel died."

I finished my glass and set it down gently, then took a deep breath and began slowly, not looking at her: "We were attacking—it was like a seesaw: attack, retreat, counterattack—anyway, there were about five hundred yards between the lines and our sector was to break through at a point softened by our artillery. 'Get the machine gunners and it's a walk over,' that's what we were told." I poured myself more wine and took a drink.

"Daniel didn't seem nervous. He never did to me, but I was terrified. Most of us were. This was the big push. No stopping. 'The armies of France are depending on you,' that sort of thing."

"And?"

"We couldn't do it."

"You couldn't break through?"

"We couldn't find any openings in the German wire." I stubbed out my cigarette and lit another one.

"Did..."

"It's not an unusual story. Happened all the time."

"Did you see Daniel?"

"He was right next to me when we went over the top." I remembered his face; the strange look in his eyes and how he had just started to say something when the whistle went off. What was he going to say?

"He was always right next to me, like he was looking out for me."

"And then..."

"We were up and running. All of us. There was so much noise and smoke. Things were flying around. Like a tremendous storm."

"Did Daniel get to the wire?"

I looked at her, then turned away.

"None of the boys had a chance. They were just cut down." I heard my voice breaking.

"Did you see Daniel?"

"I saw Daniel." I was whispering now.

"He was dead?"

I paused, staring up toward the sky.

"Please tell me the truth. It's all I have left." She was leaning forward now, holding my hands in hers.

"He was caught in the wire."

"He died in the wire?"

"Yes."

"You're sure."

I nodded.

"And how quickly did he die?"

"Not quickly enough."

"You could hear him?"

"Yes, I could hear him."

She buried her head in her hands.

After I paid the bill we got up and walked to Notre Dame and lit a candle. Then we sat near the back and looked up at the stained glass windows and wished to God we still knew how to pray.

◆ ◆ ◆

"WHO IS SHE?" Martin was standing over my sketch pad, which lay open on my bed.

"Who is who?"

"Who is the woman you keep drawing?"

"Oh, her." I gestured toward the unfinished charcoal portrait of Julia, which I had drawn the day before. "Just a woman."

"There is no such thing as 'just a woman,'" he said, picking up the picture to examine it closely.

"Okay. It's somebody I once knew."

"Why do you keep drawing pictures of her?"

I shrugged.

"She's very pretty." He gently placed the pad back on the bed.

"She was much prettier than that."

"Want to tell me about her?"

I thought about it for a moment. "What are your plans for the day?"

"Plans? I don't have any plans. My schedule is wide open." He grinned.

I spent the rest of the day telling Martin all about Julia.

◆　　◆　　◆

THE UNEXAMINED life may not be worth living, but are we sure the examined life is? After nearly a century of scrutinizing my life with forensic intensity, I have my doubts.

It's late afternoon and I'm sitting at my desk, writing, thinking, puzzling over things; an old tea drinker reading his last cup of leaves, desperate for revelation. Through the window I can see Howard and Martin playing croquet. Helen crosses the lawn quickly, as though in pursuit of somebody. I draw the blinds, then turn to a fresh page of my journal.

Julia once asked me to what extent I felt I was really my true self in public, and all I could say was very little. She said it's a pity what a gap there is between our public and private selves, probably the loneliest piece of no-man's-land in the world, she called it. Then she told me that she was devastated the first time she realized how far apart everybody really was, even close friends.

"What about you and Daniel?" I asked.

"I think we were as close as two people can get, in the time we had."

"Was it close enough?"

"It was close enough."

And that's what we all long for, isn't it? To connect, if only momentarily, clasping hands across the chasm, which is why drinking buddies at the bar seem almost love-struck as they fall over each other in rapid and raucous agreement; why friends and lovers whisper in intimate code, attempting to bridge the divide with ropes and pulleys and secret handshakes that belie their permanent solitude.

Maybe not being ourselves is what kills us, sometimes decades before we die. Daniel understood that. So did Julia. And they saved me from that, didn't they? But then they left me.

I open the blinds again and peer out. Martin and Howard are bent over, tugging at a cro-quiet wicket. Helen stands nearby, vigilant. Suddenly she looks at my window and points, a big smile surging across her face, then heads toward the building. I quickly put my journal away, hurry into the bathroom and shut the door.

◆　　◆　　◆

WE MET the next day at the Eiffel Tower. Julia was standing at the bottom waiting for me. We climbed up to the third platform before stopping to look out over Paris.

"What did you tell Charlotte?" she asked, after catching her breath.

"I told her I wanted to explore some military museums—she would hate that—and that I was meeting Page for dinner."

"Did she mind?"

"Not at all." It was true, she didn't mind. Charlotte was good about that; giving me my freedom. But not this much. How unfair. I tried not to think of her.

Julia spread her hands out along the railing and took a deep breath. "It's the most beautiful view in the world," she said finally.

"No, I have the most beautiful view in the world." I pressed up against her back and put my arms around her waist, then rested my chin on her shoulder. She leaned back against me and turned her head to kiss my cheek.

"Did you and Daniel come up here?"

My stomach tightened. "It was closed."

"He would have loved this view. He would hike all day just for a good view."

"I can never be Daniel," I said suddenly.

She turned quickly toward me. "I don't want you to." She stared into my eyes, then kissed me hard on the lips. I enjoyed the feel of her body pressed against mine.

"Let's see Paris," she said, taking my hand and heading back down the stairs.

We stopped first at Napoleon's tomb, staring at the smooth red porphyry and imagining its contents. I tried to remember the various types of coffins but I couldn't, so I read them out loud from a guidebook. Then I explained to Julia that the twelve large statues surrounding the tomb were winged goddesses of victory, each representing a different campaign. She pointed out that their heads appeared to be bent in eternal defeat. As we stood there I thought of Daniel standing on the same spot and rubbing his hands against the same smooth stone and I remembered how he was sadder that day than I'd ever seen him. Did he just know? Did he look at Paris and see all the things he would never be able to show Julia? It must have been awful for the men who just *knew*. There were so many of them.

When we left the Dôme des Invalides we walked to the Palais du Luxembourg and sat in the gardens talking, then stopped for lunch along the Boulevard Saint-Michel. We sat for two hours, telling stories and laughing and holding hands under the table. I'd never seen Julia so happy, and it made me wonder what she looked like before Daniel died.

After lunch we went for a stroll, leaning close and whispering comments about the various people passing by. "Look at those two," I said, pointing toward a squat, boorish-looking man walking with a tall, spindly woman with ferretlike features. "Do you think opposites really attract?"

"Only until all the differences overwhelm them," she said.

"So what about those two?"

"They are in the overwhelmed-by-the-differences stage."

"No sex?"

"Two or three times a year. Lights out. Not a peep," she said, wrapping her arm around mine. Then she tugged at me and said, "Look at that woman's face there, the one on the bench. What does it tell you about her?"

I looked over at a middle-aged woman sitting alone, her purse clutched in her lap. "You tell me first. I want to know what you see."

Julia studied the woman for a moment, then said, "She's married, unhappily. She's just discovered that her husband has a lover but she doesn't really care because she's no longer attracted to him. She has two children, maybe three, and it's more work than she ever dreamed of. And now she's sitting on the bench wondering how she got to this place in her life and trying to gather the strength to run her errands and return home."

I looked back at the woman on the bench. Julia seemed exactly right.

"So what did you see when you first saw me?" I asked.

She was quiet for a moment. "That's a hard question." She opened her purse, pulled out a cigarette and lit one. "I'll tell you. I saw a kind, compassionate man who was much lonelier than he dared to realize."

I felt my eyes redden. I couldn't think of anything to say.

"I don't mean to hurt your feelings."

I shrugged. "You were right."

"So what did you see when you first saw me?"

I ran my fingers through my hair, then shoved my hands in my pockets.

"You don't have to answer that," she said.

"I want to." But how to put it?

She looked at me, waiting.

"I saw what I'd always been looking for."

She smiled shyly, as though she didn't really believe me. I wanted to continue but couldn't think of what to say, not without saying too much.

We kept walking for a while, stopping to browse at the bookstalls along the quay. Then we bought a bottle of wine and sat along the embankment drinking and holding hands and watching the boats go by.

"I wish I had been able to find you, after the war," I said.

"I wish you had too."

"Things would be different."

She nodded. "At least we finally met. I think Daniel would be glad of that."

"I have to tell you that I feel guilty," I said.

"That makes two of us."

"Not just for Charlotte but for Daniel too."

"Don't feel bad for Daniel. Not because of us."

"But I do."

"Yes, I know. I see it in your eyes." She leaned forward and kissed me on the lips.

"You're so different from Charlotte. I don't understand how I could have possibly..."

"You don't need to tell me. It's not my business. Anyway, it just makes me feel bad to hear about her."

"Then I'll stop," I said.

"Besides, we can't do anything to spoil this day." She was smiling again.

When we finished the wine we got up and walked for a while, stopping to look at La Madeleine. Then we sat in a café and split a large piece of chocolate mousse cake. I dropped my piece in my lap, then dropped it again on my shoe as I tried to pick it up. Julia burst out laughing, momentarily choking on the piece of cake in her mouth. Then she hiccuped.

"Oh, Christ," she said.

"Serves you right for laughing," I said, leaning over my shoe and trying to scoop up the cake with my spoon.

She pounded her fist against her chest.

"Try holding your breath."

"You don't think I've tried that?" she said, hiccuping midsentence.

"Just a thought."

"But there is something that might work," she said, eyeing me with a sultry grin.

"Oh, really?"

"Really."

When we got to her hotel room she unbuttoned my shirt and pants in silence, then slowly ran her hands along my chest as we stood by her bed. She slowly unbuttoned her blouse and slid out of her skirt. When she finished undressing I took her in my arms and carried her to the bed, then laid over her, supporting myself with my arms so that I could look down at her.

"You're so utterly beautiful," I said.

"So are you." She raised her head and kissed me, then pulled me against her. As I slowly ran my lips along her neck, down to her breasts, to her stomach, she arched her back and gently rocked her head back and forth. When I entered her she whispered my name, then pulled me deeper into her and arched her back more. I held her with all my strength, slowly lifting her into the air.

After we made love we lay in bed for an hour looking at each other and listening to the sounds of the city below us. My mouth tasted of her sweat and every so often I pressed my nose against her flesh to breathe in the smell of her.

"I've thought about you my whole life," I said, running my fingertips across her skin.

"But you didn't know me." Her face was right up next to mine and damp strands of hair were stuck to her forehead.

"But I did, don't you see? It's the strangest thing but I've always known you, only I couldn't see your face until Daniel described you."

"Then you saw my face?"

"Yes, quite clearly. I just never dreamed I would be able to touch it."

When we made love again I was surprised by the strength of her arms and her legs and when I was inside of her I wanted to tell her that I loved her but I didn't. Or at least I don't think I did.

Afterward as we lay against each other I felt my limbs trembling from exertion and when I tried to make a fist I couldn't, which made me laugh.

"Why are you laughing?" she asked, nuzzling up against me.

"Because I feel so good," I said.

"Me too."

Her eyes watered.

"I've upset you."

"No, it's wonderful. It's just that I haven't been with anybody for years."

I pulled her closer and kissed her eyelids.

"You should never be alone," I said.

"Nobody should," she whispered.

◆　◆　◆

I DRESSED first and then sat in a chair in the corner and watched as she got dressed, pausing to sit on the edge of the bed to brush her hair.

"Let's go to the track," I said. "We could make the last couple of races at Auteuil."

"You really want to? I've never—"

"We'll hop in a taxi. Come on."

She smiled and took my hand as we headed out the door.

We sat at the top of the grandstand, watching the field through a pair of rented binoculars. Julia quickly mastered the various strategies—more than I had after a dozen efforts—and soon established a complicated betting system based on the names of the horses and jockeys. She won two hundred francs.

"I had no idea it was so easy to make money," she said, drawing stares as she tucked her latest winnings into her purse. I'd been losing precipitously.

"Maybe so, but you just don't get that sense of achievement that follows a nine-hour workday," I said, still breathless from running back and forth to the gambling windows.

Julia jumped to her feet again as the last race began and cheered her horse on. It was wonderful to see her so happy.

"I can't believe they can clear those hedges," she said, peering through the binoculars.

"Here comes the water jump," I said.

Two horses fell. Only one got up.

"Is the jockey hurt?" I asked.

"No, he seems all right. But the horse can't get up."

"Is it yours?"

"No. I don't care though, I just want it to get up." She kept staring through the binoculars. The horse remained on its side.

"What will they do?" she asked, after the race finished and the grandstand began to empty out.

"They'll wait until everybody leaves, then put it to death."

"That ruins the whole thing, doesn't it?" she said as we got into a taxi.

"Yes, I guess it does," I said. For the rest of the ride into the city I couldn't stop thinking of Giles telling me the best way to shoot a horse.

◆　◆　◆

THE BRIDGES over the Seine were lit up when we got back and we walked for half an hour along the river watching the fishermen and the flatboats and the way the light played off the water.

Suddenly Julia stopped, pushed me up against a lamppost and kissed me. I wrapped my arms around the small of her back and pulled her against me. When we started walking again she smiled at me and said, "I'm famished."

"Food?"

She nodded and said, "Then more kisses."

I kissed her again. "Deal."

We made our way to the Boulevard Saint-Germain where we stopped for dinner at a large brasserie.

As we took our seats Julia leaned toward me

and asked, "Do you think I should have visited Daniel's parents? I've thought about it a lot—they are Robin's grandparents—but I couldn't stand the idea of being turned away."

"I don't know. They'd be pretty old by now."

"It bothers me," she said.

"I can understand why." I paused for a minute, then said, "You must miss your mother a great deal."

She nodded slowly. "There are so many times when I wish I could ask her for advice. She was so good at the difficult decisions. I'm afraid that I'm not."

How was I at the difficult decisions?

"And I wish Robin could have been old enough to know her. She was all the family I've got."

"At least Robin's got a wonderful mother like you."

"But I'm not sure that's enough. I worry about her, not having a real family, not having a father or aunts or uncles or grandparents or even a house full of memories."

I couldn't think of what to say. Finally I said, "I'd love to meet her someday."

"Yes, I'd like that too."

The waiter brought the menus. "Do you understand any of this?" asked Julia, looking up at me.

"Not a word. I just choose randomly."

"Then I'll have what you have."

"Of course I may get the brains."

"Don't you dare."

She picked up the wine list. "Do you feel like champagne? I've only had it once before."

"Then let's remedy that." I ordered a bottle.

After we drank a toast I leaned forward and kissed her and said, "You know something? Daniel was right, everything does look different now."

"What do you mean?" She was smiling.

"I mean that I've never seen things this way before. Not this fork or that plate or the people at the next table or the trees or the buildings or the sky. It's all completely different."

She reached over and squeezed my hand. Then her smile slipped from her face. "When I first met you at the monument I felt scared," she said.

"Why?"

"Because certain people can change your life forever."

Did she really believe I could change her life? No, I'd never be what Daniel was to her. Nobody could. "You've changed mine," I said.

She nodded slowly. "To us," she said, raising her glass.

"To us."

She lit a cigarette, blowing the smoke up toward the ceiling. "What time do you have to get back?"

I looked down at my watch. "Not for hours."

"Would you take me dancing then? Just for a little while?"

"As long as you promise not to laugh at me."

"Why would I laugh at you?" she asked.

"Because I'm a lousy dancer."

"Good, we'll be perfect together."

We found a small nightclub not far from the restaurant, ordered drinks and then danced nonstop for an hour, laughing and kissing and trying not to fall over each other. Julia was full of animation as she tried to show me some steps and I noticed how the band members watched her and how she made them smile and I realized that she was the kind of person who changed the feeling in a room, so that others suddenly feel that they are in the right place. Is that the secret of life, to surround yourself with people who are so full of passion, people who know sadness but not bitterness? I looked into her face, which was alive with excitement, and then into her eyes, which were full of all the things you can only say with your eyes.

"Now just move your left foot like this," she said, demonstrating.

"You're gorgeous," I said, whispering into her ear.

"You're not listening."

"I was distracted. Anyway, I was raised not to stare at a woman's feet."

"I'm granting a special dispensation," she said.

"I'll take it," I said, staring down at her legs as she demonstrated a dance step once again.

When we returned to our seats my shirt clung to my chest and back with sweat but I didn't care. I wanted to stay out all night.

"This has been such a wonderful day," said

Julia, pulling her chair next to mine. "It's so different from my life."

"Mine too." I thought about that: how I felt as though I'd walked right out of my previous life and all its constraints and assumptions, if only for a few hours. Then I thought of Sean lying in his bed asleep, curled up like a tiny animal. Did he wonder why Daddy didn't give him a kiss good night?

"I think it's the unlived parts of our lives that fascinate us the most," she said, swiveling her empty glass in her hand. "So much remains dormant."

"But it doesn't have to be that way."

"No, but it usually is, isn't it?"

We sat for a while and then danced again, until I stepped on Julia's foot for the third time.

"It really doesn't hurt," she said, covering her mouth with her hands and trying to stifle laughter. "Honest."

"Let's give it a brief rest in any case," I said. When we returned to our table a well-dressed man with a friendly red face approached us.

"You like the band?" he asked, leaning over us.

"They're wonderful," said Julia.

He nodded approvingly.

"You're the owner?" I asked.

"Yes," he said proudly.

"It's a very lovely place," said Julia.

He studied us for a moment, resumed his large smile and said, "You are engaged, no?"

"Oh, no—"

"Yes, yes we are," I said. "How did you guess?"

Julia turned quickly and looked at me. I ignored her.

"I can always tell," he said. "It's in the language of the body and the eyes and the face. I never miss it. Allow me to buy you a drink." He turned and signaled a waiter. Then he leaned toward me and said, "Your fiancée is very beautiful."

"She is, isn't she?"

Julia was still staring at me, blushing.

"When will you be married?"

I turned to Julia and took her hand. "Darling?"

She looked at me, then at the owner. "That's a little tricky," she stuttered. "Things to iron out and all. The relatives. Finding the right spot..."

"Don't put it off," he said, looking at me. "Such a woman is easily lost." He winked. I hesitated before winking back.

When he left Julia leaned over and pinched me. "You're drunk," she said, smiling coyly.

"I just wanted to see what it would feel like to say that. I hope you're not embarrassed."

"Maybe caught off guard." She folded her cocktail napkin, then unfolded it. "So how did it feel?"

Again the burning in the chest, only stronger this time. "Good," I said softly. "Very good."

She blushed again and looked down at her napkin. When the band started up she stood and took my hand and led me back to the dance floor. I wrapped both my arms around her waist and she slung her arms around my neck, resting her cheek against mine so that my lips were near her ear.

"When do you go back to the States?" she asked.

"A week from today." Then I quickly added, "But I could change it, or send Charlotte and her sister and Sean ahead."

I felt her pull away slightly.

"You can't do that."

"I could come with you to Florence." Could I?

She pulled back more and looked at me. "You can't come with me, don't you see?"

I tried to think of what to say but I couldn't; the drinks had blurred my thoughts. How could I not be with her? But there was Charlotte and Sean. Too much in the way. Every choice impossible.

"Just hold me," she said, leaning against me again.

So I held her as close as I could and closed my eyes, letting the music take me.

◆　◆　◆

I'VE DECIDED to start smoking again. Just an occasional cigar out on the porch after dinner. I quit a pack-a-day habit in 1960, when a nagging cough convinced me that the surgeon general didn't smoke. That was the second biggest heartbreak of my life.

Cigarettes had been my punctuation in life, the periods, commas, hyphens and exclamation points (especially after sex) by which I divided and organized my day. Without them I felt like one endless run-on sentence; a formless, structureless bundle of anguish, always off balance, like a person forced to go weeks without looking at a clock. I groped and pawed at my shirt pocket as though searching for a phantom limb. What on earth to do with my hands, hour after hour, day after day, week after week? I studied other non-smokers to see what they did with their hands, but nothing felt natural, and my hands, particularly my right hand, fidgeted and twitched like those of a seamstress newly unemployed for the first time in decades.

After women and children—and sometimes before—cigarettes were the great love of my life, the one ever-satisfying constant. When I quit, it seemed that I was destined to spend the rest of my years in a state of acute discomfort, as though the very purpose of my life, the battle that would expend my life's energies, would be to not smoke. At bars I would position myself downwind from the nearest smoker and discreetly hyperventilate. In my dreams I sucked down three and four packs a night in desperate compensation.

Gradually, the cravings subsided, until cigarettes faded into the background like an ex-spouse; impossible to completely forget but no longer right in my face. But now? What the hell, right? So my clothes will stink again.

Not stinking hasn't helped much lately. And frankly, I could use a vice.

So it's settled. Tomorrow I'll take the bus into town and walk to The Smoke Shop and buy a box of Montecristo Double Coronas from the walk-in sliding glass humidor. That should last me.

◆　◆　◆

I WAS WALKING down the hallway to my room to use the bathroom when Erica smiled at me. Not just with her mouth but with her whole face, as though the curtains of a large stage had suddenly been pulled back to reveal a full orchestra, the instruments gleaming.

Oh, Lord.

I wonder what makes such a smile so hopeful and restorative; why beauty sometimes looks like a solution to life's most pressing problems, so much so that you want to drown in another, to wrap yourself around them like a speeding car around a telephone pole, horn blaring.

I think beauty represents a need in the eye of the beholder, a need that is never quite met. What you see isn't what you get; what you see is what you never get, which is why you can't stop staring.

"Hello, Erica."

When I got to my room I went to the bathroom, purposely avoiding the mirror, then grabbed my sketch pad and headed outside.

◆　◆　◆

I FEEL LIKE shit today, a miserable bundle of mounting symptoms. Dr. Tompkins hovered over me briefly, and someone hooked me to an IV. I think I saw Sarah but I'm not sure. I'm not sure of anything.

I remember another time, with nurses and doctors leaning over me. First the dressing station, just behind the front, where a medic administered antitetanic serum, then painted the shrapnel wound in my right thigh with iodine and taped a large absorbent pad over it. Then I was placed on the ground in a large crowded courtyard for twelve hours, until two men in bloody tunics finally lifted me into an ambulance and drove me back three or four miles to an evacuation hospital. Then more waiting on the packed floor of a dark corridor until I was carried into an operating room lit by the bare jet flame of a portable acetylene generator. The silver surgical instruments laid out on a white enamel table rattled occasionally as explosions shook the room and the overwhelming smell of chlorine, gas, gangrene, acetylene and ether made me gag. I struggled not to vomit as a tired-looking nurse smeared Vaseline on my face and then placed a mask over it and administered ether. I fought it briefly but two men held me down.

Later I awoke to another nurse cutting away my bandages. Then a doctor probed the wound with instruments and swabbed it with gauze soaked in Dakin's solution. Then he removed small red rubber tubes that had been partly buried in the wound and replaced them with new tubes, which dangled out of the wound after it was dressed again. Every two hours a nurse poured more Dakin's solution through a glass reservoir and into the tubes to irrigate the wound, until it was time to dress it again.

"How are you doing, Patrick?"

It's a soft voice, close to my face. A warm hand is pressed against my forehead. I stare upward at the light until I see a nurse. Sarah. Yes, Sarah. I nod and then slowly run my right hand down to my right thigh and feel the long scar with my fingertips. With the other hand I hold tightly to the emergency call button.

◆　　◆　　◆

I WISH GOD still worked. Or at least I wish some of the substitutes were more reassuring; that there was some plausible alternative to unretouched reality, a way to skirt the messy stuff. A rebuttal to the darkness.

Let's see, there's materialism (If I'm just a doomed creature at least I'll be a comfortable, well-attired one, God-like in my furnishings if not my chromosomes); there's science (The idea that we might outsmart God, somehow pick his locks and take over the controls—hah!); there's the woozy notion of salvation through self-knowledge, though it's awfully expensive and besides, it doesn't stop the pain (Insight alone never does, on the contrary, it can strip wounds raw); and there is love, which also seems flawed, but not as flawed perhaps.

So if I can't be writ large upon the heavens,
if I can't entrust myself to God,
then at least let me alight upon the
soul of a woman,
if only briefly
before I plummet.

♦　♦　♦

I DIDN'T SEE Julia the next day. There was no time. I took care of Sean in the morning and then we met Charlotte and Margaret for a picnic in the Bois de Boulogne. When we got back to the hotel Sean took a nap while Margaret went for a walk. Charlotte and I sat and played cards and then I went out for an hour, hurrying over to Julia's hotel to leave her a note telling her I'd try to see her the next day and that I missed her. On the way back I stopped at a store and bought her a gift.

We ate dinner that night at a small restaurant on the Champs-Elysées but left early after Sean unexpectedly hurled a spoon across the dining room, knocking a small, decorative vase off a ledge, which landed on a woman's plate, cracking it and the vase and causing the woman to erupt in expletives. (I never knew he possessed such an arm.) After I settled with the owner we went for a stroll along the Seine. Margaret was talkative but both Charlotte and I were quiet. I couldn't decide whether that was normal or whether Charlotte sensed that I was full of secrets; secrets that I feared were tumbling from my eyes.

When we got back to the hotel Margaret and Charlotte wrote letters while I read a book to Sean.

"We haven't been to Versailles yet," said Charlotte, licking an envelope. "Why don't we go tomorrow?"

"That's a wonderful idea!" said Margaret. "I've been reading *all* about it."

"But there's so much I still want to see in Paris," I said.

"You can't miss Versailles," said Charlotte.

"The truth is, I don't feel very good," I said, putting down the book and lifting Sean off my lap.

Charlotte eyed me closely.

"He has been acting strange," said Margaret, who often spoke of me as though I were in another room. I never did like Margaret, and my feelings for her now were testing new lows. "Maybe you should go and buy yourself a new suit."

"A new suit?"

"Might make you feel better."

"Really?"

When Margaret left the room, Charlotte said, "Are you all right? You seem a little..."

"I'm fine. Just tired."

"You're mad that I didn't go to the dedication with you, aren't you?"

"No, not at all."

"I should have gone. It was selfish of me not to."

"I'm not mad. I promise. Anyway, you would have been bored."

"But I should have been with you." She came closer and gave me a hug. Then she looked up at me and said, "You have to let go of it eventually."

"Let go?"

"It's been ten years."

"Ten years."

"You can't let it ruin your life." She leaned forward and kissed me lightly on the cheek. "You get some sleep."

They left at nine the next morning. I jumped out of bed as soon as the door closed, then bathed and dressed and ran to Julia's hotel. She was in the sparse dining room beyond the lobby having breakfast.

"I've got the whole day free," I said.

She stood and kissed me. "Where are they?"

"Versailles." I laughed to myself. "I can just see my sister-in-law looking at herself in all those mirrors. They'll be there for days."

"So what shall we do?" Julia asked, sitting back down and sipping her coffee.

"Why don't we lock ourselves in your room and see what happens?"

She pulled out her room key and dangled it in front of me. Her smile made me hunger for her skin against mine.

The waiter came and took my order. When my breakfast arrived I wolfed it down, with Julia watching, then paid the bill and followed her to her room. As soon as she closed the door I picked her up and spun her in the air and carried her to the bed, laying her down gently. We undressed each other wordlessly, then sat up on the bed on our knees, looking at each other and tracing our fingers across each other's skin. I ran my hands down her back and along her thighs and then up along her sides and shoulders before gently cupping her breasts and kissing them and pushing her down against the pillow. As we made love she struggled not to cry out and afterward we clung to each other in silence. I don't know how much time passed.

"There's so much I want to know about you," I said, sitting up and reaching for my cigarettes.

"There is not much to tell."

"I think there always is." I lit one, then passed it to her. We were lying side by side on our elbows, facing each other.

"Ask me then."

"When is your birthday?"

"October twenty-eighth."

"Who's your favorite author?"

"Emily Brontë. Then Tolstoy."

"Composer?"

"Chopin."

"Color?"

"Depends on the day."

"Season?"

"Fall."

"Which do you prefer, mountains or beaches?"

"Beaches."

"Are you more interested in the past or the future?"

"Oh, definitely the past."

"Do you play any instruments?"

"I wanted to. We didn't have the money."

"Are you a morning or a night person?"

"Both."

"You can't be both."

"Who says so?"

"Do you have trouble sleeping?"

"Only since I met you." She smiled.

"What's your favorite food?"

"English."

"English?"

"I'm joking. Italian, actually, though I'm not a food person. And remember, I'm an awful cook."

"I'll cook you a meal someday," I said.

"When is someday?"

I leaned back on the pillow and stared at the ceiling, noticing the cracks in the light blue paint.

"I'm sorry, I shouldn't have said that," she said. "Anyway, we have all day. Let's talk about today." She rolled over on top of me.

"First, I have something for you." I slid out from under her and reached for my coat. I pulled a slim box from one of the pockets and handed it to her.

She opened it slowly, keeping her eyes on me. When she saw the necklace she closed the box quickly, then opened it again.

She studied my face for a moment, then

looked down again at the thin gold necklace, which carried a sapphire pendant. "It's stunning," she said.

"Put it on."

She carefully pulled it out of the box and clasped it around her neck. "I've never had anything this beautiful." She stood and looked in the mirror. "You're crazy, Patrick."

"That I am." I got up and stood behind her and put my arms around her waist, running my hands slowly up her stomach to her breasts. She gradually arched her back and turned her head to kiss me. Once I was inside of her I came quickly and powerfully and then found myself on the verge of tears. *So this is it: this is how close two people can feel.*

When we got back in bed we lay facing each other and looking into each other's eyes for several minutes without talking.

"You've made everything else worth it; everything I've been through. I didn't feel that way before I met you."

"Because of the war..." she asked softly, tracing her fingers along my face.

I nodded. She kissed my forehead and then hugged me.

"During the war I used to think it was no longer right for people to laugh and sing, not with all the butchery. And I couldn't bear to think of the rich sitting on plush velvet seats in the opera houses of Paris and Berlin and Vienna, just a train ride from hell. It seemed almost criminal."

"And what did Daniel think?"

I smiled. "He thought we had to keep laughing."

◆　　◆　　◆

AFTER WE dressed Julia wanted to take her easel down to the quay for a few hours and try to paint the boats on the Seine. We stopped near the Pont Neuf across from the narrow tip of the Ile de la Cité and after she had set up I sat nearby and watched her.

"Do you mind me staring?" I asked.

"I'm flattered."

She began mixing paints on her palette, then dabbed her brush and leaned toward the canvas. I looked at her long fingers and her wrists and her arms and her legs and then back at her fingers, which carefully stroked the paintbrush back and forth.

"Do you know how I feel right now?"

She looked over at me. "How?"

"I can't really describe it."

"Try."

I thought for a moment. "I think the only reason a lot of people hang in there day after day is because they hope that one day they'll feel like this." I looked out over the river and watched a boat glide by. "Daniel once asked me if I'd ever been in love. He knew I hadn't. I think that worried him and now I understand why."

She put down her brush and stared at me. Her eyes were exceptionally clear and full of intent.

"He knew I had nothing to hold on to. No memory of utter joy and ecstasy. Nothing that could endure the desolation. Whereas even in the worst of it, he had a place to go. He had you."

She was silent for a while, still staring at me, and then she picked up her brush and began painting again. "So now you'll always have a place to go," she said, trying her best to smile.

♦　♦　♦

I SAT THERE for two hours, just watching her and feeling the sun on my face and listening to the sounds of Paris. I'd never felt that way before: so rapturous and serene, as though I had stumbled upon the answers to life's hardest questions. What I kept thinking was that I wished everybody had a chance to know such a feeling, if only for a day. Especially the millions who died in the dirt and the mud. Otherwise, what was the sense in being born?

After Julia finished we took her things back to her hotel, then went window-shopping, leaning against each other as we peered into storefronts and laughed and marveled at various items on display. As we passed a church we heard music playing and went inside and stood near the back listening to a small concert performed by university students. I tried to make out the story in the stained glass above them but couldn't, except for the last scene. Jesus again, suspended from the cross and looking down at us, desperate for a cleaning.

We stayed until the end of the concert, then walked to the Bois de Boulogne. When we reached the grass Julia bent over and took off her shoes, holding them in one hand. "Did you know that I'm very fast?" she asked.

"I didn't."

"It's true."

"How fast?"

"Probably faster than you," she said, smiling.

"That's not so fast," I said. "Bet I can catch you before you reach that tree over there."

"Only if I let you," she said. Then she kissed me quickly, turned and took off running. I followed, trying not to laugh out loud as I struggled to catch up. Just before she reached the tree she turned and spread her arms out, catching me so that I fell on top of her.

"I was closing in," I said, rolling over so that she was on top of me.

"I couldn't wait any longer," she said. "Besides, I know how much men hate to lose." She began tickling me until I rolled back over on her and pinned her down. As I began kissing her I felt overwhelmed with the desire to be inside of her.

"Do you have any idea how pretty you are?" I said.

She smiled and said, "Do you have any idea how much I love kissing you?" Then she kissed me quickly all over my face before rolling over back on top of me. I held her face in my hands and stared at her.

"Now you do," she said. She rolled off me and stood up. We brushed the leaves off each other before walking arm and arm through the park, stopping to watch a group of old men play *boule*.

After we left the park we took a taxi to Sacré-Coeur and sat on the sloping lawn, looking out over the city. Julia took my hand and kissed it. "I haven't felt this content—this peaceful—in so long that I'd almost forgotten what it's like," she said.

I turned to say something, hesitated for a minute, then said, "There is something I don't understand about you."

"What is that?" She looked anxious.

"I don't understand how you could be so alone for so many years. Especially someone like you. It doesn't make sense."

"Whose life does?"

"Haven't other men proposed to you?"

"God, no." She laughed.

"I would have."

"Patr—"

"It's true."

"You shouldn't say that. It's too much for me."

"I can't bear to think of you being so alone; of us being apart."

"At least now I'll always have you to think about." She leaned against me.

"But that's not enough. It's not enough for me. I need to see you and touch you and hold you. At night when I'm in my hotel I can't sleep because I crave you so badly."

"I'm here now," she said, putting her arms around me.

"Don't you know what people would give for this?" I tried to keep my voice steady. "*Everything*, Julia. Most people would give everything for this."

She nodded slowly, then rested her head on my chest as I lay back.

"So we're luckier than most people," she said softly.

"Are we?"

She didn't answer.

We must have fallen asleep because when we awoke the sky had changed colors and the air was cooler, portending rain. We walked through the streets of Montmartre for a while, pausing to admire the work of local artists, then stopped for dinner.

"I want to take you to the Louvre," she said, after we had finished eating.

"I'd love that. Ever since you first told me about going to the Louvre, about how the things that you saw brought tears to your eyes, well, I've dreamed of going there with you."

She looked down at her watch. "You'd better get back to your hotel."

"There's a little time."

"But not enough, is there?"

I leaned forward and took her hand. "I could leave Charlotte."

She pulled her hand back. "No. No you can't. Not your wife and son. Please don't say that."

"But what will we do?"

She was silent for a moment, then said,

"Don't you understand? There is nothing for us to do."

"What do you mean? I couldn't bear to lose you."

"I couldn't bear to lose Daniel."

"But you don't have to lose me."

"I never had you, *don't you see?*"

I looked down at the table, fighting back tears. My fists were clenched. "Goddamn it."

She put her hand on my back and rubbed it. "I should never have come to Paris."

"Don't say that." I lit a cigarette, inhaling deeply.

"I won't ruin your life, Patrick. I'd rather never see you again than know that I took you away from your wife and child."

"Do you mean that?"

She nodded slowly as she bit her lip.

"I'd always find you," I said, leaning toward her. But when I said that I thought I saw fear in her eyes. Of me? Of what she'd done?

"Please don't make this any harder," she said.

When the waiter brought the check she insisted on paying it. Outside it was raining lightly and the streets were quiet. We walked slowly back to her hotel, pausing to watch the light from the street lamps skip across the puddles at our feet. We stood out front for a while, unwilling to say good night yet too sad to make hurried love in her room. Finally she said, "Do you know why I was so upset when I visited the Louvre, why I ran out?"

"Why?"

"Because for the first time I realized what the Louvre says."

"What does it say?"

"That our lives—all of our lives—are a struggle between love and loss."

"And which wins?"

"That's what I can't decide."

I ran my fingers along her cheek, then kissed her forehead.

"I'll be waiting for you," she said, as she turned and walked into her hotel. I watched her cross the lobby to the stairs, then hurried back to my hotel and tiptoed into bed. In the morning when Charlotte asked where I had been I told her I'd felt better and gone down the street for some dinner where I met a French veteran who told wonderful stories and plied me with drink until I could barely walk.

◆　◆　◆

IN THE ROOM across the hall there lives a blind and partially paralyzed woman named April Lessing. She never comes out, not unless she has to, so I go visit her a few times a week. I sit on the small metal and wood chair next to her bed in the permanent semidarkness and we talk. Sometimes she puts her hands on my face, running her fingers slowly from my forehead down to my chin. It bothered me at first, especially when she described what my face felt like. Nice high cheekbones, but a bit thin in the cheeks, she would say. Good chin. Strong jawline. (If only she knew.) But now

407

I rather enjoy it, though it often feels more revealing than I would like.

April is ninety-two. Her voice is low and hoarse like a smoker's, though she says she quit forty years ago. She keeps three sets of rosary beads by her bed: one pink, one yellow and one white, and still complains about the reforms of Vatican II. "They took all the mystery out of it," she says. "Putting the mass in English."

"I think the idea was that it would be better if people could understand what was being said," I respond.

"People don't *want* to understand what's being said, don't you see? Once you understand the words the whole thing is not nearly so impressive."

April's husband died thirty-six years ago, at the age of sixty-seven. "I told my daughters, 'Whatever you do, don't marry an older man unless you plan to marry twice,'" she says. "It's so silly, women marrying older men when the men die seven or eight years before them anyway! Dumbest thing I ever heard."

"But if they fall in love..."

"That's what happened to me, only I didn't realize that all the men would die off in their seventies. They were dying like flies at the club we belonged to. Heart attacks on the golf course, strokes in the locker room, seizures in the dining room. Goodness, what a mess! And most of the ladies can't find a decent second husband because they are all dead or dying or married and dying."

"I didn't realize how exceptional I was."

"Oh, but we've given up on you!"

"You have?"

"Why sure, you're already taken."

"I am?"

"Of course you are. You've been taken all your life. Do you think I'm blind?"

◆　◆　◆

YOU KNOW HOW when you are young, you can't imagine forgetting how old you are, whereas once you hit middle age it becomes necessary—especially if the question is fired out of the blue—to consult your fingers? Well, when you get even older the same thing happens with what year it is, not just whether it's 1980 or 1981 but whether it's 1980 or 1970. And then you think to yourself, Good God, which young chap is president these days? And as you're trying to remember you're suddenly flooded by the childhood smell of pencil shavings, and there you are, emptying the silver and black pencil sharpener bolted to the wall of the classroom near the pretty girl in the blue and white gingham dress, which is why you're at the pencil sharpener in the first place. And then pain brings you back again, wondering what year it is and who is president.

◆　◆　◆

I JUST FINISHED reading Jung's autobiography: *Memories, Dreams, Reflections*. I was struck by his inability to go to Rome. He said he didn't have the strength for it; the strength to deal with "the spirit that broods there," a spirit suffusing every stone and layered back through antiquity. The last time he tried to go he fainted while buying the tickets.

What about me? Would I have the strength to go back to France?

◆　　◆　　◆

IT WAS ONLY after the police found me half a mile from Great Oaks after dark and without even my customary sweater that Dr. Tompkins told me, in his roundabout way, that I was losing my mind.

"Early onset," he said, assuring me that it would never catch up to and overrun the cancer.

"Brain rot, eh?"

"You might want to get your affairs in order."

"How did you know I was having affairs?"

He didn't smile.

All I remember is how happy Sarah was to see me when the officer escorted me through the front door just before midnight. And I remember that she hugged me and that she almost cried and I wondered what horrible thing had happened to her until she told me. Then I felt ashamed like a kindergartner who has crapped in his pants. And that's when it was agreed that I wouldn't be allowed to leave the grounds on my own again.

I waited a long time for sleep that night, and

when it came it whisked me far far away all on my own.

♦   ♦   ♦

NOT MUCH longer now, Julia. Not much longer at all.

♦   ♦   ♦

I THINK most of us are haunted deep within by a sense of lost perfection, by the nagging feeling not just that things could be better but that they once were better; that we can actually, in our hearts, recall a feeling of joy that we cannot reproduce, and that is our ultimate agony. It's not just that we can imagine utter happiness, it's that we've tasted it; perhaps, as Freud would say, at the breast of our mothers. And having tasted it, nothing else tastes the same, which is why so much of life is so bitterly sweet.

I don't think we ever stop trying to find it again, that sense of infinite well-being and security. Deep in our hearts we all long for a sort of Restoration. That's what love offers: our only chance back to an ethereal communion we once enjoyed. And maybe that's why love even at first sight feels so much like a reunion.

And without love? Without love we are like songbirds who cannot sing.

♦   ♦   ♦

IS JULIA DEAD? I couldn't bear to think so.

◆　◆　◆

I WAS LEANING against an oak tree near the gazebo vomiting when Martin found me.

"You all right?" he asked, putting his hand on my back.

I waved him off and retched again.

"I'll get a nurse," he said, turning to go.

"No, stay."

"But you..." I vomited again, my whole body convulsing as Martin held on to my shoulder. "Let me get someone," he said.

"No, please, it's nothing." I wiped my mouth with my sleeve.

"You're sick. I'm going to get the doctor." He turned again to go.

"Wait."

He turned back toward me.

"This isn't the big C it's the little c," I said.

"Huh?"

"Cigar. I had a goddamn cigar."

"You had a cigar? But you don't smoke."

"I know I don't smoke."

"So why did you have a cigar?" He looked confused.

"Because I wanted one."

"It made you sick, huh?"

"Yes, it made me sick." I pushed myself into an upright position.

"Here, let me help you," he said, taking my arm and leading me across the lawn and back inside.

"I don't think you should smoke anymore," he said.

"No, I don't think I should either."

◆　　◆　　◆

GOD, IT'S ME, Patrick. Patrick Delaney. Patrick E. Delaney. Room four, if that helps. I was just wondering, do the people who believe in you know something I don't? Do you give them some sort of secret understanding or insight or signal? Because if you do, I believe you've overlooked me. (A flick of the lights will suffice.) And if you don't, why then I'm baffled.

The truth is—and I'll keep this short because you must be quite pressed for time—the truth is that it's getting awfully tempting to believe in you, which is to say that the alternatives are looking rather bleak. I hate to say it, Lord, but you may, finally, have me on the ropes. But I was wondering: if you really do exist (and I still have grave doubts), any chance you could lighten up a bit? And must I always do the talking?

◆　　◆　　◆

I COULDN'T see Julia for two days. It was raining hard and Sean was sick and there was no way to get away. So all I could do was run to her hotel each day through the rain and leave her a note telling her that I missed her and that I'd try again the next day.

413

And then I would sit next to Sean's bed and put wet washcloths on his forehead and sing him "Old King Cole" and "Swanee River" and "Five Little Sailors," and whenever I thought of sailing for New York I would clench my fists and teeth and struggle not to cry out at the rain.

◆　　◆　　◆

YESTERDAY I noticed a scent of bark outside that I had not smelled in years. While the bark lingered in my nose, flushing out ancient treehouses and campfires and games of tag and capture the flag, I noticed that the birds seemed to be singing louder than usual and the leaves on the trees looked more pronounced, almost exaggerated in their lush clarity. I sat perfectly still, waiting for some evidence of a stroke or heart attack. But nothing hurt. I took long deep breaths, slowly at first then one right after another, tasting the air that swirled within my lungs and thinking how the first scent of autumn is like coming across a lost album of childhood photographs.

And today too, I feel, well, *good*. Clearheaded. Crisp even, though it fades in and out. Everything seems to have unusual depth and color as though my senses are on heightened alert. I feel a fullness in my chest. It's a pleasing fullness; like the deep welling one feels before a good, overdue cry.

Only two things in my life ever had the power to contain me wholly in the present moment: Julia and the German Army. But now? What is this?

It's death, isn't it? The encore. I smiled, trying not to laugh as some visitors walked quickly by. Well if this is death's approach, then I no longer envy those who die abruptly, never experiencing the power of death's proximity. Let me breathe as deep as I can and close my eyes for a moment. Yes, that feels so peaceful, so relaxing, as though everything is brimming over.

Oh Lord, I'm crying now and I don't have my handkerchief. But I'm not sad. No, not at all. I'm wildly happy like a boy in the rain, face up to the clouds, arms aloft, fists clenched. Alive!

◆　　◆　　◆

WHEN I SAW Julia again she was standing in front of her hotel, leaning against the wall with her hands in the pockets of her raincoat. Her hair was wet from the rain and she didn't smile when she saw me. I had only a few minutes before I had to meet Charlotte and Margaret.

"What is it?" I said, running my hands along her cheeks.

She turned her face away.

"Tell me. Please."

She turned back and looked at me. Her eyes were swollen.

"I saw you and your wife and son. I watched you come out of your hotel."

"You watched us?"

"And I followed you to the park. I watched you playing with Sean and I saw how you and Charlotte held hands as you walked." She swallowed hard. "You looked so lovely together. All three of you."

"But why—"

"I had to know what it would feel like. I had to see that you were married."

I remembered carrying Sean on my shoulders in the park and galloping like a horse and then hiding a coin in my hand and pretending to pluck it from behind his ears, a trick that never ceased to delight him, causing him to search behind his ears several times a day.

I nervously reached for my cigarettes. Julia began crying.

"It felt awful, Patrick."

"I'm sorry."

"I couldn't bear it."

"You shouldn't—"

"It's my fault."

"Don't say that."

"There is no place for me in your life. I don't belong here." She turned sideways as if to leave.

"There has to be a place." I was whispering.

"There isn't. I can't do this."

I felt my fists tighten until my whole arms were quaking. The pressure in my head caused a piercing pain just behind my eyes. "You can't leave me, Julia. You're the only person who's given me any hope. You've changed everything for me, don't you see?"

She looked up at me and began to say something but stopped, her hands held limply aloft in grief, as if in midsentence. I could hardly look at her.

"Just give me some time," I said. "Please." I thought again of Sean and how we had played in the bath for an hour that morning and how he had laughed hysterically when he abruptly peed all over me.

She didn't say anything.

I grabbed her by the shoulders. "You'll wait a little longer? Say that you will."

She looked up at me. "Yes, I'll wait," she said softly.

I spent the rest of the day following Charlotte and Margaret around Paris, stopping to look inside every shoe store—Margaret's idea—and trying my best to remember to smile as we sat for dinner at an expensive restaurant near the Panthéon.

I couldn't sleep that night. Early the next morning I took Sean out for a walk, stopping in a park so that he could chase pigeons. Then we sat together on a bench and watched the sun come up, casting an orange and then yellow hue on the streets and buildings. Sean was on my lap and it was cold so I unbuttoned my jacket and wrapped it around him. He tilted his head straight back to look up at me, then reached for my nose. After he crawled out of my jacket he began searching my pockets with his small, dimpled hands. "Bon bon?" he inquired, smiling sweetly.

I stroked his cheek. "No bon bon. Can you say, *'Bonjour? Bonjour Papa?'*"

"No, bon *bon* Papa," he said sternly, tossing his head forward as he spoke.

I reached into the inside pocket of my jacket and pulled out a small red candy, handing it to him. Then I took his hand and began walking back to the hotel. After I dropped him off at the room I ran over to Julia's hotel, but she wasn't there.

"Why do you keep disappearing on us?" asked Charlotte, when I returned. She was sitting before the mirror applying her makeup.

"What do you mean?"

"You know what I mean. You're always heading off somewhere."

"I just went out to get some cigarettes."

"But you spend hours out by yourself."

"I don't want to bore you with the military museums. And you know I can't stand shopping—especially for shoes."

"It's Margaret, isn't it? You're avoiding her. I've always known you didn't like her. And don't think she doesn't know."

I started to deny it but thought: no, let her think that.

"The sitter will be here in fifteen minutes. Margaret and I are going out. You're welcome to join us."

"Shopping?"

"You don't have to go *in* the stores."

"I'll meet you later. We'll have a nice dinner."

Charlotte looked at me through the mirror. "Margaret was right. You are acting strange." Then she stood and rummaged through her purse for her lipstick, which she carefully applied to her lips. After she was done she zipped up her dress, put on her shoes and went to the door. "You can't dwell on the war forever, Patrick."

"No, I can't."

"You could have some fun while we're here."

"Yes. Maybe I'll even buy that suit."

"Just try?"

"I'll try." I walked over and kissed her briefly. "See you for dinner."

"Dinner."

"Bye."

When I returned to Julia's hotel she was sitting in the lobby reading a newspaper. She jumped up when she saw me and her eyes were full of happiness. "I'm sorry about yesterday," she said. "I shouldn't get so upset."

"That's all right," I said, hugging her.

"I was terrified that you wouldn't come back."

"It's getting harder to get away."

I saw the muscles in her face tighten. "How much time do we have?"

"I'm meeting them for dinner," I said. "Maybe I can get away for a few hours tomorrow too."

"Let's go to the Louvre. No, let's go up to my room and then to the Louvre."

Once inside her room we made love silently and quickly. Too quickly. But everything was too quickly now, so that our time together felt increasingly compressed.

As we dressed I looked around her small room; at her suitcase on the floor in the corner and her things laid out neatly on the dresser and at the bed and the cracked blue paint on the ceiling and as I looked around I wondered how many more times I would make it back here, but I decided not to guess.

Outside as we walked down the sidewalk I struggled to keep up with her. "I can't wait to show you what I found at the Louvre," she said, looking as excited as I'd ever seen her.

"What is it?" I asked.

"You'll see," she said, smiling.

I noticed a change in her as soon as we entered the museum. She moved differently and spoke in hushed tones as though she were in a church or a mausoleum. We strolled down the vast hallways for three hours without talking, pausing for minutes at a time to stare at various statues and busts and paintings and ancient artifacts. I looked into the eyes of kings and queens and emperors and princes and peasants and slaves and old men and young children and I saw the blood dripping from a hundred Jesuses withering on the cross. I saw Mantegna's *Saint Sebastian* bound and run through with arrows and Titian's alluring *Woman in the Mirror* and Delacroix's *Liberty Leading the People*, her chest bared as she crosses the barricades, the dead at her feet. Before Velázquez's portrait of *The Infante Marguerite* I thought of Robin and then I saw Murillo's *Young Beggar* and I thought of all the orphans of war and I suddenly had a sense of losing time completely, as though the world had come to a screeching halt and I was privileged to walk about it unlocking its mysteries, both glorious and wretched, with Julia as my guide.

As we walked slowly down a statue-lined hallway toward the *Venus de Milo*, Julia turned to me and asked, "Do you feel it?"

"You mean the sense of history, of what these artists were trying to say?"

She nodded.

"Yes, yes I do. It's quite overwhelming. And haunting too, all those faces staring at you from the past."

"It is, isn't it?" She began walking again.

"It's so enormous, like a huge tribute to humanity."

"Did they get it right?" she asked.

"What do you mean?"

"Did the artists get it right? The things you and Daniel went through, what you felt and saw and did. Not just the bad things but the good things too. Did they get it right?"

I looked up into the face of a solemn statue. "Yes, they got it right."

"That's good." I could see she was biting her lip.

"Shall we go outside, have a cigarette and maybe some coffee?" I asked.

She nodded. We turned down the hallway.

"Oh, Jesus."

"What is it?"

"Charlotte's here. With her sister." I stepped back behind a cluster of tourists and watched

421

as Charlotte and Margaret slowly worked their way down the hall toward us.

"I had no idea they'd be here." I looked at Julia. Her face was stricken.

"Did they see us?" she asked.

"I don't know."

Julia began backing away from me. Charlotte and Margaret were coming closer. I looked around for an exit. When I looked back at Julia she was farther down the hall, standing next to a large statue and staring at Charlotte. I hid behind a pillar, then edged my way toward Julia. She turned toward me and shook her head no, then backed away more.

"Where will I meet you?" I said, whispering loudly.

But Julia kept shaking her head.

I pushed through a group of tourists, heading toward her, but she kept backing away.

"Patrick? Is that you?"

I froze.

"Patrick?"

I slowly turned.

"Charlotte?"

"What on earth are you doing here?"

Margaret was next to her, scowling.

"I thought...I thought I might find you here." I turned and looked back at Julia. She was watching, her face constricted.

"That was sweet of you," said Charlotte, leaning forward and kissing me. "I can't *believe* you found us."

I looked again at Julia. She was crying.

"Patrick, are you listening to me?" Charlotte turned to follow my gaze. I started toward Julia but she shook her head no and began backing farther away, her fist pressed against her mouth.

I turned back to Charlotte. "I...I thought I saw an old friend, from the war. Just a resemblance."

Don't go, Julia.

"You're sweating," said Charlotte, tracing her finger along my temple.

Julia.

"Yes, it's hot in here, isn't it?"

"Not really," said Margaret, who was wearing a sweater.

Charlotte joined her arm in mine. "I was just wishing you were here. There's a painting I want to show you. I'm just crazy about it."

More tourists streamed down the hallway. I strained for a glimpse of Julia. She was still there, but farther away now, still watching me, shaking her head. My legs begged to run. *Go after her.*

Margaret was staring at me. I stared back at her. Charlotte tugged at my sleeve. "Come on."

I thought of Sean back at the hotel. Of his hazel green eyes and his giggle and the way he smiled when I walked into the room and how he was always trying to grab my nose and pull it off. I thought of Charlotte and our wedding and our comforting routine at home and how happy we were to finally own a house and how the neighborhood children were so good with Sean. I thought of the war and how lucky I was just to be alive and how I'd never let Sean face such a thing. I thought of Lawton and Giles and Tometti and Daniel and all that they would miss in life. And I thought of the look in Daniel's eyes on the day he died; how he tried to give me strength.

Give me strength.

"Isn't this place incredible?" said Charlotte. "Have you seen the Egyptian collection? And the jewelry. Did you see the jewelry on display?"

Julia was harder to see now. *Go to her.*

Charlotte tugged again at my sleeve. I slowly followed alongside of her. Margaret kept staring at me.

Don't leave her alone. Not again.

"Isn't this one beautiful?" said Charlotte, pointing to a marble.

I turned again to look for Julia.

"Yes, it's very beautiful," I said.

Daniel, what should I do?

"You're trembling," said Charlotte, turning toward me. "Are you feeling all right?"

I shook my head.

I don't know what to do, Daniel.

"You poor thing." She put her arm around me and kissed me again, then felt my forehead. "God, you're burning up."

Are you listening, Daniel?

I turned and looked for Julia again, but she was gone.

♦   ♦   ♦

♦ ♦ ♦

WE SPENT three hours standing before various paintings and statues and reading from Margaret's guidebook, but all I could see was Julia with her green eyes filled with tears as she fled from the Louvre.

After we were done Charlotte and Margaret wanted to stop for a drink but I told them I'd meet them back at the hotel. Once I got around the corner I ran all the way to Julia's hotel but she had already checked out. The concierge said she left in a hurry.

Two days later we sailed for New York.

I could hardly breathe.

♦ ♦ ♦

IS THAT YOU, Daniel?

Yes, it's me. How are you, Patrick?

But it can't be you. Shit, I'm so confused. Did you tell Julia?

Tell her what? That you...that you died? Daniel, I couldn't find her. Not until I saw her at the memorial.

She's beautiful, isn't she, Patrick?

Oh God, yes. And you have a daughter.

A girl?

Robin. I'm so sorry, Daniel. You should have lived, not—

That wasn't for us to decide.

But I've made such a mess of things.

You love Julia, don't you?

Yes, yes I do, Daniel. But I didn't mean to—

My dear Julia.

She misses you so. If you could have seen her. The look in her eyes. She was just like you described, only sadder.

But you lost her too?

Yes, I lost her too.

◆　◆　◆

I WAITED ten months to get a letter from Julia. The envelope was postmarked New York but there was no return address. The letter itself was short and formal; I assumed she feared it might fall into Charlotte's hands. It read:

Dear Patrick:
Perhaps you'll remember me: I'm the woman you met briefly at the dedication to the memorial. You were a close friend of Daniel's, the father of my child. Anyway, I thought you should know that I'm engaged to marry. He's a wonderful man and I'm sure he'll make a good father to my daughter Robin.
I hope this letter finds you and your family in the best of health and thank you again for all your kindness.
Sincerely yours,
Julia

Married.

I stood by our mailbox at the end of our walkway, steadying myself.

Married.

I folded the letter, placed it back in the envelope and put it in my pocket.

Married.

I began walking down the sidewalk, away from our house. I could hear Sean's laughter in the backyard, then Charlotte calling for him.

Married.

I said the word out loud.

Married.

So that was it, the end of any hope. And so quickly. Not even a return address. No way to reply.

I carried the letter around with me for several days, studying the words and handwriting for something more, then burned it in the fireplace.

Married.

She'd found somebody. Somebody she could talk to. Someone who understood her. Someone like Daniel.

I was devastated.

◆　◆　◆

A YEAR LATER Kelly was born. I guess I'd resigned myself to make the most of what I had; what Charlotte and I had. I also needed another person to love and to hold. Each day as I came home from work I couldn't wait to see Kelly and Sean and hug them and roll on the carpet with them, and as I walked down the sidewalk toward our house I'd promise myself to draw closer to Charlotte, to concentrate on the things that we did have and not on the things that we didn't.

Sometimes at night I would stand in the children's bedrooms and watch them sleep and wonder if I could ever have left them for Julia and the answer was always no, I couldn't have. At least not until they were much older. Then I would look at Charlotte while she slept and I would wonder if I could ever stop thinking about all the parts that were missing— the things I'd felt with Julia—and I knew that the answer to that was no as well.

I'm not sure if there is an exact moment when you realize that you married the wrong person or whether the realization just creeps up on you, stalking you occasionally at first and then relentlessly until you can no longer deny that there is a feeling even more lonely than being all alone. But once the feeling starts, it grows like ivy over every thought and gesture. I don't think Charlotte ever figured out what happened. She just withdrew and grew angry and eventually made her own plans. I don't know how long I would have lasted if she hadn't asked for a divorce when Kelly was two. She had found a wealthy real estate agent named Arnie with shiny blond hair and a large empty house in Florida. When I asked her for the children she burst into tears and screamed and told me she would fight. So I stayed up all night thinking and crying and drinking and in the morning I told her they belonged with their mother.

I visited Sean and Kelly three times a week up until the day they moved to Fort Lauderdale. I promised Charlotte I'd sell the house for her and after they drove off I sat on the barren living room floor crying as I searched the empty walls for all the laughter and tears and birthdays and Thanksgivings and Christmases.

Before I left I went upstairs, stopping first in our bedroom, which still smelled of Charlotte. I closed my eyes and inhaled, picturing her before the mirror in the bathroom. Then suddenly I laughed through my tears. Charlotte never did smell right. Even just out of the bath her skin and hair smelled all wrong, at least to me. It didn't matter what perfume she wore, her own smell always came though. It always does. I think if the smell of a person is wrong, if the pheromones aren't right, you can just about forget the rest of the relationship and save a lot of grief.

I walked down the hallway to the children's bedrooms and stood in each one studying the crayon marks and the stickers on the walls and the stray pieces of Lincoln Logs and little blocks still littering the closet floors. When grief overwhelmed me I hurried out and drove for three hours before returning to the small one-bedroom apartment I had rented. Six weeks later I sold the house and sent Charlotte the money. Then I quit my job at the accounting firm—business was so bad then that there wasn't enough work for me anyway—and took six months off to drive across the Depression-wracked country, wondering what to do with the rest of my life.

If I drank too much, which was seldom then, I would question whether Julia had ever really existed at all, or whether she had just risen from the mist temporarily like the Angel at Mons; a vision confined to soldiers in need. That's when I started writing letters to her, unsent letters that I wrote in my journal telling her all the things I wanted to say but couldn't. Writing page after page late into the night was the closest I could come to her, though it wasn't very close at all, especially after I turned out the light.

♦ ♦ ♦

DEAR JULIA,
What do I say to you tonight, another night when I wonder where you are and if you really are happy and if you ever still think about our days together in France. I quit my job, Julia, did I tell you that? You'd be proud of me, I think. I've got a job starting in the fall teaching history at a small high school in Vermont. Remember how Daniel used to say there were only three noble pursuits in life? Well, you know I'm no artist and I don't feel strong enough for charity work right now so I've gone into teaching. You'd be pleased, wouldn't you? And did I tell you that I'll be able to take Sean and Kelly for

*the summer now? They hate the heat in
Florida and I'll have a small cottage
right near campus with plenty for them to
do. I do miss them so and I often wonder
how your family is and whether Robin
now has a brother or sister.*

Please take care of yourself.

Good night, Julia.

◆　　◆　　◆

WHAT A CRISP, clear memory today! July 1955,
and I was just about to start teaching a class
on European history when a headline in the
newspaper on my desk caught my eye. A
tremendous underground explosion in Belgium
near Messines: one of two massive mines that
never detonated on June 7, 1917, when British
tunnelers mined the German lines, killing
ten thousand outright. One more mine remains.
Waiting.

Did Julia hear about it? She would have
thought of me. She must have. The class
stared at me, waiting. I spent the hour talking
about the mines at Messines.

◆　　◆　　◆

I FINALLY captured Julia. Not perfectly. But closer
than I've ever gotten before. Certainly closer
than I'll ever get again. I spent four days on
the drawing, sequestering myself in my room
for the final day.

I've taped her to the wall above my bed.

431

Everybody asks about her. Robert said she was hotter than hot. Martin conceded she was every bit as beautiful as Lara.

I like to sit in my orange chair and stare at her. I feel so proud, knowing I'll never lose her now. It's comforting too, having her there, watching over me. How I did it, I don't know. But I've been trying for fifty years. It's wonderful to be able to look at her again.

◆ ◆ ◆

IS IT WORTH being saved if one is consequently damned? That's what happened, isn't it? I'm sitting here, looking at Julia's picture, and I realize that she made my whole life seem worthwhile, even the worst parts. And yet she ruined it too, so that I was never content again with Charlotte (might not I have been happy enough with her if I'd never met Julia?), and so that the rest of my life was haunted by the knowledge of what I had once had and then lost.

Does everything we have become a searing loss? Is that what the end is all about? And how long would the feelings have endured? Would Daniel and Julia have lasted a lifetime together without losing their passion? What about me and Julia? How would we have aged together?

I study her face on the wall; her eyes (I've got them!) and hair and lips and neck. Well, if we are all inexorably doomed in the end, then at least I've known what it's like to be saved, if only for a few days.

IF I CAN'T have love again before I die—and it's looking rather unlikely these days—I'd at least like to decant a bit of wisdom, some comforting compilation of beliefs or corpus of insight; a distillation of all I have seen and thought so that I can say, "Aha, there's the rub," and nod knowingly before I depart.

It's after midnight now and I'm sitting by the window, my journal open in my lap, my pen in hand, just sitting and thinking and listening to Martin's slow, sonorous breathing across the room.

Suddenly, it all seems so funny to me that I begin laughing, laughing so hard that I have to think bad thoughts in order to catch my breath. What wretches we are! Congenital narcissists who cling like drowning rats to the notion of a self that is fixed and strong and permanent, a delusion defended by material possessions and job titles and diplomas and bolstered by drugs and therapy and social convention. (Ironically, the more effective our false selves, the more we compromise our deeper selves.) And so if only briefly, we are emboldened by the illusion that we are in charge. Look out, world!

But alas, the pitiable little self always gets whooped in the end, pummeled by disease and humiliated by decay and finally trumped by death. Try as we might to make our little stand, we shall soon be swept from the rocks and back into the cosmic soup, and to fight back is only to suffer more.

What then is life but a desperate, hilarious, passionate and finally tragic bid to prove that we are more than hideously sensitive fertilizer? The quest! And so we stumble forth, seeking salvation through love and heroism, the royal roads to the soul. Sancho, my horse!

Martin snores louder. I look over at him, then up at Julia above my bed. Then I lean back, smiling.

Love is self-explanatory: the right person makes you feel well-nigh immortal, vaccinating you with their affections. So long as you remain in their heart you are safe, or better than safe even, for a while at least. You are, momentarily, in a state of grace.

Our quest for heroism is more awkward. Not the obvious heroism that earns medals and applause but the heroism of daily life. Go to Princeton and you're an educational hero; run a marathon and you're an athletic hero; make loads of money and you're a financial hero—the alpha hero of our culture. Each occupation and role in life has its own exacting rituals for advancement and reward, from the employee-of-the-month parking space to stock options. The point is not the Princeton degree or the marathon medallion or the money or the parking space, it's what these things say about us, that we are special and unique; that momentarily at least, we have risen head and shoulders above the clamoring masses to be giddily succored by premonitions of divinity.

The crisis of our age is not that we have proven adept at slaughtering each other in ever greater numbers (that's just a technological feat), it's that more and more of us have a gnawing sense that we are engaged in silly make-work heroism, not the stuff that's in our genes, the true heroism of tribal rituals. (How ironic that primitive cultures were so much better at offering members a heroic sense of self-worth.)

Maybe the turning point came during the Great War, when machines first made a mockery of man. Men marched into battle because they longed to be heroes, but the sheer vastness of the carnage swallowed up individual acts of bravery so that even valor became meaningless until finally it was so routinely demanded and thus demeaned that the only way to make a name for yourself was to top Corporal Alvin York, and he single-handedly killed some twenty-eight Germans and captured 132 others.

♦   ♦   ♦

TWENTY-EIGHT is not that many, really. Not for the Great War. You see, it was possible for a well-placed machine gunner to kill a thousand men in a morning's work, so long as the gun didn't jam.

It is important to understand that.

I LAY awake, unable to sleep. Or am I afraid to dream?

♦ ♦ ♦

"MARTIN? " The sun pushed through the white slats and painted bright horizontal streaks against the far wall. I could hear the nurses shaking bottles of pills and liquids as they prepared the morning medical cart, which rattled down the hallways like a small locomotive. "Martin?" I called again. He was perfectly still, on his back with the covers up to his chin. "Martin?" Then I knew and pushed the red button near my headboard again and again and I reached out and grabbed hold of him and cried out as loud as I could.

Martin.

That afternoon I called Lara. After I told her she couldn't speak so I said I'd call back and hung up gently. Sitting there in the phone booth with my hand still on the receiver I got the idea to pull out the yellow pages and make another call on Martin's behalf. And for Lara too. A proper send-off.

Then I went out back and sat on a bench beneath the largest oak tree, not far from where Howard and I had buried Eleanor Kravitski's pennies. I cried for two hours.

♦ ♦ ♦

I GREETED Martin's daughter just before the service, expecting inquiries about his last minutes or days or weeks. Instead she simply leaned forward and whispered, "We'll come by his room later and pick up his things." Then she turned and headed for her seat.

Dozens of old men and women and staff members packed the back pews of the chapel, the wheelchairs forming two additional pews. The service itself was deeply and profoundly anonymous; not one reference to Martin's life or beliefs, just a generic soliloquy on the rather pedestrian and predictable fate of all of us poor sods. I sat perfectly still, studying the large white sculpture of Jesus on the cross that hung above the altar and wondering how much it really hurt to be crucified or if there were worse things.

I decided there were worse things.

As the service ended, the door of the chapel opened and a lone bagpipe player in full kilt appeared. The minister looked confused while Martin's daughter twisted her head back to see what was happening. I winked at Howard, who sat just across the aisle from me, then closed my eyes and tilted my head back as the music began to play. I didn't bother to stop the warm tears that coursed down my face and onto my shirt.

Good-bye, my friend.

After the final note I stood up, slipped out of the chapel and hurried back to my room, where I placed Martin's favorite belongings in a small box and addressed it to Lara. Then

I flagged Robert down as he walked past my room.

"Do me a favor, Robert."

"Of course."

"Mail this for me, would you?" I placed a ten-dollar bill on top of the box and handed it to him.

"I'll pick it up after work," he said.

"Would you mind keeping it in your supply room until you leave? It's a special favor."

"Yeah sure, of course."

"And one more thing." I reached back into my closet and grabbed the helmet. "Would you give this to Hanford?" He looked at it, then back at me, then nodded and turned to leave.

"Robert..."

"Yes?"

I paused. "Nothing. Take care."

"You too, Mr. Delaney."

When he left I put "Shenandoah" on my tape deck and sat down at my desk and wrote a note to Robert, which I propped up against the tape deck. Then I wrote a one-page letter to Sarah that I enclosed in an envelope along with the best black and white photo of me I could find, which was taken when I was thirty-four, just one year older than she was now. I recently had the photo reprinted so that at least the paper it was on would look fresh.

Then I put the envelope on my pillow and began to pack. First I packed my small suitcase, careful to wrap the bottle of Scotch in two sweaters. Then I placed my journals, wallet, passport and two books into the light brown leather bag I bought at Abercrombie and Fitch in New York in 1928, just before sailing to France with Charlotte and her sister and Sean. When I finished I walked down the corridor and found an empty wheelchair, which I brought back to my room. I placed my luggage in the chair and covered it with a blanket, then sat on the edge of the bed, breathing hard as I looked around the room.

When I got up I stood before the mirror and combed my hair, then walked over to my bed and carefully took down my drawing of Julia, pausing to stare at it before rolling it tightly and tucking it into my leather bag. Then I peered down the hallway, grabbed the wheelchair and headed out. At the taxi stand I handed my suitcase to a young Middle Eastern man who smiled reverentially as I asked him to stop at my bank and then head for the airport.

PART
FOUR

> The tragedy of man is what dies inside
> himself while he still lives.
> —*Albert Schweitzer*

From the backseat of the taxi I scrutinized the driver's dashboard, which was pasted with pictures of smiling children and a flag whose nationality I did not recognize. He drove fast, too fast, but I felt no fear as we hurtled across the Golden Gate Bridge heading south. I think one of my children has a photo of me standing on that bridge the day it opened in 1937, during one of my trips out west. I remember drinking too much one evening at a bar near Fisherman's Wharf and walking all night through the city, secretly hoping I'd run into Julia again, even if she was with her husband. Did I sing aloud as I stumbled and lurched down streets shimmering from the ocean mist?

I noticed the taxi driver eyeing me occasionally through the rearview mirror, flashing smiles like a ship's signalman. "Beautiful day, eh?" he said through the mirror.

"Yes," I said to the mirror.

"You have big family?" he asked.

"Medium size, I guess. Three great-grandchildren." I smiled reflexively and suppressed an urge to pull out their pictures, though I might have if he hadn't been driving so fast.

"I have two grandchildren," he smiled. As

he pointed to the little faces pasted to his dashboard he seemed to talk faster and faster and I lost track of what he was saying. I felt disoriented and dizzy as a sudden panic tightened my chest and I couldn't explain to myself what I was doing in this taxi or where I was going. The feeling made my eyes water and I stared down at my leather shoulder bag until I could trace my way back to that morning and my decision to leave. "I'm going to Paris today," I said finally, with perhaps too little conviction.

"I hate the French," he said, still holding a smile. "Not like Americans. I lived two years in France and never once felt welcomed. Very rude people." I imagined him barreling down the Champs-Elysées in a tiny Peugeot with French pedestrians fleeing every which way.

"Americans have one problem," he continued, leaning into the top of the steering wheel. "They don't take care of family. Now everybody lives so far apart it's crazy, you know?" I nodded. "You tell me how people are going to survive without family?" I nodded again. "My mother, she's eighty-five, she's been living with me five years, since my father died. She has dementia, you know? Doesn't even recognize her own son, her own son me, Achmed, but what am I going to do, dump her on the street?" I shook my head. "Me, I respect my elders," he said.

"Glad to hear that," I said, feeling elderly indeed.

"I respect family. Even if I can't stand them, like my brother, an idiot, always borrowing money from me, can't hold a job, lazy son of bitch, you know?"

I watched his eyes dancing in the rearview mirror and wondered if he was driving from memory.

"And my wife, bless her, she's a good cook, a good mother, but after we got married she got fat, you know? Now she's a big woman. Big woman. Fat as a manatee. You know what a manatee is? Big animal, a manatee. But what am I going to do, break up my family because my wife is fat as a manatee? No way, not me. See, I'm a family man. Respect the family."

◆　　◆　　◆

AT THE AIRPORT I mailed Sean and Kelly each a packet of letters with instructions not to open them until they reached the ages written in large numbers on the outside of each envelope. I paid for the ticket to Paris with fifty-dollar bills from the large brown leather wallet I made at the crafts shop last fall and kept hidden in the back of my closet beneath some dirty clothes. (Even greed has its limits.) The woman at the ticket counter asked if I was traveling alone, which I think surprised her because she quickly offered to have an employee wheel me to the gate. To make her feel better I told her I had family waiting at the other end and I tried to smile even though my hips ached from the walking.

445

I was the first to board and I slipped the young man who had pushed me through the airport a five-dollar bill before steadying myself with my cane and walking back to row nineteen. I had a window seat which was good in case I managed to sleep during the flight. After I placed my bag beneath the seat and tightened my seat belt I waited for the other passengers and watched the luggage glide up a conveyor belt and disappear; some of it, I imagined, never to be seen again.

As I sat there staring out the window I suddenly remembered how during our last night together in Paris Julia had asked me if I thought that love was the purpose of our lives and I had said yes, it has to be, because it's the only thing we have that's stronger than our pain. I hadn't thought about it that way until I'd said it, but I'm certain now that I was right.

I pulled down the window shade and rested my head against a pillow and when I closed my eyes I could see Julia sitting across the table from me and leaning forward the way she did when she had something important to say.

"I feel lucky then," she had said, bringing that smile into her eyes.

"But you're still young. You still have—"

"But I have been lucky, don't you think? I mean compared to most people?"

"In some ways."

After the waiter refilled our glasses she looked up at me and said, "Do you feel like anyone really knows you?"

"A few people," I said, though I knew it wasn't true.

"You're rare then," she said, gently extinguishing her cigarette in a small white china ashtray.

"You think so?" I felt foolish now.

"Oh yes, because I think most people are so well hidden that they lose the very meaning of their lives." She paused, then said, "That's what I don't want."

"To feel lost?"

"From myself. To feel that I'm betraying myself."

"But surely..."

"It's hard to say what you feel sometimes, isn't it?" she asked. "Maybe that's why the really important things in our lives have hidden meanings."

"You think so?"

"Oh, I'm quite sure of it," she said. "That's how we keep our dreams alive." I looked at her hands and noticed they were shaking. She began talking quickly: "What I'm trying to say is that I think we all look for clues that we are not utterly alone. Clues we find in literature and paintings and music and even in someone's eyes; clues that demonstrate that someone else has felt the same indescribable feelings, seen the same things or passed by the same spot even if it was by candlelight three hundred years ago. It means everything, like finding footprints in the sand of a deserted island."

◆　　◆　　◆

I LOST YOUR footprints, Julia.

◆   ◆   ◆

I BROUGHT along William Manchester's *The Arms of Krupp*, which I now pulled from the seat pocket and placed on my lap. I am curious about the family that made all those guns that were once pointed in my direction. As the plane lurched back from the gate a stewardess offered me a blanket, which I took. Then I watched closely as she demonstrated the safety procedures.

I stare far too much at stewardesses, as if I'm part of the audience watching a show, forgetting that they can see perfectly well that I'm staring and it's not a show but a poor-paying job. There were two female flight attendants, a tall, bony brunette with sharp features and a shorter blonde with heavy makeup. I immediately decided that the brunette was divorced two or three years ago from a heavy drinker who fails to make child support payments and now she's struggling to raise two pimply boys in junior high who desperately need orthodontic work. The blonde is single and rooms with two other flight attendants who all dream of marrying well and decorating huge houses in floral patterns with all-white carpeting and huge kitchens with really functional center islands. I wondered if she'd tolerate an old man worth $100,000 but assumed she's set on a flight captain or better. Anyway, I prefer the brunette.

As the plane took off I stared out the window

and smiled, enjoying the dull drone of the engines. I slept through the layover at JFK, which was confusing, but at least I got some rest. When I noticed that it was just after midnight I looked out the window and imagined the black waves miles below, and beneath them miles of cold and silent darkness. I thought of Oscar Bellamy and his checkerboard and his endless fears and I wondered how he felt about flying over oceans. Not so good, I decided.

The young man next to me—he boarded in New York— appeared about thirty, with neat sandy blond hair that looked as though it was cut exactly one week ago and again exactly one week before that. From his expensive leather shoes I assumed he was in finance or at least represented those who were. He was dressed in a dark blue suit, worsted wool I think, and wore a crisp white shirt adorned with a yellow paisley tie. His cologne, recently applied, was a bit too sweet and reminiscent of nothing more than other affluent men his age who smell too sweet. I assumed it was called Wall Street or Attaché or VIP or Portfolio and I imagined him leaning into the mirror each morning as he slapped some on his cheeks, POW! POW! just like in the commercials. His face was handsome, strong chin and straight nose, but lacking in animation. A good face for poker but not for striking up friendships. How much are we the product of our faces and how much are they the product of our personalities? I've known people whose faces rested naturally in a smile and I'm certain their lives were much different because of that.

I watched as he stuffed a pillow beneath his lower back and then pulled a thick leather-bound notebook from his briefcase, opened it and stared at the pages. From the graphics I surmised that it was some sort of schedule book.

"Looks like you're pretty damn busy," I said, startling him.

He eyed me for a moment, then waved the book and said, "It helps keep me from completely falling apart."

I wondered what I would write in an appointment book. Take medicine? Review living will?

I plucked the in-flight magazine from the seat pouch and struggled to recline my chair until the young man noticed my difficulty and put a hand at the top and pushed it back. I thanked him and thumbed through the magazine, then closed my eyes and imagined I was a seagull skimming just a few feet over the waves which marched below me in perfect formation across the ocean.

◆　　◆　　◆

As fast as one wave was mown down, another rolled up behind it. Our machine-gunners say they were absolutely sick of killing them.
　　　　　　　—*Harold Coulter, British Army.*

I WAS TEN when my father took me to Antietam to study the battlefield and learn about strategy and courage and most of all to stare at his father's (and my namesake's) thin white slab jutting from the wet grass. That was 1908, and it was cold and foggy as we walked across the fields and down along the Sunken Road, which my father explained was also called Bloody Lane. He carried a large jug of fresh apple cider in one hand and with the other pointed out where each army stood and I listened carefully for the sound of cannon and pounding hoofs and the clash of metal but I heard only the sound of the cider sloshing in the jug. Still, I felt afraid as I stared across the meadow toward the woods and imagined it full of soldiers drawing a bead on me and preparing to charge.

"Your grandfather fell somewhere right around here," said Father, surveying a grassy field. "Died fighting slavery and to keep this country together." Even then I realized that such a death was about as good as it gets and I carefully selected a spot about equidistant between two stands of trees and stared at it until I saw grandfather Delaney lying there with a glorious glow about him as he died again and again for freedom and justice.

"We still have the letter from his captain that said he died in the second charge, dead by the time he hit the ground. Took a minié ball right in the chest."

I was doubtful but said nothing as we walked across the grass to a cemetery bordered by a low stone wall. To me the rows of tombstones looked like dominoes and I wondered if I pushed the first one hard enough would they all fall? Beneath the grass I saw rows and rows of skeletons still dressed in blues and grays and some even holding swords by their sides.

When we reached my grandfather's headstone Father knelt down before it. "I still remember the day that letter arrived in the mail," he said quietly. "I'll never forget the look on my mother's face."

I tried to feel their grief but I was more interested in looking at the worn letters of my name etched in white stone and wondering what my namesake looked like down in the rich black soil beneath my feet.

♦ ♦ ♦

TRAFFIC USED to come to a complete standstill in New York City every year for one minute at eleven A.M. on November 11. It's true. The police would blow their whistles and everybody stopped.

Does anybody remember that? Could they all be gone?

♦ ♦ ♦

DANIEL? Daniel? Daniel! I feel fiery hot and there are hands pressing on my shoulders. Julia? I can't get to him, Julia, I can't!

Who's shaking me? My hips and stomach hurt and I breathe faster and faster until suddenly it's bright. I stare into the light until gradually I see a face. A young man's face.

"Sir, are you all right?"

"Huh?" I sat motionless for a minute, waiting for everything to stop moving. Then I squinted and looked around. I'm on a plane. A plane to Paris. Just dreams.

"I'm sorry," I said, coughing. "Bad dream. The medications do it."

"No problem." He looked worried and I wondered if he feared I might have some sort of seizure or simply expire right here next to him on the 506 to Paris. I felt embarrassed and apologized again as I pulled my seat forward.

He returned to his paperwork and I to my book. But I couldn't focus for long on the words and soon I closed the book and stared at the flight attendants. When they were out of view I watched the young man shuffle through his papers.

"What sort of work do you do?" I asked.

"I'm an attorney. Corporate law."

"Interesting?" A cruel question, but I was bored.

"The money is."

"Ever think of doing anything else?"

"Oh, lots of things, but they don't pay enough."

"Like what?"

"Oh well, let's see, I guess in my heart of hearts I would have liked to have been a professional musician, but I don't have the talent."

"Funny, I always wanted to be a musician too."

"Did you play an instrument?"

"No, never got around to it. I guess everybody wishes they were a musician. I wonder what musicians long for?"

"Probably a paycheck."

"Yeah, right. You know, you kind of look like a musician."

"Really, you think so?" He sat up.

"Hair's a little short. What instrument do you play?"

"Guitar. It's a great outlet after work, though my neighbors might disagree."

"Ever write your own songs?"

"Haven't for a while because I've been so busy, but I used to, especially in college." He smiled. "After breaking up with a girlfriend the muse came on strong. The problem is, I only wanted to write when I was depressed."

"That's the thing about art. It *really* helps to be unhappy."

"Maybe that's why so many musicians stop writing good music once they make it big."

"So be glad you never hit it big." He chuckled in a way that belied his youth and made me like him.

The blond stewardess served our dinner: chicken, a small salad, a roll and a brownie with nuts sprinkled on top. I traded my brownie for the young man's roll and we ate in silence. After I finished I pulled out my small black kit bag, unzipped it and began opening pill bottles one by one, returning each bottle back into the bag after I had removed and swallowed a pill.

"Why are you going to Paris?" he asked, as the trays were being removed.

"Job interview." I popped the last of eight pills into my mouth.

He looked puzzled. I winked. I've done a lot of winking since I got old. One quick wink meaning "right-o." Two rapid winks with mouth agape meaning, "Our little secret, right?" Winking is one of the few things you can do better when you're older. In fact, I don't think anyone under sixty-five can really execute a wink properly. When young people wink, they look like they're having problems with their contacts. When old people wink, it's like they are firing off great big smoke rings, dense with cryptic meaning. Maybe winking is the secret handshake of old age. But I can't help but notice that I got really good at winking just about the time I got really bad at screwing. Maybe that's why old people wink so much, kind of an inside joke like: you can't keep it up either, huh? (Isn't God a scream.)

"Actually, I thought I'd look up some old friends while I can still get about," I said.

"I admire that. I think we're only as old as we feel."

"No, actually, I feel quite young, at least inside; your age really. It's the rest of me that's so dreadfully dated."

He laughed. "Good point. I suppose there are some limitations."

I folded my arms on my chest. "It's interesting, when you think about it. I mean, you've got what I need and I've got what you need."

He looked puzzled.

"You're wondering what I've got, eh?"

"Wisdom, experience," he said, uncertainly.

"Something even more important."

"What's that?"

"I've got physical proof that people your age really do turn into people my age. And fast."

"Time flies," he said.

"In my case it has flown." I waved one hand in the air and made a whooshing sound. Then I leaned into him and said, "Do you want to know a little secret?" He nodded hesitantly. "It's simple, really. Once you become my age, you finally realize that the things that people your age consider important are actually bullshit." I jabbed my finger into his chest. "Total, absolute, worthless bullshit. But by the time you realize it, it's too goddamn late to do anything about it, which is *really* bullshit! But at least I've warned you."

He put his tray up and leaned back. "I was debating whether to have a 7-Up or a Scotch, but you've just made up my mind."

"I'll have one too," I said, turning back to look out the window.

Two drinks and several confessions later, the young man turned to me and said, "I have a problem." I looked at the way his eyebrows huddled together and I knew he was serious so I raised my eyebrows in invitation and waited. "I think my wife is having an affair."

"You *think* she is?"

"Well, I'm not positive, but let's just say that my marriage is a mess."

"Do you have children?"

"Thank God no," he said. "Though I suppose children might have held us together."

"Let me tell you something—and I love kids—but having children to improve a marriage is like shooting the dog to kill the fleas."

"I'll remember that."

"What does your wife do?"

"She's a stockbroker, very successful."

"You two powerhouses ever see each other?"

"It's hard, juggling our careers and all."

"Do you like the way she smells?"

"What?"

"Your wife. Does she smell right to you?"

"No one's ever asked me that. I guess so. Sometimes. I don't know."

"Think about it," I said.

"I will."

"Are you having an affair?"

"No, but I can't say I'm not attracted to other women."

"Trust me, you'll never be able to say that, not with a straight face. What makes you think your wife is having an affair?"

"There's this guy she works with. We were at an office party. They weren't flirting or anything, but I saw this look."

"Ah, *that* look."

"Yeah, I mean don't you think it shows, on people's faces, when they've slept together? I think I could walk into a room and pick out people who slept together thirty years ago."

"It's my experience that everyone who is the least bit interesting has at least one terrible little secret, usually about sex or money."

"The scary part is, I'm not sure that I care anymore. I'm not sure I still love her. And we've only been married for three years."

"Married years are like dog years," I said. "And you don't even have kids yet; you're not even incorporated."

"I can't imagine. Even sharing a bathroom is trying. It looks more like a trauma center when she's done. You'd think people had been brought back from the brink of death in there."

"It's tough, them being human and all."

"But when I see other women and imagine being with them, I know it would be only a matter of time before I took them for granted too. That's just human nature, right?"

I shrugged.

"Maybe my expectations are too high," he said.

"Mine were so high that I'm still single."

"Your whole life?" He looked incredulous.

"No, I was married once. But not happily."

"Do you suppose everyone who is married secretly wonders if they could do better? Find a better fit?"

"Of course. And some not so secretly. Do you want in on a terrible secret?"

"Sure," he said, hesitantly.

I lowered my voice. "No matter what you do, you'll always be plagued by the sense that your life is slipping away and that other people are having better sex than you. Much better."

He buried his face in his hands.

"But if it's any comfort, everyone else feels that way too."

"That's *so* depressing," he said. "I remember when Ann and I were just dating. We must have talked on the phone five times a day. We slept on top of each other. Do you think there is any way to sustain that feeling, at least a little longer?"

"Restrict your conjugal visits to a minimum. Don't look in each other's closets. Use separate bathrooms. Don't ask too many questions."

He finished off his glass of Scotch and looked around for a flight attendant. Then he said, "I had this English teacher once—God, he really ruined literature for me, tearing it into little shreds and then demanding to know what each shred meant, when of course only he had the correct interpretation, which probably eluded even the poor author himself. I wanted to tell him that maybe Byron was hammered when he wrote that stanza but I couldn't afford to flunk. Anyway, this teacher used to say that romantic love was false love, just a temporary intoxication based on idealization and mystery, while true love—or rational love—was based on knowledge and respect and compassion and maturity, which sounds fine until you actually compare how the two feel. Wow, what a difference. I'll take romantic love any day. Do you remember your first crush? *Shit*." He turned and looked back down the aisle for a flight attendant.

"I do."

"Or how about when you found out that a girl had a crush on you. What a *feeling*, like you were omnipotent."

"Didn't happen much."

"Me neither." He waved his hand at a flight attendant, who ignored him. "So what do you do, just keep them on a pedestal? Never consummate the relationship? That's torture! I nearly had a breakdown in seventh grade sitting next to Sally Manley every day."

"The dues we paid in the hard coinage of puberty," I said, which made him laugh. "It's torture because you'll always wonder if maybe that love, that feeling of romantic love, could have been sustained with the right person."

He paused a moment, biting the edge of his thumbnail, then said, "I wonder how long it would last, if you loved somebody from afar. Somebody you couldn't be with or even touch."

"I suppose the feeling would last a very long time."

"I wonder if it's worth it. If it's bearable. Like the wife who secretly longs for her neighbor's husband all her life, or the man who secretly wishes he had married a former girlfriend or who falls in love with his brother-in-law's sister. That sort of thing."

"I don't think people who love from afar have much choice in the matter."

He rubbed his eyes and ran his hands through his hair, a gesture I haven't been able to pull off for several decades. "I think I'm getting a headache," he said, as he rose and headed for the lavatory. When he returned he turned toward me and said, "Do you mind if I ask how old you are?"

"Pushing eighty," I lied.

"Wow. You don't seem that old."

"That's because I'm still breathing."

"What were you dreaming about earlier, when you woke with such a start? You looked terribly frightened."

"I was." What was I dreaming about? I couldn't remember. "At my age it gets harder and harder to distinguish dreams from reality, the past from the present. My life is now so heavily weighted toward the past that I feel sometimes like a listing ship."

"A lot of flashbacks, huh?"

"Tons of flashbacks," I smiled.

◆　　◆　　◆

DEAR JULIA:
I'm finally going back, back to France. I'm on a plane now, somewhere over the ocean. Technically, I think I've run away. But don't worry, I feel good. And I've met the nicest young man.

Did you ever go back again? Was it

*harder or easier the second time? I hope
it's not much harder.*

*Anyway, I've been thinking that maybe
I'm not such a fool after all, that maybe
my choice in life wasn't between loving
you and finding someone else to love;
maybe it was between loving you as I have
or being like all those people who don't
have any love at all, people without any
magic in their lives; without any stars to
guide them. So I don't feel so bad. I've
got the Northern Light. I always have.*

Love,

Patrick

◆　　◆　　◆

I SLEPT AGAIN for half an hour and awoke with
stomach cramps. I carefully made my way to
the bathrooms, where I had to stand in line
behind a tall teenager with headphones on.
Once inside I carefully latched the door and
began unbuckling my pants. Just as I sat
down the red return-to-cabin light flashed
on and the plane began to shake. I ignored it
and held tight to a handgrip. When I finished
I glanced down in the toilet before flushing.
Blood. I washed my hands, careful to clean the
sink area with my towelette, then struggled with
the door latch before opening it. When I
returned to my seat, the young man was back
at work, a pile of papers in his lap. From the
way he kept blinking and rubbing his temples
I could tell he was having trouble concentrating.

"Was your father a lawyer?" I asked.

"Oh no, he was a small-time businessman, always jumping from one thing to another. A deli, a bunch of car washes, that kind of thing. He was always on the verge of the big breakthrough."

"He's dead?"

"Died three years ago. We had to put my mother in a nursing home last winter. She's got Pick's disease. One of those dementia diseases."

"That's tough."

He stuffed his paperwork into the seat pocket. "We tried to keep her at home as long as we could but she was starting to set off the smoke detectors every time she got near the kitchen. I was afraid she'd end up at the grocery store in her bathrobe."

"Or without her bathrobe."

"Yeah." He slowly shook his head back and forth. "We're paying a fortune for this rest home—it's the best one we could find—but God it's so depressing. I hate even going to visit her. Keep out of those places if you can."

"Sounds like good advice."

"I go in to see her and there are all these people sitting around spoon-feeding their parents and wiping their mouths and it smells like—"

"Piss. It smells like piss."

He looked at me for a moment. "You're right. Piss. And it's kind of—"

"Musty. Tomblike."

"Exactly," he said, pointing a finger at me.

"First thing I did after she got sick was to make a living will out for myself. I say, 'Pull the plug friends. *Sayonara*.'"

"Master of your fate," I nodded.

He nodded vigorously, then stared up at the ceiling. "You know, the thing I never forget is that my parents never seemed happy their whole lives."

"Of course not. They were your parents, right? They weren't supposed to be happy. They're supposed to haunt you like the ghosts of Christmas future unless you mend your ways. Don't you ever hear the rattle of those chains at night?" He chuckled. "Your job is to make amends for their failures."

"That'll keep me busy."

"So what do you really want to do?"

"Want to do?"

"With your life."

"Ah, with my life. Well, let's see, a lot of things. I guess I really just want to be successful."

"What do you consider success?"

"A good salary, recognition in my field."

"That's all bullshit."

"Bullshit?"

"Yeah, men have defined success all wrong, which is why they are such crotchety old farts when they get to be my age and realize what fools they've been, sacrificing their marriages, their children, their health and their souls to their careers, all so they can be considered a somebody at work, which is like hitching your star to the nearest fire hydrant. Who gives a shit, except the other careerists who've made the same catastrophic mistake with their lives, and so are desperate to defend the entitlements of being a somebody, lest somebodyism be exposed for what it is: an ill-fated pyramid scheme." I laughed out loud, then took another big swig of Scotch. "It's a self-esteem problem, which is why men jumped out of windows during the stock market crash. It wasn't the money—you know damn well they would have paid all that and more to ransom their life—it was the fact that their money represented their sense of worth. Without it they felt worthless; already dead."

"Well, since you're so goddamn wise, why don't you just tell me what you did so I can just emulate the maestro?"

"I'm afraid that would be disastrous."

"Oh really?" He leaned toward me. "How did *you* fuck up?"

"In more ways than I can explain."

"I'm listening."

I paused for a moment, then said, "I guess I was always waiting for things to happen that didn't happen. I married the wrong woman. I never spent enough time with my kids. That kind of thing." I picked up my drink and finished it.

"Well, at least you didn't keel over at the office."

"That's a real relief."

"So what would you do if you were me?" I could see him brace himself.

"If I could be in your shoes for a day? I suppose the first thing I'd do is to get laid—and I am being serious—then I'd figure out whether I really loved my wife for the right reasons, and if I did I'd try to get her back. If I didn't, I'd move on."

"You make it sound so easy."

"Hey, this is make-believe. I mean, if I were really you I would probably make things even worse. That's the thing about life: even if we had a second chance we'd probably blow it, right? In fact, I think that's the only consolation for blowing it the first time, knowing that you'd probably blow it a second and third time too, so why sweat it. It's just human nature."

"I've often thought about being old, what it will be like," he said.

"Kind of morbid, huh?"

"Well, I guess I think of it in terms of wanting to be able to look back on my life and feel that I did the right things."

"Good luck."

"Gee, thanks," he said.

"The problem is that while happiness is well within our reach, so is a lot of unhappiness. And frankly, the unhappiness is considerably closer."

"Naturally."

"I knew a woman once who thought we should work backward from our deaths to make our lives more fulfilling," I said.

"How do you mean?"

"Well, the less time one has, the more valued that time is, right?"

"Sure."

"So conversely, the more time one thinks one has, the less each moment is appreciated, right? So maybe death—acceptance of our mortality—can liberate us."

"I can't deal with death."

"Then you can't deal with life."

"You really think that way?"

"Let's just say it's getting a lot harder to pretend like I'm going to be the one exception who lives forever—though it's only recently that I've conceded this point."

He bit down hard on another piece of ice. "I don't know. I just hate the idea that I'm just a worthless sack of cells on a measly little planet circling a sun that"—he pointed his finger in the air—"is just one of three hundred billion stars in the Milky Way galaxy, which is one of billions of galaxies in the universe, which is itself probably just a mole on God's great big mushy behind." He flung himself back against his seat.

"It does take some getting used to."

"Maybe people my age have unrealistic expectations. I mean, we really expect to be *happy*, and if we aren't, there is going to be hell to pay."

"I was every bit as greedy, only I never figured out how to make hell pay. A friend of mine used to say that happiness is like an erection: great while it lasts—especially if you can share it—but unsustainable for any length of time. And boy can it fade fast."

"Most of the people I work with are too busy to be happy," he said.

"That's just the point. They are also too busy to be really unhappy. Ever watch a workaholic—one of those rich, corpulent ones—try to relax on a beach? It's hysterical. You'd think they were in detox: Day One."

"That's why insomnia is so brutal," he said. "No distractions. Christ, I'm up half the night running worst-case scenarios."

I leaned back, closed my eyes and whispered:

> *Then save me, or the passèd day will*
> > *shine*
> *Upon my pillow, breeding many woes;*
> *Save me from curious conscience, that*
> > *still hoards*
> *Its strength for darkness, burrowing like*
> > *a mole;*
> *Turn the key deftly in the oilèd wards,*
> *And seal the hushèd casket of my soul.*

"You wrote that?"

"I'm flattered. No, that's Keats. A poem called 'To Sleep.'"

"I should memorize some poetry."

"One thing at a time." I sat back, enjoying the momentary cessation of all physical pain thanks to the Scotch, which was mixing beautifully with my other medications. After years of mounting aches and pains, the absence of any pain is a sensation in itself, like a moment of silence in a huge crowd.

"How do you keep from getting too nostalgic? I think I'll be terribly nostalgic when I'm old. Hell, I'm already nostalgic about college."

"You just get crabby instead."

He raised his glass. "Cheers."

"Cheers," I said.

"What was that?"

"That's the wheels coming down. Or the engine coming off. You can never be sure."

"Thanks." His hands were locked on the armrests, and I noticed that his thumbnails were bitten to the quick so that he'd even begun grazing on the skin running up toward the knuckle.

After a few minutes he asked, "Anyone meeting you at the airport?"

"No, I'm taking a taxi to the Gare de l'Est. Then off to Reims."

"Tell you what. I'll have a rental car so why don't I drive you to the station?"

"You wouldn't mind?"

"I'd be happy to, really."

"That's very kind of you, thanks. I'd like that."

◆　　◆　　◆

I'M COMING, Daniel. I'm coming back.

◆　　◆　　◆

THE YOUNG MAN pulled up to the curb in a blue SAAB and opened the trunk. "Sorry it took so long," he said, grabbing my suitcase. "Terrible line at the rental agency."

"I'm in no rush."

We were both silent for most of the drive.

I looked out the window and watched cars and buildings slide by. Nothing looked familiar.

"Have you ever been to the Louvre?" I asked as we approached the station.

"No, I can't say that I have. I hear it's quite something."

"You should spend a day there. It might do you some good."

"I'll see if I can sneak away for a while." He looked at me, then added, "I'd like to buy you dinner sometime, if you're ever in New York."

"Sure. Maybe we'll even find some action." I winked approvingly.

He chuckled that chuckle again.

At the station we shook hands good-bye and then I stood at the curb, watching him drive away. After I could no longer see his car I went looking for a place to sit down so I could familiarize myself with the station and figure out how to buy a ticket for a train to Reims.

◆　◆　◆

I KNOW, I shouldn't. But I couldn't help staring at the young woman sitting two seats down on the left. She boarded the train just after me. I watched her walk slowly down the aisle, searching for just the right spot. Then she tucked her olive-drab canvas suitcase in the overhead before sliding into a seat next to the window. As soon as we pulled out of the station she took a book from her black leather purse, opened it slowly, pressing up and down along the seam with the flat of her hand, then began to read. After no more than a page she turned and looked out the window, sometimes twisting her head to follow some object as the train hurled by.

We were headed east, east toward the front. Did she think of the front? I doubted it. Now we were perhaps ten miles east of Paris. In September 1914 the German Army got within a dozen miles of Paris before French reinforcements shuttled in commandeered taxis held them at the Marne. Did she know that? I looked out my window at the fields and houses and trees streaming by when a sudden stabbing pain in my abdomen caused me to jerk forward. I leaned back again slowly, pulling a white handkerchief from my coat pocket and dabbing my forehead, which was damp. Then I placed one hand on the back of the seat in front of me to steady myself and turned and looked out the window, feeling much too hot.

There was a man marching along the railroad embankment. No, more than that, a soldier; a soldier marching with his head down and a rifle slung over his shoulder. I squinted and stared, then blinked and stared again. Her grandfather. Of course! It was the girl's grandfather, off to meet the German onslaught; marching off to save Paris and France. How young and handsome he looked, though tired and hungry. I knocked on the glass.

Should I tell the girl? Perhaps she could at least wave or throw him a kiss or shed a tear?

No, it's not something to tell, though I feel certain he won't come back. But what is she looking at out her window? Does she see something? That field there on the left, does she wonder if that is precisely where her grandfather fell, the grandfather who disappeared somewhere along the front in 1914? What about that brown house up ahead, might not that be where her father was killed twenty-eight years later by another German Army, lined up against the wall with seven others and summarily shot for sabotaging the railroad tracks? Or did her parents resign themselves to the Aryan conquest, even collaborating with the sharply dressed and swaggering occupiers?

She turned back once and looked at me, a brief, point-blank stare. An ancient longing gripped me by the throat. I smiled, trying not to look too eager. Did I look too desperate? Too pathetic? Could she see the tears coming? She smiled and then turned back to look out her window.

I remained perfectly still, hands wrapped tightly around the cane between my knees. Wishing.

◆　◆　◆

MORE PAIN. Much more, so that I must concentrate on remaining conscious. Keep the eyes open. Breathe slowly. That's it.

Strange how the pain brings me closer to them: to Giles and Daniel, to Page and Lawton and Tometti; and to the others, to all the forgotten millions, and to all their unspeakable agony.

Just try to imagine it. Even momentarily. Try to imagine the most horrifying, grotesque wound possible and then know with absolute certainty that that precise wound has been sustained exactly so hundreds and even thousands and hundreds of thousands of times, that every possible burning, searing, tearing jagged-edged slice, rip and trauma to the human body has been endured again and again by young men from Germany and England and France and Russia and Italy and Austria-Hungary and Belgium and Portugal and Montenegro and Australia and Canada and New Zealand and India and Ireland and Turkey and Bulgaria and Greece and Serbia and South Africa and Romania and Scotland and everywhere else and they had names like Henry and Karl and George and Sergei and Antonio and Erich and Dominic and Albert and Yuri and Étienne and Alexei and Heinrich and Miklos and Pierre and Janos and Kemal and Dieter and Jean.

Maybe there is a comfort in that, in all that multilingual pain. Maybe in our own final suffering we at least won't feel so terribly alone, knowing that every possible torment has already been suffered, that even on the most excruciating descent toward our own vile end we are in the company of millions. Millions of people who just like us could not bear the pain for even one minute longer and how could this happen to me I cannot endure it I cannot I cannot.

Millions of them. Can't you see the faces?

◆　◆　◆

I STOOD UP too early. That's why I fell when the train lurched suddenly before stopping. A young man helped me to my feet. Then the woman stood before me, holding out my cane and my leather bag. I thought she was going to say something but she didn't; she just smiled shyly, as though sorry for me. I thanked her and sat down, waiting until everyone else had gotten off. From my window I watched as she walked quickly across the platform and into the crowd. Then I stood and made my way to the door.

◆　◆　◆

NUMBERS. I remember the numbers. The clean, crisp and unyielding numbers. The irreproachable godforsaken numbers.

Verdun, February 21, 1916. One million Germans attack along an eight-mile front. (Watch them coming.) In the first five months 23 million shells are fired. (Listen.) Ten months later, 650,000 men are dead. (Kneel.)

It's a draw.

Battle of the Somme, day one, July 1, 1916. Following a massive seven-day artillery bombardment, 60,000 British troops, fortified by tots of navy rum, emerge from their trenches and start across no-man's-land, walking. Within hours, more than 20,000 are dead. (20,000 mothers, 20,000 fathers, 20,000 letters home, 20,000 headstones, how many sons and daughters and sisters and brothers and lovers?) Four months later the British dead totals 100,000; French, 50,000; German, 160,000. The British line has advanced six miles, less than the intended gains of the first day. Count 'em: one, two, three, four, five, six. Or 51,666 men a mile; twenty-nine men a yard; nearly ten men for every twelve inches. One man every inch and a quarter. A limb every few centimeters. Blood every millimeter. Tears every ...every what?

November, 1918. Armistice. Final tally, estimated combat-related deaths only (bullets, shells, bayonets, knives, gas, bare hands): Germans: 1.8 million; Russians: 1.7 million; French: 1.4 million; British: 900,000; Italians: 600,000; Austrians/Hungarians: 1.3 million; Romanians: 340,000; Americans: 50,000 (and another 60,000 to influenza); Australians: 60,000; Canadians: 60,000; Bulgarians: 90,000; Indians: 50,000; Serbians: 50,000; Belgians: 50,000; Turks: 330,000...

♦   ♦   ♦

In November came the Armistice... The news sent me out walking alone...cursing and sobbing and thinking of the dead.
—*Robert Graves, British Army.*

WORLD WAR II begins in 250 months. Count 'em. One, two, three, four...

♦ ♦ ♦

SOME NUMBERS are more interesting than others. In 1919 a row of rifles and bayonets was discovered protruding from the earth at Verdun, where two dozen French soldiers were buried (alive?) in their trench in 1916. You can still see them, pointing to the sky. The French call it the Tranchée des Baïonnettes.

There are other names for it too.

♦ ♦ ♦

I FOUND the memorial without much trouble and parked the dark green Fiat I had borrowed from my hotel on the gravel shoulder of the road, which was still rural but now lined with much larger trees. Everywhere the trees were taller, dwarfing my memories. I was glad for that.

I turned off the ignition and sat in the car for a few minutes, staring out the window. How unbelievable to think and feel that tomorrow it would be exactly sixty-two years to the day when the 152 names on the memorial became just names, names to be etched in stone; long enough so that even anniversaries pass unnoticed, until one day perhaps the monument itself cracks and crumbles and is finally bulldozed to make way for an office building, like Indian graves in Manhattan.

It took three attempts to get out of the seat, which seemed ludicrously close to the ground. I closed the door quietly and then leaned against the car, wheezing. The air was damp and sweet, as after a rain, and the gravel beneath my feet crackled loudly as I made my way down the path to the monument, clutching my cane tightly in one hand.

After a few yards I paused to catch my breath again, uncertain whether I suddenly felt much too cold or much too hot. Looking up I squinted and saw a young woman kneeling next to the monument and trimming the grass with hand clippers. There was a basket of fresh flowers on the ledge behind her. I didn't want to frighten her so I tapped my cane loudly on the ground as I approached. She turned to look at me, and her face quickly relaxed as she saw that I was far too feeble to pose a threat.

I waved my cane and continued toward the far side of the memorial, where I could look out across the field to the low ridgeline several hundred yards away. The woman, who appeared to be in her early twenties, stood and approached me.

"*Bonjour,*" she said.

"Hello," I said, turning toward her just as I felt a series of sharp spasms in my abdomen. Her face was beautiful and I tried not to wince as I pushed down hard on my cane to keep my balance. With my left hand I felt for a bottle of pain-killers in my coat pocket.

Oh but her face.

"You're American?" she asked, in perfect English.

I nodded.

"You must be a veteran," she said, walking closer.

"I am." I tried to stand straight.

"Of this battle? Were you here?"

"Afraid so. It dates me a bit, doesn't it?"

She put down her clippers and wiped her hands. "I was just tidying the place up a bit," she said. "I come by every year...."

"For the anniversary?"

"Yes."

"I didn't think anyone remembered anymore," I said.

"You're the only other person I've ever seen here." She took a few steps toward me, staring.

"It's kind of you to visit," I said. "Do you live nearby?"

"I grew up near here but I live in Paris now. What about you?"

"I'm traveling." Was that it?

"Have you been back often?" she asked.

"Only once before, many years ago."

"Is it very different?"

"A lot of it, yes. But it feels the same, at least right here."

"Do the changes bother you?"

I shrugged. "You get used to it."

"I'm not sure I could. But I'm talking too much. Here, let me gather my things and leave you in peace."

"No please, don't mind me. I just want to sit for a while."

"You're sure?"

I nodded.

She picked up her clippers and walked to the other side of the memorial. I listened to the sound of the shears slicing through the grass.

"There, that's enough for today," she said, wiping her forehead with the back of her hand. She put the clippers into her blue nylon backpack and then sat down near me.

"I love this time of day," she said. "Just when it starts to get a little hard to see things."

"Between night and day." Then I laughed to myself.

"What is it?"

"I was just thinking how the war ruined dawn and dusk."

"Ruined them?"

"That's when attacks were most likely so we always had to stand-to with fixed bayonets for an hour at sunrise and sunset."

"I see."

"And the pity was that's all we had, just a small slice of the sky to stare at when it changed colors."

"God, I've never thought of that. From a trench you really couldn't see much else, could you?"

"It was kind of like living in a tall box with the top open," I said.

She kept staring at me. "You look familiar," she said, leaning toward me.

"Old people tend to look alike," I said, feeling flushed by her attention.

"No, there is something about your face, your eyes." She peered at me as though I were on display in a museum.

"My God, you're the man in the portrait, aren't you?" She looked almost awed and I noticed how clear her eyes were, as though they'd just been made.

"The portrait?" I stood up and tightened my grip on my cane, taking fast and shallow breaths and struggling to maintain my balance.

"Yes, the portrait my grandmother painted years ago. It was in her living room for, God, forever."

"Julia?" I leaned harder on my cane.

"Yes, Julia!"

I staggered toward her a few steps.

She talked quickly: "There was one portrait of Grandfather Daniel, he was walking across a field. There was a church steeple in the background and he looked so tired and dirty. Sad, really. And then there was another painting of a man—of you—standing here, right in front of this memorial, standing in an overcoat like it had just rained. She said you were the only two men she ever really loved. But I thought you were, well I thought you were dead, that she'd lost you too."

She loved me. Julia always did love me. I looked up at the sky.

"You thought I was..."

"Well, she didn't exactly say dead. It was just the way she talked about you. How both you and Daniel were frozen in time for her. Forever young. Her young soldiers..."

"What about her husband?" I asked.

"What husband?"

"The one she married, around 1929?"

"She never married."

"*What?*"

"Oh no. We used to tease her about it. She was so beautiful."

"Are you sure?"

"Of course I'm sure. What makes you think she married?"

I looked at her but couldn't say anything. What did that mean? Was the engagement called off? Why wouldn't she have told me that? Or was there no engagement? The thought suddenly overwhelmed me: *there was no other man.* Not for Julia. Certainly not that quickly. No, the letter she sent was to protect me, to keep me from looking for her. That was it, wasn't it? She couldn't bear to pull me away from my wife and son, even if it meant spending the rest of her life alone. And yet I was alone too.

All those years.

The young woman was still staring at me, her bright green eyes studying my reaction. She waited a minute, then said, "Your portrait is quite handsome, really. It's hanging in my apartment in Paris. You and Grandfather were on either side of the fireplace at her house for years."

"Her house..."

"Not five miles from here."

481

"Here?"

"Yes, she came to visit in, let's see, 1928 I think it was, and never left."

So you stayed behind. Someone else must have mailed the letter for you from New York. All those years in France. Alone amongst the ruins.

"She sent for my mother...."

"Robin?"

"Yes. Are you okay?"

"Tell me, Julia is..." But your face just told me. Don't fall. Don't fall.

"I'm so sorry. She died just last year."

I sat down again quickly and she sat next to me, this time closer. "She did quite well for herself with her art gallery. I always admired her so much; her work in the underground during the Second World War, her independence, the long walks she'd take in the countryside right up until the end. I think the land held some sort of magic for her. And she always took special care of this memorial. We scattered her ashes around it. After she died, I decided it was my turn."

I glanced over at the basket of flowers, then rested my cane along my knees, unable to talk.

"I'll leave you for a moment," she said softly, backing away and walking toward the trees. I stared up at the sky and watched as a flock of birds flew by.

When she returned she stood, staring at me. That's when I saw the necklace.

She put her hand on it. "You recognize

this? It was Julia's." She took it off and handed it to me. I laid it gently in my palm, then ran my fingers along the length of it, stopping to rub the sapphire pendant.

"Did you give it to her?"

I nodded.

"Then keep it, please."

"No, I want you to have it."

"You're sure?"

"Yes," I handed it back to her. She self-consciously clasped it around her neck.

"You look like her," I said.

"Oh yes, everybody used to say that. I'm quite flattered, really."

"You're..."

"Natalie. I'm studying art at the Sorbonne. Painting."

"You've got the right ancestry."

"It's a start."

"A good one."

I looked closely at her hair and her hands and the slenderness of her face. Then I turned toward the open field that stretched from one ridgeline to another. "Onions," I laughed. "There are onions growing in no-man's-land."

She followed my eyes toward the field, which was now cultivated, and smiled.

"Your grandfather hated onions," I said.

"I don't know very much about him, I'm afraid. But I'm very curious. He's always seemed like sort of a hero to me, not just because of the war but because of the way he and Grandmother met and ran away. It always sounded so romantic, especially when I was a young girl."

We sat in silence for a few minutes, close enough to each other so that I could smell her hair.

"Would you like a drink?" I said, reaching into my leather bag.

"Oh, I've got some water, thanks."

"Ah, but you don't have Scotch."

"Scotch?" She raised her eyebrows and her cheeks tugged playfully at the sides of her mouth.

"I've brought along a bottle of Scotch—if you don't mind sharing a glass I purloined from my hotel."

"Why sure, thank you." She sat next to me and watched as I carefully removed the lid from the bottle and poured a glass, pausing to look at the signatures.

I watched her take a drink and made sure to sip from precisely where she sipped without her noticing. A slight breeze brought her perfume right up against me and into my chest.

"I'm sorry to stare but you bring back a lot of memories," I said.

"That's all right," she said with almost a giggle. "I stared at your face for years." She turned and traced her fingers along a name carved in the granite: John Giles. I thought of his dog and his dreams of opening a movie theater in Cleveland.

"I have to meet someone for dinner tonight. Can I offer you a ride back to your hotel?" she asked.

"Thanks, but that's my car there," I said. "Or at least I borrowed it from the concierge at my hotel. It's just down the road. Did you know I'm too old to rent a car? A bad risk, it seems. Couldn't convince them I could see my hands in front of my face, not that I can. Anyway, I'd like to sit here awhile." I looked over at Jack Lawton's name and thought of him lisping one of his dirty stories.

"Oh, I understand. But it must be rather sad, thinking about all those poor men." She put her hand on my forearm. "I've always hated being somewhere where loved ones once were and now they are not and I still am. It's haunting."

"It was a long time ago," I said, watching our arms together, hers white and smooth and mine gray and wrinkled.

She started to say something, stopped and then said, "May I paint you?"

"Me?"

"Yes, I'd come back tomorrow—if you'd meet me. Would you sit for me? Here, in front of the memorial?"

"You really want to paint an old codger like me?" I thought of Tometti and his Italian love songs and I wondered whether Teresa was still alive.

"I was going to come back anyway to paint. It's something I always promised myself I'd do. And now with you here, well, to think that I could paint the same man my grandmother painted...."

"Yes, of course."

She stood up. "So it's a deal?"

"It's a deal."

"How's noon?"

"Shouldn't we catch the morning light?" I asked.

"Oh yes, you're right. If you don't mind."

"Not at all. How's seven A.M.?"

"That's great. You mean it?"

"I'll be here."

"And you'll tell me what happened to you and Julia? She was very tight-lipped about you and I'm dying to know more."

"It's not a long story."

"Please, I'd love to hear it."

"Then I shall tell it to you. I shall tell you the story."

"Wonderful." She studied my face for a moment as if wondering where she would begin, then shuffled her feet and said, "Well, good-bye, then."

"Yes, see you tomorrow."

"Tomorrow." She took a few steps, then turned back toward me and waved and walked away with a remarkable lightness that made me smile. I watched as she faded into the dusk and I waved several times though I knew she could not see me.

As her car pulled down the gravel road and slid into the light gray mist I poured another half glass of Scotch and carefully placed the bottle on the ground. Then I pulled out my journal from my bag, opened it and placed it on my lap. After I took a sip of Scotch I took out my pen and started a letter to Julia, telling her that I had met her beautiful granddaughter and that she was going to paint my portrait in the morning. I also told her that I missed her terribly and that I was sorry I was too late and that I didn't know how I was ever going to say good-bye.

When the rain started I closed the journal and tilted my head up and opened my mouth and let the drops fall on my tongue. Then I took another sip of the Scotch and raised my glass to the monument and squinted until I could read the names etched in stone out loud one by one from beginning to end, over and over again as loud as I could.

EPILOGUE

I had to paint him from memory. I put him just next to the memorial in the morning light, standing with his cane and that leather bag over his shoulder with the sun casting shadows in the names etched in stone behind him. I couldn't finish it at first; maybe because it made me so sad, especially after I read his diary. Once I began to read it, I realized that it was the story he was going to tell me: the story of Patrick and Daniel and Julia.

The last thing he wrote was to Julia, telling her that he had just met her granddaughter here in France and how I looked just like her. What got to me were the last lines, where his beautiful handwriting suddenly comes apart. He wrote:

When did you know you'd never leave, Julia? When? Was it because you'd fallen too? Is that what you meant about the things that couldn't be said, that you'd always love me, even if it meant being alone for the rest of your life? And that was you in the night, wasn't it? You talking to me and listening and holding me. So maybe all those years we weren't really alone. Maybe we had what other people will risk everything for, if only they get the chance: a place in our hearts we could always go, a place that was safe and hallowed and full of wonder; a place where love conquers loss. I've come back now, Julia. I've finally come home. It's not easy for me, being here. Such memories! The laughter. The screams. Your eyes. But it's the right place for me. It's where I belong.

Being last is the hard thing; the awful sense of being left behind. But I'm ready now. After all these years I'm finally ready. I'm not even scared. There is just one thing left I want to ask; one thing I want to know from you: if our love really is stronger than death, if our souls can defy even that, then would it be too late to ask if I could consider you my...

I sent his belongings to his children. We've written each other several times and they promise to visit soon. They also volunteered to say something to the people at Great Oaks, particularly Janet, Erica, Hanford, Robert, Sarah and Jeffrey.

One Saturday a few months after Patrick died, I was walking along a street in Paris and suddenly I realized what was wrong with my portrait. So I ran all the way back to my apartment and pulled it out and I worked on it for three days. When I finished I wept, not just because I was upset but because I knew I had gotten it right this time. Julia was there now, standing right next to Patrick so they were almost touching, with the morning dew just beginning to dry on the granite monument behind them and the light just coming through the trees.

Oh, and I put smiles on both of them, even though it's a memorial. I just thought that if they were together, they'd be smiling. I don't think Daniel would mind anymore. After all, I think of him as the sunlight.